Crescent

www.dragonmoonpress.com

PHIL ROSSI

Crescent

www.crescentstation.net

ISBN 10 1-896944-52-3Print Edition
ISBN 13 978-1-896944-52-4

Dragon Moon Press is an Imprint of Hades Publications Inc.
P.O. Box 1714, Calgary, Alberta, T2P 2L7, Canada

www.dragonmoonpress.com
www.crescentstation.net

[Acknowledgements]

The journey to bring *Crescent* to the page began, as of this printing, two years and two months ago, almost to the day—when I released the first episode of a podcast that became bigger than I could have imagined. In that span of time, there have been many late nights and just as many early mornings spent doing my damndest to craft the best story I could possibly tell. I've now come to realize that the journey began long before I wrote the opening sentence to *Crescent*. Many people have inspired and supported me along the way. I'm going to use this page to express my humble thanks to the following: Jen, for the seemingly endless solo nights and the unflagging support, for being one of the first sets of eyes to read the very first iteration of *Crescent*. Bren, for your laughter. Zach, for being the other first set of eyes and for your general demeanor as a surly bastard. Scott, for taking me under your wing and giving me honesty. Tee, for the beers, ears, and shoulders. Gabrielle, for making me a better writer. Lindsay, for coming in and influencing my writing at the right time. Steve, for keeping that barstool warm. Gwen for taking this book on. All of my listeners, for making this happen.

And thanks to Mom, Dad, Lisa, and Laura for being there from the beginning. I had this dream—there was an alligator… and a baby.

[Dedication]

This novel is for Jennifer and Bren

[Prologue]

Warm morning light fell from sun globes suspended high above Main Street, Crescent Station. The bazaar buzzed with activity as residents of the station went to and fro on their Saturday morning errands. Some shopped at rickety stands of metal and fake wood, examining fruit and vegetables with discriminating interest. Squealing girls stepped out of fashion booths, showing off potential purchases to their friends. Merchants shouted the merits of their goods, each seller trying to out-yell the next. A sidewalk cafe bustled with waitstaff ferrying out omelets and coffee to hungry patrons. A pub was across the busy causeway from the cafe, and the raucous sounds of a televised sporting event drifted through its metal batwing doors.

"This is boring," Brian said as he tossed a few empty aluminum cans at the big, black collector robot's feet. The machine looked foolish when it bent over to snatch up the scattered drinking containers. Its multiple arms whirred and clicked as they swept down and came back up with Brian's trash, then crushed each can and placed it into the bin on the robot's back. "I'm sick of playing with the bots, Will. We've been doing it all morning long." Brian ran a hand through the mess of red hair atop his head.

"Yeah. I know… " Will picked another can out of the trash and cradled it in his chubby hands. In truth, he never really got bored on Main Street. He liked to watch the people come and go. Fussing with the bots was Brian's idea. Will would have been happy to sit in the cafe eating hash browns and watching the girls in the fashion booths. His stomach growled.

Brian looked up at Will and smiled, his green eyes twinkling. "I found something cool the other day. I haven't checked it out yet, though. Thought we should go there together." Brian glanced around and said in a conspiratorial voice, "Think I can trust ya?"

"Waddya mean?" Will said. "Yeah. Tell me what is!"

"I dunno, man. You're not gonna tell your parents, are you?"

"What? No. Why would you say that?" Will's round cheeks flushed. He knew why.

"Remember how they tanned our hides when they caught us playing on L Deck?" Brian asked. There was no way that Will could have forgotten, but Brian enjoyed making Will feel inadequate at every opportunity.

"Well, yeah." Will said. It had been Will's fault that they were caught playing where they didn't belong. Will had slipped up when his parents asked him why he had come home so wet and dirty on that fateful day.

"I found a special hatch on L Deck," Brian said.

"You went back to L?" Will couldn't believe it. Brian's parents had given their son such a whooping that Brian had hardly been able to walk for the better part of a week.

"Yeah, man. I found this little hatch in one of the alleys. It looked like it had been welded shut, but it was f'd up from the floods. I got the thing off without even trying. Wanna go explore?" Brian tossed a can to the collector. The robot caught it in midair, orange eye nodes flaring as it placed it into the bin.

"Do I? Shit yeah, I do," Will said. He hoped he sounded convincing. He didn't *really* want to go exploring. But he was afraid of Brian giving him a hard time.

"Even though we're not supposed to be on L Deck?" Brian prodded.

"Whatever, man. Beats messing with the collectors." Will placed his can back into the refuse bin.

[•••]

L Deck was quiet. The residential level had been abandoned for nearly a month after a water line busted in the worst possible way. L had been completely submerged. It had happened in the middle of the night, and as a result, a lot of people had died there. L was drained now, but it would be months before people were allowed to live there again. The result was a ghost town. Will looked around at the dark, gaping doors of abandoned apartments and shuddered. The place felt like a morgue. A week ago, Will and Brian had snuck down there to see if they could find any salvageable items in the empty apartments. Will had hated the idea, but Brian had a knack for being persuasive.

Will glanced at one of the open apartment doors. Starlight filtered in through a grimy window and illuminated a child's stuffed animal, coated in black mildew.

The two boys wandered up and down the dimly lit station corridors for hours. Brian was paying no heed to the abandoned homes this time. Will was grateful. He felt dirty going through people's things. Dead people's things, at that. It just wasn't right. No, Brian was set on finding his supposed hatch, and that was just fine by Will.

"Are you sure you remember where this hatch is?" Will said, hoping that Brian would say no and they'd be able to go back to Main Street.

"There it is!" Brian was pointing at a dark hole in the wall of the alley; the metal grating had been cast aside and lay in a pool of standing water. Will peered into the opening and could see nothing but darkness. He didn't want to go in there. There were probably a dozen rats the size of housecats crawling around.

"Geez. I dunno, man. We probably shouldn't do this. What if we get lost?" Will shifted his weight from one foot to the other.

"What if we get lost?" Brian mimicked. "Geez, Will. Grow a freakin' set, will ya? I've already checked it out. It's a straight shot." Brian pulled a small black flashlight out of his pocket and clicked it on, shining it directly into Will's eyes. The boy squinted into the glare and grabbed at the light, but Will was too slow and Brian snatched it away. Laughing, Brian got onto his hands and knees and spared Will a final look before disappearing into the shadows. Suddenly, the vacant corridor felt very much like a crypt, and although Brian was being an asshole, Will didn't want to be alone. He took a deep breath and crawled after him.

The narrow passage was damp and reeked of mold. The air was choking, and Will's nostrils burned. He could see the glow of Brian's flashlight bobbing up ahead and crawled as fast as he could to catch up. Will worried that he was too fat to be in the tunnel and that he would get stuck, but when the tunnel descended at a steep angle that made it difficult to keep traction, he was thankful for his extra padding.

Will came out into a large compartment. Brian's light disappeared, leaving it too dark to see. Will fumbled for his own flashlight, clicked it on, and screamed. Several hulking figures loomed in the center of the room. He heard Brian's laughter somewhere close by. Will focused the beam of his light on the things. They were only collector bots, old and rusted, covered in a thick layer of dust. The big, multi-limbed robots were probably from the station's original complement of worker bots.

They looked scary, all rusty like that, but their power cells had run dead a long time ago. These collectors couldn't hurt him. Will shivered, all the same. There was an open panel at the far end of the room, and Brian's face appeared in the dark space.

"What are you waiting for? Come on, scaredy cat."

Will ducked through the opening and came out into a wide causeway. A few ceiling panels glowed with a tawny light. Behind where the boys stood, the tunnel extended into alternating patches of weak light and complete darkness. Ahead of them, Will could make out a large door. Brian leaned against a bulkhead across from the hatch they had come through. The bulkhead looked like it had been sealed shut with a plasma caster; the seams were bloated with brownish, oxidized chrome. Brian tapped his foot with growing impatience. His arms were crossed over the chest of his now-dirty tee shirt and his pale, freckled complexion looked sickly in the flickering light. He gave Will the middle finger, turned, and ran into the shadows.

"Come on, man!" the slim boy called over his shoulder. "You gotta see this!"

Will caught up to Brian toward the end of the corridor. The tunnel terminated at a massive, black door. On it was painted a crude, red X. Written across the door in big yellow letters, Will read: Authorized Personnel Only. No Access.

"Holy shit," Will gasped. "Is this … "

"The Vault, Will. The freakin' Vault. Can you believe it? I found the Vault. I thought I couldn't get any more awesome than I already was. I guess I was wrong."

"I didn't even think it was real!" For a moment, Will forgot he was scared.

"What do you think is behind it?" Brian asked. "Biological waste? Dead things? They closed this part of the station for a reason." Brian approached the door and reached out a hand to touch it.

"Don't do that! What if there's an alarm or something?" Will took a step forward.

"Oh, give me break. This place probably isn't even on the grid. I mean, it's not even supposed to be here."

The air seemed to grow cooler. Will glanced up, expecting to see an air vent above his head—there was only a guttering light panel.

"Brian, let's go. I don't like it here." The chill had reminded Will of his fear. A rat squealed in the shadows.

"Wanna run home to mommy? Go, run home, then. I'm gonna touch it," Brian said, and smirked.

"No, Brian. Come on. This isn't cool. Let's go," Will protested. Brian shook his head and placed his hand on the door. He recoiled.

"Wow. This thing is ice cold."

"Happy now? You touched it. Can we please go?" Will turned to leave. A low groaning sound made him stop in his tracks. His breath caught in his throat.

"Did you hear that?" Brian said. He didn't sound so brave anymore.

"Yeah. I heard it. Let's go… " Will said. Suddenly, he had to pee really bad.

"Wait." Brian paused. "There it is again… Shit. Do you see that?"

Will turned back to the big door. A growing shadow seeped out from around its girth now, devouring the meager light. Brian was staring at it as it grew, his jaw agape. Will took another step back. The liquid darkness twisted toward Brian, growing and reaching like charcoal tentacles.

"Brian!" Will shouted, but Brian didn't move; he stood transfixed. The shadows wrapped around him, an ethereal shroud of sable. Brian's form seemed to go fuzzy, out of focus, for an instant. Then Brian finally moved. He turned his head at a sick angle and emitted a choked scream before the shadow completely enveloped him, cutting off the sound. Will took off running back the way they had come, flashlight pointed ahead of him to beat back the darkness. Hot tears ran down his face.

He dove through the small opening in the corridor wall and cried out at the sight of the rusted collector bots. Their dusty eye spots flared orange.

The joints of the robots whined and chirped as they moved for the first time in centuries. Will stood transfixed. Large segmented arms, thick with rust, reached out to embrace him. They were the last thing Will ever saw.

(Part 1: 15 Years Later)

Gerald Evans tapped a floor vent with the toe of his boot.

The heat was blocked again.

Nothing but a vague whisper of warmth rose from between the metal slats, but Gerald was far too busy marveling at the backlog of messages that choked his communications terminal to worry about a blocked vent. Flushing the heating system was far from his mind. Much like with the vents, the comm system's hard drive went months without regular purges. Even still, Gerald wondered why he had gone six months without a flush. He was bad, but not *that* bad.

Gerald hit the next page of messages. A video sat at the top of the queue. *Oh. You again.* The communication was six months old, to the day, and was the very reason Gerald had put off cleaning out the system. *Liam's last rites,* Gerald thought and frowned. The message was the last time he'd heard from his brother. Sure, he could've deleted the message or, just as easily, he could have saved the message, but both actions would have represented final acceptance that he'd never hear from Liam again. Instead, Gerald had let the message linger until he had all but forgotten that it was still there. Gerald hit play and sat back in the control couch. The monitor blanked and then filled with the image of his brother. Liam's dark hair was just beginning to gray. His delicately creased features were bright with the flush and smile of hopeful anticipation. Liam's wife stood at his side. Long, thickly braided hair hung over one bare shoulder and she held Gerald's nephew in her arms. The kid was just scraping at the one year mark. Chubby fingers tugged at his mother's braid; she kept pushing the small, pink hand away.

"Hey Gerry. I was hopin' you'd pick up," his brother said. "We'll be outta radio contact for a few weeks while we make this last cargo run and... Man, that feels weird to say. But, shit. This is it, little brother. The last run, and then retirement." Liam smiled wide, as if he couldn't contain his happiness. He paused and glanced at his wife and child and then returned his attention to the camera. "Look. Believe it or not, I didn't call to give you a lecture. I know Mom always lays into you about this crap but, it *is* important. You haven't saved a penny as far as any of us know. You're not all that much younger than I am, Gerry. You can't fly forever. The odds of something happening out there, they're just not in our favor. Sooner or later…" Liam shook his head and smiled. "Ger, it's never too early to start planning for retirement. So, that's it. If I don't get a chance to talk to you, be safe and be well. I'll shoot you a line when we get to Habeos. Seriously, though, do call me back if you get a chance."

"End of message," the terminal stated in a clipped and metallic voice. *And end of the line, brother.*

He noticed the lack of warmth, then.

Gerald Evans harbored no particular love for space. It was always cold. The chill possessed a knack for entering uninvited. Tenacious as hell, even the thickest of hulls couldn't keep the cold out. It didn't even knock. The quiet—that was another thing. Reinforced plating wouldn't keep that silence out, either. Gerald Evans didn't have a hard-on for space; but between the stars, the floating rocks, and the endless dust, lay the salvage. And hauling salvage was how Gerald made a living.

He reached out and removed one of several photographs taped to the control console. The snapshot showed a picture of Gerald, standing between Liam and his wife. How long ago had the picture been taken? A year? Maybe a little more? Gerald laughed. He was nearly bald in the picture—a victim of a tragic haircut. His dark hair, previously thick and wavy, had been cropped so close to the skull that his scalp was visible. The playful ridicule from Liam and his wife had been without mercy.

That was the last time Gerald had actually seen Liam and his family.

He ran a hand over his head; the hair was longer again.

Liam and his family had never arrived in Habeos. The search for the missing cargo pilot and his family was given up after just two months; Gerald's mom just didn't have the money to pay for an extension, and Gerald was no help there, either. Space had claimed itself another victim—three of them, for the price of one.

But those were the odds.

Gerald had shed his tears and spent his time grieving. There was nothing left to do to but…

"Message deleted."

[•••]

Crescent was visible through the front viewport. The station was a disembodied talon, black-silhouetted as it floated six hundred and fifty kilometers above the gray-green expanse of the planet Anrar III. Starships, appearing as tiny globes of light from Gerald's current distance, came and went from the bulbous docking hub at the top of the sickle. Gerald waved his hand over a swatch of controls and engaged the final approach. He watched as Crescent grew larger in the octagonal glass viewport. The space station's hull bore the scars of centuries of small impacts. The metallic skin was pockmarked and scorched in spots. In other places, old breaches were mended with a patchwork of scrap material.

The thrust of Gerald's ship increased gently, pressing him into the control couch, and Crescent increased in size at an exponential rate. Before long, it was all Gerald could see out of the forward port. Weathered hull raced by at a blinding speed—so fast that he couldn't make out any details. It was all a multi-colored blur. The ship shuddered as it slowed.

Melodic laughter chimed from the oblong speaker mounted above the control couch.

"Something funny?" Gerald asked and looked around the empty bridge for a spilled cup of coffee, or maybe a stow-away space monkey come out of hiding.

"Yes. Would you like me to elaborate, Captain?" A metered baritone drifted from above his head—the voice of the ship's computer.

"Yes, Bean." Gerald could not put together why the previous owner of the tug class hauler had named the ship Bean, and Bean refused to elaborate.

"Thank you, Captain. I find it humorous that this is your fourth visit to Crescent in the past six months."

"That tickles your circuits?" Gerald arched a brow.

"It does, Captain. You yourself said you'd never be caught dead on Crescent."

"When did I ever say that to you?"

"You never said it to me directly, but you have said it on numerous ship-to-ship communications," Bean commented.

"You always were one for eavesdropping, Bean."

"It can't be helped. It is my ears that you speak into ever so tenderly."

Gerald grunted and glanced over at the main scanner overlay. A shimmering holographic projection floated to the right of the control couch. It showed a green schematic of the station and its relation to Bean's tight orbit. A handful of colorful radar blips circled the image in three dimensions. The proximity indicator flashed the decreasing distance between Bean and the docking hub.

"Bean. Open the comm channel to Crescent ATC." Gerald paused. "On second thought, send the landing request for me, will you? I'm feeling antisocial."

"When are you ever feeling social?" the computer asked.

There were a few seconds of silence before Bean spoke up again.

"Permission has been granted, Captain."

A portal of brilliant light loomed ahead, making it impossible to see much of anything else. Bean glided toward the opening in a graceful pirouette. Silvery tethers uncoiled from dark compartments on the station-hub. There was a shudder as docking clamps on each tether's end engaged. Bean was pulled into Crescent's main hangar. And like that, the salvage hauler—proclaimed "Bean" in faded, stenciled letters—was no longer moving.

Gerald dropped from the small disembarkation porthole on the underside of Bean's hull. It felt strange to be on a solid deck. Stillness for the first time in three days. *The crawl is gonna get me,* Gerald thought. *The second my head hits that pillow.* The deep space equivalent to sea legs, the crawl was a persistent sensation of motion most pronounced after long trips between stars. Maritime folklore said a seafarer's soul didn't always reach the shore at the same time as his body; the sailor still felt the waves because his spirit remained at sea. When mankind sailed to the stars, the folklore traveled with him, nearly unchanged for thousands of years.

Gerald wondered if Bean felt anything similar to the crawl. Doubtful. Bean was, after all, only a ship.

A woman stood waiting on the hangar deck; her arms were crossed over the dark blue of her Crescent Security uniform. The blues, as they were called, were the standard Core Sec threads. Hers were embroidered with an arc of gold just above the Core Sec starburst insignia on the breast pocket to indicate her as a member of Crescent Station's crew. The officer had dark hair, woven into a tight braid that fell down her back in a coil tighter than the docking lines that had pulled Bean in, leaving her pale face framed by a few stray ringlets. Her lips were set in a straight line. She was pretty—very pretty—and looked just as fierce. She had a mean-looking stun rod slung in a hip holster. Typical welcoming party. Gerald set his yellow duffle on the flight deck.

"Back so soon, Mr. Evans?" she asked.

"Officer Griffin." He smiled. "Did you come to say hello or to break my stones?"

"Just checking for the usual, Gerry. Weapons?"

"Just the widow makers." He balled his hands into fists and raised them.

She snorted a laugh and shook her head. He bowed with grace.

"It's hard to believe you're even real, Mr. Evans," Griffin stated.

"Thank you very much. The 11:30 show is different than the 7:30," he said, and bowed again. Although he joked, Gerald was no idiot. The weapons policy on any space station was strictly enforced. On Crescent it was a matter of life or death. A projectile traveling at near sonic could easily puncture Crescent's old hull if it hit at the right weak spot. The station had a hard enough time maintaining pressure and atmosphere without having holes punched in her skin. Gerald raised his arms. "Commence the pleasuring, Officer Griffin."

She smirked and waved a slender black wand up one side of his body, along his arm, and repeated the gesture on the other side.

As Officer Griffin scanned him, Gerald glanced down the length of the hangar deck. Black-clad members of some religious cult swarmed a merchant. No sooner had the fat bastard set foot off his ship than black leaflets were shoved into his face. *Every station has its crazies—especially this far out,* Gerald thought. *At least they're not playing tambourines.* Even still, Gerald would be sure to avoid them all the same.

"Mayor Kendall would like to see you."

"What'd you say?" He returned his attention the officer.

"Mayor Kendall would like to see you," she repeated.

"Now?" He looked to his duffle bag as she probed it with her magic contraband detection stick. "I've been dying for a shower and a shave these past few days. And I need to stow my sack of underpants and socks." He gave the yellow duffle a shake.

Officer Griffin looked up at him with green eyes and batted her long lashes.

"Take it with ya, pard," she said in a mock-drawl and then shrugged. "Like with most personal appointments from the Mayor's office, it seemed important."

Swell, he thought. Getting summoned by Crescent's Mayor, the de facto iron fist of the deep space outpost, smacked of getting called to the principal's office—nothing good ever came of it.

[•••]

Gerald rejoined Officer Griffin on the other side of the decontamination causeway. Sound, light, and people exploded from everywhere he looked. His head spun. The second he stepped out of the DC he wanted to turn right around and head back to his ship. Main Street, Crescent Station blew the mind like a Euro-Chin firecracker after any length of time in the sensory isolation of space. The wide and vaulted station level was the nexus of station life. The chamber, roughly one square mile of metal, glass, and support pylons, was a mismatch of colorful tent-shops, bazaars, taverns, and people—lots and lots of people.

Light the color of salmon drifted from large sun globes suspended high above. Gerald had arrived just before the night cycle of the station. Activity on Main Street was ramping up and Gerald couldn't seem to keep pace with Griffin as she wove through the crowd. They passed Heathen's, Gerald's favorite of the Crescent watering holes. Music and raucous laughter drifted through the brushed-chrome batwing doors, mingled with the fine stench of tobacco. A drink and a smoke was exactly what Gerald wanted. Officer Griffin turned to look over her shoulder, frowned, and grabbed him by the arm.

"Did you forget how to walk?" she asked.

"What? No."

He was thankful when they dodged out of the crowd and into a service tunnel. Homeless people slept in the shadows, their limp bodies propped up against the walls. Thick cables ran above their heads like black serpents. Conduits hissed overhead. Officer Griffin had slowed her pace. Was this some kind of short cut? Gerald was pretty confident they were headed away from the station's administrative suites. Officer Griffin halted beside a wide door labeled Storage 15. Her fingers danced over the keypad set in the wall beside the door. There was a chime and the door shuddered open. She gestured with a cock of her head. Gerald arched a brow.

"The Mayor is in … there?"

"Just go, asshole." She gave him a small shove and followed in behind him. The door slid shut in their wake.

It was dark as pitch in the small room. The air was thick and musty.

"Are we… " Gerald began.

"Alone?" The word almost sounded like a laugh as it passed over Griffin's hidden lips. "Quite." He felt her hands wrap around his collar and before he could react he was pulled forward. He lost his balance and both he and Officer Griffin tumbled to the hard, metal floor.

"Son of a… " he muttered and she was on top of him in an instant, peppering his face and neck with kisses. "The Mayor doesn't really want to see me, does he?"

"He does." She kissed him on the mouth. It was a long and greedy kiss that made Gerald all the more aware that he had neither brushed his teeth nor showered in more than three days. Griffin didn't seem to mind. "Kendall wants to see you. But not 'till morning. You think you're important enough that Kendall'd disturb his precious dinner for you? Not bloody likely."

"Jesus, Marisa. You had me worried. Bringing me in here… " His fading concern wasn't stopping him from unbuttoning the front of her uniform with fast and clumsy fingers.

"When are you going to learn to trust me, Gerry?"

"That, my dear, is a loaded question. Let's get reacquainted first and I'll consider it."

A large paint can fell off a high shelf and Gerald thought he saw something move in the shadows. He attempted to sit up. She forced him back down with the palm of her hand.

"Just fuck me, fly boy," she said.

They spent the next three hours getting reacquainted.

[•••]

His name was Taylor and he was more mountain than man. The behemoth had little to say as he led Gerald down the low-lit metal and glass corridor that bisected the station's administrative suite of offices. Gerald eyed the hulk as he followed him and wondered if he favored salvage pilots for breakfast. *And I'm on the menu,* Gerald thought.

Taylor left Gerald in the antechamber of the Mayor's private office. Gerald proceeded to examine the walls, not out of boredom, but out of suppressed awe. Real wood panels obscured the chamber's more mundane surfaces. Gerald leaned in close. The panels had an aged look to them, like the trees had come from Earth herself—very expensive stuff. They were stained a deep red and lined with shallow shelves that contained actual paper books. The only things paper was used for nowadays were administrative nonsense, archiving, and cheap advertising. That meant the books were older than god himself.

Gerald sat down on a leather couch. The piece of furniture made a squelching sound and conformed to the shape of his body. The sensation was supposed to be pleasant, but Gerald felt groped from all sides by the furniture. He got up as quickly as he had seated himself. The cushions were reluctant to let go and did so with a hiss. He walked along the Mayor's personal library instead, and trailed his index finger over the ancient spine of one of the tomes; the title was in a language he'd never seen before. There wasn't a single fleck of dust on the book—quite a feat of caretaking in a place like Crescent, considering that three quarters of the universe's dust originated on that very station, or so Gerald believed. As he moved along the neatly organized rows of books, Gerald couldn't help but notice the door to Mayor Kendall's office was open a sliver. He approached the door and heard what sounded like a good old fashioned scolding.

"Dr. Cortez, we are happy to accommodate you on Crescent. As I'm sure you've seen in your short stay, your donations have gone a long way. However, I cannot allow you and your daughter to snoop around where you don't belong, trying to find some place that doesn't even exist. There is no buried treasure on this station. Those decks are off limits for safety reasons. If it were anyone else, they would have been kicked off the station. In fact, the guard that your daughter bribed is being sent away on the next transport. I take these matters seriously. I am tolerant, Dr. Cortez. Extremely tolerant, I'm sure you'll agree. But I can't have you going down there. Consider this a warning. You are a smart man. You know next time I won't be as forgiving. Your daughter is a very pretty girl. Let's keep it that way."

"Yes," Gerald heard a soft, male voice say—heavy with the sound of acquiescence, and trembling ever-so-slightly. "I apologize."

"Do not apologize. Just assure me that it won't happen again."

"It won't happen again."

"Good. In that case, Dr. Cortez, You and I are done for today."

Gerald hurried back to the hungry couch and sat down; the cushions purred and enveloped him. The office door opened fully and a trapezoid of light fell across the dark carpet, revealing a woven pattern of vines that coiled and twined on one another like verdant barbed wire. Roses the dark color of wine blossomed along the green tentacles. It struck Gerald as more beastly than beautiful. His reverie was broken as a shadow spread across the rug. A stocky man with a crazy mop of curly white hair dashed out of the office; he clutched a small, flat personal terminal close to his chest. Tiny eyes darted to Gerald and then to the exit. The man, presumably Dr. Cortez, was escorted by two roughnecks. One of them was tall and fiery stubble covered most of his freckled cheeks. The shorter one was all grease and slick hair with a wad of tobacco stuffed into his cheek that was so big it looked like his face might burst. Cortez's escorts didn't spare Gerald a single glance.

"Come in, Gerald," the metered drawl of Mayor Kendall drifted from the office.

The Mayor's office continued the theme of the antechamber. The walls were stained burgundy and volume-lined. A wide desk with wood side-panels and a dozen or more liquid crystal displays set into its top stood at the aft of the room. Each monitor glowed with a different scene, showing a combination of security camera feeds and news feeds. A big, octagonal viewport stood beyond the desk and showed the night face of Anrar III; the deep orange sun, Anrar, blazed as a necklace of light over the curve of the large planet. Its light flooded the office like day glow. A shimmering hologram hovered above one of the camera feeds, appearing as a diffuse negative from Gerald's perspective.

"Gerald, I won't keep you long. I am well aware that you just arrived from a lengthy salvage trip. Men have needs after trips like this." Mayor Kendall's tall, lanky frame was silhouetted by the glow of the star. He had his back to Gerald. "Far be it from me to deny you of these needs." Kendall turned and stepped out of the glare. He extended his hand to Gerald. Blazing sunlight caught in the wisps of Kendall's thin, gray hair making the strands glow like heated filaments. Gerald took Kendall's slender hand for a quick, firm hand shake. Kendall's pink lips curved into a grin, but the smile did not spread across his pale face. He let go of Gerald's hand and strolled back behind his desk. The mayor waved a hand through the floating holographic projection that still hovered above the desk. It winked out of existence.

"Sit, Gerald. You're making me nervous." Kendall's lips twitched with another smile, but there was little fondness in the mayor's watery eyes.

Gerald smiled and gestured to the large, leather chair behind the desk.

"You first, Mayor," he said, and Kendall laughed. The sound of it set Gerald on edge.

"Very well, then." Kendall seated himself and Gerald sat down across from him. Gerald was thankful when the chair didn't try to cop a feel. "In short, Gerald, I'm looking for a good salvage man. Core Sec has appointed Crescent the salvage hub of this system and the neighboring Tireca system. With all the recent raids on miners and the like, Crescent stands to do very well with the influx of scrap, ore, and whatever else is floating out there. I need a reliable man to get out there and haul. A trustworthy man who won't siphon off some of the salvage for himself."

"And why exactly am I that man?"

"You've done four jobs for me in the past, Gerald." Kendall paused and spread his hands out over the monitors. "Four jobs and I haven't had to order you killed yet. That's a pretty good track record in my book." Kendall laughed again, though he made no joke. "You will be paid three times your non-contract commission."

Gerald knew he would have to say yes or he'd never get a job from Crescent again. Not that that would have been a huge loss. Crescent wasn't exactly a vacation resort. Not to mention, Gerald wasn't thrilled about being contractually obligated to a man like Kendall. It was one thing to do a job or two for someone. It was another thing entirely when they *owned* your ass. But, three times Gerald's non-contract rate—that was a lot of cash. More than Gerald could make in a year. He thought of his brother's message. Was Kendall's offer a coincidence or a chance to get on the right track, with a head start to boot? Fate or fool's luck. Kendall placed an envelope on the desktop.

"There's a data wafer in there. It has the details of the contract. Take it with you. Review it and let me know tomorrow. It's a big decision and I won't rush you. We're done here for now."

Gerald placed the envelope into the breast pocket of his flight jacket and left the office.

[•••]

Gerald tottered out of Heathen's and onto Main Street. A faint blue glow trickled down from the sun globes—the shadows held sway now. A big clock disc floated over the distant Main Street exit tunnel. It was 3:45 a.m. Gerald's head felt like it was stuffed with gauze. He had finally managed to have that drink, and countless more had followed. The occasion for the revelry: he had decided to accept Kendall's offer and felt obliged to celebrate.

Now, swaying on the sidewalk, he began to wonder if drink number ten had been such a great idea. He reached out a hand and grabbed a nearby lightpost to steady himself. The globe atop the onyx shaft cast a sphere of dull, wavering orange. Chin-to-chest, he began the trek back to his apartment, hoping to high hell he could figure out how to get there. When he successfully exited Main Street, he figured he was at least going in the right direction—away from the bar.

"Look out, boy."

The voice startled him. He felt a hand on his chest. "You almost ran old Naheela down, ya did." He lifted his head and in his shadow stood Crescent's resident crone. She was the epitome of old age. Naheela's dark skin was so wrinkled it didn't even appear to be flesh. Her face reminded him of a crumpled ball of rice paper, with chaotic and equally intricate creases and folds. She smiled a crooked grin; her few remaining teeth glistened in the low light of residential corridor 2B.

Her breath was fetid.

"Sorry," Gerald managed. "Late. I'm… drunk. Sleep."

"You are, you are, young'n." *You are* came out of her dry, spittle flecked lips as one word—*yar*. "Best get your handsome self to bed," she said. A vein-painted eyelid fell in what he thought might have been a wink. It made his skin crawl. *Old people are scary when you're loaded,* he thought.

Gerald was thankful to discover he was standing outside the door to his apartment.

"Crescent is waking, my boy. Pray sleep with the light on and with one eye open," she whispered in a conspiratorial voice. "At least until you get used to its creaks and groans."

He turned his head away from the key access pad beside the door and she was gone. He could still smell her breath.

Fingertips that felt three times fatter than normal punched in the seven digit key code. There was a chime and the door to his apartment slid open. *First try, thank god,* he thought. He stepped over the threshold, grateful to be home—his new home. The dim night disappeared behind the hissing bulkhead. With the door closed, the room wrapped him up in its velvet darkness. It was ice cold. Environmental zones were never steady in 2B, or so he had been cautioned. He shivered. Maybe with the increase in salary, he could afford something more... comfortable. He fumbled at his belt.

"Lights," he said.

The overhead lights flickered on.

Three drops of wine-colored liquid splashed to the metal floor of the apartment.

Gerald looked up from the floor.

A body dropped from the ceiling, suspended by dark cables that wound around its outstretched limbs like serpents. It was a woman. She was naked and split open from pelvis to sternum.

He stumbled backwards and tripped over something. There was a clatter as metal surgical tools fell to the floor, knocked from a cart that hadn't been there a second ago. Scalpels, forceps, and instruments he didn't recognize littered the now blood-soaked floor of his apartment. All of the tools were polished to a reflective shine; the implements sparkled with light gone red. He fell over the cart and brought it down with him, shattering the glass top. A metallic, guttural groaning came from everywhere and nowhere. Gerald struggled to get to his feet, slipping and sliding in the viscera that covered the soles of his shoes. Where the door had been seconds ago, was now a dripping wall. He turned—the body of the woman was gone. He felt a small dose of relief and turned forward, expecting the door to be there, but it wasn't.

Hands gripped his shoulders and spun him around. Gerald fell again and when he hit the ground the wind was knocked out of him. The corpse of the woman straddled him; very much animated, she supported herself with one hand on his chest.

"The Three. It's because of them!! It was a mistake!" The dark cavity of her wound oozed blood, its edges ragged and black as if they were covered with oil. "We can't save her. We were wrong!" The metallic groan sounded anew and her head cranked to one side at an unnatural angle. There was a cracking sound, and blood sprayed from her gaping mouth. It spattered warm across his face.

Gerald closed his eyes and screamed like had never screamed before. He felt the pressure of her body ease off.

When he opened his eyes, she wasn't there anymore. He looked around and screamed again for good measure. The blood was gone. The cart was gone. The surgical tools were gone.

There was his bed against the far wall, unmade. There was his yellow duffle bag at the foot of the bed with the contents strewn around it, just as he had left it hours ago. And that was all. Gerald blinked and rubbed his eyes with both hands.

Sticky. His hands were sticky. He brought them away slowly and wiped them on his jeans.

He didn't need to look. He knew what it was that covered them.

(Part II)

"You look a little fragile, Gerald. Paper thin and just as blanched. You feelin' all right, son?" Mayor Kendall sat with his arms crossed over his chest. His slight frame was dwarfed by the big leather desk chair. He eyed Gerald with a curious, if not slightly suspicious, gaze.

"The crawl," Gerald said. He wanted to rub his eyes; they stung with a persistence that was distracting. "I had a hard time getting to sleep last night." That he'd had a hard time sleeping was no lie. Fear of a repeat hallucination of the bleeding, screaming ghost woman had kept him awake—the crawl, not so much. Kendall dipped his chin in a nod and then swiveled his chair to accommodate a look out the large viewport. The surface of Anrar III was tarred with night fall. Stars glittered above the blackness.

"I'll confess, Gerald. That's somethin' I don't know all too much about. I keep my trips off station as short as possible. I pay people a lot of money to go to far off places for me." Kendall paused and swiveled back to look at Gerald. "Are you going to be one of those people I pay a lot of money, Gerald?"

"I am. On one condition," Gerald said. He wanted to get it over and done with before he could change his mind. Both of Kendall's thin, gray brows arched.

"*You're* giving *me* a condition of employment?"

"Yeah. I'm your man on the condition that you give me somewhere to sign right now. We need to cut this meeting short. I gotta get some damn sleep."

Kendall did not laugh, but his eyes glittered. He seemed genuinely amused.

"Very well, Gerald." Kendall slid a rectangle of paper across the glowing expanse of LCD monitors. Gerald took it and glanced down the length of the sheet. Standard contractual verbiage. He'd be an employee of Crescent Station for a period of six months, sol-time, after which his contract would be renewed based on necessity. There was a non-compete clause that stated Gerald could not work for anyone else in this time of employment. The pay was good—there'd be no need. Gerald took a pen from the exhaust port of a cargo vessel modeled in dark clay. He thought of Liam and his family and then signed in a large scrawl.

"There's my mark, Mayor." He slid the page back to him.

"You sign like royalty, Gerald." Kendall smiled.

"I guess I missed my calling by a long one. We done here?"

"Of course. Do get some rest. I'm sure you'll be busy here soon." Kendall winked at Gerald. The gesture was suggestive—of what, Gerald wasn't quite sure. If he stuck around that office much longer, he might find out. And he probably wouldn't like it.

[•••]

Gerald sat in the cafeteria, a cheap automated mess hall two levels below Main Street. It was always quiet in the cafeteria, because the food sucked. The coffee was even worse than the grub—the shit tasted like motor oil, but goddamn if it didn't open your eyes wide. It was as good a spot as any for Gerald to wake up and sort out the jumble of thoughts in his throbbing head.

The air handlers whispered above him.

A door whined opened, but Gerald didn't look up from his steaming mug—at least, not until a chair went crashing to the tiled floor. His eyes swept across the rows of long tables to the far side of the room, eager to shoot his best menacing gaze at whoever's bumbling had defiled his sanctuary. A thin woman strode past the fallen chair with her eyes cast to the floor, tucking a tangle of long, blonde hair behind an ear and mumbling to herself as she went. Gerald watched her without saying a word. She was a pretty girl, outward appearance of insanity aside.

"I didn't *go* there," she said to herself and made a beeline for the tarnished, cylindrical food vendor. Then she noticed Gerald. She stopped dead in her tracks, only meters away from his seat. A flush crept high into her pale cheeks.

"Sorry," he said. "Did I scare you?"

"You can't go around sneaking up on people like that," she said.

"Sneaking up?"

"It's not the proper thing to do, especially when a lady is involved!" She stabbed a finger in his direction.

"Whoa, whoa!" He raised his hands in a surrendering gesture.

"Are you always so rude?" she asked, hands on her hips.

He immediately regretted coming to the cafeteria. Clearly, all the crazies came here for breakfast.

"Sir!"

He snapped to attention.

"At the very least, apologize."

"I'm... sorry?"

"Like you mean it!" Her eyes flashed and she crossed her arms over the small but perfectly adequate swell of her breasts.

"I'm sorry, Miss."

"And you should be."

She harrumphed and continued on her way to the food dispenser. Gerald got to his feet and made a quick exit, fearful of what she might drop in his lap once she had gotten her breakfast.

Gerald returned to his quarters. He hadn't gone back since he had been spat out of that terrible hallucination. *No,* he told himself, *terrible dream.* He looked at his hands. There was still a little rust-colored grime caked beneath his nails. But even that didn't sway his conviction that the ghost lady had been a figment of his space-weary, drunken mind. Hell, bad cases of the crawl were usually accompanied by hallucinations. But you had to be in space for weeks to feel the crawl that severely—not days. *See, then, it was a dream. Not the crawl. Not a ghost.*

It made sense.

"If you're so convinced it was a dream, why are you staring at your door like an idiot?" he asked himself. He took a deep breath and punched in the key code. The door opened, and Gerald prepared himself to flee at the first sign of any thing off kilter. A talking duffle bag, a bleeding ceiling fan—he'd run straight back to Bean and that'd be that. But the room was empty. The bed was still unmade. There were still clothes scattered around the gray floor. The ceiling fan creaked as it spun on a wobbly axis. It was not bleeding. Dirty as sin, but not bleeding.

There was a communications terminal set into the wall beside the disheveled bed. Fingerprints left behind by the apartment's previous resident were greasy marks on the dull screen. The comm flashed with the words: *one missed call.* Gerald pressed his thumb to the overlay marked "message retrieval." *Downloading message,* the comm informed him in a friendly but clipped voice.

"A brief word from our sponsor, and then on to your message!" a voice said in a nauseatingly cheerful tone. A purple cartoon octopus with a bulbous body and wriggly, puffy arms floated into center of the otherwise dark screen. It began scratching at its body furiously.

"Do you suffer from itchy, dry skin?" a male voice said. The octopus nodded its head.

"Are you ready to strangle the first person you see because of it?" From behind its back, the octopus revealed a cartoon puppy, a purple tentacle tight around the small critter's throat. The puppy's eyes were little black x's and its tongue hung out the side of its cartoon mouth. The octopus fluttered its single large eye in a look of innocence.

"Then you need Gemar's body cream!" The octopus tossed the puppy aside. A tube—it looked something that'd hold toothpaste—fell from above and the octopus caught it with a sucker. *Gemar's Body Cream* was written on the tube in bubble letters. Identical tubes rained in from off-screen to land on each of the octopus' outstretched tentacles. The octopus shook the tubes over its head. Out poured thousands of tiny, glittering drops of light. A white glow soon covered the octopus. A big smile curved across the creature's face. The octopus floated off screen, expelling a realistic looking cloud of ink. The ink cloud filled with sparkling red letters that proclaimed: Gemar's!

"Gemar's! A trusted brand for 175 years! Available at a pharmacist near you!"

A rapid voice added:

"Warning, Gemar's body cream may cause constipation, loose stools, abdominal pain, and blindness. If you experience any of these symptoms, discontinue use and immediately notify your physician."

The body cream logo dissolved and was replaced with the face of a man who was the picture perfect definition of ugly. Gerald would have rather watched the commercial on loop than look at him. The face was as long as a horse's; the nose hooked up at an unnatural angle. A patchy beard poorly concealed pockmark-ridden cheeks. Gerald's first thought was that the man could use a shave, but he realized that shaving would only reveal more of his ugliness to the world.

"Mr. Evans." The man spoke as if he had a mouthful of marbles. "This is Walter Vegan. I'm Crescent's Chief of Operations. I'll be your point of contact for Mayor Kendall's contract with you. We've got your first salvage mission. It is waiting to be downloaded to your ship's computer. Mayor wants you to leave immediately. You sent a read receipt when you opened this message. We're timing you. Please don't delay."

"I'm going to need some more coffee," Gerald muttered.

[•••]

Walter Vegan's coordinates brought Bean into the Tireca system—a system of six planets that revolved around a massive blue star. The system was one jump between the Anrar system and the New Juno system, the gateway to the wealthy colonies on the frontier. Bean approached an asteroid belt that orbited a nameless blue gas giant. The asteroids were floating black specks against the planets roiling clouds. But not for long. As the hauler neared, the spots soon became boulders, massive and rotating slowly. Bean throttled toward them. Gerald looked to the radar overlay—the 3D image projected from a flat, control console-mounted screen as a shimmering, colored hologram. Bean's proximity to the nearby asteroids trailed around the bottom of the hologram in glowing green letters.

"Bean, give me a little less zoom," Gerald said. The displayed field of view increased, resulting in a choked expanse of colored blobs.

"The cluster is dense, Captain. A condition you are more than familiar with. I probably don't need to say that at this resolution you will not be able to detect even the largest of starships."

"Thank you for that pearl, Bean. Why in the hell would miners want to fly into this dense bastard?"

"Captain. You and I are here, aren't we?"

"We're not miners, Bean. What I need you to do is this: Plot the safest possible course using field density variance. We'll take that route in. Monitor it and remap as necessary for the haul."

"Yes, Captain."

Bean crested the craggy ridgeline of a shadowed, drifting mountain of ore. Open space swung into slow view. The radar overlay cleared ever-so-slightly to reveal a fair berth between rocks, but the dark strait between the colored blobs was shrinking fast. A glowing orange blip pulsed close to their present location. *The salvage. It shouldn't still be hot,* Gerald thought. As the interference cleared on the flickering display, the orange dot was flanked by several smaller red dots. Gerald cut the engines and took control from Bean, then called up the telescopic overlay. A glowing rectangle blossomed midair. It showed three metallic spiders orbiting a mining barge. The orbiting vessels each had eight curved projections that jutted from a central globe. At the end of each projection was a plasma thrower. Just a single thrower was capable of cutting the unshielded Bean right in half. Eight would turn Bean into a small sun. Gerald squeezed out a burst of retro thrust—just enough to reverse Bean out of view. On the radar overlay, the red blips spread out suddenly. Gerald looked up and saw several white flares streak out of the asteroid field. He ran a hand down his face.

"Bean, take us back the way we came."

"Take us back, Captain?" Bean inquired. "I'm reading life signs on the mining barge."

"We're not a rescue ship, Bean. Get us out of here."

"Yes, Captain. Drives coiling."

[•••]

Walter Vegan ambled toward Gerald, his horse-face set in a frown. The tall, lethal looking man that Gerald had seen in Kendall's office was at Vegan's side. He wore a wide-brimmed hat drawn low over his brow. Gerald couldn't see his eyes. The shorter man from Kendall's office was in tow behind the space-cowboy. A ruddy cheek bulged with a wad of tobacco. His black hair was slicked back close to his scalp. Vegan began to speak and Gerald placed a palm on his chest, forcing him into a nearby maintenance cart. Several tools fell to the ground with a clatter. Vegan's bloodshot eyes went wide. His mouth worked soundlessly for a moment. There was dry spittle, caked white, at the corners of his lips. Mr. Slick Hair snickered and hawked a dark wad of tobacco onto the flight deck.

"What are you doing?" Vegan managed.

"Getting ready to lay you out, Walter," Gerald hissed. "The raiders were still out there. What kind of salvage mission did you think I was equipped to run? Was it an SOS you received?"

"What? No!" Vegan protested. "Standard beacon picked up by a scout."

"Right. That's why raiders were taking potshots at the poor bastard."

Gerald glanced between Vegan and the two other men who were now posturing to intervene; the redhead's hand disappeared into the folds of his jacket. Not a good sign. Gerald removed his hand from Vegan, wiped it on his pants, and took a single step back.

"Who are your friends, Walter?" he asked.

"They're the mayor's boys, Gerald. This is Albin Catlier," Vegan said, and pointed at the taller of his two companions, "and this is Jacob Raney." Raney hawked another black wad of tobacco spit onto the deck and grinned with stained teeth. "Mr. Catlier and Mr. Raney are here to make sure you go directly to his office."

"Uh huh," Gerald said.

Catlier's hand came out from beneath his coat. Gerald felt himself about to flinch, but eased as Catlier perched a smoke between his lips. He struck a match on his boot heel and lit the cigarette.

"Whenever you're ready, Mr. Evans," Catlier said around the filter.

[•••]

Taylor stood—as intimidating as ever—beside the door to Mayor Kendall's office. The man-mountain's gargantuan frame dwarfed Gerald, Raney, and even Catlier. Taylor's arms were crossed over his keg of a chest. The bulging biceps created the appearance that the tribal-tattooed limbs were, in actuality, recently fed pythons. Surely, the cords of muscle that stood out under the bodyguard's decorated flesh were fiber-reinforced. His girth blocked the closed office door. He wore a strange little smile on his remarkably disproportionate and pug-like face. Raney stepped within centimeters of the man's barrel chest and looked up into Taylor's small eyes. Gerald surmised that the hulk could crush Raney with just a little finger. Taylor dropped his eyes to Gerald.

"Mayor Kendall is expecting you," he said, ignoring Raney and sounding bored. Taylor shoved Raney out of the way and opened the door. Gerald stepped into the office and the door was closed behind him. Mayor Kendall sat behind his desk, fingers twined together atop the LCDs. The blue glow of the monitors lit the mayor's face unevenly, creating menacing slashes of shadow on his cheeks. Kendall did not look pleased.

"Gerald," he said in a calm voice. "Your first job for me and already you've let me down. How disappointing for the both of us."

"Look, Kendall. Mayor. That mining barge was a fresh kill. It would've been suicide for me to try to haul it out. The raiders were still there when I showed up." Gerald was pissed. He tried to keep his voice even and his temper low, but his hands began to tremble.

"I know Mr. Vegan provided you with a mission brief. I had expected you'd read it. But maybe you're not capable of perceiving letter-combinations as these meaningful things we learned folks call words. The raiders, they're from the Stronghold clan. They hit, take what they can fit in their cargo holds, and then don't come back."

"They were still there!" Gerald felt himself slipping.

"Sit down, Gerald, please."

"I don't want to sit."

"Son, do not get into the habit of making me repeat myself." Kendall's tone did not waver.

Gerald sat.

"Here's what you're going to do to remedy this situation: You are going to go back to that belt and you are going to pray that derelict is still floating out there and that it hasn't been smashed to pieces by the rocks. You're going to haul it back here and that will be that. We will never have a repeat of this conversation."

Gerald found the calm in Kendall's voice unnerving. He almost wished the Mayor would lash out at him.

"Believe me when I tell you, Gerald, I will cause you far more pain than these raiders are capable of. Let me down again and you'll learn firsthand. Now go."

Gerald did not argue. He left Kendall's office and headed back to the hangar.

Gerald found Walter Vegan leaning against Bean when he returned to the flight deck. Vegan smiled a gap-toothed grin and Gerald felt the urge to knock the horse-head right off the man's slumped shoulders. Instead, he brushed passed him.

"You're dirtying my hull, Vegan," Gerald said and climbed back into the ship.

The computer chimed as Gerald harnessed himself into the control couch.

"Captain, you still have your arms," the computer said. "I take it things went well?"

"Bean," Gerald said, "I'm starting to think this contract was a big mistake."

[•••]

Bean glided back into the asteroid field. The ship rolled and yawed to avoid the floating rocks. The mining vessel drifted in a mess of its own debris. Each bit had to be scooped up individually. The process would take some time. Gerald scanned for life signs and saw right off there was no point in hailing the barge. Life support was offline. The pilot was dead.

"Bean. Flag all the debris and we'll scoop it."

Gerald looked at that radar overlay. Amoebic masses of color filled the glowing hologram. He swept his eyes over the ever-changing patches of stars. He was alone.

For now.

[Part III]

Grinding, pumping, thumping. The cacophony blaring from Heathen's speaker system sounded less like music and more like something you'd hear in the heart of a refinery. The sounds blended with the din of conversation to fill the bar with the sort of aural stew that makes you feel more drunk than you actually are. Gerald had only been at Heathen's for an hour, but he already felt the hem of his consciousness tugging itself closer to the floor. He sat at the far end of the bar with several spent bottles of beer at his elbow and watched a group of mercenaries at the opposite end of the bar, his interest shifting from wary to amused and back to wary every five minutes or so. For one thing, the meatheads were clearly not shy about their vocation—they still wore their empty holsters at their hips, over their backs, chests, ankles, and thighs. You name a body part, and there was a spot for a weapon, a vacant home for something meant to blow your head off or slit your throat. The mercenaries weren't paid to pick flowers, that was for goddamn sure. They huddled over Heathen's juke-core, their bearded and dirty faces lit up by pinks, purples, yellows, and blues. The colors oscillated madly to the beat of the music.

"This used to be such a nice place," Gerald grumbled.

"What's that?" Maerl, the owner and bartender, happened to be standing right in front of him. Gerald lifted his gaze. Based on Maerl's sour look, he must've thought the comment was directed at him. Gerald gestured to the mercenaries with a cock of his head.

"Ah." Maerl nodded. "Just got here today. Rumor has it they're off to one of Darros Stronghold's newly… acquired colonies in the Habeos system to settle some sort of border dispute. Apparently, the crime lord offers great benefits." Maerl grunted. "Here's to hoping they don't stay on Crescent much longer. If have to take a second night of this… music… I'll put lit cigarettes out in my ears."

"No shit," Gerald said. Maerl pointed at Gerald's empty bottle; Gerald nodded.

"Sometimes, Gerald, I can't wait to sell Heathen's and move off to New Juno."

"Yeah?" Gerald said.

"I'm building my nest egg. That's why I opened Heathen's in the first place." A few more patrons bellied up to the bar, and Maerl winked and moved off to take care of them.

Gerald turned his attention to the widescreen LCD above the bar. It showed some poor news correspondent getting pounded by a blizzard and looking completely miserable about it. From what Gerald could pick up over the noise, there had been a colonial uprising in Habeos system—two jumps away. According to the report, the rub was that no one could figure out how the colonists got so many guns so fast. A lot of people had died in the violence. It was presumed that Darros Stronghold, local raider warlord, had had some involvement. Stronghold was always involved.

One of Maerl's bartenders switched the channel to a pre-recorded vatter concert. Vatters were a special breed of musician. Decorated head to toe with metal studs called trodes, vatters splashed around in bio-conductive goo to make their music. The combination of the liquid and the trodes enabled the vatter to communicate with their gear, resulting in the display of noise, color, and light that filled the screen above the bar. Even though Gerald wasn't a fan of the vatter currently on the LCD, he would have taken anything over the news. It was always so sensationalized and depressing.

"How was the first day on the job?" Marisa sidled up next to Gerald. Her uniform jacket was unbuttoned, exposing the taut white tee shirt beneath. The shirt was blank, save for a black stencil between the swell of her breasts that depicted a hand with the middle finger extended.

"It was work." Gerald didn't care to elaborate. He was drinking to forget about his *first day on the job*, not so that he could relive it. He looked away from Marisa to watch two of the mercenaries punch each other in the chest. They yelled the word "bro" at the top of their lungs with each successive blow. Marisa glanced in their direction and rolled her eyes.

"I think those wastes of flesh were drunk when they landed their spider a few hours ago."

"Spider." Gerald looked her. He thought of mentioning his little encounter. Glancing back at the testosterone-fest, he thought better of it.

"Not a fun weapons inspection," she said and shuddered. "Grab-asses." She wrapped her long fingers around the neck of Gerald's beer bottle and took an exaggerated pull. She smiled and licked her lips. "Thanks, hon. Been a long day for me, too." She waved Maerl over. "Shots. Stat."

"House special, Officer Griffin?" Maerl inquired.

"I'm off duty. Somethin' stronger than that. I think Gerry's had a bad day."

"Marisa. I really don't want to… "

"Be a man?" She rubbed his thigh. The full line of her lips curved into a grin that spelled disaster. "You're under my care now. You'll feel swarthy again before this is all said and done."

Two steaming shot glasses were placed before them. Maerl crossed his arms over his chest. His blue eyes swam with sympathy and no small amount of concern.

"I don't care what trouble you two get into. Just don't get into it here. Understand?"

Marisa looked up at Maerl and batted her lashes, her lips pursing into an innocent pout that belied the glimmer in her green eyes.

"I'm not a bad girl, Maerlie. You know that," she said as she hefted a shot glass; Gerald took his own and they clinked them together. "May we find your balls again by the end of the night!"

Gerald laughed. He tossed the steaming liquid into his mouth. It splashed against his throat and burned like holy hell. He set the glass down hard and slapped the bar with his other hand.

"Sweet merciful crap!" he managed.

Marisa nearly gagged and then sat up straight, as if she had just had a brilliant idea. She raised her hand and pointed a finger skyward.

"Another round, executioner!"

An hour later, Gerald could no longer recall why he'd been having a bad day.

"I'm going to have to check the grounding because that damn panel keeps shorting out, no matter what I do. It doesn't happen all the time. It only seems to happen when I'm in a bad mood. I can only take so much voltage in my finger. I swear." He looked around conspiratorially. "Bean is messing with me. Goddamned bucket of scrap." He looked at Marisa, who was no longer paying attention. Instead, her eyes were directed down to the far end of the bar and locked with a mercenary's narrowed gaze.

"Gerry," she whispered sidelong, "this fuck won't stop staring at me."

"Maybe because you're staring at him."

She turned and looked directly at Gerald, and shook her head.

"Don't get jealous on me, Gerry. Just letting him know who the alpha is."

"Great," Gerald said and moaned.

The mercenary walked an uneven line in their direction. His cracked lips were set into an ear-to-ear grin. Some green, mystery juice stained his crooked teeth. His eyes didn't so much as blink in Gerald's direction. No, the mercenary's sights were one hundred percent fixed on Marisa's exposed skin.

"Hello, darlin'," the mercenary said in a thick and slurred voice. He leaned against the bar. A tingling sensation rose from the base of Gerald's beanbag, up the length of his spine, and settled in at the back of his neck, causing the hairs to stand up there. Honor-defending time was fast approaching.

"Can I buy you a… .?" the mercenary began.

"Drink? I already have one. Thanks anyway, love."

"How about a screw?" He reached over and grabbed her crotch. Gerald was too stunned to engage in any kind of chivalrous act—his inability to react was moot. Marisa already had a handful of the mercenary's hair. She slammed his dirty, bearded face nose first into the bar. Cartilage and bone flattened with an audible crack.

"I've already got one of those, too." She let go of his hair and he slid to the ground with his hands on his face. He was too drunk and in too much pain to do anything other than repeat "my nose, my nose" over and over. The mercenary's compadres, dumb and dumber, were already on their feet at the other end of the bar and coming in fast. Gerald slid off his stool and looked to Maerl, who shrugged almost apologetically. Gerald looked to Marisa and she winked. She was enjoying this; the crazy bitch actually looked happy. A nasty, scar-faced bastard was the first to reach them. Gerald stepped right in front of him, fists raised. The mercenary reached into his furry overcoat. Gerald's eye caught a glimpse of something disturbingly similar to the butt of a gun.

"He's packing," Gerald spat at Marisa. She dropped her hand to her waist for the stunner that usually rode there, but holster and stunner were back in her locker at HQ.

The lights went out and the music died.

The bar-goers yelled in protest.

Then it got loud—real loud. A grinding, shrieking noise erupted from all around, immediately overwhelming the yells of the half-drunk crowd. It sounded like the metal ceiling was being sheared in two. Gerald put his hands to his ears. There was a bright flash of blue light—like high voltage electricity. Gerald thought he saw a black shape seeping through the crowd, ink dropped in a bucket of water.

Another flash.

Silver stalks—*no, not stalks, spikes,* Gerald thought—sprouted from the floor. The spikes overturned tables and impaled a handful of unfortunate souls through the chest and other less savory spots before the people could even scream.

Black.

Another flash.

Limp bodies slid down the length of the strange metal protrusions. Blood snaked down the shafts in glistening, slithering veins. The flashes of light that illuminated the horrific events lasted for no more than an eye-blink. So fast, in fact, that Gerald wasn't sure that he had seen any of it.

There were screams as the darkness held them captive. He reached out and grabbed Marisa's hand. It was ice cold.

"Marisa, did you see… "

"No," she said. "No. I didn't see a goddamned thing. I didn't see a goddamned thing."

And like that, Heathen's light panels flickered to life. Marisa's eyes were on him. For an instant, her eyes were like polished onyx—but when she blinked, the green reappeared. The music was back up. The metal shafts Gerald had glimpsed were gone, but there were bodies. They lay in growing pools of dark red with arms and legs contorted. Gerald counted at least five of them. Two of the cadavers belonged to the mercenaries that had been ready to brawl no more than sixty seconds earlier. The scar-faced one had a slab gun clutched in a bloodied hand. His friend gripped an identical ceramic, snub-nosed weapon. Grapefruit-sized holes bloodied their torsos. Had they shot each other in the chaos?

The batwing doors slammed open.

Blue uniforms began to flood into the room. Maerl mopped at his brow with a bar rag. He looked like he was about to have a coronary. Marisa gaped at the dead mercenaries where they lay, her slender hand at her throat.

“They shot each other,” Marisa said. Gerald looked at her; she was still staring.

“You saw what I saw.” He grabbed her arm. “You did, didn’t you?”

“They shot each other.” She pointed at the guns and tore her green eyes away to meet Gerald’s. She waved her hand in an arc to indicate the rest of the barroom. “And they shot those innocent people. I did the weapons check myself. How could I have missed slab guns? This is bad.” Gerald rubbed his eyes with the heels of his hands—a gesture that was becoming way too familiar. Maybe Marisa hadn’t seen anything. Maybe it was another hallucination. Her skin was positively blanched, though—like she had seen a ghost. He wasn’t going to push the issue. Security ushered them out of Heathen’s and onto Main Street.

Marisa was talking to a security officer just out of earshot. She no longer wore the terrified look, but surveyed the area with a sweep of her eyes that did not make eye contact with Gerald. She looked in control of herself again. Gerald wished he felt the same, but he was so goddamn tired. He felt like he was going out of his mind with exhaustion. Three-quarters of the bar crowd milled around in the vicinity of the pub like lost souls. They peered into the windows of the neighboring dark shops, talking in low voices and hoping that Heathen’s would reopen soon. The meat wagon rolled up, treads creaking. The coroner followed behind the body-hauling cart with a data-pad tucked underneath one arm and a cigarette burning low between two spindly fingers. He went into the tavern.

“I can’t see how they shot those other folks,” a voice said from below.

Gerald looked down. A diminutive man, arms corded with muscles and painted with tattoos, rubbed at a goateed chin with stubby fingers.

“What?”

“I can’t see how they shot those folks all the way across the bar. Guess it’s a good thing I’m short or else that would’a been my head.”

Gerald didn’t respond. He had nothing to contribute. A security guard stepped out of Heathen’s and brushed past him. Before the doors swung shut again, Gerald could see Maerl talking to the security captain; a red flush was creeping out of the bar owner’s collar and onto his face.

“But crazy shit can happen in the dark, huh?” the small man said.

Gerald dropped his eyes and nodded.

“You okay, brother? You look like you just caught your daddy fucking your sister.”

Gerald raised his eyebrows and sighed. He felt around for his cigarettes, but knew he had left them sitting on the bar.

"It's been a long day," he said. "How about you give me a smoke and I'll promise not to tell you about it."

[•••]

The comm terminal's incessant chiming pulled Marisa out of a restless sleep. She sat up and rubbed her eyes; her legs were tangled in the sheets. She could see the comm unit from her bed. The glowing, glossy display screen was a manifestation of the dread that had kept her tossing and turning all night. Security HQ was calling her. Captain Benedict was no doubt feeling unsettled by the ugly night at Heathen's. He was calling to blame her, and why wouldn't he? After all, Marisa herself had cleared those mercenaries to enter the station.

She rose, went to the terminal and activated the unit. The screen filled with a sea of static, and then went blank.

"Hello?" she said.

The screen winked back on. It showed a grainy security feed for a dark and empty corridor. A few light panels cast flickering patches on a dirty floor. Marisa leaned in close. She didn't recognize the part of the station she was looking at. A woman walked through the camera's field of view. She wore the blues of a security officer. The woman glanced up at the camera as she walked by. This prompted Marisa to lean even closer to the screen. Was it... ?

No. It couldn't be.

The camera changed angles to show a large, black bulkhead. Yellow letters were stenciled across its surface. They read *no entry, authorized personnel only.* A large, red X was crudely painted over the span of the bulkhead.

Good lord. It was the *Vault.* A Crescent myth, the Vault wasn't supposed to actually exist. Even if someone could find it, the whole area where it was rumored to be was strictly off limits. Everybody knew that. The station level had been sealed off due to some catastrophic event in its early history—or so said the rumors.

A delicate thing of a woman with thin arms, long legs, and blonde hair that fell past her shoulders knelt in front of the bulkhead. Her cheek was pressed to the black metal. The security officer stepped back into view and Marisa now saw what she hadn't believed at first. The officer was her. There was no sound, but Marisa could tell by her onscreen mannerisms that her pixelated alter-ego was confronting the blonde woman. The woman reached out so quickly it was all but a blur. Slender fingers wrapped around the wrist of the onscreen version of Marisa. She was pulled forward into the black bulkhead. In her apartment, Marisa put her hand to her forehead, which had begun to ache. The screen started to fill with growing black patches, as if the LCD was burning out. Soon, the whole screen was black.

It didn't stop there. The darkness seeped out around the edges of the comm panel and drifted toward Marisa in long, thin tendrils. She stepped back to avoid them but she was too slow and they brushed against the bare skin of her arms.

She had never felt so cold.

[•••]

Marisa's eyes fluttered open. She stared at her ceiling. Her sweet, familiar ceiling. *A dream*, she thought. It was a strange one, at that, and probably a reaction to the stress of the previous night. It felt really early to her. She had woken up before her alarm had gone off. Two hours early, according to the ovoid PDA strapped to her wrist. A bottle of carthine sat open on her night stand. Apparently, the sedative had not done its trick.

Judging by the flashing clock display, there had been another power failure—the second in as many weeks. The power was back on now, though, and that was a good thing. The last power outage lasted so long; the entire apartment block had to be emptied out. It got so cold, people's crappers were freezing; the water in the bathrooms had turned to solid ice. For an hour, she lay in bed watching the clock above the comm flash a row of glowing green eights. She spent the next hour showering and mentally preparing herself for a day that was sure to be full of questions. She kept expecting the call from Captain Benedict, but it never came.

Marisa pulled the uniform jacket over her tee shirt, pushed the wet hair out of her face and tied it back. She slid the slender stun rod into the curved holster that hung on her hip and looked at the wall clock. Eights. Crazy eights.

She stepped out of her apartment. There was a splash when her boot came down.

"What the fuck?"

Black water covered the deck and rippled around her shins. Overhead, fluorescent panels flickered dim, and dapples of light trembled faintly on the walls and neighboring apartment doors.

"This is ridiculous," Marisa said through clenched teeth. The water was cold and her calves began to twist into painful knots. The door to her apartment slid shut with a gurgle. She entered her keycode. There was a crackle and nothing happened. "Of course. Makes sense," she said to no one in particular.

Most of the lights were out—more than three-quarters of the translucent ceiling panels were dark. Water dripped from around their edges in steady drip-drops. She could see her breath in the meager light that fell from the few lit squares. She was the only one in corridor, as far as she could see. The hall curved into darkness in front of her and behind her. She began to walk in the direction of the lifts. If she knew one thing, it was that she was freezing her ass off and none too happy about it.

There was splashing up ahead, just around the bend of the corridor. The sound was almost frantic in its intensity. It sounded as if someone were playing, and having a gay old time, to boot. The station was filled with such freaks; she could hardly believe it sometimes. She went around the hallway's curve and suddenly her foot was no longer in contact with the floor. There was an instant of freefall, and then Marisa was submerged in the cold water. She broke the surface with a coughing gasp. Panic whispered *hello* somewhere in the back of her mind. She looked around and felt an approaching scream for help tickle her throat. Was there a hole in the deck?

She looked up and saw the rectangle of fluttering light above her. From the looks of it, Marisa surmised she had fallen at least three meters. Maybe more. Water trickled down the face of the close, dark walls in a slow moving sheet. It looked like living glass. Drops of it rained from overhead.

Again came the sound of playful

Violent.

splashing. It wasn't far off. She removed the small flashlight from her belt and turned it on. A white shaft of light cut through the narrow chamber. Mist lifted off the rippling surface of the dark water in ghostly filaments. She lifted her face upward, and pointed the flashlight beam overhead, where she could make out rusted chains hanging from the shadow-veiled ceiling. Water rained down on her again. Marisa closed her eyes as it hit her face in big drops. She had seen enough to know where she was—one of the condensation cisterns that were part of Crescent's life support system. How the hell had she ended up in there? The cisterns were a long way from home. The answer didn't matter too much at the moment. What mattered was to keep moving and find the exit before hypothermia put her to sleep for good. She was shivering so violently it was difficult to walk straight.

As she had suspected, Marisa wasn't alone in the cistern. A man, hairless and shirtless, was waist deep some five meters ahead of her. His back was to Marisa and he was dashing around in the black water. His arms flailed in and out of the dark liquid. The water trailed above his bald scalp in arcs that caught the light of Marisa's flashlight. The droplets glittered like diamonds before spattering back into the murk.

"Hey!" she shouted. He didn't answer her. As she got closer, she could see he had tiny, silver studs poking out of his skin. He was a vatter.

"Hey!" she shouted again. The man went still with such suddenness that Marisa took a step backward. He turned and looked at her with sable eyes. They were darker than the water. Marisa took another stuttering step backward and the vatter began running at her. The water was still up to his waist, but he managed to cut through the liquid with a horrible speed that left her paralyzed. He closed much of the space between them by the time Marisa convinced her body to move. She turned and began to trudge away from him. Well ahead of her, the rectangle of light stayed no bigger than a shoe box. Marisa knew the water was slowing her down way too much. There was no way she could escape. Terror poked holes in her brain stem. Breath puffed out before her in quick white clouds. Panic spoke up full now, and it said, *Scream for your life, bitch!*

Marisa screamed. The rectangle of light began to fill with black—slow black, like tar. The light from above was choked out. It reminded her of the dream.

Around her, the shadows began to slink off the walls. Penumbral tentacles reached out to wrap around her.

An icy hand grabbed her by the back of the neck and plunged her beneath the water's black, undulating surface.

[•••]

"Is she going to be okay?" a distant and familiar voice asked. Her eyelids were so goddamned heavy. They felt gummed together.

"I think so. She was mildly hypothermic when the maintenance crew stumbled across her. I managed to get her core temperature back up with little problem. And her circulation is fine." She didn't recognize that voice.

"Doc, how long was she down there?" She liked that voice, but she felt bad because he sounded so concerned.

"I'd say at least several hours."

"Good Christ. Did she say anything to you? Like why the hell she was in the cistern?"

Were they talking about her? Marisa couldn't figure it out. Understanding teetered on the edge of her struggling mind, but she could only brush her fingertips against it. She didn't remember anything about being in any cistern. Not really, anyhow. For some reason, she *did* remember water. Regardless, she thought the people in the room were talking about crazy things and she wished they would stop. She opened her eyes and the light hurt. She saw Gerald. He was facing away from her. She tried to reach for him, but was too weak to lift her arm. He was talking with a man in a white coat. A doctor.

"She mumbled something about a vatter—about having to find something for him," the doctor said. Marisa's skin prickled at the word and she felt herself jerked closer to full consciousness. *The cistern. The vatter. The Black. Yes. The Black.*

She blinked and behind closed lids, she saw Heathen's. She saw the chaos from the night before, but it moved in still frame. Cords of shadow slinked through the shuddering crowd.

The Black had been at Heathen's.

She knew the Black from somewhere else, too. *Where?* Somewhere deep.

Her whole being felt suddenly heavy again. She let the thoughts slip from her like sand through extended fingers.

"That was pretty much it," the voice of the doctor said. "That, and that she was cold—obviously. The tox screen showed carthine in her system. Does she use it regularly?"

"Only when she can't sleep. We had an interesting night last night. I'm not surprised she took some."

"At high levels, carthine can and generally does cause powerful hallucinations."

"How much did she take?" Gerald asked.

"It's difficult to say. The body metabolizes it pretty quickly. Her blood alcohol level was also high."

Marisa had heard enough. She was tired. Too tired to deal with any of it. She closed her eyes and waited for sleep.

She did not have to wait long.

[Part IV]

"ETA fifteen minutes, Captain. Time to wake up."

"Thanks, Bean. I'm not sleeping."

"No?" said the ship's computer. "You have been awfully quiet since we left Crescent."

"I feel bad for leaving Marisa alone at that hospital, Bean. That's all. I'm not a self-absorbed prick all the time, you know."

"Captain, I had not previously detected this level of sensitivity in you. Perhaps instead of taking off, I should have run you a hot bath?"

The star Tireca took up most of the front viewport. Blue-green solar prominences flared off the sun's surface as gossamer threads of glowing plasma. The nanites embedded in the four-centimeter-thick smart-glass automatically polarized so as not to blind Bean's occupant. Gerald shielded his eyes. Even with the polarization, the view was almost too bright.

"What do you make of a colony ship being this far off course?"

"A faulty guidance system would be my first guess," Bean replied.

"Right. Because it's impossible to know when you're headed into a sun." Gerald scratched one stubbly cheek. "Bean, we've done strange salvage runs before. Some really weird shit. But something about these last two has rubbed me a little funny. Call it a gut instinct." Gerald yawned. He remained trapped in a maze of cotton-skulled exhaustion. It had been one thing after the other since he landed two days ago. *Two days?* Gerald thought. *Is that really all? Feels like two weeks.*

"I won't ask why, Captain. I confess. I do not understand the human *gut instinct.* Will you cancel your contract with Kendall?"

"I don't think that'd be a good idea. Another gut instinct. Kendall's not the type to let contractors terminate their own work orders."

The ship began to slow.

"Bean?"

"We are approaching the limit of my hull's heat tolerance."

Gerald looked over at the radar overlay and then out at the mottled blue brilliance that filled the viewport.

"The colony ship is," Gerald checked a display, "twenty-five hundred meters off. The retrieval line won't reach that far."

"I can fire the drones to haul it within tug range."

"And what's the chance that the drones will survive the heat?"

"Better than your own chance at survival if you return to Crescent without that ship."

Gerald laughed.

"Bean, your capacity for humor in the face of adversity amazes me."

"I wasn't joking, Captain."

"Yeah, yeah. Go ahead, launch the drones. That's why I have'm," he said, and then added, "They're on their last leg anyway." Still, Gerald felt little comfort.

Gerald called up four holographic overlays, each representing cameras mounted on each of Bean's drones. Each individual overlay was quartered, showing infrared, x-ray, microwave, and visible spectrum views. The colony ship appeared as a dark hulk against the hot, blue backdrop of massive Tireca. Gerald switched the visible spectrum camera to manual operation and began cycling through the polarization filters until the view became crisp. There it was. A floating, bloated mass of slag in a degrading orbit. The metal was glowing, almost white from the heat. It looked more like a terminal asteroid than a ship.

"Bean. Did you pick up any lifeboat beacons?"

"Negative, Captain. No indication that lifeboats had been launched."

Gerald sighed and cursed under his breath.

"These ships carry easily two hundred passengers and you're telling me not one got off? How the hell could this have happened? What were they doing going toward the sun?"

"A bad sub-light drive?" Bean offered.

"It sucks. That's what. Hook up the tethers the best you can when the drones haul that thing in. If they manage to haul it in."

Several minutes went by before Bean spoke up again.

"The drones have successfully latched onto the salvage. They are on their way back. Five hundred meters and closing."

"Whatever. Just tether the colony ship and take us back to Crescent." Gerald's mood was only worsening. The longer they were out there, the more he felt like hitting someone.

Twelve hauling tethers uncoiled from Bean's belly with serpentine grace. Gleaming, the lines twisted out to meet the oncoming drones and their burden. The arachnid-like robots doused the surface of the derelict with coolant. The ship's skin was glossy and distorted, an unbroken sheet of rippling glass.

The hauling tethers had nothing to latch onto. They slid repeatedly off the hulk.

"Bean?"

"Captain. Do I have to remind you that I am not a mining vessel? My tethers are designed for ship and cargo container hauling. This colony ship is a small asteroid."

"Switch to manual and I'll give it a shot."

"What makes you think you have a better chance of securing the colony ship than a computer?" Bean asked.

"Watch and learn, Bean."

Panels in the top of both control couch arms slid open. Six small joysticks protruded from each panel; one by one, a green light winked on at the tips of the controls.

"Manual control engaged, Captain." An overlay shimmered into view directly in front of him; it showed the slagheap, the tethers, and Bean.

"Rotate camera Alt 50 degrees, Azimuth 90. The friggin' thing looks like a potato."

Gerald began to manipulate six of the twelve joysticks using his fingertips, sending the tethers toward the dead colony ship. Three of the shining lengths of segmented metal cable slid beneath the target while the other three slithered across the top. The tethers met at the aft of the target and tied themselves together. The remaining tethers snaked out and Gerald manipulated them in the same fashion as the first six, only perpendicular to the first set, effectively netting in the bloated, misshapen colony ship.

"Viola. Simple as that, Bean-bag."

"I hate when you call me that," Bean said. The synthesized voice sounded wounded.

"Like you have feelings."

"My complexity would surprise even you, Captain Sensitivity." Bean paused. "The hauling configuration is not stable. I fear the tethers will not hold the colony ship indefinitely."

"Who said anything about indefinitely? We just have to get it back to Crescent."

[•••]

Bean shook violently when the sub-light engines disengaged.

"What the hell was that?" Gerald gripped the arms of the control couch.

"That was the colony ship decelerating at a different rate from us, and there is another problem."

"And that is?"

"The colony ship is about to hit us."

Gerald was thrown hard against the restraints, the wind belched out of his lungs. Crescent, Anrar III, and cold space spiraled in the viewport. A klaxon began to wail as the hull moaned. Gerald caught his breath and watched as several of Bean's drones—smashed nearly beyond recognition—floated by the viewport. Bits of hull drifted like metallic confetti in the wake of the robot carcasses. The ship's structure groaned again. This time, louder.

"Bean! Status! And turn off the goddamned alarm."

"Captain. The drone bay has been ruptured. The ship will depressurize any second now."

"Oh crap."

"I recommend you put on your EV suit."

Gerald was out of the control couch and across the small bridge in an eyeblink. The emergency locker was open and he was ripping off his pants and then his shirt. Bean began to vibrate beneath his feet.

"Detach the tethers, Bean. Get control of the ship and bring us in. Send out a distress call to ATC and get the pattern cleared." He pulled on the close-fitting pants and the jacket of the life suit. The hem of the jacket sealed itself to the pants with a muted, sucking sound. Next came the helmet. It was almost too small for his head. Gerald wished he had tried the damn thing on before he bought it. He forced it on and heard the click of the seal. His neck was scrunched and already beginning to cramp. In short, quick *I-have-to-pee-really-bad* strides, Gerald dashed back to the control couch and strapped in. The maintenance bulkhead that led to the smashed drone bay blew out and there were thirty roaring seconds of escaping atmosphere and several loud crashes as whatever wasn't bolted down was blasted into space.

And then silence.

[•••]

Gerald pressed the door buzzer. There was no answer. He pressed it again. And again. And still one more time for annoyed good measure. He knew she was home. The hospital told him they had discharged her two hours after he had left her bedside. He was ready to hit the button again when the door opened, revealing a bed-ruffled Marisa. White cotton pants hung low on her waist, creating a gap beneath the gray tank top she wore. The space showed off a taut belly painted with a tattoo of the mythical beast that shared her namesake. Her hair was piled atop her head in a nest of stray locks.

"Sorry, I was… " she began.

"Napping? I see that. From what the doctor had to say, sounds like you had a long night."

She sighed.

"Come in, Gerry."

"Never thought you'd ask," he said, and brushed past her.

Her tiny apartment was immaculate as always. Despite some of her more wild inclinations, Marisa had proven herself to be a neat freak, time and again. He sat on the edge of the shelf-bed that protruded from the wall. Marisa pulled up a plastic chair and sat across from him.

"Some night, huh?" she said.

"You could say that," he replied.

"You sound… irritated."

"Irritated? Maybe. I don't know. I haven't recovered from my trip here. I haven't gotten any sleep. I'm hung-over. Bean got fucked up today. Kendall is an ass face, and my girlfriend is overdosing on carthine."

"Oh, I'm your girlfriend now?" she said, openly ignoring the carthine comment. Gerald looked up at her and frowned at her dodge.

"What happened last night, after we left Heathen's?" he asked. He wasn't going to allow her cuteness to disarm him. Not if he could help it.

"Look, Gerry. I don't know what happened. I do know that I didn't OD. Don't trust me?" She reached over to a nearby table and tossed him a pill bottle. It was nearly full. "See? Ever think we had too much to drink last night? How much of the end of the night do you remember?"

He didn't respond. *Hello pot,* he thought, *my name is kettle.*

"Exactly. So be pissed that you don't feel well, be pissed because Kendall is a… what did you call him, ass face? But don't be pissed at me, okay? I didn't do anything wrong. Or rather, I didn't do anything more wrong than taking that last shot." Marisa leaned toward him and planted a kiss square on his lips. She slid out of the plastic chair to kneel between his knees and twined her fingers into his hair. She kissed him a second time and then pulled away.

"Friends?"

"Yeah. Yeah we're fine."

"Good, because you really shouldn't be mad at your girlfriend, especially when she does things like this." She slid her hand into his pants and squeezed.

"What other things does she do?"

[•••]

"They keep you closed all night?" Gerald pushed around a few digital brochures Maerl had been showing off. The flimsy things, appropriately called flimsies or flims, shimmered with images of several pieces of attractive real estate in the New Juno colonies.

"You don't remember coming back in here a few hours later?" Maerl arched a dark brow and placed the brochures under the bar. Gerald felt even worse about having been pissed at Marisa.

"Right," Gerald said. "More shots."

"Is Mari okay? Heard she ended up in the hospital. That true?"

"Yeah. She's fine now. She was in rough shape when I walked her home. I shouldn't have let her out of my sight," Gerald admitted.

"And where is she now?"

"Out of my sight." Gerald smiled and shrugged. He took a sip of his beer. "That is to say, she was coherent when I left her, and at this time is taking a nap."

Maerl placed two cocktails on a tray and moved out from behind the bar. Gerald stared at the large LCD above the racks of liquor. A large-breasted cartoon girl with even larger eyes, was flying across the void of space toward a giant, neon-green can of a soft drink called *Wheezie!* She stripped off her space suit as she went. The screen dissolved into a news story. He was about to look away when he saw that the feed was about a missing colony ship bound for New Juno. Apparently, the ship had disappeared a few days back. Several important political figures had been onboard, on their way to a summit to discuss the escalating violence in the Habeos systems. Gerald didn't want to know.

The anchorman segued into a local story. Apparently, a young mother of two had also gone missing, leaving her toddlers home alone for days. Hungry and confused, the toddlers were otherwise no worse for wear, but there was still no sign of the mother. *What kind of person just walks out on their kids like that?* Gerald thought. He wondered why the hell Maerl insisted on playing the news in the bar.

"That's the third missing person story they've aired on the news this week," Maerl commented as he stepped back around the bar. "Better keep an eye on that girl of yours."

"She can take care of herself, provided she's not too drunk." Gerald finished his beer and slid the empty bottle away. Maerl placed another before him. Gerald reached for his wallet, but the bartender held up a hand to stop him. He pointed over Gerald's shoulder.

"Courtesy of Dr. Donovan Cortez and his daughter, Dr. Ina Cortez. They want you to join them for a drink."

Gerald turned on his stool. He recognized Donovan Cortez from Kendall's office. Cortez sat in a booth on the far side of Heathen's beneath a glowing caricature of a shapely female figure. Beneath the shape were the words *Drink Femalien!* Cortez wore a suit, minus the jacket. His shirt collar looked too tight for his chubby neck. Curly gray hair, matted at the top, sprung out around the doctor's ears. Ina Cortez sat beside the doctor, half in and half out of the booth. Her cornsilk hair was combed straight and parted in the middle. It fell past thin, pale shoulders that were exposed save for the narrow straps of her small dress. Her eyes were pointed downward and hidden behind long lashes. She looked uncomfortable. And both she and her father looked woefully out of place. Gerald stood and made his way over to them.

"Dr. Cortez?" Gerald said amicably enough as he stepped to the booth. The older man looked up at him and smiled. Cortez tried to stand too quickly; the olive green table shuddered and threatened to spill the two drinks that sat atop it. Cortez's plump lips spread in a wide smile.

"Mr. Evans!"

"You just bought me a beer, Doc. You don't need to act surprised to see me." He paused, waiting. When Cortez said nothing, Gerald spoke again. "Generally, this is when you'd ask me to sit."

"Oh yes, yes. I'm sorry. I'm not used to… doing this sort of thing. Please, sit."

"Hello," Gerald looked to the daughter. "Ina, is it?" he inquired. She raised her eyes to him and offered a quick smile before averting her gaze again. She was the crazy girl who had spoiled Gerald's morning coffee. Her blue eyes didn't hint at recognition, so he decided to keep his mouth shut. No sense in heightening the awkwardness. Gerald sat. "So, what sort of *thing* is this, anyway?"

"It is my understanding that you are Crescent Station's salvage man."

"Yeah, that's right. For how much longer, I don't know. Things haven't been going all that smoothly."

Donovan frowned and looked perplexed.

"Chalk it up to Kendall and I not exactly seeing eye to eye on the definition of *salvage.*" Gerald took a sip of the beer Donovan had bought him. He set the bottle down and noticed Ina's bare ankle. It was delicate and pale. There was a tattoo there, nestled just below her ankle bone. The artwork looked like a small rose, but Gerald couldn't be sure without staring, and he didn't want to make her or her father any more uncomfortable than they already were.

"I have a job for you. If you are interested. I don't know what kind of contract you have with Crescent. I don't really care, to be honest with you. I don't want Kendall to know about this. I am prepared to compensate you very well—better, I'm sure, than Kendall is paying you for your entire contract."

"I wouldn't be too sure about that, Doc. Kendall is paying me pretty damn well," Gerald played coy, but his interest was piqued. If he could manage to take in enough cash on the side, maybe he could buy his way out of the contract with Kendall.

Cortez waved his hand.

"Money is no object, Mr. Evans. There is a ship—a shuttle. I want you to haul it back to Crescent for me."

"A shuttle?"

"A shuttle," the elder Cortez echoed. "It is very old and likely very fragile. I've been over your files. You have a commendable record, Mr. Evans. So many salvage runs with such a high success rate, and quite the variety of hauls. I think you can handle picking up my little shuttle."

"Right. So, you want me to tug a shuttle into Crescent without anyone getting wind of it? How do you propose I do that? Take it apart and stow it my bunk?"

"No, no. Leave that to me. Vegan and his crew can be bought. The deck hands can be bought. None of that should be your concern. All you have to do is go to the coordinates that I will send you, grab the shuttle, and bring it back to Hangar 19."

"And what else can you tell me about this shuttle, Doctor?" Gerald asked.

"In truth, little. I have reason to believe that this lifeboat is from an old, abandoned mining colony on Anrar III."

"Lifeboat or shuttle, Doc? That makes a big difference."

"Well. More likely the former than the latter. It should be in the small asteroid belt orbiting moon III of Anrar VI."

Gerald tapped at his chin. He looked from the elder Cortez's eager but cautious face to the daughter's, which was hidden behind a fall of golden hair.

"Do you have anything to offer here, Miss… rather, Dr. Cortez?"

"No." She didn't bother looking up.

"Doc, how did you come by this information?" Gerald asked.

"I can't say," the elder Cortez said.

Can't say, or won't, Gerald thought.

"Right. Let's say I go out there and it's not there," Gerald said over the mouth of the beer bottle. He emptied the contents and set the bottle down on the table.

"It'll be there," Donovan insisted.

"Let's say I go out there and it's not there. I'd expect to get paid in full."

"Yes, of course, Gerald. I will compensate you for your time, either way," Donovan kneaded his pudgy hands.

"And I'd expect a hefty down payment even before I set foot on my ship," Gerald added.

"Yes, yes," Donovan said. He sounded impatient. "All that can be arranged easily."

"You know I'm without a ship, right? For at least a day." Gerald figured the Cortezes had the right to know.

"What? No. I didn't know that," Donovan sighed and looked away.

"Little accident this morning. Bean is dry-docked until the day after next."

"I was not aware of that." Donovan sounded disappointed, but a moment later he was smiling again. He had the tiniest of spaces between his front teeth. "Two days is a sufferable delay. I have waited this long, after all."

Gerald slid the empty bottle across the table.

"Thanks for the beer." He stood and began to walk away, but Donovan grabbed him by the hem of his shirt.

"Wait!"

Gerald slapped his hand away.

"Come on now, Doc. That's no way to behave."

Donovan took a deep breath and regained his composure.

"I'm sorry. This is just very important. That derelict could answer a lot of questions."

"If it's out there."

"It's out there."

"Let me sleep on it, Doc. I'll let you know tomorrow, either way."

Gerald left Heathen's without another word.

[•••]

Gerald didn't wake up so much as he half jumped out of his bed. The creaking ceiling fan cooled a sheen of sweat on his bare chest. The dream faded fast from his memories—tatters of red and engine-oil black. Violet stars and dust. Planets. Death. Gerald shuddered. His mind wouldn't form anything substantial from the dream other than a sick feeling in the pit of his stomach and the urge to shit. He looked at the time display that floated on the screen of the wall terminal. It was 3:45 in the morning.

He saw movement out of the corner of his eye and turned so suddenly that a hot lance of pain shot down his neck. A pudgy kid, clutching a small flashlight in one hand, dashed into Gerald's washroom. The narrow door slammed shut behind him.

"Hey, kid! What the hell?" Gerald shouted.

A heartbeat later, Gerald was standing; any hope of getting back to sleep fell to the floor like the cast-off bed sheets. If this kid was trying to rob him, he'd have more success going out the front door, not into the bathroom. *Stupid.* Gerald pulled the door open and snapped on the light.

The bathroom was empty. Every single hair on his body stood on end. Gerald's reflection stared back at him from the mirror. He had seen the kid go in there, plain as day. Gerald swallowed hard. He pulled back the plastic shower curtain. Empty.

He dropped his eyes to the floor. A metal object sat on the oval bath mat. Gerald knelt down and picked it up. It was an aluminum soda can.

The thing looked old; the material had begun to oxidize. Gerald felt another chill coming on and tossed the can into the garbage.

He stepped out of the washroom and looked at the bed. There was no way he was going back to sleep. He clicked on the rack light and rummaged around in his discarded clothing until he retrieved Donovan Cortez's card. Gerald went to the terminal and inserted it into the reader. It went directly to voicemail.

"Donovan. Gerald. Send me the coordinates and send me the cash. I'll leave as soon as Bean is ready."

Getting off the station as often as possible would be a good thing.

[Part V]

Gerald frowned and ran his hand over welding points that were both bloated and ugly. Bean might not have been the prettiest ship in the galaxy, but one thing was for damn sure: he'd been a hell of a lot prettier before the colony-ship-turned-slagheap rearended him.

"Good morning, Gerald."

"It's afternoon," Gerald countered and turned. Donovan Cortez stood on the flight deck along with Ina at his side; his bespectacled eyes examined the hauler.

"Actually, it *is* morning," said Donovan.

"Whatever. I got your coordinates. You didn't have to come and send me off. I do appreciate the gesture."

"We're coming with you," Cortez said and took a step toward the ship, a bright smile on his face.

"That is entirely out of the question." Gerald held out a warding hand.

"Gerald, I'm paying you quite well. Well enough that you should have no problem taking two passengers with you."

"Bean is a hauler, not a transport vessel; she can't hold more than two passengers. Sorry, pops."

Donovan looked back up at the ship. His brow creased for a moment before he spoke again.

"Well, in that case, I've never enjoyed space flight. You'll just have to take Ina with you. I'll wait here."

"No." Gerald didn't want anyone green on his ship. Different people reacted to space in different ways. He didn't want to take the chance that Ina Cortez would go nutso on him.

"Gerald, I need to send *someone* along to make sure my interests are kept in mind," Donovan insisted.

"Are you saying you don't trust me?" Gerald raised his brows.

"Would I place my daughter's safety in your hands if I didn't?" Donovan said. "I will pay you an additional fee for taking Ina as a passenger."

Gerald sighed—more money was more money. A dock hand holding a welding torch stood at the far end of the flight deck. His face-shield was raised and he watched the exchange with vague interest. Walter Vegan was nowhere in sight. Gerald returned his attention to the dynamic duo.

"Great. Fine," Gerald said, and eyed the bag at Ina's feet. He pointed at it. "Get that stowed. We're leaving in five minutes. And you might want to hand Sparky down there a fifty on your way out," Gerald gestured to the dockhand with a tilt of his head.

[•••]

Security HQ was quiet and largely deserted. Marisa was grateful. The few officers that were present went about their business, paying more heed to their work than to Marisa. She stepped into a monitoring station and set her bag on the table. A row of LCDs showed multiple sections of the station—blocks of Main Street, views of the hangar, views of the living levels and the farms. Crescent had a lot of cameras, that was for sure. No one was stationed at the feeds. Likely, the missing attendant was in the head or getting food from the compiler. That was fine by Marisa; she didn't feel like talking to anyone. She didn't want to talk about Heathen's, sure to be the conversation du jour. She sat down on the monitoring station's backless stool and shifted her weight this way and that, but it was impossible to find a comfortable sitting position. Back pain, after all, meant eternal vigilance—at least according to El Capitan. Visit any monitoring station on Crescent and there'd be an officer sitting on a stool, massaging a cramp out of one sore muscle or another. Marisa yawned wide; her jaw popped. She still felt tired and her brain was muddy, even though it had been a couple of days since her hospital visit.

"Welcome back, Lieutenant," said a voice from behind her. She suppressed a frown and swiveled on the stool.

"Hi, Captain."

Captain Walter Benedict stood in the doorway, black mug of coffee forever attached to one hand, cigarette between the fingers of the other. His long, pepper black hair was matted to the sides of his head and it was a curled mess where it hit his shoulders. Expressionless, he watched her with his one good, blue eye. Benedict's other eye was made from glass and was as unnatural and protruding as ever. Marisa always wondered why he hadn't opted for an implant when he had lost the eye in a knife fight so many years ago.

"How did your meeting with Kendall go?" he asked.

"There was no meeting," she replied.

"That a fact?"

"Yes, it is."

"I thought he might've had something to say to you about those armed mercenaries shooting up that fine tavern. He requested a personnel list of hangar security on duty the afternoon those assholes arrived," Benedict took a drink of coffee. "I told him I would deal with my crew and that I didn't need him involved. He gave me the impression he'd pursue it anyway—you know how Kendall is. I went to bat pretty damn heavy for you, Mari. If he does talk to you, I'd expect nothing more than a slap on the wrist." Benedict nodded once.

Marisa felt relieved, though at the same time she wanted to shout, *People died because of me!* She bit her tongue—exhaustion was making her feel dramatic. She was happy that the captain had stuck up for her. When it came to locking horns with Mayor Kendall, most people backed down. She saw no reason for her captain to behave any differently. Benedict held her gaze and Marisa felt herself lips tug themselves into a grin. It felt good to smile. She had made a mistake at the docks. That was all.

That's not all, she thought. *There's no way I could've missed those guns.*

"Well. He hasn't bothered me yet and I'm not going to go to him. So. We'll see." Marisa did find it a little odd, though. Kendall was always quick to come down on anyone who fucked up. He came down hard and in a timely fashion. But, there had been no one waiting for her when she was discharged from the hospital. There had been no one sitting in her apartment smoking a cigarette—no messages on the comm.

Benedict said, "To that end, I've decided to take you off of hangar detail for a while. To give you some opportunity to mull over where you screwed the pooch."

Marisa chewed on her bottom lip for an instant, keeping back a rebuttal.

"Welcome to your new job. You'll work the monitor station here in this office for the time being," Benedict said, and sounded satisfied.

"Great." Marisa turned her attention to the monitors.

"I knew you'd be pleased." He tossed her a wink. "Now, get to work."

[•••]

"We have arrived, Captain," Bean's voice drifted from the comm.

"I see that, Bean."

The asteroid field drifted over the frozen surface of Anrar's most distant planetary body. This field was nowhere near as dense as the site of Gerald's first haul for Kendall, and for that Gerald was thankful. All the same, he felt out of his comfort zone. Gerald was used to flying alone. There was something about having a passenger aboard, as mouse-ish in her silence as Ina was, that made him nervous.

"Shall I take us to the coordinates, or would you rather show off for the lady?" said the ship's computer.

"Take us in, Bean."

The hauler banked and the thrusters fired. Bean brought them into the heart of the asteroid field on a slow approach. Dark, rolling boulders drifted past the viewport, breathtakingly close. Gerald glanced at Ina, who for once was not looking at her feet, but instead gazed out the viewport in wide-eyed wonder. A stray lock of hair had fallen across one high cheekbone. He felt the irrational urge to brush it away. Her eyes were like bits of blue-gray glass; they moved from the viewport to meet his.

They both looked away.

"I haven't spent all that much time in space," she said, her voice almost a whisper.

"I can tell." Gerald smiled. "I see crap… rather, things like this every day. I've gotten used to it."

"I don't know how you could ever get used to it."

He looked at her again and she was watching him with keen interest. He shrugged and glanced over to the radar array.

"Now, who the hell is that?" Gerald said.

"What's wrong?" Ina asked.

There was a red blip eight thousand meters out.

"It's a ship," Bean replied, "but not *the* ship."

"Has it spotted us?" Gerald leaned forward.

"It would not appear so; however, it is difficult to say. There is a lot of magnetic disturbance out here," Bean said.

"Kill all non-critical systems. Let us drift."

"Captain, you might be interested to know the transponder code is registered to Crescent."

"Very interested, Bean. Can you activate the cameras? Or would that put off too much of an energy signature?" Gerald asked.

"Shuttles have a weak sensory array. Our cameras will not alert them to our presence."

The visual camera display shimmered to life in front of the control couch. It showed not one, but two specks against the milky body of Anrar VI. The camera zoomed in, each frame increasing with a jerk. Two ships were tethered together.

"Son of a bitch," Gerald said. "There's two?"

A space-suited figure crawled out of an unmarked cargo carrier's top hatch. He was followed by another individual. The pair pumped their legs, leapt from the cargo ship, and floated a short distance to a Crescent cargo vessel's open rear hatch.

"Are we safe out here?" Ina asked. Faint rose petals blossomed on her cheeks. She looked from the viewport to Gerald, her eyes reflecting the same sense of unease that he was feeling. Something glittered in her liquid blue gaze. She asked with such anticipation in her voice it seemed to Gerald that she wanted the answer to be no.

"Well." Gerald brought up the radar overlay with a wave of the hand and zoomed out several clicks with a twirl of his fingers. "So long as we don't see any more colored dots in this view, yeah, we should be okay. And if *they* don't notice us floating out here." Gerald gestured to the camera view that now showed the two suited figures floating back to the unmarked cargo vessel; they were guiding a long, heavy-duty crate into the ship's hold. *What is that?* Gerald wondered.

"So we wait?" Ina asked before Gerald could speculate any further.

"Yeah. Pretty simple. We wait."

Ina sighed. Gerald could see her breath. He was surprised at how quickly the heat had dissipated once the life support systems were cut to a minimum. Bean shouldn't have cooled off so fast. Clearly, there was still collision damage that needed repairing. He was about to ask Bean to check into it when Ina placed her hand on his cheek. It was cool and soft. Gerald looked at her, his brow rising in surprise and more than mild confusion.

"Is my hand cold?" she asked.

"Yes. A little bit. I'm sorry about that." He was about to go on to an explanation of bad circuits and clogged vents when she put her other hand on his cheek.

"How about this one?"

"Yeah, that one too." Gerald felt his cheeks getting hot despite the cabin temperature.

"How long do you think we'll be waiting?"

Ina inched toward him, close enough that he could smell her hair. It smelled clean—like spring time, planet-side. The scent made him feel a little light-headed.

"I don't know. Not long? Long?"

"Oh." Ina trailed the fingertips of one hand down the line of his jaw and down his neck to rest on his collarbone. She closed the distance between them, her arms sliding out over his shoulders. She brushed her lips over his. Gerald was not surprised that they were as soft as her hands. He brought his head back, but she was still only centimeters away. Her breath drifted toward him in warm puffs.

"Ina. I'm flattered, but I've… "

"Got a girlfriend millions of kilometers and two hulls away?" She silenced him with her index finger. "Or is it a wife? A boyfriend? I don't really care. I don't know what's come over me, Gerald. But, were I you, I'd consider myself lucky to be here." She kissed him again, this time with a fierceness that caught him off guard. Ina pushed him back into the control couch and straddled him. Her hair hung down over his face and tickled his cheeks. For an instant, he thought he glimpsed a shadow behind her. A trick of the light.

"Gerald." She paused, rocking forward and back once. "Captain." She bit her lip. "You no doubt have a bunk on this ship? With blankets?"

He nodded in response.

"Good. Take me there."

[•••]

At first, it was cool in the small sleep quarters. Gerald had closed the overhead vents to preserve what little warmth remained. Forty-five minutes later, he wished he had kept them open. Their lovemaking turned the four-by-four meter enclosure into a sauna. The smell of their combined sweat and the tang of sex was pungent, but not unpleasant. Ina lay beside him, her arm and leg draped over Gerald's naked body. His chest rose and fell as his breathing returned to normal. Either he had set the life support systems too low or he had to start hitting the gym.

"Thank you," Ina said and looked up at him, blinking her wide, clear eyes twice. She gave him a tentative smile, closer to the shyness he had witnessed at Heathen's and again in the hangar.

Gerald didn't reply, but only returned the grin. Ina had been far more adept between the sheets than he would've expected. It's always the quiet ones.

"Don't tell my father."

"Not a word." Gerald slipped from her slender arms and pulled on his pants. He smiled, trying to make his face appear as safe as possible. He placed a hand on her bare thigh. "Really, I'm not such a bad guy." *Just weak willed,* he mused and thought of Marisa. He pushed the guilt down before it could sneak up on him.

"I'm counting on it," she said, strangely.

"What's that supposed to mean?" He removed his hand.

"I don't know. That's not what I meant to come out." She looked away. "I'm not... I never... Sorry."

"It's okay. About that day in the cafeteria... " Gerald said. "I wanted to ask you about it in Heathen's, but... "

"What day in the cafeteria?" She looked confused.

"You seemed very upset about something? Gave me a stern talking-to."

"I don't ever remember being in the cafeteria," she said, and sounded perfectly sincere. Gerald nodded and shrugged.

"Maybe I dreamed it. Look, I'll be on the bridge. Come out when you're ready."

"Thank you," she said again.

"And that's enough of that. No more apologizing or thanking—don't make me lock you in here."

Her lips quirked in a ghost of a grin and he left her there to get dressed.

[•••]

The mystery ships were gone by the time Gerald returned to the bridge. He sat in the control couch and watched the empty camera feed for several seconds, tapping his chin as he contemplated the next move. He waved away the camera overlay, replacing it with the radar. The field was clear, which meant nothing, Gerald knew. It could fill with a dozen red blips at any second. He reinitialized the ship systems one by one and Bean began to hum to life around him.

"Bean," Gerald said.

"Take us to the coordinates?" the computer replied.

"You got it."

Ina returned to the bridge as the engines fired. The change in inertia caused her to stumble. Gerald grabbed her by the waist and she placed her hands on his. He settled her into the couch beside him. He didn't look at her. It was time to focus now. It didn't matter if Bean was in control of the ship or not.

[•••]

The comm crackled.

"Captain," Bean's voice sounded tinny in the small helmet speakers. "The lifeboat's reactor core is still hot." Gerald stopped his descent and gripped the hauling tether with more force. Starlight glittered on the tiny, interlocking plates of the cable. It looked like the hide of some chrome-scaled, interstellar snake.

"You're kidding me," Gerald said.

"Older model ships relied on heavy fusion cores for propulsion. The lifeboat's core would still be hot three hundred years from now. You are going to have to jettison it."

"At the risk of sounding repetitive here—you're kidding me."

Bean was right, of course. When they dislodged the vessel from the crater wall, the lifeboat would be under more stress than it had been in hundreds of years. The stress just might be enough to agitate the reactor and blow the whole ship into pieces, taking Bean, Gerald, and Ina along with it.

Gerald ran his hand over the edge of one of the lifeboat's tail fins. Dust came away in a milky cloud that hung suspended in the cold starlight. He looked to the gaping opening in the lifeboat's side. The metal was twisted and sharp. He hoped that...

"You'll have to go in through the opening in the starboard side of the lifeboat."

"I can manually pop one of the belly hatches," Gerald said.

"Captain. I'm sure the mechanisms that allow for manual hatch release are sealed from exposure to hundreds of years of space dust."

"I could tear my suit if I go through that hole." Gerald let go of the tether and fired one of the suit's small air jets, propelling himself to the lifeboat's hull. He landed silently and the magnets in his boots automatically adjusted to simulate 9.8 gravities. Measured steps carried him along the curving hull to the underside of the vessel, his booted feet kicking up small, cream-colored clouds of dust with each silent step. The helmet lamp grew brighter as it adapted to the darkness. Gerald crouched and began wiping the hull-plates clean until he found one belly hatch. After several attempts at turning the manual release, Gerald realized that trying to open the thing by hand was futile. For a moment, he considered letting a drone try to open it, but in the end he knew it would only be a waste of time. The hatch was sealed. He grumbled as he returned to the starboard side of the lifeboat, looking up to Bean's bulbous body when he halted. Ina was watching him through the viewport, and he waved. He felt like an idiot for doing so. She waved back.

"Captain. Bear in mind, I am not making you go through with this. Neither is our guest."

The comm crackled and it was Ina speaking now.

"Why don't you send a drone to release the core?" she asked.

"We're wasting time talking. The drone would be just as likely to blow us all to bits—if not more so. I'm going in."

Gerald walked to the edge of the wound in the lifeboat's side. He wiped away some of the dust with the pad of his thumb, exposing more silvery material. There was no sign of charring. An explosion within the shuttle hadn't made the opening. Gerald could not begin to imagine what had.

"Bean. What are the rad levels like in there? Am I already frying?"

"I would have informed you if radiation levels were not within tolerable limits."

"All right, then. Here we go."

Gerald released the magnetic hold of his boots. Firing the suit's jets for an instant lifted him off of the hull by several meters. He guided the suit above the opening and then began his descent, drifting into the lifeboat at an excruciatingly slow rate. The metal tatters that had once been hull plates were as jagged as they were sharp—they looked serrated. Gerald heaved a dramatic sigh of relief when he cleared the opening.

"I'm in."

Gerald continued to settle toward the port wall of the compartment he had entered. All he could see was the lifeboat's deck in front of him and darkness to either side. The deck was riddled with debris. Everything was covered in a creamy concoction of frost and dust. He startled when his feet contacted with solid paneling and bit his bottom lip to keep from yelping. Re-activating the magnets in his boots, he walked down the port wall to the floor. His helmet lamp cut a shaft through the consummate darkness—he had entered at the hibernation chamber. The floor was lined with rows of long, slender sarcophagi. He couldn't tell if they were occupied or not. Their interiors were dark; ice crystals obscured the glass surfaces of the tubes.

The way he had entered was a path of destruction. A single row hibernation tubes had been busted apart. The damage seemed to culminate with the gaping hole. Gerald began to feel a rising tingle of fear, starting first at his balls and then clawing for his chest. His breath came hard and his head darted from side to side.

"Captain, your respiration rate is increasing rapidly. You will hyperventilate if you don't control your breathing."

He heard Bean's voice but he didn't comprehend it. He took several staggering steps backwards and got tripped up—it almost felt like something had grabbed his ankle. His boots detached from the deck and he drifted to the port wall. His heart pounded in his ears. He couldn't concentrate. He couldn't breathe.

"Gerald. Calm down. You're okay in there," Ina's voice came across the comm channel.

I'm freaking the fuck out, Gerald thought. *Far from goddamned okay.* He forced himself to take a deep breath.

"Gerald?" Ina's voice came again.

Another deep breath. Gerald looked for what had tripped him. There was nothing but empty floor. *I tripped on my own foot,* he thought.

"I'm okay," he said at last. He could hear Ina exhaling on the other end of the comm. She didn't say anything. "Where do I have to go, Bean?"

"There is a bulkhead at the aft of the hibernation cabin. Go through it and you'll be in a corridor. Follow that corridor one hundred meters. There is a portal in the floor with a ladder that will lead to the engineering deck. Descend that ladder. I'll instruct you from there."

The corridor seemed to go on for a featureless eternity. The narrow, arched passage had not seen light since the shuttle had crashed, Gerald was sure of it. He half expected to see albino, cave dwelling spiders skitter from his path. He was glad that he did not. He desperately missed the patch of stars that had been visible in the hibernation chamber. With each step into the dead interior of the lifeboat, he felt the panic try to resurface. He bit it back as best he could and focused on moving one foot in front of the other. Just ahead, he could see the portal to the next deck; a ladder emerged from a black hole in the floor and disappeared into an opening in the ceiling panels. *A few more meters,* he thought. A few more meters and he'd have to go into that hole. Further away from the starlight. Further away from Bean. If the lifeboat harbored any more mysteries, they'd been down there, in the dark. They'd be the kind of mysteries with glowing eyes, dripping fangs, and an appetite for salvage boat pilots.

Gerald expected to hear his boots clank on the rungs of the ladder as he made his descent. All he could hear was the air handler within his suit. Beyond the helmet's thin face plate was the silence of vacuum. The lack of sound was more unnerving than ever.

"Where to now, Bean?" Gerald fought to keep his voice even. He had been on too many derelicts to count, some even older than the lifeboat, but this ship felt different. There was a sense of being in the wrong place that nagged at him with every soundless step.

"There is a panel in the lower aft wall. Remove it by depressing a small release in each of the four corners. Crawl an additional fifty meters and you will come to a small ovoid chamber. This sits directly above the reactor core. You'll find the release in this chamber."

Gerald removed the panel and it floated over his shoulder to bounce silently against the ceiling panels. He got onto his knees and peered into the service tunnel. It was far from spacious. Wall-to-wall and ceiling-to-ceiling, it was no bigger than a coffin.

"Ina, your father's rates have just gone up. A lot."

Gerald got onto his belly and used his elbows to drag himself forward. The going was slow. He kept his eyes down, only glancing up occasionally. There were dark smudges on the flooring and on the walls, the color of engine oil. He came to an oculus hatch that was frozen three-quarters open. It was just wide enough that Gerald thought he'd be able to get through, but when he tried, his shoulders got stuck. He started to jerk frantically, filling his lungs in preparation to scream bloody murder, but he managed to wriggle free. He exhaled and continued on.

His head lamp beat back the darkness as he finally floated into the ovoid chamber. Walls curved into ceiling which curved into wall and back into ceiling again in an unending geometry. Gerald bit his lip and squeezed his eyes shut.

No. No. No. I'm not seeing this, he thought, not just in denial, but in blatant refusal of the signals his optic nerve transmitted to his brain. *No.*

"Gerald?" It was Ina's voice. "Your respiration is spiking again."

"I've found the passengers," he whispered.

Bodies filled the center of the room, piled in a tangled heap. Thin, sinewy arms and legs were twisted together in inhuman contortions. Mouths gaped; peeled-back lips exposed teeth that returned the light of Gerald's head lamp in gleaming death-smiles. What the hell were the crew and passengers doing in here? He looked to the ceiling. There were more bodies up there, spread-eagled and just as black and as space-mummified as the others. *What the hell happened on this ship?* Gerald engaged the boots' magnets and came in contact with the curved deck. A few hesitant steps brought him to the cadavers. Some of the passengers had been naked when they died. Their members were shriveled like the curl of a spent match. The passengers' ragged flesh told of old wounds. Most, if not all, of the bodies had severe lacerations covering their torsos. In some instances, their bellies were torn wide open revealing dark, empty cavities.

"Bean. Where is this goddamn release? I need to get out of here now." He wasn't even sure why he was bothering. The lifeboat should be left where they found it.

"It is in the center of the room. There will be a protruding handle. Pull and turn it one-hundred and eighty degrees."

Center of the room. Beneath the pile of death.

Gerald began to move the bodies, trying to his best to not to think about what he was doing. He lifted the desiccated and frozen remains of the lifeboat passengers, first one at a time, and then in armfuls, casting them aside. The bodies drifted away from him in graceful cartwheels, raisin-like eyes staring, jaws set in perpetual grins. It was too strange. Absurdly, Gerald felt like an intrepid explorer who had just stumbled into the lair of some savage, long-tusked beast.

Lair. Was that what this room was—a lair? *Don't even think it,* he thought. *Keep digging.*

Gerald thanked a god, he wasn't really sure which one, when he got to the bottom of the heap and saw the metal protrusion Bean had said would be there. Gerald grabbed it and pulled. It gave easily. He began to turn it, finding that it moved freely in its close-fitting socket. A stroke of luck at last. The release caught and Gerald felt a vibration in the handle.

"Bean?"

"The core has been jettisoned, Captain."

"I need to retire. Today," Gerald said.

There was a loud, concussive bang. It came from a black opening at the opposite end of the room. *I didn't hear that. I felt it,* he thought. It happened again. Stronger this time. Something had caused the chamber to tremble with such force that it reverberated in his suit.

"Bean? Is the ship falling apart?" Gerald was already on his belly, dragging himself back into the cramped service channel.

"Negative, Captain. The structure is stable."

He felt it again—a rhythmic *thump, thump*. Like something was moving. Moving toward him. *Whatever it is, it's still here,* Gerald thought, *and I'm in its lair.* He pulled himself down the tunnel as fast as he could. The vibration was getting more intense.

"Captain. I'm picking up a strange energy reading on the ship. It's emanating sixty meters to your rear."

Faster, Gerald thought, *I've got to move faster.*

The tremors continued to increase. Gerald could feel them between his legs as a growing tingle. *Faster, come on.* There was light in the tunnel. Cold and violet, it leaked around the small space between his body and the channel wall, casting sharp, writhing shadows.

Murhaté. The word was whispered in his ear, the dry husk of a nearly incomprehensible voice.

"Motherfucker."

The light was getting bright enough that Gerald could see his exit and the corridor beyond it. The dark smudges on the tunnel walls stood out in the lilac glare. How had he not realized it before? It was long-dried blood that stained the walls.

Make us whole.

Gerald burst free from the service channel and ran for the ladder.

"Gerald, are you okay?" Ina sounded panicked. He didn't spare the breath it would take to answer her.

Gerald hazarded a look over his shoulder.

The light bled from the service channel hatch in a painful blaze.

"Gerald!" Ina sounded frantic.

Gerald had to squeeze his eyes shut against the cold radiance. He stumbled. *Fuck me,* he thought defeated, *this is it.*

Make us one!

Darkness. The light was gone. Gerald sensed that he was alone again, but that didn't slow him down. He was up the ladder, down the hall, back in the hibernation chamber and floating toward Bean in a fraction of the time it had taken him to enter the ship.

"Gerald?" Ina said over the comm again. He could see her, pressed against the glass of the viewport. Her voice was small.

"You call your father," Gerald said, struggling to catch his breath, "and tell him there is something very wrong with this ship."

[PART VI

"Yes, dear. I like you just fine," Ezra Kendall said and slipped into a pseudo-silk robe. It was the truth. He did like her just fine. His fondness for her or lack thereof had nothing to do with his inability to finish the job. Mayor Kendall eyed the prostitute's bare breasts. They were the real thing. He was *sure* of it. A prostitute with real tits was not something you found every day, Kendall knew. Even that fact hadn't helped him finish the job. He looked at her face now. He could see that she had been pretty once. That was fairly certain. Now, a scar ran from her chin to her left eye, the cornea was milky and malformed; the blemish detracted from her looks. But, she was a real woman. *I'm too uptight lately,* Kendall thought. *Might be that I'll just have to try again later.* He went to the small, oak bar that stood along the far wall of his bed chamber and looked up at the framed LCD suspended there. The shimmering pixels showed a super-station floating over a backdrop of stars; two rings glittered as they rotated on a shared axis. The portrait was a vision of Crescent—Kendall's vision of what the station would look like, were it to be completed. One of these days, he vowed, he would finish the construction that was halted so long ago. *And soon,* he reminded himself.

"My money?" the girl said in a voice that was almost a whisper. It was like she was afraid to ask for her payment. If there was one thing that Kendall appreciated, it was making good on a deal. He filled a snifter with a brandy that was as genuine as her breasts.

"You'll be paid on your way out. I'm old fashioned. I'd rather not be part of the money exchange. Understand?"

"Yes, sweetheart. I believe I do."

The bed linens whispered as she slipped from between their soft confines; the sound was followed by the clack of heels on the hardwood. She click-clacked her way to the door; it hissed open. She clacked through, the door hissed shut, and Kendall was alone again. He lifted the ɔs and inhaled deeply. Yes. Real was the only way to go. in one hand, Kendall padded barefoot past the antique gh bed and drew open the curtains that hung above the circular viewport showed a toss of stars, snaked with faint wisps of nebulosity. He placed his hand on the glass; it was cool to the touch. Kendall depressed a finger beneath his ear and there was a click.

"Taylor, please have Catlier and Raney go retrieve Ms. Griffin. *Officer* Griffin. I will meet with her here."

"Right away, sir," Taylor's voice crackled over the cochlear implant.

[•••]

The door slid open on its track; Kendall still stared out the window, enjoying the lingering taste of the brandy. The glass was empty now. He'd have to see about that.

"You wanted to see me, Mayor." There was the slightest quaver in the alto voice. She probably didn't even know it was there—most wouldn't notice it—but he did. It was like blood in the water; Kendall licked his lips.

"Yes, Officer Griffin." He moved from the window and settled into an antique, cushioned chair; the plastic and metal frame creaked as it adjusted to his weight. "Your first name is Marisa, is it not?"

"It is," she said. She was in her uniform; fitted, blue sleeves tapered to hands that were at her sides. Her hair was piled atop her head in a tight bun. She was a pretty girl. Fetching, even. Perhaps a little old for his taste. Kendall preferred his females young. According to her personnel file, Griffin was approaching thirty. Even still, exceptions could always be made.

"May I call you Marisa?"

"I don't see the harm in that." Marisa smiled. The gesture was forced. Kendall appreciated the effort.

"Sit down, Marisa … sit down, please." Kendall gestured to the tousled bed. Was that a little blood on the sheets? Marisa hesitated, but only for a moment; she crossed the polished floor and seated herself on the thick mattress, just across from the mayor.

"Do you know why I've asked you here?" Kendall looked into his empty snifter and got to his feet; the robe parted slightly and he felt a draft on his member. Marisa's eyes snapped up to his face; she had noticed. Good for her.

"I think so," she said. Snifter refilled, Kendall returned to his seat.

"Good. No sense in beating around the bush then. I appreciate that. It was unfortunate. The incident at Heathen's. Core Sec is sending someone to audit the operations of this station. Imagine that. An auditor. Here. You know as well as I, Marisa, that I—we—run a tight ship here. Still, there's bound to be a mistake or two, here or there. It is a crying shame that your superior saw fit to file an official report on one small incident. Not to mention, place a permanent mark on your record as an officer."

Marisa's face remained calm; there was no hint of emotion. He admired her control. The supposed betrayal must have been hard to swallow.

"I thought Captain Benedict was a man I could rely upon. I'm sure you felt the same. But his prudence in this matter seems to be lacking, wouldn't you agree?"

Marisa didn't answer. Her features remained still and she almost appeared disinterested. Kendall imagined the rage that must be bubbling up inside her. He felt his cock give the weakest of twitches.

"Of course you would. After all, you're the one who took the blame for the whole incident. Marisa, as Mayor of Crescent, I'm in a fairly powerful position. I could have your record wiped clean." It was a lie. He had no strong relations in central Core Sec. He cared as much about the lie as he did about her record. The incident at Heathen's was not even the impetus for the auditor's visit, Kendall knew. *General Audit* was the only reason given on the notification. Heathen's was but a footnote. *None* of that was important, what was important was that her eyes brightened. Kendall had her. He was pleased.

"Go on," she said in even tones.

"Nothing is for free, Marisa. I'm sure you understand that. If you want a shining record of service again, you're going to have to work for it, dear."

She stood suddenly, cheeks flushed, and she wrapped her arms around herself protectively. Her dark eyes fell to the twisted sheets and then moved to the door.

"No, no, sweetheart. Nothing so dramatic." Kendall smiled, attempting to lace the grin with as much reassurance as possible. They'd get into that bed together in due time, but not now.

"It is clear to me that I'm going to need a second set of eyes, ears, and hands within Crescent's security force when this auditor arrives. It is also clear to me that I cannot trust Captain Benedict with the task. Do you think that's something you could do for me? Act as my eyes and ears?"

"What would it entail?"

"Whatever I ask. That is what it will entail. If you please me, then I will make sure your record reflects your stalwart service. Get us through this rough spot with Core Sec and we can move forward from there."

"Okay," she said.

Kendall nodded. He got to his feet and extended a bony hand. She took it in her own for a single, downward shake. Her skin was soft and warm. She began to withdraw, but he gripped her fingers for an instant longer, his smile going from sweet to venomous.

"Don't fuck this up, Officer Griffin. I wouldn't want to have to punish you as much as you wouldn't want to be punished." Another lie—he'd love to punish her. He released his grip.

"Are we done here?"

"Unless you want to join me for a brandy, yes. We are done here."

She began to move toward the door.

"One more thing, Marisa. Let's keep this little talk between you and I."

"Of course," she said, the words almost lost in the whine of the door motors.

Kendall felt better. He activated his cochlear.

"The young prostitute with the scar and the real tits. Find her and bring her back. I don't care if she's *busy*. Deal with it and bring her here. And Taylor. Make sure she's clean."

"You have a four thirty with the finance minister, Mayor." Taylor responded.

"Well, send him here. He can watch for all I care."

Kendall was going to fuck the hell out of the little whore, picturing Officer Griffin's pretty face the whole while.

[•••]

Marisa looked at Gerald. Gerald looked at Marisa. Neither spoke.

I saw that motherfucker's prick, Marisa wanted to scream into Gerald's face. But he seemed to be unable to make eye contact with her, or even to speak. He seemed more interested in the top of their table; the LCD above the bar came in close second. Instead of yelling, she lifted the pint of amber lager to her lips. The beer was Heathen's own special brew, made right on the station. She took a shallow sip. Although a favorite, the beer wasn't doing all that much to settle the chaos in her gut, but she thought it smart to feign normalcy. Despite her best efforts, nothing felt normal. Her world seemed to be fucked every which way from Tuesday and showed no signs of righting itself.

The batwing doors of the club swung open. Both Marisa and Gerald looked over and watched Taylor amble into the bar. Marisa had never seen him walk before. It was almost comical. Taylor's legs were so damned huge, he had to keep them slightly apart to accommodate movement. It looked like he had just pinched off a loaf in his knickers. *I bet his prick is as shriveled as his boss',* she thought, and actually laughed out loud. Gerald arched a brow but still didn't say anything. He lit a cigarette and watched Taylor make his shit-pantsed way to the bar. The big man leaned in toward Maerl and said something to him. Maerl frowned and dropped his eyes. Taylor leaned in closer and the bartender pointed a finger in the direction of Marisa and Gerald's table.

"Great," Gerald said at last.

"What'd you do to piss off special K this time, Gerry?" She attempted to sound lighthearted, but she didn't know for sure that big and ugly wasn't coming for her. Maybe Kendall had decided he did want to check under her hood.

Taylor crossed the empty dance floor and stepped up to the small round table. He crossed his massive, painted arms across his equally gigantic chest. His small, black eyes were on Gerald. Taylor's lips bore a lopsided twist that Marisa assumed was supposed to be a grin. A shit-eating grin? He had plenty of it in his pants.

"Gerald," Taylor said.

"Taylor," Gerald replied. "You know, I always have a hard time calling you that. I feel like you should be called Killer or Mangler or something." This made Taylor bark with laughter. The giant actually grabbed his sides like some overstuffed and tickled cartoon character.

"I like you, Gerald. Mayor Kendall—he's not so convinced."

"That is a shame. He seems like such a nice man." Gerald looked at Marisa. *What did you do?* she thought, and took another sip from her beer, pretending not to pay attention or care. *He must've done something—he looks guilty.*

"He wants to see you," Taylor said. Gerald drained the contents of his pint glass and got to his feet. "No sense in putting up a fight, right?" He winked at the man-mountain and then looked down to Marisa. "Don't wait up. I'm going to be late."

Marisa's eyes followed them as they headed across the barroom. Gerald must've made some other wisecrack because Taylor started roaring with laughter again. The outburst didn't do much for his walk. She watched them pass through the batwings, and then Marisa raised a slender hand for another drink. Maerl was quick to fill a fresh glass and ferry it over to her. She smiled up at him gratefully. Maerl looked to the door, scratched his chin, and then looked down at Marisa. He frowned.

"I wonder what that was all about," Maerl said, and Marisa shrugged.

"I don't know. Maybe Gerry just isn't doing the job the way that Kendall expected he would." The pint was filled to the brim. She bent her head over the beer and drank without lifting the glass off the table. Then she raised her head and spoke. "I'm sure Gerry's not doing a bad job. He just has his own way of doing things."

Maerl glanced back at the door. "Maybe that's true. But you know as well as I do, on Kendall's station, you do things his way."

"Or the airlock," Marisa finished.

"Off the record and off the station." Maerl laughed uneasily.

"Core Sec is coming soon," Marisa said as she trailed a fingertip down the condensation that had formed on the glass. "Benedict notified them of the incident. He thought it warranted an investigation on their part."

"Yeah—I got an email from your captain. The auditor is going to interview me or some such crap."

"I didn't let those guns into the station, Maerl. There is *no way* I could have missed that. Those were standard weapons—nothing special that would pass through our scanners undetected."

"Faulty gear?"

"I checked it. More than once. Everything at the docks is working fine," she sighed and took another sip of the malty beverage.

"Maybe the guns were already here?" Maerl said in the most nonchalant of tones. To Marisa, this seemed like the wrong kind of question to ask—the variety of question that Kendall would want her to prevent Core Sec from asking. Marisa shrugged it off and offered a weak smile.

"You know," Maerl added, "I bet when Core Sec comes here with their fancy gear, they'll find something wrong with the dock scanner system. Nothing will be to blame but old wiring."

"You're right," Marisa nodded, and smiled.

"Get you anything else?"

"I'm good for now, thanks." She didn't think her angry stomach could make it through the current pint, let alone another.

Maerl went back to the bar and left Marisa with her thoughts. *Maybe the guns were already here.* She heard Maerl's voice repeat this in her head. Maybe? There was no maybe about it. Those guns had been on the station. They had been handed to the mercenaries. By who? By Kendall? Why would Kendall give them guns in the first place? Did he want that whole thing to go down at Heathen's? That didn't make any sense. *Easy, Marisa. Keep your nose clean and it won't get broken.* She pushed the beer away and pressed a credit wafer to the clear disc at the center of the table. It chimed. She instructed the computer to place a five credit tip on her tab, and waved to Maerl as she left the bar.

Marisa stepped out onto Main Street. Several of the station's large, multi-limbed collector bots trudged by, emptying refuse bins into compartments on their wide backs as they went. A pack of children chased after the robots, throwing stray pieces of garbage at the machines. The bits of trash—aluminum cans, glass bottles, and the like—were caught with ease and placed into the back compartments for recycling.

The overhead globes flooded the drag with fiery orange light. Sunset. If you didn't look up to the high, arching ceiling you might believe it was a real sunset. The cool recycled air smelled of spices and cooking meats. Main Street was *almost* as good as a real planet-side market, but not quite. She was willing to concede its imperfections for the peace of mind brought on by a brief waft of curry and an artificial sunset. And why the hell not?

A man in a dark sweat shirt and cargo pants stepped up to her so suddenly she almost knocked him over. He held out a stack of black paper leaflets with a hand that was painted with a small beetle tattoo. Marisa growled at him for ruining her moment. She pushed him out of the way and the stack of fliers went skyward. In an instant, the weirdo was on his hands and knees collecting and Marisa was on her way down the street. There was a group of similarly clad youths handing out the same bits of trash just ahead of her. She crossed to the other side of the street and made her way into a bazaar choked with people drifting from one tent-shop to another.

A bald head, buried deep in a throng of market-goers, caught her eye. Dark tattoos snaked up to the shaved scalp. *It's him,* she thought, and stopped short. *The vatter.* He turned and seemed to see her. Marisa couldn't make out his face. It hurt her head to look directly at it. In an instant, he was moving, weaving through the crowd. Marisa reacted in the span of a heartbeat and ran after him, weaving in and out of meandering station folk. She followed him out of the bazaar and down a side alley choked with cardboard crates. Marisa burst out the other side, taking a few boxes with her. The bald head disappeared around yet another corner. Marisa leapt over a news stand in quick pursuit. She knocked over a rack of news flimsies and nearly careened into a rack of gaudy sunglasses. The pursuit led her into another narrow alley, but the small dead end street was empty save for a single lit storefront. Ramshackle, decorated with animal bones and gaudy, glowing beads, it bulged from the station wall. It wasn't a shop at all. It was a residence.

The vatter was nowhere in sight. Something glittered on the bleak floor-space just in front of the apartment's split and warped metal frame. Marisa approached the burnished object; her feet were increasingly hesitant with each step. She shuddered. Something was wrong here. Marisa could sense it in her fillings. She looked down at the shiny object. It was a small, metallic stud, like vatters wore in their skin.

"Come in, Officer Griffin," Naheela's unmistakable voice floated from inside the hut. "I would say I was expecting you—but I think you already knew that."

(Part VII)

"I've been hearing some distressing things, Gerald." Kendall stood behind an LCD-filled desk. At his back, the velvet drapes had been drawn shut, obscuring the large viewport. The blue light that came from the multiple displays illuminated the room and cast dark, slanted shadows on Kendall's face. The mayor's features seemed more narrow and angular than usual.

"And what things would those be, Mayor?" Gerald folded his arms. Kendall did not respond. "You have no proof that I shoved my little sister off of the bunk bed. Not a shred. She's always trying to get me in trouble!"

Kendall remained silent. Gerald admitted to himself, that yes, he was perfectly uncomfortable. He had every right to feel that way. Of course, this was Kendall's desired effect. And that Gerald was falling prey to it irked him to no end. Crescent's mayor finally turned. On his face was a mask of impatience and irritation, the corners of Kendall's thin lips sagged to the ground. He waved a long-fingered hand over one of the viewscreens and a two dimensional projection shimmered out of the display. Kendall twirled his fingers above the wavering image, rotating it to face Gerald, and the pixels coalesced. It showed Gerald helping Ina into Bean. It showed him climb in after her. It showed the ship lift off the flight deck and exit the hangar into space. Kendall snapped his fingers and the image froze on Bean's flaring exhaust cones.

"That," Kendall pointed at the image, "is what is distressing me. I was told you did not return to your hangar. I am an intelligent man, Gerald. Please do not insult that intelligence."

"Okay. I took a pretty girl for a joyride. So what?"

"You're running salvage for another party on Crescent," Kendall said, his voice matter-of-fact. "In blatant disregard of our agreement. In violation of our contract. All area salvage claimed by your ship—by contract—belongs to Crescent."

"Kendall, you've got it wrong. I didn't land in a different hangar because I was hiding anything from you. I landed in a different hangar because I was hiding from my girlfriend." Kendall's brow lifted. "I didn't want her to know I was… sampling other wares? That can't be covered under my contract with you, can it?"

"You have no way of proving that, son," Kendall said. "By all accounts, you are in quite a pickle." Kendall depressed a small black button atop his desk. An instant later Taylor was in the room, a meaty hand on Gerald's shoulder.

"Wait, goddamnit. I can prove it. Just check the security feed for hangar… " Gerald blanked, what hangar number was the cover-up location. *Think, damn you, think.* "Hangar thirteen."

"Hangar thirteen, you say?" Kendall sat behind the desk and clucked his tongue. "What do you think, Taylor? Would you like to tear his arms off or would you prefer to watch the security feed from hangar thirteen?"

The man-mountain guffawed. "What do you think, Mayor?"

Kendall nodded and Taylor knocked Gerald from his chair, the floor rising up to slap him hard in the face. Taylor's thick fists rained down blows before Gerald could register he was no longer sitting. Kendall circled the pair and spoke as Taylor delivered his beating.

"Gerald, I'm willing to give you the benefit of the doubt as we look into your story. Why? It has nothing to do with any sort of fondness for you. I'm actually starting to *not* like you. But, you happen to be the *only* salvage man on Crescent," Taylor's fist caught Gerald in the side of the head and his ears began to ring. He could barely hear the mayor as he continued. "I'd send Walter Vegan out to do the job, but he's already destroyed three—no, four ships. He's more of an, how shall I put it, administrator. In the future, if you decide to leave Crescent on an unscheduled joyride, you had better go through the proper ATC channels." Kendall held up his hand and Taylor ceased his assault. "This is my only warning, Gerald. I'm beginning to regret my decision to hire you. Why don't you consider restoring my faith?"

[•••]

The stink in Naheela's hut was unbearable. It was an amalgam of incense, rotting things, and the undeniable smell of old age. Visually, the space was a disaster area. There were boxes and crates piled everywhere.

Knick knacks—small statues, dim holo projections, candles—were anywhere there was a flat surface for them to stand upon. Marisa had to fight the compulsion to organize the place.

Naheela sat at the only trinket-free piece of furniture, a small round table with a heavy, metal base. The table looked like it might at one point have been anchored to the floor of a diner. Naheela beckoned to Marisa with the arthritic claw of a hand. The hag opened her mouth; viscous saliva spanned the dark space like spider silk and caught the candlelight before breaking. Flecks of white spittle remained on her cracked lips. Either oblivious, or just not giving a crap, Naheela did not wipe it away.

"Are ye jus' gonna stand there all day, dearest? You're lettin' a draft in." Naheela tossed her head back and cackled as if she had just told the funniest joke in the universe. Marisa remained frozen in the doorway. The laughter ceased so suddenly it was startling. "Come in and sit down," Naheela barked as an order and Marisa found herself in motion, moving across the cluttered floor in short steps to seat herself across from the crone. The rancor of the old woman's body odor made Marisa's eyes water and she wondered when the hag had last bathed. She dropped her eyes to the table. The dark wood grain swirled and writhed beneath the gloss of polyurethane. Marisa placed her hand on the slightly scarred surface. It was real wood.

"This table is the oldest thing on Crescent Station, ye know," Naheela said. Her words floated on a cloud of foul breath. Marisa wasn't sure how much more she could take.

"Why have you invited me here?" Marisa asked.

"Why have *I*?" Naheela pointed to herself with a curved, yellow nail, "Invited *you*?" Naheela cackled again. The sound was like breaking glass to Marisa's ears, and she cringed. "Need I remind you, girlie, you are the one who showed up on Naheela's doorstep. No, no. I didn't invite you here, but I did expect you sooner or later. Pushed by the need for answers, and by winds you can't explain but can only feel."

"You're not making any sense." But that was the rub. Naheela *was* making sense. Marisa knew she was right where she belonged. And that made her feel all the more batty.

"You followed him here."

"What?"

"The vatter. But that was just a reflection. He is not here yet, but I've seen him more than once and so have you. The glass shudders,

Marisa. And from these vibrations come the reflections, like ripples on a pool. They dance to our shore and show things yet distant. Things are changing on Crescent every day. I see them all." Naheela clapped her hands together. "Strange and terrible things. You can feel it. You stand in it waist deep in the well. The *Three*, Marisa."

Marisa started to speak, but Naheela held up a hand to silence her.

"The Three are close, and you are just a pawn. You brought the darkness to your boyfriend—and he is a pawn. You opened his eyes to the Black. And his new slut. There is another—your boyfriend's new slut—she was touched as you were touched. At the Vault," Naheela intoned the words. "You best be heedful of that girl. I cannot see what is planned for her. Your roles are different in all this and I have already made my decision. I can only help you."

"Help me what? Why am I even listening to this?" Marisa pushed away from the table and stood. The old woman was only preying on Marisa's deranged, sleep deprived state. The hag was probably about to ask for money.

"Soon, you will go back to the water. There is something there that the Black would have you keep. Something that would open the door for the Three. But you must go there and ruin it. Destroy it. Destroy it good."

"I've heard enough. Enjoy the rest of your short life." Marisa turned to leave.

"Wait!" Naheela cried out. "I have to give you something." The old woman got up from the table with a speed that was nothing short of amazing. So amazing, in fact, Marisa remained planted where she stood. The crone hobbled behind one of the crates and returned with a small leather sheath. She tossed it onto the table. "Take that." Marisa leaned over the table and reached out to smack the object away. Naheela grabbed her around the wrist with one hand and shoved the sheath into Marisa's hand with the other. Her spotted hands were strong and cold. Marisa tried to pull away, but Naheela refused to let go.

"Destroy the thing you will find," Naheela said in a voice that sounded like a thousand and echoed inside Marisa's skull. The words seared onto her brain like a brand. The sensation passed, and Naheela let go of her. "Take it, Marisa. Take it."

"I don't want it," Marisa said.

"Take it, take. Or I'll be there every second of the day askin' ye to. Even when that comely man of yours has his prick in you. Take it. Take it." Marisa frowned, but did as she was instructed. She slid the sheath into her pocket and patted the bulge there. Naheela nodded, satisfied.

When Marisa was far enough away from the stench of Naheela's hut, she leaned against a dumpster—the trash bin smelled sweet by comparison. She retrieved the leather sheath from her pocket and removed the object it contained. She held in her hand a hammer not much bigger than her open hand. The head of the mallet was a thick disc of crimson so red, it was almost black. The hammer's two prongs were metal and covered in flecks of what she thought might be rust. *Destroy the thing you will find.* Yes, of course. As her fingers curled around the object, she knew what she had to do. She had a purpose. The realization glittered in her mind. Something compelled her to rap the hammer against the dumpster. When she did, the prongs rang with the most beautiful note she had ever heard. It made her head feel clear. She returned the hammer to its sheath and returned the sheath to the pocket of her jacket.

[•••]

Albin Catlier sat on the top rail of the metal fence; his boots were hooked under the bottom rung. For an instant, he thought he heard singing and looked up and over to Jacob Raney, who sat beside him. The other man was silent, playing with some multicolored puzzle-trinket he had stolen from Kendall's office.

Down the slope from where he and Jacob sat, Crescent's plump and happy cows meandered and grazed on vibrant green grass. Big collector bots moved across the field carrying bales of hay. The cows were a new stock to Crescent. Genetic engineering had graced the animals with the ability to produce three times more milk than the naturally-bred station livestock that preceded them. The bovine wonders were graciously paid for by Donovan Cortez, and upped the station's production of all protein-related products significantly.

"Let's go, Jacob," Albin said, and the two men hopped off the fence.

The farm extended for almost a mile in either direction. The ceiling here was lower than Main Street's, but still high enough to give you a crick in your neck if you stared too long. Sun globes, similar to those on Main Street but a fraction of the size, pumped life-providing light to the grass below.

Albin and Jacob drove a small hover down the slope and to the squat and angular structure at the massive chamber's aft: the Farm. The Farm was the main agricultural plant on Crescent. All material for the station's food compilers was processed here. Agricultural goods were packed at the Farm's broad loading docks for export to the neighboring systems.

Albin never cared much for the farm level on Crescent, or on any other space station, for that matter. There was something that was too unnatural about it. Sure, it shared some qualities with any planet-side open range. Grass. Open space. The smell of hay and manure. But none of it was genuine. Beyond the false sky, below the artificially-grown grass, there was vacuum. It just didn't stroke him right. It was like someone smiling and buying you a drink right before they stabbed you in the gut.

Robyn Prior sat in the front room of the Farm's office space. Her eyes were cast down to the data terminal set in the top of her small desk. She looked up when the two men entered and her cheeks immediately blanched. Jacob smiled one of his tobacco grins and Albin lifted his hat back with his thumb before lighting a cigarette. Robyn looked back down at the terminal, but Albin placed a hand on the screen, obscuring the view. Her flinch sent a glass ornament shaped like a penguin flying to the ground, where it shattered into a thousand pieces. A small robot chirped out of a hole in the wall and began sweeping up the fragments with a series of beeps.

"Relax, Robyn," Albin said. "Where is Jasper?"

"I... I don't know where he is," she sputtered. Jasper Prior, Robyn's husband, was the owner and operator of the Farm. He was always there somewhere. Albin frowned and slid his hand off the terminal.

"Robyn, don't make me have to go looking for your husband. I'd be forced to leave Jacob behind to keep an eye on you and, well, you know Jacob. He's a little twitchy when I'm not around."

Jacob nodded solemnly and then he laughed. The sharp, slightly crazed sound of it made Robyn jump again. Albin looked at her. She wasn't an ugly woman. A little homely, perhaps. She was showing the signs of age around the mouth and eyes, but looked to be keeping things together. Jacob began wandering around the small office space, examining the various pictures hanging on the walls. Some showed the fields, some showed the facilities. Another showed an old and long-forgotten wood and shingle farmhouse on a span of countryside that likely no longer existed.

"Okay," Robyn said at last. "He's in process monitoring station sixteen. I'll light the floor panels. Follow the blue ones."

"I knew you'd be reasonable. Jacob, you stick around here. I'll be back soon. Play nice."

Robyn shot him a look that said *please, don't leave me alone with him.* But she didn't dare say it—Jacob, after all, was quite sensitive.

[•••]

Jasper was crying like a little girl. Albin had only had to bash his head twice against the railing to bring on the tears. He let go, and the fat, balding man fell to his knees, clinging to the rails with his pudgy arms. Below the men, the elaborate conveyance system clacked away. Albin leaned against a support pillar and lit another cigarette as he glanced around the works. The room was belts and bulbous kilns from wall to wall. It was noisy, and smelled faintly of ozone.

"Who else, Jasper? Who else you been selling Kendall's guns to?" Albin gestured with a cock of his head to the prefab weapons that were rolling by on the belts and into the kilns for super heating. It wasn't only milk, cheese, and veggies that came out of the farm, but guns. Lots of guns—Kendall's magical share of the outer colonies' black market. The operation was a big one. The steady output of weapons had become extremely useful in maintaining good relations with Darros Stronghold and his raider clans.

"No one else. Just those mercenaries. They were the first. I pulled the ad from the nexus the second there was that incident at Heathen's."

"You know Core Sec is sending an auditor here, right?"

"No. I didn't know that," Jasper slid the rest of the way to the floor. "What are we going to do?"

"You're going to stand up, for starters. And you're going to stop sniveling like a little girl."

Jasper did as he was told. He almost lost his trousers when he did so. Albin caught a glimpse of the man's underwear. They were recently stained. And now he was pretty sure he could smell shit.

"This just means more work for the rest of us, Jasper. You shouldn't have gotten greedy. A shame you only know how to think of yourself." Albin pushed Jasper hard. The fat man yelped like a small dog and went careening over the railing. He landed hard on the wide conveyor channel. There was an audible crack—something definitely broke. Jasper began to wail and writhe. Tears steamed out of the corners of his squeezed shut eyes. The conveyor belt drew Jasper's wriggling body into the kiln chamber, where there was a final choking scream followed by a glare of white light. The completed weapons rolled out the other side and there was no trace of Jasper Prior—not even a filling.

When Albin returned to the front office, he found Robyn bent over the terminal desk with her suit-dress hiked up past her hips. Jacob rammed her hard from behind. Robyn's screams were muffled by what looked like her pantyhose. The flesh-toned stockings had been shoved into her mouth. Blood trickled from a lacerated cheek—obviously where Jacob had hit her.

"When you're done, kill her. Toss her in the kiln. I know you're gonna make a mess, so clean the place up, too, for god's sake."

Jacob flashed his teeth and continued to fuck away. *He really is a goddamn animal,* Albin thought as he slipped out the front door. The magnetic bolts clanked as the door locked behind him. Prior Farm was officially closed for the afternoon; at least until the new management arrived.

(Part VIII)

"I just thought you'd want to know," Walter Vegan said and inhaled through his teeth, making a wet slurping sound. Donovan Cortez tried his damndest not to breathe through his nose. Vegan smelled fouler than usual that afternoon. It was as if the ugly man had been crawling around in raw sewage. "If you don't want Kendall sniffing around here, you might want to pay me more."

If you're here much longer, Vegan, no one will ever want to sniff around here, Donovan thought and actually snickered out loud. There was a rustle behind the large and obscuring canvas drop sheet that hung from the ceiling girders in the otherwise empty hangar. Ina's head poked out of a seam between two flaps that marked an entrance. Vegan waggled his fingers at Ina and gave her a tobacco stained grin. Donovan gritted his teeth and took a deep breath. He tried to ignore the fuck-me eyes that were trained on his daughter.

"You want me to pay you more, Mr. Vegan?" In truth, Donovan wanted to hit Vegan for looking at his daughter, not give him more money. Donovan had never hit anyone in his life, but Vegan's hungry, mongrel gaze had stirred up a deep, searing anger. For a spilt second, Donovan wondered just what he had been thinking, bringing Ina to a place like Crescent. *I should hit myself, if anyone.*

"There are some happenings on Crescent that have made our good mayor a little more than uneasy. These empty hangars. There are quite a few. I use them for storage." Vegan made a sweeping gesture with one hand. "I'm responsible for documenting their inventory—or lack thereof. Things come into this station, I put them somewhere. Now I can't put them in this hangar. Understand? Kendall knows that Gerald left Crescent with your pretty daughter." He gestured with his eyes. Ina slipped out of view.

"Okay," Donovan said and gestured for Vegan to go on.

"I don't know what you are hiding in there. I don't want to know. This can go a few ways. I can start storing things in here. And suddenly, your secrecy is gone. I can tell Kendall that the good doctor is hiding something. Or, you send more credits my way and I'll keep this bay off limits for as long as you need it to be. How does that sound?"

Donovan took a deep breath. This was a waste of his time. He cleared his throat. "That all sounds fair. Ten thousand credits and you keep your mouth shut."

"Fifteen," Vegan countered.

"I don't understand why you need so much of my money, Mr. Vegan."

"I'm not going to work the Crescent decks forever, Doctor. I'm investing in my future. I plan on … "

"Yes, fine. Fifteen thousand credits." Donovan waved his hand dismissively. He was done with Vegan, and he didn't care to hear what the chief of operation's retirement plans entailed. "I have much to do. I will walk you out. This conversation is over."

"Yes, Doctor," Vegan's yellowed teeth flashed in a grin. "You will have to tell your daughter I said goodbye." Vegan looked up at the canvas drop and stared at it for several seconds. Donovan wasn't sure if Vegan was trying to figure out what was hidden behind it or if he was trying to picture Ina back there. Cortez took Vegan by the elbow and led him away from the canvas drop.

Donovan escorted the smelly man across the length of the expansive hangar floor and glanced up at the big, trundle airlock as they went. Small stripes of reinforced glass showed slices of Anrar III's gray-green surface. Vegan stepped through an exit bulkhead and into the narrow access hallway beyond it. He turned, his round belly brushed the wall, and he opened his crooked mouth to say something else. Donovan was certain it was nothing that he wanted to hear. He swung the bulkhead shut and locked it. Vegan smiled through the circular portal and then disappeared.

[•••]

The lifeboat took up at least a quarter of the hangar's deck space—maybe a little more. Its curving body extended almost all the way to the cobweb-laced ceiling girders. There were several big floodlights set up around the base of the lifeboat. The ship looked like a slumbering leviathan in the glaring light of the stand-mounted halo-globes. Chalky dust from the asteroid caked the lifeboat's long, rounded hull in places; clean patches revealed gray, pocked hull plates. The twin tail fins—both were severely damaged by ages of small impacts—jutted from the side of a wide tail section like tattered wings. Most of the hull plates at the nose of the ship were missing, exposing the ship's skeleton. The bands of metal had been severely bent by the impact that had ended the lifeboat's short journey centuries ago.

It was a small wonder that Gerald had been able to guide the derelict into the bay using only his small tug. The salvage captain had seemed thrilled to be rid of the lifeboat. Gerald had acted like he was afraid of the thing, but didn't say why. Ina explained that Gerald had had a bit of a panic attack while on the derelict, but Gerald hadn't told her why he had panicked. Claustrophobia was Donovan's guess.

Donovan strode toward the aft of the vessel with wide, quick steps. He could hardly contain himself as he rode the small, portable lift to the lifeboat's main loading hatch, excited to set foot on the ship for the first time.

Donovan hesitated at the edge of the lift. He squinted into the shadowy interior of the lifeboat's boarding area and tried to imagine Anrar III's miners and their families shuffling in procession onto the ship. Or perhaps they had fled onto the ship. He clicked on his flashlight and stepped into the darkness.

It was a straight shot to the control bridge of the lifeboat. Donovan resisted the urge to disappear down the various dark corridors he passed along the way. Ina was waiting on the bridge, he knew, and she'd give him holy hell for starting to explore without her. When he stepped onto the bridge, he saw her with her back to him at a bay of six large trapezoidal windows. The windows were arranged in two parallel rows of three; the top row was angled upward to afford a view of whatever was above the ship—in this case, the dusty hangar ceiling. The bottom row of windows looked down over the fore of the lifeboat. Ina was staring down at the collapsed nose of the ship, seemingly oblivious to his presence. Donovan walked around the perimeter of the bridge. He was impressed. Everything was remarkably intact—only a few of the control panels were charred from apparent shorts. He stepped beside his daughter and looked down through the scarred and dusty glass at the crushed nose-section.

"Dad," Ina said. He looked at her; her attention was now fixed on him. Her delicate brow was creased.

"Yes, dear? What's wrong?"

"How'd you know, Dad? How'd you know this lifeboat would be out there?"

Donovan knew it was only a matter of time before Ina asked the obvious. He had expected the question sooner. Ina was a curious girl. She always had been. Not to mention, she was also always vocal with him. But lately she seemed to be holding back. Her demeanor had changed since he had reprimanded her for venturing into the station's bowels. She was keeping strange hours lately, too. There were nights when she didn't come home, and he thought he even heard a man's voice in the apartment on one occasion. Ina's interest in their goals had seemed to wane, at least until the discovery of the lifeboat. That had perked her up.

She was young, and should have fun being so. She missed out on a lot with the aggressive pursuit of her various degrees, yes, but...

"Dad," she said, regaining his attention. "Stop thinking about nine thousand things. Please, answer my question."

Donovan inhaled until his lungs were filled and then let the air out slowly. His gray eyes flitted around the bridge. It was now or never.

"There was a good reason I didn't tell you, Ina." He opened his mouth, closed it, and then opened it again. "There was no scientific basis for this expedition. None whatsoever." His cheeks reddened instantly with shame.

Ina folded her arms across her chest and leaned against the viewports. She waited for him to go on.

"The truth is, it came to me in a dream. The asteroid. The lifeboat. The coordinates. This dream... it was largely nonsense, but the details of those three elements were like crystal. So clear. So hard and real. They were right there in the front of my mind when I woke. Ina—you know I'm a pragmatist. But, the impression this dream left in its wake, it was so strong. I had to investigate further."

"Was this a dream, Dad? Or a vision?"

Donovan raised his bushy brows and laughed. He could hardly believe he was having this conversation. He was beginning to wish he had just fabricated an answer.

"Is there a difference?"

"Of course there is a difference. A dream comes from your own head. A vision, someone else puts there for you."

Donovan felt a chill run up his spine. He did not like her definition. It felt entirely too accurate. He also didn't like her matter-of-fact tone. He looked back out the viewport. Long shadows draped the support struts and pooled around the belly of the lifeboat.

He felt cold and suppressed a shiver.

"It doesn't matter," Donovan said. It did matter, but that did not stop him from wanting to banish the thought from his mind. "What matters is that this," he spread his hands wide, "this ship was out there, and we have a lot of work to do."

And at that, he was excited all over again—to the point of giddiness. He had no idea where he to begin. He wanted to explore the whole vessel, every possible nook and cranny. Gone was the scientific will. Gone was the pragmatic. Now it was all about the boyish desire to go crawling around in the dust and spider webs in search of treasure.

"Where do we start, Dad?" Ina asked him, as if she were reading his thoughts.

Donovan hesitated. "Where better to start than right here? The brain of the whole works. Let's see what data we can get out of these computers."

[•••]

Marisa sat on the floor of her apartment, her bare legs crossed beneath her. The overhead halos were set at their lowest so that only a diffuse, milky light filled the gray-walled room. Furniture painted only the vaguest of shadows on the gray carpet. In front of her sat the leather sheath containing the strange mallet that Naheela had given her. Marisa touched it with a fingertip and felt a stirring inside her—a pleasant warmth between her legs. She took her hand away from the object. Marisa had been repeating that routine for the past two hours. There was a purpose for the hammer; Marisa was sure of it. But the shadows in her apartment had been doing their best to make her forget and now she almost had. The shadows had new life; a life she had come to call *the Black*. The Black had been a phantasmal presence in Heathen's, within the cisterns, and from her nightmares—and it wouldn't let her think things through. The twinges in her womanhood were from the Black, and were stronger than Naheela's hexing. They were stronger, and they felt much better.

Now she was fumbling to get the hammer out of the sheath. *Destroy it,* Naheela's voice intoned. *Destroy it!* The words were commanding and harsh. *Destroy what?* Marisa thought. *God, I know this is important.* She held the hammer's head between the thumbs and forefingers of both hands. The tingling started again. Hot. Wet. Marisa groaned and lay back on the floor. She placed one hand over her mouth and maintained her grip on the implement with the other. Waves of sensation swelled between her legs and then crashed over her body. She cried out each time. And each time the tide of sensation drew her further and further out into a sea of darkness. Like a rip current, it was pulling her under. Each time, the disembodied voice of Naheela was further away. The hammer struck the floor and rang with a warbling note. She climaxed into a black void.

There were voices in this black place. Men and women. Some people laughed. Some shouted. Marisa opened her eyes and gasped. She found herself stumbling down crowded Main Street. Her hand still clutched the hammer. Marisa looked down at her lap in dawning horror. She had put on pants at some point before going on her little walk, at least, but there was an alarming dark stain where she had soaked through her underwear and jeans. She hadn't wet her pants. She wasn't menstruating. *Good lord,* she thought, *Oh my sweet lord.* Her eyes darted around for familiar landmarks to measure how far down Main Street she had wandered. The glowing neon scrawl that proclaimed Heathen's was just a block away—she had somehow traversed almost three quarters of Main Street's bazaar. She ducked into a terminal booth and closed the curtain. Had security seen her? Surely the cameras had picked up her trek. She looked at the rusty hammer and wondered if those old flakes were really rust at all. Revolted, she threw it down. It sang for an instant as it clattered to rest. The sound made her head spin. Her fingers worked fast to enter a number into the terminal.

The screen glowed to life. She leaned in close, one arm draped over her head.

"Gerry!" she gasped.

"Marisa?" He paused and his forehead creased with concern. "Are you crying? What's wrong?"

She hadn't realized it, but she was crying—in big, shaking sobs.

"Come get me. Please."

"What's going on, what's wrong?" he asked her again.

"I don't know what's happening to me. Please, come get me." She wiped the tears from her eyes with the back of her hand. Gerald looked down and she concealed the wet spot by pressing her hand there. It felt good and she recoiled. Then she realized that Gerald couldn't see anything below her neck. He was only reading the address bar on the screen of his apartment's terminal.

"You're at the booth by Heathen's?" he said.

"Yes. That's the one. Please hurry."

"I'll be right there," he said and the screen went dark.

Black.

[•••]

Gerald threw back the curtain of the terminal booth and stuck his head in. It was empty. He spun and looked up and down the length of Main Street. The sun globes shone with a fading purple light; nighttime was coming on strong. People glided up and down the sidewalks, orange street lamps cast long, caricatured shadows. He didn't see Marisa anywhere. He spent another ten minutes weaving through crowds of people and poking his head into storefronts and fashion booths, but she was still nowhere to be found. Gerald was worried. She'd been acting so damn strange lately. He knew he should've been keeping a closer eye on her.

He thought of Ina then, of the way her hair had hung into his face and smelled like flowers. A pang of guilt stabbed him directly in the chest. He was a bastard. Bastard or not, he had to find Marisa.

Gerald strode through the batwings and pushed his way toward Heathen's main bar. It was happy hour, and the room was packed shoulder-to-shoulder with bodies. Maerl was behind the counter, mixing up drinks and pouring beers in a flurry of shakers, ice, and foam. One of Heathen's female bartenders—a pretty girl with long, black hair and large breasts that nearly spilled over her black corset—smiled at him.

"What'll it be?" she asked sweetly.

"I gotta talk to Maerl," he said. She held a hand behind her ear in the universal *I-can't-hear-you* gesture. Gerald leaned in and spoke into her ear while he pointed at the bald bartender. "Maerl! I've got to speak to Maerl!"

Her smile widened and she nodded. The bartender turned away and went over to place her hands on Maerl's shoulder. Balancing on tiptoes, she spoke into his ear. Maerl looked over to Gerald and grinned. He finished filling a round of shots and slid them over to a group of young women. Once he had taken their credit wafer, he went over to Gerald.

"What's up, kid?" Maerl asked, leaning over the bar. "Why so pale? See a ghost or something?"

"Marisa—she's in some kind of trouble. Did she come in here?" Gerald looked around. Some of the bar-goers seemed lost. Their eyes were ringed with dark circles. Some faces were slack-jawed and utterly without expression. Pint glasses traveled listless paths to frowning lips.

"Sorry, Gerry. Haven't seen her at all today," Maerl said, and Gerald turned his eyes back to him.

"If she comes in here, don't let her leave. Call my PDA, all right?"

"Sure thing. Hope she's okay!"

"Yeah, me too."

Gerald left Heathen's twice as overwhelmed as he had been when he had gotten there. He looked up Main Street first, and then down. The scattering of storefronts and alleys all looked the same—painted in identical swatches of artificial night glow and streetlamp light. He had no idea where to begin looking, but he started walking anyway. He would find her. He had to.

[•••]

The water was ice cold on Marisa's naked legs. It didn't matter. Fire radiated from the hammer, up her arms, into her belly, and then into her crotch. There it exploded as a supernova and spread through every single nerve ending. If some part of her was cold, it was distant. She submerged herself again and felt around the floor of the cistern. It was rough with mineral deposits, but otherwise featureless. *Keep looking,* Naheela's voice had been joined by a chorus of a thousand others. Marisa came up for air and went back down. It was ink black under the surface of the water, but she found she could see when her eyes were closed. It was as if something else was seeing for her, in a relief of chartreuse and onyx. A raised area stood out on the cistern floor in her vision. It was the height of a credit wafer and no wider than the palm of her hand.

Yes! the voices in her head gasped; she felt another wave of warm tingling. She swam toward the shape. Centuries of mineral deposits had fused the object to the floor. She began to hack to at it with the hammer's prongs. Hunks of deep red deposit drifted away. She hacked and hacked.

Gentle, now, the voices in her head told her. Naheela's voice was no longer part of the chorus. *You've almost got it now.*

She came up for air, taking it in gulps and gasps, and then went back down again. The shaft of the hammer clenched between her teeth, she used use her fingers on the object. Marisa felt it give, like a loose tooth ready to come out of its socket. She pushed and pulled on it, and finally the thing was loose and in her hand. She resurfaced and a shiver ran through her body. Cold. She was so goddamned cold now. The sound of her swimming echoed into the darkness.

[•••]

Marisa was in her apartment. She lay on her back. Naked. Her hair was still wet from the cistern. The hammer lay out of its sheath on the carpet. She was no longer interested in the hammer. The object that she had retrieved from the floor of the cistern was demanding her full attention. She had the thing pressed to her heart. The peculiar optical disc was cold on her hot skin. She held her prize up in front of her face and the deep, red glass-like substance first reflected but then seemed to devour the light from the halo-globes.

She didn't care about its purpose. Marisa was focused on her reward.

You must do it now. Destroy it! she heard Naheela say.

Marisa sat up and took the hammer in hand. She held the crimson head of the mallet just above the disc's reflective surface and the object immediately began to warm in her hand.

Shadows drained down the wall. They flowed over the carpet and wrapped around Marisa's naked body like a shroud. Marisa's head felt like it was filled with cotton candy—sweet and gauzy. The Black whispered into that space and told her to stop. The Black told her the crone had only given her the hammer out of jealousy so that Marisa would ruin the true gift: the beautiful glass disc. *How evil of Naheela!* Marisa thought dreamily. She crawled over to the garbage chute and opened the panel, then threw the hammer in without hesitation. It rang as it fell down the shaft. The sound grew distant and then died altogether. Marisa felt a pang of deep sorrow at the sudden silence. But she was becoming very sleepy, so she ignored the sadness. There was no time to be sad. She had one more task to complete before she could rest. She had to hide the disc. She had to keep it safe.

Marisa was in bed when Gerald finally came to her. She stirred, only vaguely aware of his presence. He was talking to her, but she didn't understand the words coming out of his mouth. She heard herself tell him she was fine now and that everything was okay. Of course, that was the truth. She felt Gerald slide beneath the covers of the small bed and wrap his arms around her. He was warm, so warm. It felt good.

You can't trust him, the Black said.

Yes, I can. Marisa responded. *He's Gerry. He takes care of my shit.*

The voice didn't answer, and Marisa fell into a deep, fitful sleep.

[Part IX]

Nigel Swaren wiped his hand across the mirror, leaving a wide streak in the condensation. He tilted his chin up and turned his head first to the left and then to the right. His stubble was shaved down low, but Nigel was cursed with a beard that grew like hellfire. In half a day, the shadow would be dark again. His short hair was combed back, the strands in perfect rows. Dark strays were tucked back neatly behind his shower-pink ears. The air handling system hummed and hissed above his head and cooled the still-damp flesh of his bare chest and shoulders. He took the white tee shirt that hung from the washroom door and pulled it over his slender and toned torso. He tucked the tee shirt into the waistband of his blue, straight-legged Core Sec security pants and dropped his eyes to the octagonal PDA that was strapped to his wrist. With a thumb, he cleared the fog on the small LCD.

The merchant vessel *Oasis* would be arriving at Crescent soon.

Someone began to beat upon the bulkhead that separated his quarters from the rest of the ship. Nigel hated hitching rides. Privacy was a horrendous thing to maintain. He grimaced and opened the washroom door. The pounding continued. Nigel paused, washed his hands, dried them, and then examined his well-manicured nails. He turned the light off and stepped into the narrow berthing quarter. More pounding. Nigel took his time pulling the uniform jacket off the sleep-rack and slipping it over his shoulders. He buttoned it up and then went to the door. When he flipped the lock toggle and the door slid open, the captain of the *Oasis*, Wrenfeld, stood on the other side, fist raised mid-knock. The captain's gap-toothed grin beamed from the dense forest of a dark, springy beard. His chestnut eyes shone with a peculiar eagerness.

"Mr. Swaren, we're about to begin our final approach to Crescent. Figured you wouldn't want to miss it," Captain Wrenfeld said before perching the stub of a cigar between his wet lips. The brown thing was unlit and Nigel was glad. He detested the smell of cigar smoke. During the trip, the recycled air on the *Oasis* had been laced constantly with the stale odor of tobacco.

"And why is that, Captain?"

Wrenfeld raised his dark, bushy brows and barked a laugh around the unlit cigar.

"Crescent is quite the gem. Everyone wants to see her."

"I'm not everyone, Captain Wrenfeld."

Wrenfeld laughed again; the sound was followed by a litany of dry coughs.

"Be that as it may—you're still gonna want to see it. Trus' me."

"Do I even have a choice in this?" Nigel asked.

"'Fraid not," Wrenfeld said, his tone apologetic.

[•••]

Nigel stood alongside Captain Wrenfeld in an observation lounge that was no wider than Nigel's washroom. The small space was a haze of smoke. Nigel wanted to gag. The dark side of Anrar III could be seen through fingerprint-smeared viewports. The planet's girth blotted out more and more stars as it continued to grow with *Oasis'* steady approach. Droplets of fire grew along the planet's fringe and the sun rose in a blinding flash of yellow-orange light. Nigel squinted; the viewport polarized to accommodate the change in visual radiation. Wrenfeld pointed.

"There."

A small black hook was silhouetted against the cresting sun in the direction of Wrenfeld's pointing finger. It looked like a nail clipping; not what Nigel would have categorized as awe-inspiring. But as the *Oasis* drew nearer, that fingernail clipping grew into something less than ordinary. Nigel pretended to be unimpressed, but in truth, of all the stations he'd traveled to as a Core Sec internal security auditor, he'd seen nothing like Crescent. As it grew in the viewport, it appeared almost as a living thing—an ancient creature you'd see dwelling at bottom of an ocean. The station's long, curved hull was weathered, beaten, and crudely patched. The surface looked like it had grown its fair share of tumors in the form of repairs and modifications. The mismatched hull plates, docking tubes, and sensory arrays looked natural—the adaptation and evolution of this ancient, void-dwelling beast.

"She's somethin', ain't she?" Wrenfeld said and stabbed his cigar out in an ashtray. "You can stay here. I'm needed on the bridge so we can dock."

"They never finished it. The original engineers... " Nigel said and his voice trailed off. He didn't know much about Crescent. It was just another station to him. He'd heard plenty of rumors that it was a nasty place, even before it had come into his mission dossier. Security reports confirmed that it was no vacation spot. But still, he didn't expect to see a quarter-completed, seemingly abandoned space hulk.

"Didn't do your homework?" Wrenfeld waggled his brows. "Never heard of the curse, then?"

"I did my homework, Captain—folklore wasn't part of it. When I'm dispatched to a station or outpost, I don't make it routine to study up on the design history."

"Well, that might've been helpful in this case. As you can see, Crescent isn't like most Core Sec facilities. She's old. I won't say she's the oldest, but she shows her age. She was built before the Core. Something bad happened on her—something downright evil. And that was it. The buildin' stopped and she was abandoned. Only thanks to the New Juno colonization efforts did she come back into service."

"Quaint. I'm sure there's a more logical explanation to things than a campfire story, Captain. I don't care either way. I'm not here about this station's past—I'm here to see if Crescent has a future."

"And I'm just here to drop ya off." Wrenfeld winked. "Enjoy the view."

Wrenfeld took his leave and Nigel moved closer to the viewport to examine the station. He'd been to some rough places—mining depots that were under riot, research facilities in need of outbreak containment—but when he looked upon the strange, incomplete space station, there was a tingling in his nethers. The sensation told him with certainty that Crescent was going to be a somewhat different experience.

[•••]

Nigel inhaled a lung full of hangar air. He could not have been happier to be off the small and smoky *Oasis*. Nigel looked to where Captain Wrenfeld was supervising a crew of Crescent deck hands, a fresh cigar planted between beard-obscured lips. The crew carted various crates down the docking ramp to be hauled away by station collector bots. Wrenfeld was making one wisecrack after the other. The dockhands seemed either not to understand the jokes, or not to care. Their slack expressions never changed, and their eyes—they looked downright weary—were focused on the crates as they should have been, not on the comedian ship captain and his antics. That fact did not seem to deter Wrenfeld one bit; he went right on with the humor between plumes of heavy smoke.

Duffle bag in hand, Nigel made his way down to the deck to where two individuals, a man and woman, were waiting for him. Nigel guessed the man was middle-aged, it was hard to tell—the fellow's long horse-face was covered in patchy hair growth. In some places the curling strands wanted to be a beard, in others they weren't quite so sure. Salt and pepper hair, greasy and stringy, hung to his shoulders. At the man's side stood a woman who wore the Core Sec blues. Her hair was twisted onto the top of her head in a tight bun. Her pale features were delicate but her expression was stern as her green eyes regarded him. When Nigel reached them, the woman extended her hand, which he took for a single, downward shake before letting go.

"Welcome to Crescent, Captain Swaren," she said, flashing a brief and polite smile. "I'm Lieutenant Marisa Griffin. This is Walter Vegan, Crescent's Chief of Operations and deck master." Officer Griffin looked up at her beastly companion. He didn't speak, but he wore a scowl on his horse face that said plenty. Walter Vegan did not welcome Nigel to his station.

"How was the trip?" Officer Griffin asked.

"If you won't be needing anything more from me, I've got some work that needs doing," Vegan said. He looked to Nigel and offered a tight, little bow. "Captain Swaren." Nigel nodded and returned his attention to Officer Griffin, who was far more pleasing to the eye than Vegan.

"Just to clear the air right off the bat, Officer Griffin, most people instantly believe me to be the *bad guy*. That's not the case. When given a chance, I'm actually pretty much okay. I only become the bad guy when people interfere with my audits. If I ask for your help, you should give it to me. You'll find that we'll get along just fine."

Officer Griffin flashed one of her polite smiles. "Of course," she said. "As your liaison during your stay here on Crescent, I will be of as much assistance as I can possibly be."

"I appreciate that," Nigel said.

"Now, if you don't mind too much, I need to check your bag and perform the standard security checks on your person."

"See? You've already passed the first test." Nigel smiled.

[•••]

Kendall leaned forward in his chair; the leather creaked beneath him. The security feed from the main docking port floated above his desk and he listened intently to the exchange between Officer Griffin and this Captain Nigel Swaren. Griffin was being polite—not too polite, Kendall was glad to hear. Too polite would be suspicious. She just had to do her job. Kendall narrowed his gaze at the pixelated image of Swaren. At the current level of zoom, it was hard to make out too many distinguishing features. Swaren looked young. But to misconstrue youth as naïveté would be a mistake. According to Captain Swaren's Core Sec profile, he was a highly decorated auditor. If there was something wrong at a station or outpost, Nigel was sent there. And when he left, that problem no longer existed. There was nothing wrong on Crescent, Kendall knew. He ran her tight as always. Kendall's side activities didn't interfere with the station's day-to-day operations. If anything, the special goods being produced the beneath the Farm assured the station's safety in this volatile region. Kendall wouldn't let an auditor fuck with that. In truth, Kendall did not know why Core Sec had sent the auditor to the station.

Kendall's reverie was broken by a rattle in the anteroom. The sound was followed by several loud thuds.

"Taylor?" Kendall said. There was an instant of static in his cochlear.

"Yes, Mayor?" Taylor's voice responded.

"What are you doing out there?"

"What are you taking about?" Taylor replied.

"In the antechamber. It sounds like you're moving the goddamned furniture."

"Mayor Kendall, I'm not in there. I'm with Raney and Catlier."

Kendall felt a tightening in the pit of his stomach. He activated the office door lock and called up the security feed for the anteroom—it showed only static.

"Taylor, there is something wrong, then."

"I'm only a minute away, Mayor."

"Well, hurry up, goddamn it." Kendall moved out from behind his desk and went to the door. He pressed his head against the cool wood. There was another bang as something slammed into the door. The door shuddered and Kendall jumped backwards, scanning the room for the closest potential weapon at hand. He bent over an awkwardly shaped flower pot and was hefting it when Taylor's voice crackled over the intercom speaker.

"What the—? Mayor. This is… really weird. You should come out and see this."

"Is it safe? Are you sure it's safe?"

"Yes, Mayor. I locked you in when me an' the boys left to get dinner. No one has access to this antechamber when it's locked but me and Captain Benedict and he's in a meeting with the auditor now." Kendall deactivated the door lock and the swung the old thing open. He wasn't quite sure what he was looking at when he entered the outer room.

Half of Kendall's book collection had been pulled off the shelves and lay scattered across the floor. It was as if someone had yanked out volumes at random and had thrown them around the room. A fat dictionary lay at Kendall's feet. Obviously, the book was what had hit the door minutes ago. The furniture had been completely rearranged. Chairs were stacked in the middle of the room, tables stood on their heads. *A practical joke?* Kendall thought and looked at Taylor. *He's not smart enough to play a practical joke. Better yet, he's not stupid enough to pull that shit, either. No one is. So in that case… what is going on here?*

[•••]

"This is Crescent's Core Sec HQ." Marisa gestured with the sweep of a hand that encompassed the multiple banks of security feeds. "As you can see, the room is not large enough to accommodate overlay projection for the number of feeds on Crescent. So, we employ a more classic video feed system." She pointed to the widescreen LCD that was suspended above the rows of smaller displays. "That screen is five times the size of the others and in high definition." She then pointed to the two bulkheads at the far end of the room. "The door on the right, cell block is down there—temporary holding only. Criminals are processed and then either moved off station or to Crescent's small penitentiary. The bulkhead on the left—showers, lockers, and the toilet."

Marisa did not have to be psychic to know that Captain Swaren was not impressed. He had said very little on the trip down to the Core Sec HQ. He eyed HQ with same tight-lipped expression that had regarded the scenery on their trek down there. Marisa wanted to grab him, slap him, and yell in his face, *Are you too pretty for a place like Crescent?* He was rather pretty, it had to be said. Not that Marisa was attracted to him; she wasn't. But, she couldn't ignore the strong chin, high cheekbones, and glass-chip hazel eyes. His stuffiness didn't affect his good looks, but the attitude rendered them a non-factor.

"I was told I'd have a private office. Where would that be?" he said, folding his arms over his chest. He moved over to the banks of monitors and squinted. "This resolution is crap."

"Captain Benedict has the only office. Generally, in this monitoring station, there is only one Core Sec officer assigned. Most times, at least. You're welcome to use this room."

"Only one officer for all those feeds? That strikes me as understaffing."

"As you will see in your audit, Crescent has been extremely clean for the past fifteen years. Besides, there are more than a few satellite monitoring stations on Crescent that are always manned. Core Sec is always watching," Marisa said and forced a smile. Exhaustion began to throb as a headache behind her eyes. She hadn't been able to sleep in her apartment without chemical assistance, not after recent events. Now, the pills hardly worked.

The effort of being enthusiastic was killing her slowly. Captain Swaren was no help.

"We'll see," Nigel said. "Are we done for now?"

"Well, there is certainly more of the station to see, Captain." She looked at him; a quizzical expression drew fine lines into her brow.

"I've seen enough for now. I have plenty of work to do. If you'd be so kind," he gestured to the door. He wanted her to leave. Marisa was insulted.

"Look, I'm your liaison here. Effectively, your assistant. Don't you think ... "

"I think I'll be contacting you if I need you. Please. I'm not trying to be rude," Nigel said. If he was trying to be polite, he was failing miserably.

"Okay." She didn't know what else to say. She had no idea what she would do in the meantime—Swaren was her only assignment. She was inclined to go to Heathen's and not answer when Swaren called her. That would be career suicide—likely real suicide, she knew. Kendall would have her head. No, she would go to the mayor and give him a preliminary report. He would like that, and she would earn some points. Maybe it would hasten a discharge from his personal employ.

"Griffin," Nigel said, and she halted on her way to the door. "Yes. Now I know why I know your name. You were wrapped up in a bit of a gun club scandal, no?"

"I...what?" Marisa stammered. Damn him—he had managed to catch her off guard.

"Be a love and, while you're out, fetch the dock scanner data records for the past month and a half, and the maintenance logs for the last... say... fifteen years?"

Speechless, she turned on her heel and left him there.

[•••]

Marisa decided to head to Kendall's office first. After that, she'd go to the bar. If she could still walk following the bar visit, she'd go to the dock scanner. At least now she could tell Kendall that Swaren had already asked about Heathen's. Marisa found Taylor shelving books when she arrived in the antechamber. The room was a mess. Amongst the scattered old and rare editions, furniture stood cockeyed and upended. Taylor looked at her and grunted, but didn't make any sound that approximated speech. Marisa imagined he was having a difficult time alphabetizing and almost said as much before he got off his big knees and pressed a thumb behind his ear.

"Marisa Griffin is here to see you, Mayor," Taylor said and paused. "Go on in."

The door didn't even have a chance to swing shut behind her before Kendall was beckoning her over with his hand. "Officer Griffin. Will you come take a look at this, please?" he said. The door banged shut. "There is something not quite right with one of my feeds." Marisa went behind Kendall's desk to stand next him. He had one overlay pulled up and it hovered as a dark square. A diagnostic window floated in the glass panel that comprised the surface of the desk. Marisa glanced at the readout; it indicated that the feed was working just fine.

"What's the problem, exactly?" she asked.

"The problem, my dear girl? You can see the overlay as well as I. It's gone blank. But according to the computer it's... "

"Fine, yes. Is there something obscuring the lens?" It was an obvious question.

"Taylor made sure the camera was free of obstruction."

"Did you hard reset the camera?" she asked.

"Did I do what? No. I've never heard of such a thing."

"The feed cameras contain their own CPUs. Sometimes—and it is rare—they overload."

"And how do I hard reset the camera?" Kendall asked.

Marisa led him out to the antechamber. She hadn't expected to be teaching Camera Maintenance 101. She pulled two chairs over and stood on one of them, then indicated for Kendall to do the same. Marisa found it a strange experience to stand on a chair next to the mayor. It felt like they were playing some silly kid's game. *The floor's lava, touch and you die!* She looked at Kendall; he was watching her intently. Marisa pointed at the rectangular button on the side of the camera. She could feel Taylor gawking at them.

"That one?" Kendall said, reaching out to touch one of several buttons on the camera's side panel. She pushed his hand away.

"No, Mayor. The red button."

"Ah, I see. I just press it, then? Or rather, I order someone to press it for me?" He curved his lips in a grin that made Marisa's skin crawl. She offered a short laugh at his attempt at humor.

"No, you press it and hold it down for thirty seconds. The red LED on the front of the camera will go blank. If you see that LED relight, you're in business." She got down from the chair, leaving Kendall up there alone.

"Well, aren't you going to press it?" he asked.

"No. You are, Mayor. I'm going to watch the diagnostic window back in the office to see if I can't determine the problem."

Marisa made it back behind the desk just as the camera rebooted. The diagnostic window showed endless rows of command line text—it scrolled by fast and most of it was unintelligible computer language. The feed floating above the desk exploded with a burst of static and went black, only to be replaced with four colored squares. The squares went black and, like that, she was looking at Kendall's thin and wrinkled face in the overlay. He was squinting into the camera. The diagnostic screen on the desk display told her the system was functioning normally. She scrolled back through the boot log and couldn't find anything off. At least, not at first. After a few seconds of perusal, she found a portion of code-text that was garbled beyond anything she'd ever seen. The symbols weren't from any programming language she knew of. Strange. A virus in the security system? None that the diagnostic routine had picked up. Kendall returned to his office and the door closed in an arc behind him. He slumped into his big leather chair.

Marisa leaned over the arm of the chair; she was close enough to Kendall that she could smell the pomade in his hair. The smell was spiced and almost overbearing. Kendall looked up at her with watery eyes. There was a glimmer in those eyes that she did not like. He smiled. Apparently, he did not mind her proximity.

"I apologize, Officer Griffin. I realize you were not coming down here to repair my security feed."

"No, I wasn't. Nor was I planning on reviewing your feed. But that's just the kind of girl I am—a real team player."

"Certainly. Certainly, my dear," Kendall said.

"When did the feed go out?"

"Ten minutes ago, five minutes ago? I heard some banging out there," he pointed at the closed door. "Yes, five minutes ago."

Marisa rolled the security feed back by eight minutes and let it play. It showed Taylor speaking into his comm. Marisa turned on the sound and heard the tail end of Kendall's dinner order. Bratwurst with sauerkraut and hot mustard. The exit door slid open, and Albin Catlier and Jacob Raney stood on the other side it. Taylor stepped out to join them and once the door slid shut, the red light above it winked on. The feed tracked forward another several minutes, then went black at minute three.

"We'll slow it down," she said.

"Yes, let's take our time." She could feel Kendall's eyes on her body, not on the feed overlay. She was used to attention from the opposite sex, but she didn't relish how Kendall's gaze made her feel. She glanced at the styrofoam container that sat at the corner of the desk.

"Your dinner's getting cold, Mayor."

"I've lost my appetite for bratwurst," Kendall said and winked.

She shrugged off the comment and played the blackout portion of the security feed. The footage crept forward at one quarter its original speed.

"Now, what the hell are we looking at?" Kendall said.

At first glance, Marisa thought there was a defect in the charge-coupled sensor chip within the camera. A dark blotch grew in the center of the feed, devouring the pixels. But as she watched the shape grow, it became clear what she was seeing. She shivered. Up to that very moment, she hadn't been convinced that the living shadows and their accompanying disembodied voices weren't imaginary things—images created by her psyche as she sailed off the deep end. *Hallucinations aren't something that can be captured on a security feed,* she told herself. This was a chip defect. The similarity was only coincidental.

"I don't know," Marisa admitted and took a deep breath. She glanced to the mayor. Tiny beads of sweat had broken out on his forehead. "I'll play it back slower," she said.

Ink dropped into a glass of water. The blackness twisted out with curling tendrils that grew and thickened. They spread out over everything, turning it all black. She took a step back from the desk, her hand on her heart. Her breath was short. The headache that had been a low throb now blossomed white-hot between her eyes. She managed to wrench her eyes away from the overlay before they could explode in her head. The floating hologram swelled; its glowing boundaries bowed outwards and looked about to rupture.

"Turn it off," Kendall gasped. "If there's a god, turn that fucking thing off." The mayor's eyes were frozen, open. Marisa thought they might fall out of his skull.

She pried her fingers from her chest and swiped her hand through the overlay. A lance of ice shot up her arm. The hovering black square exploded into light and was gone. Kendall let out a gasp and a cry and then began sucking in air like a drowning man. Marisa found she was doing the same. Consciousness became gooey for an instant and then she was on her knees and breathing hard. As she managed to slow her respiration, the glittering floaters that had been encroaching on her field of vision began to drift away. She looked up from the floor to Kendall; he lay slumped in his chair. The mayor was out cold and there was a trickle of drool on his suit jacket. *I don't know what's happening,* Marisa thought, *and I promise not to care, if you just let me wake up and let this all be a dream, I'll never question it. Just let me wake up. Let me forget this.* Suddenly, Nigel Swaren was far from her mind.

Kendall stirred; a moan escaped his lips. His face remained slack, like he had taken a strong sedative, or had had a stroke. His eyelids sprung open and he was on his feet backing away from the desk. His eyes darted to Marisa who was still sitting cross-legged on the carpet. He looked afraid.

She didn't blame him.

"Erase," Kendall said, his voice a croak. What was that in his eyes? Recognition? "Erase the whole array. It can't be good—what's on there.

Erase the damnable thing." Kendall stormed out from behind the desk. The office door swung open and he disappeared through it. The door slammed shut and she was alone.

Marisa sat behind the big desk; the leather chair was still warm from Kendall's body. She gazed down through the thick pane of glass at the rows of LCDs beneath. They cycled with a hundred feeds, each showing a different aspect of Crescent. There were LCDs dedicated to news feeds, too. A young girl had been murdered. There were environmental instabilities on Decks H through K. The Farm had reopened for business. Marisa looked away. She was afraid if she stared too long, she would see the feeds black out one by one until the whole desk panel was dark and a tar-colored wave of god-knows-what sucked her into its lightlessness. She called up the original feed again. It showed Taylor moving a couch against one of the far walls in the antechamber. She paused it and then called up the options menu. Her fingertip hovered above the words "purge record."

Marisa hesitated. Captain Swaren was sure to audit the security feeds, and surely he'd be curious about what went on in the mayor's office. She sat back from the hovering options menu and folded her hands in her lap. Had Kendall staged the whole thing so that she would delete the record unknowingly, only to be blamed for it later? She looked around the room, and felt the office camera watching her. She could hear Kendall saying to Swaren, *I left her there alone for just a few minutes. I had no idea what she was up to.* Marisa was *almost* convinced she was being played. The bizarre imagery she had watched on the feed had evoked a strong and terrible reaction, but it could have been a trick perpetrated by Kendall. Easily. All the rest could be coincidence—a strong fucking coincidence at that.

But, she was willing to believe it was all part of her general slip into madness. She'd believe anything that would let her feel in control, even if for a few minutes.

She closed the options screen. If Kendall asked, she'd tell him she had deleted it. And if there was something on there that Swaren was not supposed to see, that was Kendall's problem—and his ass. Marisa would play the mayor's little game, but the rules had just changed.

She was in control.

[Part X]

The Crescent botanical garden was an expansive atrium filled with vibrant, green foliage. Artificial sunlight leaked around thick, obscuring leaves of rubber tree plants that reached all the way to the glass ceiling. Hidden nozzles sprayed cool mist that clung to the greenery in trembling beads. Gerald seemed to get caught by the nozzles just as they would go active and, as a result, was getting fairly wet. He moved down a dim garden path, trailing his fingers across the narrow trunks of trees whose growth had been stunted by thin constrictor bands around their bases. He wondered how the plants did in the wild. They probably got three times as big and ate small woodland creatures. The path brought him into a courtyard. Six identical stone-lined trails ran through the clearing's center and disappeared back into the vegetation that hung obediently behind the courtyard's marble-fenced perimeter. In the center of the crossing paths was an honest-to-goodness thread garden. Blossoms of multicolored bacteria—vibrant clumps like bouquets of small flowers exploding with petals—hung suspended from individual strands of nutrient-providing nano-threads. The thread garden was sealed behind four transparent glass walls. There was a metal sculpture, bronze and glinting at the heart of the thread garden—a likeness of Crescent. Gerald pressed a hand to the glass. It gave ever so slightly; not glass at all, but moisture-permeable film.

"Don't touch it, please," a voice reprimanded Gerald from not far behind. He turned to see a man in a gray, multi-pocketed jumper absently sweeping the slate stones of the central area. He was an old man. Nowhere near as aged as Naheela, but his face was set with deep-etched wrinkles and the thin hair atop his head was cotton white. The hands that pushed the broom were dark with liver spots, the skin thin enough that the codger's veins were visible. "That film lets jus' the right amount of moisture in there. Thread gardens are delicate creatures, you know."

"I know," Gerald said. He watched the old man continue to sweep with his big, yellow broom. Gerald found it odd that the man should be sweeping when there were plenty of bots that could do the same job—a bot would do a better job.

"The only place they're successfully grown without a film is on desert worlds," the old man nodded. "So, like I said, don't you go touching at it with your moist hands."

Gerald was pretty sure no one had ever accused him of having moist hands. He stepped away from the garden and raised his hands.

"That's a good boy." The man dipped his chin to Gerald and swept off into the foliage.

Gerald seated himself on a stone bench facing the thread garden. He crossed one leg over the other and yawned. It was serene in the atrium. The hum of the air handling system was barely audible. An occasional bird chirped. Gerald wondered if the melodic calls were real or digitized. Every once in a while a pleasant breeze drifted by. The currents circulated the tangy aroma of the blossoms and leaves, making the experience all the more immersive. This garden was one of Mayor Kendall's improvements to Crescent. There had been no garden in the original station plans. Gerald looked around, baffled. The place must have cost a huge chunk of change. Gerald didn't even feel like he was on the station anymore. It made him want to find a planet of his own and hide there as he faded into age and obscurity. Maerl had the right idea. A hand on Gerald's shoulder made him jump.

"I'm sorry," a familiar voice said from above him. "I didn't mean to startle you."

Gerald looked up over his shoulder at Marisa; she was in uniform, and judging from the scowl on her face she looked to be in a bad mood. Gerald patted the bench beside him and showed his teeth in a beaming smile.

"Have a seat," he said and she smirked. Marisa sat beside him, her hands folded in her lap. She looked at the thread garden.

"How many years have I been here, and I had no idea we had a thread garden. Did you know that this was here?"

"I didn't even know Crescent had a garden," Gerald confessed with a laugh. "But, I haven't been living on this hunk of metal nearly as long as you have. So what's your excuse?"

Marisa shook her head and frowned. Her gaze trailed down the strands of color to rest on the slate that covered the ground. The gray stone was covered with tiny flower petals.

"What's the matter?" It was Gerald's least favorite question to ask anyone. Not because he didn't care, but most times, if something was wrong with a person, they didn't want you asking. It was his experience that if there was something the matter, they'd offer it.

"Nothing. I just saw some strange things again today," she said in a quiet voice. *Exactly,* Gerald thought. *Stupid to ask.* Marisa looked at him. "I'm sorry, Gerry. I haven't been myself lately." Gerald was about to speak and she cut him off. "Don't act like you haven't noticed. You've been keeping yourself pretty scarce."

"I've been keeping myself scarce? The only time I see you these days is when you're on the vid terminal in your underpants. Or in the hospital." He felt like shit the instant the words left his lips. Marisa narrowed her eyes at him and her cheeks flushed. He anticipated a resounding *fuck you* at any second. Gerald was shocked when she looked away and said nothing. He had tried to convince himself, when her strange behavior began, that maybe he didn't know her all that well and she probably had problems. *But you know your behavior has been a little strange lately, too,* a voice said in his head. Kendall's voice. An interesting choice for his subconscious. *And let's not forget—you've been seeing strange things too, son.*

He took her hand. Her touch was ice cold, so he rubbed her hand between both of his. She forced a smile.

"That was an asshole thing of to say," she said.

"I'm sorry."

"Gerry, something's not right here." Marisa said. He wouldn't deny it. Their relationship had felt markedly strained over the past few weeks. "Crescent has never been a normal place." *So, this isn't about us,* he thought. He gestured for her to go on. "Don't get me wrong. It's fucked up in its own special way. That's why I've liked it here. But now? There is something weird going on. Something's in the water." She paused. "I see it your face—you can sense it, too. I look at the people in the market. I look at the people on Main Street. I look at the people in Heathen's. They sense it. They don't know it outright, but they feel something is off. It's like they keep getting out of bed on the wrong side."

Gerald considered it. The dreams. The seeing shit. The lifeboat. Marisa's issues. He hadn't drawn a correlation between what she'd been going through and the few strange experiences he had had, maybe because he just didn't want to go there. The strange vibe of the station was suddenly hard to ignore. He was torn between sharing his own less-than-normal experiences, and just giving her a sympathetic smile and an understanding nod. He went with the smile and the nod.

"You're just under a lot of pressure with this Core Sec audit. That's all."

"Pressure?" She spat the word out as if it tasted sour. "Nigel Swaren isn't putting me under any pressure whatsoever. As a matter of fact, he sent me off to do whatever I want until he needs me for something. And I have a good hunch that Nigel Swaren isn't the type of man that needs assistance in anything."

"Sorry, didn't mean to strike a nerve. Free time off, then? That can't be a bad thing."

"Can't it? It drives me mad to know that he's looking over all our security records looking for fuck-ups. Fuck-ups like my fuck-up."

"The incident with the mercenaries. That was a mistake," Gerald said.

"A mistake that ends up with people dead is a pretty big mistake in my book. I know you're trying to make me feel better, Gerry. I appreciate that. I'm just a basket case right now."

Gerald's PDA began to chime from his pocket. He smiled thinly and apologized.

"Nice moment for that thing to go off," Marisa said and sighed.

Gerald slid the small PDA into his palm and looked at it. The LCD told him it was Donovan Cortez calling. He slipped it back into his pocket and took both of Marisa's hands. He kissed them. "You just need a vacation. When this Nigel Swaren is done with whatever he's doing … "

"Maybe I'll get a permanent vacation," she cut him off and grinned, sans amusement.

"That's one way to look at it. Or, maybe you can just get off the station for a few days."

"And go where? Not much to see in the Anrar system," she countered.

"Okay, Marisa." Gerald raised his hands. "I give up. Be miserable, then."

Her pale cheeks reddened anew and she stood and straightened her uniform. Her mouth opened to speak, but nothing came out. She tugged at the navy blue jacket again and took a deep breath.

"I'm trying to keep it together here, Gerry. I'm sorry if I'm not doing a good enough job." With that, she strode off into the fronds of a fern-lined path. Gerald remained still. He wasn't sure if he should follow her. He wasn't sure if he should feel bad or feel annoyed. He wanted to feel bad, but instead he was irritated by the whole exchange.

Gerald couldn't help it. He was well aware he was being selfish. He was irritated with himself, too—at least partially. The heart of the matter was that Marisa's dance with craziness was making him question his own sanity. *You can see it in their faces,* she had said. He hadn't bothered to look for it. If he did look for *something* in the faces of Crescent's residents, would he be able to notice a difference? Maybe. And that was what prevented him from looking.

When was the last time I looked in a mirror? he thought.

Heathen's had certainly been crowded as of late. More people drinking meant more people trying to drink something away.

Gerald snapped open the cover on the PDA and it informed him that he had a single message. Gerald played it back. The small display showed Donovan Cortez. Over the short man's shoulder Gerald could see the curving hull of the lifeboat. It made him feel squeamish just knowing that thing was on Crescent. *And whatever was living in there—that's on Crescent now, too.* Gerald was quick to force that thought to the back of his mind. He focused on watching Cortez's mouth move and concentrated on each word.

"Gerald. Things are going quite well here, I must say. We've learned a lot of interesting information. I have you to thank for this boon. Perhaps I can repay you with more work?"

"Yeah, right," Gerald said, and actually guffawed.

"Please, call me back so I can share this with you. You're the only man I can trust on Crescent."

"Because it'd be my hide, too, if Kendall and Core Sec got wind of what you're up to in there." *How does Donovan plan on keeping the auditor out of that cargo hold if he decides to snoop,* Gerald thought.

[•••]

Gerald waited at the small, non-descript access door. Black paint obscured the door's small round window. Cortez had told Gerald to meet him there, and Gerald had agreed—although against his better judgment. The thought of seeing Ina again had been the deciding factor. After the dramatic exchange with Marisa, Gerald needed some positive female attention. The logic was flawed, but he needed it all the same.

Gerald stuffed his hands into his pockets and began to whistle an absent melody. He had no idea if the Cortezes knew he was out there.

He called the doctor using his PDA, but there was no answer. Gerald was getting ready to leave when the heard the locking mechanisms in the door release. Ina stood on the other side. There was a peculiar smile on her lips and he thought he saw something in her eyes—an odd darkness swimming amongst the pretty blue. But when she blinked, it was gone. *Is this what Marisa was talking about?* he thought. *Everyone just seems off for a second and then it's fine?*

"Hello, Gerald."

"Ina."

She stepped aside and gestured for him to enter.

"Thanks for coming down here. My father will appreciate it a great deal."

"Uh huh," Gerald said and stepped through the hatch. He looked up. Mineral-rich dust caked the underside of the ancient lifeboat. The vessel's skin looked organic and sickly in the floodlights. He began to regret his decision to come.

"I appreciate it, too. You left so quickly after you hauled the lifeboat, I thought… " Ina looked down at her feet. Gerald knew what she was getting at.

"Thinking complicates. Where's the old man?"

She looked up at that, the smile returning, and pointed up. "On the bridge, at the moment."

Gerald took a deep breath and exhaled slowly. Of course Donovan was on the ship—it was the last place that Gerald wanted to be.

"I'll take you to him. I don't want you getting yourself lost." Gerald nodded gratefully and cocked his head toward the opening in the belly of the lifeboat.

"After you."

Gerald found Donovan muttering to himself on the bridge. Strings of white diodes suspended within small cones had been strung in a makeshift criss-crossed pattern along the ceiling panels, casting wide pools of light. Most of the lifeboat's control consoles were dark. Most—but not all. A few consoles showed dull blinking lights that looked like they wanted to go out. Some of the surfaces on the bridge were covered with dark, rusty smudges. Gerald was pretty sure he knew what that was all about.

"I managed to get power restored to the ship with out blowing it up. How do you like that?" Donovan looked up at the cone-lights. "But the lighting system throughout the whole ship is nonfunctional. Go figure." He chuckled and got off his stool. "Thank you for coming, Gerald."

"Yep. Don't mention it." Gerald craned his neck to look over Donovan's shoulder. Navigation charts were spread out over a dark control console. On closer inspection, Gerald saw that the charts were, in actuality, terrestrial maps. "What is all that?" Gerald pointed.

"Those are maps." Donovan seemed very pleased about this.

"I can see that. Maps of what?"

"They are maps of Anrar III's surface. But these maps came directly from the data banks of the lifeboat. Some of the only salvageable data—most of the wafers were all but shot."

"Looking for buried treasure on Anrar III, Doc?"

"Precisely what I am looking for."

Gerald shook his head. "I don't think I want to hear any of this."

"You're more than welcome to leave." Ina piped in. She had crossed to the other side of the table and was looking down at the maps. She blinked up at Gerald, her eyes wide and surprisingly beautiful in the dazzle of the cone-lights. *Goddamn it. Stop that,* he thought.

"All right. Give me a break here. Tell me about your wonderful maps, Doc."

"Let me ask you a question, Gerald. Doesn't it strike you as odd that as an archaeologist, I'd choose to come to Crescent rather than spend my time in all the older places closer to Sol?"

"It doesn't strike me as odd, no. I figured you're an eccentric, wealthy retired surgeon who fancies himself an archaeologist. Maybe next week you'll fancy yourself a ballerina." Ina laughed. Donovan frowned and shook his head.

"Wealthy and eccentric—I might be both of those things. Graceful? Not by a stretch. But, we're rapidly straying from the topic at hand."

"No more interruptions, Doc. You have the floor."

"There are a multitude of archaeological sites throughout the seventeen systems of the core—the leavings of several centuries of colonization efforts. These sites have been studied again and again. I have visited many of these places, Gerald. They are fascinating, yes, but the thrill of discovery? Bah. Can you discover something new in a museum?" Donovan laughed softly. "Impossible. So, I began to look for other *possibilities.* Lost colonies, ships gone missing, and other unsubstantiated claims. Yes, it has been like grasping at straws." Donovan waved his hands around, as if the things he was mentioning floated in front of his face. "I found some claims from an early Anrar mining and survey team reporting strange geological formations. Anrar III led to Crescent Station and its very own rich and mysterious history. That is why I'm here. To shed light on this station's past and that of Anrar III."

"Nice story." Gerald tapped his chin. "But, I think whatever happened here, Doc, we missed it."

"Of course we did. But there *is* still a quarter mile of station that has never been explored. That part of the station is bound to be a treasure chest."

"Or contaminated with some horrible biological agent. Moot, anyway. Core Sec won't let anyone near it," Gerald said.

"Yet, Gerald. Yet. If I can find out what happened here—maybe it was just a revolt? Maybe it was some biological disaster, the effects of which have likely dissipated to a non-toxic level. But here I am digressing again. There is too much to focus on at times, it would seem. The maps on that table were generated from the few shards of data left in this lifeboat's computer. There are some interesting annotations on this map. Come, look for yourself." Gerald stepped alongside the table. Donovan moved to the opposite side and placed his finger on three closely distributed red circles.

"Site one," Gerald read. Donovan moved his finger to a second circle. "Site two." And a third. "Site three. Okay, fair enough. What are these sites?"

Donovan clapped his hands together, causing Ina to startle. "I would guess, the original mining colony. I need to get down to Anrar III for a closer look. I asked to requisition one of Kendall's shuttles—for an exorbitant amount of money, no less—and he wanted nothing to do with it. In truth, I think he was afraid of me getting killed down there. If that happened, he wouldn't have me padding the Crescent budget."

"You're paying Kendall?"

"It was the only way I could conduct my research below the radar. Core Sec would not allow it, were they to know about it. Curiosity is not encouraged in this part of space—for whatever reason. However, even Kendall has been stingy about letting me do my work."

"You are aware there is a Core Sec security auditor on this station, at this very moment. Right?"

"Yes. It makes me nervous that he is here. But, hopefully he won't bother us. If he does come snooping, I'm sure he can be bought as easily as everyone else."

Like me? Gerald thought.

"So, you want me to take you down to Anrar III's surface to investigate these sites."

"That is exactly what I want. I'll pay you twice what I paid you for the lifeboat haul."

It didn't sound half as dangerous as the lifeboat salvage had been. Gerald couldn't deny that he was at least a little bit curious and more than a little greedy. Each credit had the potential of taking him that much further from Crescent.

"I don't know." He met Ina's eyes. She remained silent, but the expectant look was hard to ignore.

"Okay, Doc. Why the hell not?"

Gerald took his time walking home. He looked at the people he passed. Some of them—most of them—looked perfectly normal: fine and happy. All there. But there were people who stared off into space; they looked exhausted, and some of them looked downright ill. Was there something wrong with these people?

Or was it his newly hatched paranoia?

(Part XI)

It wanted Marisa to look at it. To touch it. The goddamn thing thrummed every time she neared the place where she had concealed it. She laughed. The hiding spot was foolish. After all, only six year olds and cats hid shit underneath furniture. But that was the spot. Marisa didn't know why. It probably didn't even fucking matter.

The big recliner looked rattier now than it ever had. The fabric had been slowly unraveling itself and now pooled around the sides of the old piece of furniture. The disc was underneath the chair, wrapped in three thick towels. It had been Marisa's hope to smother the thing's call, but it only seemed to accomplish the opposite. The object's pull was, at times, almost irresistible. The sensation was tangible, like thousands of tiny hands nudging and prodding her. She'd resisted going to the thing for days. How many days, she couldn't count. Time was becoming a mere footnote on the rapidly shuffling pages of her existence.

I shouldn't look at it, Marisa thought. *I should get rid of it. There's still time.* She emptied a few white pills of carthine onto the plastic table at which she sat, and pushed the pills around with her fingertip. She'd been taking the drug more and more. It wasn't just to help her relax at night. It wasn't just to help her sleep. It was to quell the urge to look at the glass disc she had brought back from the cistern—to stifle the desire to lay with the thing for days on end until she died from thirst and starvation. She started with one pill every other day. Now she was taking three daily. It made the thrumming more bearable, but Marisa still saw the Black everywhere she looked—just out of the corner of her eye.

There was a distant chime. She glanced up at the wall clock—time to go. She looked back down at the pills and then over to the recliner. The chair watched her like a grim, age-faded sentinel, guarding the charge that sat beneath it. She flicked the pills—one, two, three—off the table and onto the floor. She stood slowly and moved toward the door. As she went, she picked up the discarded pills and popped them into her mouth.

One. Two. Three.

[•••]

Nigel was at the monitoring-station-turned-office when she arrived. He'd been on time every day, while Marisa only seemed to be showing up later and later. Her punctuality didn't matter. It wasn't like Swaren was giving her all that much to do. He glanced up at her from a stack of fan fold paper and frowned.

"You feeling okay, Lieutenant Griffin?" Nigel asked.

"Yeah. I'm fine." She wasn't lying. The carthine was kicking in.

"You look exhausted. I don't think ever seen such dark circles."

"Thanks, I'll take that as compliment. What do you have there?" She leaned over the long, slender table that served as Nigel's makeshift desk.

"This?" He waved one of the pages. "This is my least favorite part of the job. Hard copy logs. Hard copy Crescent ATC logs. I'm making sure that everyone that has come and gone from the station was cleared to do so. Flight plans in Anrar and the neighboring systems must be pre-approved by Core Sec, without exception. There's been a lot of raider activity in Habeos and Tireca as of late. Keeping track of these things has become particularly important to Core Sec with the New Juno colonization initiative ramping up."

Marisa stared at the stack. It looked fifteen centimeters high. The last thing she wanted to do was look over Swaren's shoulder as he went through the pages of condensed printout one by one.

"Marisa?"

"Huh?" This was the first time he had called her by that name. The sound of it was strange coming out of his mouth and it caused her to look up.

"You're sure you're okay?" Nigel asked and placed his hands atop the stack of data.

"Ask me again and I won't be okay, and neither will you." Despite her best intentions, Marisa felt her eyes narrowing to menacing slits.

"Easy, Lieutenant."

"And don't you make any fucking jokes about this being my time of the month." Marisa frowned and looked away.

"I wasn't planning on it," Nigel said.

"Good. Are we done here, then?" She looked back to him.

"Actually, no, we're not done here." He began thumbing back through the stack of pages, speaking casually as he did so. "Core Sec procedure specifies hard copy data review—the brass says looking at a piece of paper is more reliable than reading data on a terminal or overlay. I'll tell you, we're the only people who look at paper this often in this day and age. If it weren't for Core Sec, I bet paper wouldn't even be produced anymore." He stopped the page-flipping at a sheet that was flagged with a red sticker.

"That's very interesting," said Marisa.

"Not really. But this is." He placed his finger on a line marked by an adhesive red arrow. "Bean. Transponder number 48967, made an unscheduled trip from Crescent three days ago. It looks like someone tried to delete the entry. The record had been backed up prior to the deletion. Whoever deleted the entry didn't bother to take care of the backup. Careless, really. I looked up this "Bean." Turns out she is a Class 2A hauler specializing in salvage, captained by one Gerald Evans. His records are all clean, but I think this should be checked out nonetheless."

Marisa wondered if this had been one of Gerald's salvage runs for Kendall. Kendall's people should have no cause to delete a record if the run were legal. Which meant that maybe the runs weren't? Truly, what else could it be? She wasn't wondering so much as she was fretting. *Gerry,* she thought, *just what have you gotten yourself into?* Marisa stuffed her hands in her pockets and rocked back on her heels. She offered a weak smile.

"And what would you like from me?" Marisa asked.

Nigel was squinting at the page. "Go find this Gerald Evans. He should be on the station if he's not making another unscheduled run. Find out what he was up to." He stopped studying the sheet to look up at her.

"That all?"

"That's it."

"Do you want to question him yourself?"

"Only if necessary. I'll be tied up the rest of the day mapping crime trends. There seems to be no lack of data there. Use your discretion, Officer. If you think I need to question him myself, I will," Nigel said.

"Okay." Marisa knew that if Gerry's salvage work was illegal, Kendall would sell him out in a heartbeat. If Gerald was doing work for someone else, Kendall would have Gerald beaten into a pulp. She didn't want to see

Gerald get hurt, even if he was being an aloof and unsupportive asshole. The fact that she would be the first to question Gerald was a reprieve for the pilot—even if only a small one.

"Well, get to it," Nigel said.

"I'm sorry, Nigel. Sir. Captain Swaren. I'm just getting over the shock of being handed an actual assignment," Marisa said, and he laughed.

"You have proven reliable when being sent off to do nothing. Now, I'm sending you away with something to do. If that goes well, we'll talk about beefing up your responsibilities even further." Nigel returned his eyes to the thick stack of log entries.

She smirked but didn't say a thing. Instead, she turned to leave.

"Look. I like you, Marisa," Nigel said and returned his eyes to her. "I'm a work alone kind of guy. Don't be offended. This is just how I operate," Nigel said.

"I'm not offended. The way I look at it, Core Sec has been paying me to take strolls in the park and catch up on my grocery shopping these past few days. It's been far more relaxing than working dock security detail." A lie. Having nothing to do was giving her more time to get stoned and go crazy.

"I do have to ask," Marisa took a deep breath. "The Heathen's incident ... the ... gun club, as you called it."

"I have yet to look into it. The shoot-out is low on my list of priorities. Now go and find this Evans."

"Yes sir." She found this news more than a little relieving.

Marisa raised her hand to her forehead in a salute, which was a ridiculous gesture. There was no Core Sec salute. She needed sleep. Sleep that was not drug or alcohol induced. She blinked and offered a meek smile. Nigel looked at her like she was insane before returning his eyes to the reports. Maybe she was insane. At least now she had something to focus on. Something to get her mind off the secret treasure in her apartment.

And the shadows with their smiles.

[•••]

Marisa found Gerald in Crescent's main hangar. From the looks of it, her timing could not have been better. Bean's exhaust cones were still steaming. Gerald stood with his arms crossed over the chest of his flight suit as he examined what was clearly his most recent salvage—a mining barge with black and jagged scars marring an otherwise featureless and undamaged hull. The barge seemed no worse for wear. Gerald's brow was furrowed and he appeared to be in no small state of distress. Marisa approached him with her hands in her pockets. Her eyes went from the barge to Bean, and then to Gerald. He didn't seem to have noticed her. He was too busy trying to burn holes into the salvage with his eyes.

"Gerald," she said. His eyes flitted over to her and then back to the barge. Recognition dawned on his slack features. He looked back to her and smiled briefly.

"Hi, Marisa. I didn't think you had dock duty while that Swaren character was around. Already got the standard shakedown and ball cup by your compadres."

"That's not why I'm here, Ger," she said. Her scalp tingled and so did her face. The carthine. She wondered if he could tell she was on it. She hoped not.

He frowned and ran both hands through his hair.

"Oh," was all that he said.

"No. It's not about our conversation in the garden, either. I'm here on… business."

Gerald cocked a brow and then began to tug on some stray lines that were attached to the mining barge's hull. He picked up a data pad and tapped in some notes. Marisa continued to watch him and he continued to study the ship as if she wasn't there.

"I don't want to tell you how many mining ships I've been sent to haul out of Tireca. From the same goddamn dense asteroid field. This patch of space is so thick with rocks, I don't know how any raider could find these ships in there… "

"Gerry, I'm here on business," she repeated.

"I don't know why these guys are mining this patch in the first place. There are fields that are a lot safer to mine. And right here in Anrar… " Gerald continued to ramble. She grabbed him by the arm.

"Gerry. There are some things we need to talk about."

"Okay then," he said. "I'm here, you're here, and we're both on the clock. Start talking and I'll listen." She wondered for an instant if he was irritated because he could tell she was on the drugs. She pushed the thought aside. She didn't feel all that doped up.

Marisa glanced around the deck. Maintenance crews worked on a few nearby ships. Collector bots stacked crates and loaded them onto a freighter, whirring and clicking in their absent way. Walter Vegan hobbled near the hangar office with a cup of coffee clutched in one gnarled hand; some of its contents sloshed out with every step. He waved to her. She waved back.

"We should really talk about this somewhere a little more private."

Gerald put the data pad beneath his arm and turned around to face her. The frown had resurfaced. Marisa hadn't expected he'd to be thrilled to see her—not after the little scene she caused in the botanical gardens—but she didn't think he'd be outright pissed off. It wasn't like Gerald.

"You're serious, aren't you?" he said.

"Yes, Gerald. I'm here on Captain Swaren's order."

"The auditor? Shit. Well." He slid the data pad into a duffle bag that sat on the flight deck. He hoisted the bag and slung the strap over his shoulder. "I guess let's talk, then. Your place or mine?"

[•••]

Marisa looked around the small maintenance closet. Storage 15. Little 15. Last time she and Gerald had shared the space, she had been tearing his clothes off. Now, the salvage pilot felt worlds away from her. He sat in a creaking metal chair, and she sat on a stool across from him. He looked both annoyed and worried at the same time. She was sure she looked just as pleased to be there. She retrieved her own data pad and activated it with the wave of a hand. The entries that Nigel Swaren had flagged in the hard copy ATC logs pulsed on the screen in ominous green letters. She tapped the first entry. More information dropped down below the initial line. She held up the data pad so that he could see the display.

"Do you remember leaving the station at this time on this date?" She pointed a few lines down. "And then returning at this time?"

"I… "

"Let's keep this simple, Gerry," she said, cutting him off. "Yes/no answers to start off with." There was a moment of silence. A duct fan squeaked above them as it pumped recycled air into the closet.

"Yes," he said.

"Okay. Did you delete this entry from the ATC records?"

"No."

Marisa's head was beginning to feel clear. How could the carthine be wearing off already?

"Do you know who deleted them?"

"Yes and no."

"Either you do or you don't, Gerald. Was it Kendall? Was it someone else?"

"This is a mess," he said. The hand he raked through his dark hair made it stand up comically. He crossed his arms and leaned back in the chair, rocking the thin front legs off the gray floor.

"What's going on, Gerry? Is Kendall breaking the law? All kinds of laws? He is, isn't he?" *Say fucking yes,* Marisa thought, but didn't say it aloud. She wanted Gerald to answer yes more than anything in the world. Her suspicion—her knowledge—that Kendall was up to no good was useless when she didn't have the first clue as to the nature of his activities. There was nothing to incriminate him on but his blackmailing at this point. And in that case, it was his word over hers. But, if Gerald confessed to something, that just might be enough to lock Kendall up. The road to salvation stood out in sudden contrast. She would be able to continue with her career and Gerald would be out of hot water, too. With a record as clean as Gerry's it would be simple enough to convince a Core Sec jury that Kendall had threatened Gerald into going along with whatever plans were in action. Life could go on.

"No, not Kendall," Gerald said. "Well. Not Kendall in this instance."

That was not the answer she was expecting or hoping for.

"What the hell does that mean?" She sat back on her stool and frowned.

"What it means is, if Kendall were to find out I was doing some off-record work for another… party, I'd be as good as dead. Not that there's anything good about being dead."

"Let's go back to the yes or no for a minute, here." She wasn't ready for more complicated details. "Are you engaged in any illegal operations?"

"No. Not in this regard," he replied.

"In this regard?"

"In regard to my *other* employer."

"What about in regards to Kendall?"

"I have no idea," Gerald said. *Kendall,* she wanted to scream. *It has to be about Kendall. I have to get off this station and Kendall is the key.*

Marisa groaned in frustration.

"Let me finish, Marisa. Kendall tells me to pick up a salvage and I pick up a salvage. I never get any more details than that. And I don't ask. I just do as I'm told."

The lights went off and the fan stopped spinning. The data pad blinked out. The small space was flooded with silence. Marisa inhaled sharply; the air was cold as it hit her lungs. She could hear Gerald breathing.

"Gerry?"

"I think there's someone in here," he whispered.

The hair on the back of her neck stood up. The air grew colder and the sense that someone else was in the closet with them became stronger. The air was heavy and it wrapped around Marisa like a numbing cloud; her senses went dull. Marisa was falling.

And like that, the sensation was gone. The presence receded and the darkness lifted like a veil.

Marisa was no longer in Storage 15. She was in a much larger space. A single light panel blinked on and off above her head. It was still dark, but there was just enough yellowish light to get a sense of the room's enormity. She was in the Crescent auditorium. A sea of gray, featureless flooring stretched out around her in every direction, swallowing her in its emptiness. The stage looked naked and lonely with nothing covering it but pools of shadow. Marisa was drawn to the platform. She walked slowly, placing one foot ahead of the other as if she didn't believe the floor panels beneath her feet were made of solid matter. When her chest hit the stage's beveled edge, she halted and placed her hands on the cool metal surface.

"It will start here..." she whispered.

[•••]

Gerald heard Storage 15's door shudder open and then slam shut. The overhead light flickered to life and the vent fan began to squeak again. The darkness seemed to fold in on itself. Marisa's stool was empty. Gerald sprang to his feet and turned in a shuffling circle. Equipment leaned against the wall. Corrugated crates lined the dusty shelves. And Marisa was gone. Gerald made it out just in time to see Marisa disappear around the corner of the deserted hallway. He ran after her. She was already a good distance ahead of him by the time he rounded the bend. The distance grew between them in a way that didn't make sense.

Marisa looked blurry, as if his eyes were having trouble focusing. But the walls and lights, the cross-hatched pattern of the floor panels—those were all clear. He rubbed his eyes, but she still looked fuzzy. He followed her at a jog and then a full-out run, but despite his efforts, Gerald could not seem to gain any ground on her.

He followed her down random and seldom-used empty corridors, dodging scattered crates and dislodging cobwebs and dust. He almost lost her with each turn. The last let him out at a dead end. The only exit Marisa could have taken was a narrow service channel clearly meant for the station's smaller service robots. The gap was barely tall and wide enough to accommodate his frame. *Not again,* he thought as he squeezed himself through the opening.

Gerald stumbled out of the channel into a large, barrel-shaped chamber. He nearly fell down a spiral staircase that curled down either side of the room's curving walls. Polished chrome handrails gleamed in light cast by dim halo-globes suspended above the center of the room. The luminous spheres orbited one another slowly. He was in the foyer of the Crescent auditorium.

A reverberating bang drew his attention downward, where Marisa yanked open a large, red lacquered "employees only" door with such force it crashed against the wall. She stepped into the darkness beyond. Gerald hurried down the staircase two steps at a time until he reached the bottom. He hesitated when his fingers wrapped around the chrome handle of the red door. The metal was ice cold—almost too cold to touch. It sent a shiver up his arm. He pulled the door open. Marisa was all the way across the concert hall's floor. She looked small at that distance. She stood with her hands on the stage and her head bowed. The image of her was as crisp as everything else in the space.

"Marisa!" His voice echoed. She turned at the sound of her name. High overhead, parallel rows of translucent panels flashed on, flooding the room in a milky white light that pooled on the floor. The gray, photosensitive floor material began to swirl with muted color. Gerald and Marisa walked toward each other in wide steps. They were running by the time they met in the center of the floor. When they threw their arms around one another, Gerald felt Marisa trembling against him.

"Are you okay?" he asked.

"I'm fine… I think." Her voice was even and calm, but she continued to shake. "You felt it too, right? I know you felt it too."

"Yeah. I felt it," he admitted.

"I don't remember leaving, Gerry. The lights went out and then, like that, I was in here. I don't know how I got here. How did you get here?" she asked.

"I followed you," he answered.

"I walked here?"

"Yeah. You did."

Marisa pulled back and looked up at him. Her eyes were wide and tired. They were clear, though.

"I was brought here," she whispered.

"I know." He thought of the lifeboat. He couldn't help it. The presence that Gerald felt in the derelict's tight engineering shaft was very much like what he had felt in the closet. The similarity was impossible to ignore, as much as he would've liked to. "What I felt in the closet when the lights went out." He took a deep breath. "I felt that before."

Marisa kept her eyes on his, and Gerald saw something blossom on her face. A look of hope? A look of relief? He realized then her face was a mirror of his own. If he'd known that opening his mouth about this crap would have been so damn liberating, he would've done it after his first night on the station.

"Gerald. When did you feel that before?"

"The deleted entry on the data log." He let go of her. It was confession time. "I was running a salvage mission for Donovan Cortez."

"The surgeon?"

"The archaeologist. Doc Cortez had reason to believe there was an ancient lifeboat somewhere out in the asteroid field that orbits Anrar VI. Well, whatever made him think that a ship was out there—he was right on. We found an Anrar III lifeboat just sitting there in an asteroid's crater. I had to go on the boat to eject the reactor core so I could haul it back to Crescent." He stopped talking. He didn't want to go back there in his mind—the memory still made his stomach clench. But expectation was creasing Marisa's brow, so he went on. "I couldn't tell you how many so-called ghost ships I've found myself on over the years. The lifeboat felt different than any old and dead ship I've been on. It felt bad, Marisa. Do you know what I mean?" She nodded and waited for him to continue. "I found the crew and passengers of the lifeboat. Dead, frozen, and ripped to pieces. I heard shit. Voices. Sounds. Impossible, because there was no atmosphere on the ship, right? And the noises weren't coming through the comm, either. When I was leaving the boat, I got this feeling. Fuck.

I don't how to describe it. It was like I wasn't alone on the ship... There was something *almost* there with me. Almost. Like this thing only partially existed on the lifeboat—in this reality—and the rest of it was somewhere else. This... whatever-the-fuck it was, came after me. I don't know how I got off that boat. I think it must've wanted to let me go. Like it knew that I'd be taking it off that rock."

"Gerald." All the color washed out of Marisa's face. "You should never have brought that lifeboat back here."

(Part XII)

It was quiet in the auditorium. With no other bodies or obstacles to break the sounds of soft conversation, Gerald and Marisa's words drifted and reverberated with a gentleness that made the sounds seem like they would hang in the auditorium forever.

"How long have we been sitting here, Marisa?" Gerald asked.

"I'm not sure," Marisa replied and looked to the PDA strapped on her wrist. Gerald followed her eyes. According to the small display, the two of them had only been talking for an hour, but it felt much longer than that. "Has time felt strange to you lately?" Marisa said, as if she could read the thought on his face. "How do I put this… Inconstant? Some days fly by like mere minutes and some hours feel like they last for weeks."

He knew what she was taking about and nodded. Time *did* feel sketchy. Like something was causing the whole shebang to tremble at random.

"Perfect example. Don't think—just answer. When did all that shit go down at Heathen's? How long ago was it? Don't think, just answer," Marisa said.

He couldn't answer. He opened his mouth to speak, but realized there was no concrete timeline of events. Which was ridiculous, because the Heathen's incident was some traumatizing shit.

"It's like time is a pool, Gerry. And something keeps twitching in this pool, disturbing the water. And this something doesn't belong in our pool. Every time this thing moves, it makes new waves. New currents. That's what we feel. We feel it twitching. Moving. Waking." Marisa's voice trailed off and she looked away. A dreamy expression softened her features. "It's struggling," she said after a long pause and climbed to sit on the edge of the stage, her legs dangling below her.

Gerald sighed and shrugged. The conversation was giving him a solid headache. He decided it would be best to rein things in before Marisa brought out the crystals and incense.

"We're going on a big tangent here," Gerald said. "Let me ask you this, because this matter is immediate. It's now. What should I do about good Doc Cortez and his burning desire to visit the surface of Anrar III?" It was strange for Gerald to talk about the Cortezes with Marisa. It didn't seem right to have Ina anywhere near the front of his mind when he was with her. Marisa was clearly going through some serious shit and needed him in a big way. He had to focus.

"Gerry, I think you have to take his offer. You have to go down there," Marisa said. He looked past her and beyond the dance area in front of the stage. The far reaching auditorium floor was reacting languidly to the dull light falling from the parallel rows of panels above them. The colors in the floor shifted from muted oranges to pinks, to whites, and to deep blues.

"Are you kidding me? I'm of a mind to get off this orbiting bucket of scrap metal altogether. In the next day, if I can manage it. I might've been on the fence before we had this talk, but in truth, this is all freaking me out a little bit. There are other places to make money out there," Gerald said and climbed onto the stage to sit beside her.

"I read somewhere that it's not just places that get haunted, but people too. What's to say, if you took off, it would be over for you?" Marisa said. Her eyes narrowed ever so slightly. "What's to say the walls will stop bleeding and phantom children will stop playing in your washroom."

"Whoa, whoa. Who said *anything* about haunted?" Gerald gritted his teeth. "There is something going on here, Marisa. But, this isn't like some goddamn scary holo-vid."

"You still can't think it's all coincidence—the things we've been experiencing. And what about finding that lifeboat and the shit you experienced there? You can't still be blaming it on the crawl." She paused, clearly waiting for him to respond. When he didn't, she spoke up again, "You might find answers down there on Anrar III."

"Look, I have to go," he said. It was official. The conversation had spiraled out of control.

"Where do you have to go, Gerald? Gerry? Where you gonna go? Gonna go drink it off?" Marisa said. Venom laced her words.

"Maybe."

"Five minutes ago you were fine to talk about this." The anger faded from her voice and was replaced by the sound of raw hurt. "And now you're acting like I'm crazy again."

He wanted to tell her that he didn't think she was crazy and that he didn't really think he himself was crazy. But he couldn't get the words out; instead, he only looked over her shoulder to the exit.

"Whatever this is—we can't get away from it, Gerry. So, we...you... have to follow it down to that planet. Maybe this all has something to do with what happened here way back when... "

"The ghosts don't solve the fuckin' mystery, Marisa. This isn't some stupid holo-vid."

"I'm not saying that it has to be like that," she protested. "I'm just saying. Crescent has never felt... normal... but now. Now. Gerry. You know you have to go down there. You know you do," she said. Her agitation grew with each word.

Marisa's wrist PDA chimed; an incoming call. *Saved by the bell,* Gerald mused.

"Shit. It's Swaren. I bet he wants an update on our meeting," she said and took a deep breath. She let it out slowly and ran her hands back over her hair, which had begun to spring out from the now not-so-tight bun.

"What are you going to tell him?" Gerald asked. Relief made a quick exit at the sound of Swaren's name.

"The truth, maybe." She paused. "That you did a job for Cortez. A salvage job on a derelict and that you didn't want Kendall to know about it."

"You don't think he'll be curious as to why I didn't want Kendall to know?" Gerald asked her.

"I hope he *is* curious. As a matter of fact, I'm counting on it. You're going to tell him all about the work you're doing for Kendall. And then Swaren will look into it and bust Kendall for whatever scheme he's got going here."

"Who says there's even a scheme?" Gerald hopped down off the stage. The sound of his boots hitting the floor was jarring in the stillness.

"Fuck that, Gerald," Marisa said, slipping off the stage and onto her feet. "I've seen your face after each of your hauls for Kendall. You're no idiot. You know there's something up. Why else would you be doing side-jobs if not to buy your way out of the contract?" Marisa said.

Gerald had nothing to say to that. Marisa had his number. She was good.

"All right, then. Let's say there is something up. I'm working for Kendall. Doesn't that make me just as guilty?" Gerald said.

"Your record is spotless, Gerry. I've seen it. It wouldn't take too much to convince Core Sec that Kendall had threatened you with bodily harm. We won't have to be all that creative to take him out once there is evidence, and we can vindicate you in the process."

"I gotta ask this, Marisa. Why are you so eager to take the mayor out?" Gerald was glad that the topic of conversation had shifted, but the new direction represented little improvement.

"Why? Well, for one, Kendall is blackmailing me. He says the shooting at Heathen's was due to my carelessness. But I know those guns were already on the station. There is no way I let them through. No fucking way. I'm not going to take the fall for that. And no matter what I do or say, I'll be dropped right into the meat grinder. Guns getting through security might not be a big deal for a mayor, but this shit will ruin me," Marisa said and shook her head. "My career is all I fuckin' have, Gerry."

"When did shit get so complicated?" Gerald asked.

"I don't know," she said. "But it is. And it seems to be getting a little more complicated every day. Maybe we can figure all this out. All of it, Gerry, not just Kendall's plans, either. Wipe that look off your face. You have to go down to that planet. You do your part and I'll do mine. I'll figure the shit out with Kendall for the sake of both our asses."

"You don't think that Swaren will have Bean grounded?" Gerald asked.

"I'm sure he will. That's why you need to go down there right away." She stretched. "When were you planning on going down there, anyway?"

"I wasn't."

"Well. Now you are. So, when?" Marisa asked.

"If I was planning on going down there, I'd go down on the station's night cycle," Gerald said at last.

"Well. Gerry, it's close enough now. You call Cortez and you tell him you're going down there now. Like I said, I'll take care of the rest."

Gerald wasn't convinced that the plan was a good one. But, it was a plan. Whether he liked it or not, Marisa was going to tell Swaren that Bean's captain was running questionable salvage missions for Kendall. Gerald figured he may as well pull the job for Cortez, since there was no telling when he'd be able to make his next buck once the shit hit the fan. Gerald sucked in a deep breath. He felt around his pockets for his pack of smokes but they were missing. He extended his hand. Marisa took it and squeezed; hers was ice cold.

"All right, Marisa. You do your part and I'll do my part. I hope you have more success than I will. Because if you don't, that's both our hides." Part of him, a big part of him, hoped she'd change her mind when he was down there on Anrar III. He'd take Cortez's money, and he and Marisa could just run. Or hell, if she didn't want to run, he could run without her. Gerald was having a hard time envisioning things going well. Marisa smiled suddenly and pulled him forward for a kiss. It felt good to kiss her again. He realized then that he had been missing her—the real Marisa, not the terrified girl he'd come to see recently. This was her, all right, insistent as ever, sliding her arms around his back and pressing herself close enough to him that he could feel her heartbeat. When she broke the embrace, she left him there with a hard-on and a sense of growing unease.

[•••]

"Who's joining me this time, Doc?" Gerald said as he stepped onto the bridge of the lifeboat. Donovan Cortez spun around so fast, Gerald thought the round man was going to topple over. Cortez's fat arms pinwheeled as the archaeologist attempted to regain his balance. The sight was comical. Gerald dropped his eyes to the floor and did his best not to laugh. He felt his lips quirking into a grin despite himself.

"Gerald. For all that is holy. You scared me half to death."

"A little on edge, Doc? Sorry." Gerald couldn't blame him for being twitchy. Hell, just thinking about the lifeboat made Gerald nervous. "I thought you heard me come in." Gerald said and leaned against a dark console.

"No, I was busy. Distracted. What did you ask me? I was too startled to comprehend it."

"I said, who is going join me on Bean this go 'round. You or your daughter?"

"Does that mean that you are going to do this for me? You'll go down to Anrar III?"

"Couldn't mean anything else, Doc. The price has more than doubled, but yeah. I'm in. I emailed you the new quote. I think I'm going to need the money soon. Might be out of commission before long."

Donovan lifted a puffy eyebrow.

"Don't worry about it. I'm not grounded yet. So, answer the question, you or Ina?" Gerald cracked his knuckles and then perched a cigarette between his lips. Donovan gave Gerald a reproachful look until the cigarette was returned to the case from which it had come.

"Oh, most decidedly my daughter," Donovan said. "The

atmosphere is very thin down on Anrar III. I don't think it would bode well for my asthma."

"All right then. Fair enough. Where is she? We need to leave very soon."

"Why so soon?" Donovan just wasn't getting it; Gerald shook his head.

"Like I said. Don't worry about it. But, if you want to get a look at that planet, we need to leave this station… about fifteen minutes ago."

[•••]

Donovan looked around the hangar bay in furtive glances. Unease was written in flushed circles on his chubby cheeks. His eyes danced over to Walter Vegan, who stood with his strangely thin arms crossed over his sagging chest. Vegan watched Gerald, Ina, and Donovan with casual interest. Ina did not appear to share her father's sense of unease. She didn't seem to even notice Vegan watching them. Her eyes sparkled above a wide and eager smile. After all, Ina had a new-found love for space flight. There was no sign that she cared about Vegan paying them interest.

"He's going to want more money, that one," Cortez said and sighed. He gestured over to Vegan with a cock of his head. Vegan noticed and waved one gnarled hand.

"Probably. This is his hangar, after all, Donovan," Gerald said and smirked. He looked over to Ina for a moment, watching her shove a large duffle bag into Bean's belly hatch. Donovan was just about to speak, but Gerald didn't give him a chance. "Just be happy Vegan is greedier than he is loyal. By the way, this Core Sec auditor… He discovered the deleted departure record. Doesn't sound like he figured out where we parked your little lifeboat, but you might want to be a little more careful with this run. That is, if you don't want Core Sec or Kendall knowing about your… intellectual pursuits."

With that, Gerald patted Cortez on the thick arm and then climbed up the docking ladder.

When Gerald poked his head through the bridge hatch he found Ina already seated in the control couch, the black harness crossed over her chest. Her smile turned into a pout as Gerald climbed the rest of the way onto the bridge.

"Hurry up," Ina said. "I don't know how much longer I can wait."

He wasn't sure if she was kidding or not. She seemed not to be.

"Just be happy we're going at all. I had my doubts and I was ready to say no," Gerald said. He still couldn't believe he was going through with the trip after the trauma of the lifeboat job.

"Well, don't you worry. This is for the best and you know it," she said.

This struck Gerald as a strange response.

"It means the world to my dad," she explained, "and so it means the world to me. Since he retired, my dad has been so lost. You see, he threw himself into being a surgeon after mom died. And when he hung up the smock, he didn't have his work to focus on anymore… he started to fade away. When I introduced him to archaeology… or rather forced him into pursuing it as a hobby, well, it… it really got him going again. Look at him now. It's his life. So, you do you see how helping us means the world to me?"

That's not what she was getting and you know it, Gerry. His subconscious had adopted Marisa's voice, and her voice sounded pissed off. *That skinny little bitch isn't telling you something. And it has to do with what's going on here on Crescent. She knows something, Gerry. Better be careful.* An added level of caution was not a bad idea. He seated himself in the control couch and crossed the harness over his own chest. It locked into place with a click.

"We'll be on the surface in just under two hours," Gerald told her. "Prior to entry we're going to have to put life suits on, in case we lose pressure or anything else goes wacky. Okay?" Gerald was none-too-thrilled at the prospect of donning the too-small life suit again.

"Sure," Ina replied with a serious nod. "You can never be too careful."

She knows something.

Gerald could see Walter Vegan approaching Cortez via one of Bean's external camera feeds. Gerald felt bad for Ina's father. Vegan was not only a slimy fuck, he smelled like asshole, too.

"Bean. Do you have the updated coordinates for the Anrar site synchronized with current surface scans of the planet?"

"Of course, Captain. A foolish question."

"Well then. Let's go. Time isn't on our side here."

Bean lifted from the deck. The hangar's auto-guidance system carried the ship toward the large, shimmering docking porthole. The ion field that stretched across the big opening kept the station's atmosphere and the vacuum of open space politely sequestered to their respective sides. The barrier shifted like heat rising off hot asphalt. Ina put a hand on Gerald's knee and blinked up at him. He patted her hand and called up several control overlays. He felt ill at ease. Touching her cool flesh only seemed to amplify that feeling. When they were free of the hangar, Bean banked and then rolled until the ship was inverted. They flew back over the docking hub and toward Anrar III. A few ships came and went as they sailed by, but overall, the traffic pattern was quiet.

Time stretched endlessly between beats of awkward conversation. Gerald was thankful when Bean finally spoke up.

"Captain. The entry window will be reached in T-Minus fifteen minutes," Bean said.

"Thanks, Bean." Gerald looked to Ina. "Time to put on your life suit. I bought an extra. It's stowed underneath the control couch." He unhooked the cross harness and got to his feet. "You can put it on over your clothes," he added. The last thing that he needed was Ina getting frisky as Bean throttled toward the hard surface of the planet. She'd be able to fit into the suit with her jeans and tee shirt still firmly in place. Gerald, on the other hand, had to lose most of his clothing to don his suit. He left Ina on the bridge to dress in the privacy of the small sleep quarters.

Gerald and Ina were suited up and restrained in the control couch just as Bean began to tremble from the first molecules of thin atmosphere bouncing off the hull. Ina's smile broadened as the sympathetic vibrations began to increase. She gripped Gerald's knee again, this time harder. The hull began to glow a feral red as friction worked its magic.

"Bean'll shake more than a normal lander," Gerald shouted over the racket. "Haulers aren't the sleekest of vessels—not really meant to go planet-side. Capable, but still won't give you the smoothest ride."

"This is wonderful!" Ina cheered in return. "I love it!"

"I do not love this, Captain. Were I capable of feeling pain, I'd have aborted five minutes ago. Structure is in the yellow. Thermal monitoring is in the yellow. Still below tolerance thresholds, however. Eighty percent of our systems remain in the green. Regardless, I'm not enjoying this."

"Let me know if we explode," Gerald said.

The shaking subsided to a low vibration, and then all seemed still as Bean began to glide. Tangled wisps of cloud dashed the viewports with condensation. Ahead of them, the sun crested the craggy ridge of a distant mountain chain. Beads of moisture on the fore viewport captured the light and threw it back out as the colors of a rainbow.

"Captain," Bean said, "I'm detecting man-made structures close to our destination coordinates."

"Mining facilities," Ina said. "A geological outpost. A refinery.

Crescent's initial materials were mined right out of this planet. The yield was low, though, and there were a lot of accidents. Quite a few people died down here in the early days. The mines were quickly abandoned in favor of asteroid mining. The asteroid mining actually turned out to be the cheaper route in the end. Can you believe that?"

"You know more about Anrar III than you let on, Ina," Gerald said.

"Obviously, the precursor to any successful archaeological expedition is research."

"Captain. I am altering our vector now." The ship banked hard. Gerald's belly dropped to his feet. There was a big difference between space and atmospheric flight. His stomach had never quite gotten used to the latter. He glanced over at his adopted copilot. She still seemed thrilled; pleasure glowed rosy on her cheeks.

"There are probably some really nice finds here," Ina said. "I wish Dad were here."

Would he be squeezing the life out of my other knee? Gerald thought, and detached her hand from his leg. He then proceeded to call up an overlay that showed the topography of the area below them in a shimmering relief. The cluster of sites pulsed crimson. According to the overlay, they were less than 15 kilometers away from their destination. Gerald dipped his thumb into the hologram. Ripples of light trembled outward, and he chose a landing spot where terrain looked reasonably level. When he removed his thumb, a yellow circle glowed in its place.

"Set us down there, Bean. Looks like as good a place to land as any."

Hydraulics whined as all-terrain landing struts extended from compartments on Bean's round belly. There was a crunch when they touched down. The ship lurched forward, jerking Gerald and Ina hard in their chest harnesses, and then all was still.

"We good, Bean?" Gerald inquired.

"We're good, Captain."

"Time? Weather?"

"There are eight hours until sunset in this region. Doppler radar indicates a sizable storm front one hundred kilometers south of our location, traveling north by northeast at thirty kilometers per hour."

"Hope you brought our umbrella, Ina," Gerald said.

"Well, no," she said and laughed. "But, I'd like to stay as long as we can." She unbuckled her harness. "It's been a long time since I stepped foot on a planet."

"Well, this won't be any kind bargain. It's cold, the air is thin, and gravity is three percent greater than Crescent's artificial gravity. We're going to be dead tired long before that rain gets here."

She got to her feet, her eyes bright.

"We shall see about that… Captain."

[•••]

The air was thin, but bearable. Gerald had once gone mountain climbing on the planet Caen. Just a mile and a half into the ascent, his lungs had burned with the effort of each step. That air had been thin. That atmosphere of Anrar III didn't seem that lacking at the outset. He looked to Ina. She stood toward the aft of the hauling vessel, hand shielding her eyes from the sun as she gazed back at the mountain range they had passed over on their descent. It was barely visible on the horizon. Gerald glanced at his PDA. The LCD showed their position as blinking white dot. The first site was within short walking distance. They could be there in less than twenty minutes—if the terrain cooperated.

The wind lashed out at them as they moved out of Bean's protection. Thick clouds were rolling in from the west, diffusing the light. The assaulting air was cold; small bits of dirt and grit bit at their exposed flesh. Gerald pulled up the hood on his excursion suit. Ina, her own hood pulled tight over her head, was already on the move ahead of him, eyes cast down to her PDA. He jogged to catch up to her, the effort sucking the breath right out of him. The extra gravity felt like weights around his ankles. He reached out and wrapped a gloved hand around her elbow.

"You'll want to look at the ground just as much as you look at your PDA. You don't want to trip and break your ankle. Not here," he said.

She looked up at him and batted her long lashes.

"Gerald. Are you being chivalrous?"

"Don't call it chivalry, sweetheart. I just don't want to have to carry you back in this gravity. Don't think I could do it," he said.

"You *are* my hero!" she exclaimed, then spent the next several seconds catching her breath. When she spoke again, her tones were more serious. "I see what you mean. Sometimes, I'm a little over eager." She paused and looked at him with a slow grin. "But you knew that."

The display on Gerald's PDA counted down the meters that remained until the pair reached first waypoint. When the digits reached zero,

Gerald looked up. The dark rock plain was strewn with large and curled pieces of charred, weather-worn metal. The scraps had clearly been part of some unknown larger whole that had likely met its demise in a powerful explosion. Gerald nudged a piece of metal with his foot. It was heavy and didn't budge. Upon closer inspection, it looked like a hull plate. He knelt beside it. If there had been any defining characteristics on the plate, they had been stripped away by hundreds of years' worth of blowing grit. Beyond the debris, there were towering rock formations; the protrusions looked like weather-worn pillars. It looked like the things had grown there. The wind howled through the stone grove.

"What is this?" Gerald called ahead to Ina.

"I'm not sure." She had her hands on one of the pillars. Her glove was removed and she was running her fingers across it. "It's ice cold." Ina quickly slipped her fingers back into the glove and then she disappeared into the rocks. Gerald crouched beside the hull plate and turned it over, expending more effort than was wise. He sat cross-legged, panting for air. *Everything is heavier down here,* he told himself; *don't waste your energy. You don't want her to carry you back to the ship, do you?*

Gerald caught his breath and got back to his feet, moving into the stone grove after Ina. He came out the other side to see her standing dangerously close to the edge of a gaping maw in Anrar III's face—so close that the toes of her boots were over the edge. Gerald approached her with caution; he didn't want to startle her and risk her falling in. He stepped alongside her and forced her back a step, then leaned over for his own look. The hole was large enough to accommodate Bean. The walls of the pit were smooth—smooth to the point of appearing polished. Pieces of metal sprung up around the opening's perfect circumference in tatters. There had been a man-made structure over the hole. That much was clear.

The clinging bits of the structure were all that was left of the first mining site, as indicated by the PDA.

Cold air rose from the abyss—colder than the wind that roared across the planet's surface. He turned to Ina, but she remained silent. Her unwillingness to speak was a sign of growing fatigue. He felt it, too. His urge to say, "What the fuck is this about?" translated to a mere lift of his eyebrows.

Gerald pointed beyond the opening to where a dark structure stood at the top of a nearby slope. It wasn't far, but it was a decent incline. He glanced at the PDA. The building was their next waypoint. By the time

Gerald lifted his eyes, Ina was taking the first hesitant steps of her ascent. He stopped her by grabbing the thick material of her excursion suit. With a few quick hand gestures, Gerald showed her how to hook up the supplemental oxygen supply that was contained in her parka. Once Ina was situated, Gerald took care of uncurling the oxygen line from his own excursion suit and inserted the small tubes into his nostrils. He increased the air flow gently and made sure it wasn't set too high. Supplementing the air he was breathing was one thing, getting high off it and falling into the bottomless pit—that was another.

Ina inhaled deeply. "Much better."

"No way we'd make it up that hill without help. I should've thought of this sooner. I'm not used to crawling around on empty planets like this."

"Isn't it exhilarating?"

"I was thinking it was cold and tiring," Gerald said. She looked at him and gave a shake of her hooded head. "Yeah, yeah," he said. "This is all very scientific and wonderful. Let's go. Maybe we can reach that place before the rain starts."

"Think so?" Ina said.

"Nope, but it's worth a shot."

[•••]

The pair walked for what felt like an endless stretch of time. With each thin inhalation Gerald took, he thought the rain would start falling to deepen his misery. He cast his eyes skyward and then brought them back down to look at a destination that had come no closer.

At long last, Ina and Gerald stood panting in front of a long, single-story building constructed from dark slabs of concrete. The concrete looked to be made up of the same dark material as Anrar III itself. An unimpressive metal door with a wheel protruding from its surface seemed to be the only way inside. From their vantage point, Gerald couldn't see any windows. If there were any, they'd be obscured with ages of grit and dirt kicked up by the forces of nature.

Wind roared across the surrounding plains and flattened the parkas against their bodies. With the wind came more clouds. Gerald placed a hand on the building to steady himself. It wasn't raining yet, but it would be soon.

Gerald looked at the door. He'd have put money on the entrance being sealed shut from prolonged exposure to the elements. Words were written on the pocked metal face in faded block letters that were obscured with clots of dirt and grime. Ina pulled the sleeve of her parka down over her hand and began to rub at the lettering with it. Gerald watched her for several minutes, then left her there and started around the perimeter of the building in slow, shuffling steps. He came across a slanting system of shelves that hung lopsided from the side of the building, ready to fall at any second. Long, metal tubes were scattered around the base of the shelves. He picked one up and wasn't surprised to find it almost too heavy to hoist. He set it against the side of the building and unscrewed the top. Gerald nudged the tube with the toe of his boot and it fell over, allowing bits of dark rock to spill out onto the ground: core samples. He returned to Ina, who was looking at the door, perplexed.

"What is it?" he asked and she pointed at the block letters.

"Strange name for an outpost," she said. "Does that word mean anything to you?"

At first the word teetered on the edge of legibility, but the block letters seemed to grow clearer the longer he stared at them. In an instant, they stood out starkly against the dark metal of the door. Gerald took two jerking steps backward, unaware that he was moving at all. M-U-R-H-A-T-É.

"Murhate?" Ina asked. She was staring at the door and not at Gerald.

"No," he said and shook his head. "No. It's pronounced Mur-ha-tay."

"How do you know that?" Ina turned to face him. Half of her face was concealed by the hood; within, her eyes sparkled.

"I just do." His first instinct was to run, but he felt a tingling of suicidal curiosity that made him incapable of fleeing. *Let's see what's behind door number one!* He found he was unable to speculate. Each time he tried to think beyond the door, a fog settled over his mind. He took in a deep breath. The air tasted of minerals and rain.

"Let's get that door open," he said at last. He heard the words falling past his lips, but couldn't quite believe it was he who was speaking them. "We'll check it out." He cast a glance over his shoulder. The rain was still a good ways off.

Gerald wrapped his fingers around the metal wheel that protruded from the door's face. The thing refused to budge. He looked up at Ina. She nodded and added her hands to the wheel. Together they grunted and pulled. Nothing still. They stood gasping for air with their hands on their knees. Gerald stared at the dark, pebble strewn ground. Luminous spots floated across his field of vision.

There was a squeak. They both looked up, the breath catching in their throats. They looked first at the wheel and then at each other. Squeak. Right before their eyes, the wheel turned.

"Can there be someone in there?" Ina asked.

"Jesus. No. Of course not. You yourself told me how long these fucking mining stations have been here."

"Maybe Kendall and his people beat us down here?" Ina took a step away from the building.

Squeak.

"Maybe. But I don't think so," Gerald said. He felt his bowels shift. "Fuck. It's gotta be automatic," he said. "Machine assisted bulkhead. I'm sure that's it." Yeah. He sounded sure, but he felt a lance of ice run through his veins every time the wheel chirped. The sound was too damn out of place.

The wheel began spinning at blurring speeds and then stopped abruptly. Its chirp was replaced by a terrible moan of metal rubbing stone as the door grated open. Darkness thicker than peat lay beyond. Ina waved something in front of his face. He looked at her stupidly, unable to focus on the object.

"Are you all there, Gerald?" she asked.

"Yeah. Just... Shit." He shook his head and took the object from her. The heft of it told him it was a flashlight before it registered to his eyes.

If the darkness in the long building wasn't impenetrable, it was damn near close. It wrapped around them like a thick blanket. The cones of light cast by the flashlights did little to hold it at bay. There were more of the shelves inside, climbing all the way the ceiling and stacked high with core samples. The whole interior of the building seemed to be a large storage facility, Gerald thought as they pushed further into the darkness. The tall shelves began to recede and the floor sloped downward.

"A geological outpost," Ina stated matter-of-factly. The beam of her flashlight painted the dusty shelves with light as they passed. "Scientists were stationed here and they analyzed core samples that were brought in from all around the planet."

Gerald didn't respond. He couldn't respond. He had stopped walking and was busy trying to determine whether his knees were about to give out.

His flashlight was aimed dead ahead.

Gerald had seen death before. Recently, even. But what he was looking at now—it was unnatural.

(Part XIII)

Gerald had been a brave kid, growing up. Without fail, he had always been the one sent to check out the haunted house while his friends waited on the other side of some rusty fence, shaking in their hand-me-down boots. Gerald was brave because he had never been superstitious. He didn't believe in ghosts, the boogeyman, or monsters—none of it. Not even god. It was difficult to fear something you didn't believe in. So why, he wondered, was a god he didn't believe in putting his convictions to the test now?

The storage shelves inside Murhaté, the geological station, were pushed back against the thick walls, creating a wide clearing. The shelves leaned one against the other, and based on their cockeyed angles they had been pushed there in a hurry. The resultant open space was filled by a large circle of roughly hewn, black stones. Gerald surmised the rocks were carved from Anrar III's surface. Long, jagged shadows cast by the invading beams of Gerald and Ina's flashlights cut through the circle. Gerald raised his beam to illuminate a ring of soot-colored metal that was suspended above the center of the circle of stones. The ring was almost as wide as the clearing itself. It was hung in place by a high criss-crossing of thin cables. Shards of black Anrar III bedrock were set into the circumference of the metal ring at regular intervals.

The sight was creepy, but the abstract art display was not what had Gerald shaking in his boots like his young friends so many years ago.

The misshapen *thing* dangling at the center of the metal structure—that's what had Gerald's knees threatening to fail him. It might have been a person at one time. Tatters of fabric hung from petrified flesh so dark that it looked to be made from the rock of the planet itself. The poor creature's wrists were bound by cables, its arms spread wide. Splintered, blackened bones and shreds of obsidian material were all that remained of a midsection. The pieces were bent outward, like the person had exploded from the inside. Two limp cables snaked across the floor. These flaccid cords were attached to two black stumps—all that was left of the poor bastard's lower half. A pile of debris littered the center of the circle. Twisted bits of metal and hunks of stone. As Gerald moved closer, fragments crunching beneath his boots, he trained his light on the strange cadaver. A few long strands of golden hair still hung from a scalp that was lumpy with protuberances.

Ina knelt beside where the debris was concentrated. The pieces of metal and rock obscured the dusty floor. Her fingertips sifted through the scatter. Ina was looking for something. For what? She muttered to herself under her breath—Gerald could not distinguish what she was saying, but her whispers carried like phantoms in the dark, cold space. The shadows seemed to be creeping in closer around them. Ina continued to work her gloved hands through the bits of metal and stone. He aimed his flashlight where she was working and for a second Ina went out of focus. Gerald blinked and she was clear again. It's just a trick of the light, he told himself.

He looked up at the hanging thing. Maybe it wasn't even real. A sculpture or some such nonsense. Everything did have an abstract art sort of feel. But Gerald knew that wasn't true. A sculpture didn't belong in the geological storehouse, any more than the circle of stones or metal ring. It wasn't a damn art show. But, shit, there it was. He panned his flashlight around the scene. There was a cart off to the side of the circle with a dirty plastic box atop it and two holes in its face. It reminded Gerald of the incubators that premature infants were placed in. There were two sizable black boxes mounted atop short tripods. These boxes looked to be speakers, the kind you'd see with a public address system. An optical disc player sat below one of the speakers. He returned the flashlight beam to Ina.

"What are you doing?" he asked her, his voice was swallowed by the wind that howled outside the structure. The storm was almost upon them. "Ina, what are you doing?" He spoke louder this time.

"It has to be here somewhere." She looked up at him; her eyes flashed onyx in the beam of his flashlight. "This is the only place it could be. There should be some of it left. A piece, at least. Right here." Her voice trailed off.

She's talking like a crazy person again, he thought. *Like in the cafeteria when I first met her.*

Gerald decided that it was best to ignore her for the time being. He'd let her play in the dirt for a few minutes while he attempted to make sense of things. He moved away from her and deeper into the circle, beneath the metal ring, but when his foot crossed over the ring's lower curve his stomach did an abrupt somersault. A shock, electric and cold, jolted up his leg and knocked him off balance. He landed on his ass. *It just keeps getting better and better, doesn't it?* he thought. He was ready to cut the visit short when Ina shrieked—in delight. He clambered to his feet.

"This is it!" Ina exclaimed, and stood so abruptly that she tottered back over. She got onto her knees, where it took her several moments to regain her breath. "I knew it," she said, between gasps. "I knew it." She held something up in the beam of her flashlight: a palm-sized piece of stone. Gerald at first mistook it for more black stone, but when it caught the light of the flashlight, it took on a deep crimson hue. It was a stone knife.

"What the hell is that?"

"This, my dear, dear Captain Evans, is sanguinite."

"Miner's Bane? That shit is just a myth—a made up mineral to blame accidents on." There was a rustle somewhere deep in the station. The wind howled. Gerald looked around uneasily. "Geology lab is over, Ina. Time to go." She was ignoring him and continued to speak.

"This has got to be it!" She held it in front of Gerald's face. "Look!" She shone her flashlight through it. Red again. *Yes,* he thought, *I get it.*

She was out of breath again and Gerald took the opportunity to interject.

"Great. Lovely. Why is this such a big deal? What does it have to do with archaeology?" Gerald began to move toward the way they had come. Ina remained planted.

"No one has ever presented, for lack of a better word, hard proof of its existence—even after entire mines had been shut down because of it."

"So say the rumors," Gerald interjected but she ignored him and went on.

"And now we have it." She pointed the knife in his direction. "The stone is a clue to what happened here—it's part of all of this, somehow." She gestured to the stone circle, a frown creasing her pretty features. "You don't understand."

"And I don't really care, to be honest with you. Even better, I don't want to know. I want to finish my job and get paid. To finish that job, I have to get you back off this rock. And now, it's time to go. I don't give a shit about pebbles," Gerald said. He reached out, grabbed her by the arm, and yanked her to her feet.

"But there is more to see down here, Gerald. I didn't come here for pebbles..."

"Some other time," he said. Ina pulled herself out of his grasp and took a step away from him. *Here it comes,* he thought.

"We're paying you very well, Gerald," she said. *And there it is.*

"I understand that. And you're paying me well for a reason—my expertise. And my expertise tells me it's time to get going."

A rumble of thunder shook the entire building. Large, puffy clots of dust floated down from unseen ceiling rafters; the motes looked like large snowflakes in the shafts of light. The hanging cadaver trembled and began to sway.

"I could always leave you here and come back later," Gerald said, but he wasn't serious. He was annoyed, and nervous.

"You certainly could leave me here. Maybe that's what you should do. And come back later to get me." Ina nodded once.

"How long do you think the power cell in that flashlight will last? I can't remember for the life of me if I charged it or not." This blow seemed to connect. She glanced back up at the corpse that still swayed, and then to Gerald.

She frowned, then nodded."Fine, fine."

Gerald ushered Ina ahead of him and turned for one last look. A flood of shadows had washed over their path, and in those shadows Gerald heard something flutter. Before he could even think to indentify the sound, it was gone. He turned to step through the open door and heard a whisper, harsh and dry. He looked to Ina to see if she had spoken, but her face was already obscured by the thick hood of the parka. For him to hear her whisper, she'd have to be up to his ear with her mouth exposed. Gerald quickly stepped out of the geological station and into air that felt super-charged with static electricity. He cast his eyes to the angry sky as thunder rumbled. Then came the impression of something rushing past him, causing Gerald to spin in evasion. The outpost door slammed shut in his face.

He took a deep breath and gazed up. It wasn't raining yet and the sight of open sky helped bring back some sense of composure. The sky was bruised with dark, roiling clouds that looked absolutely swollen. Lighting arced to the ground less than a mile off—a little too close to their present location for Gerald's comfort. He started away from the building. Ina followed in step.

The hike back to Bean was going to be anything but safe, but Gerald didn't want to weather the storm in that *place*. The wind gusted. The assaulting particles of grit felt like a thousand tiny needles poking at his cheeks. He cinched the parka hood tight around his face and pulled the goggles down over his eyes. Ina did not have to be told to do the same.

[•••]

Albin Catlier finished the last drag of his cigarette. The tightly rolled stick of tobacco had burned past his knuckle, unbearably hot on his fingers and lips. He dropped the butt to the deck of the loading dock and stomped it out. The overseeing detail had taken longer than he would have liked. Had Albin known this task would have turned into eight hours of tedium, he would've rolled twice as many cigarettes. The farm workers were slow to fill the last of many long, gray crates. They were tired, which was no surprise. There were a lot of guns to move. Not to mention, they had spent the previous night disassembling the elaborate manufacturing systems that had been set up in the Farm's belly. At least now the workers were filling the final box. If he had to endure another hour of overseeing the idiots, Albin would likely eat the barrel of one the rifles they had packed and shoot off the back of his own fucking head.

The workers placed the top on the crate. Magnetic locks activated with a loud *clank* that rolled off into the night. Two collector robots hefted the heavy container and disappeared down a service corridor. With the job done, the workers dispersed without a word. The entire stock of guns was now officially out of the Farm. Shipping and production would begin again in a new location, but not until the Core Sec auditor was gone.

That meant no sales. The stream of income from the gun running was officially dead for the interim.

Albin was damned if he wasn't getting paid, though. It wasn't his problem if Kendall wasn't able to make shipments. He glanced up at the security camera. A thick smudge of shoe polish covered most of the bug-eye lens.

Albin hopped down from where he sat on the loading dock's concrete platform and squinted into the empty shipping area. Only one of the large floodlamps was activated. It served to illuminate the area where he stood. That was it. The light was unable to penetrate into darkness that surrounded loading platform nineteen. The clicks and groans of the station echoed in the shadows. Albin shuddered involuntarily. He wished he had another cigarette. Distant eye nodes of a collector robot floated in the black void beyond the floodlamp's dome of light, glowing sensors floating like a small swarm of orange fireflies. Albin stepped back into the Farm's shipping and receiving office. The bulkhead slammed shut behind him, closing off the darkness.

"The fuck'sammatter wit' you?" Jacob asked and looked up from the several feeds that monitored the exterior of the farm house.

"Nothin'." Albin seated himself at the table where he had left his tobacco and rolling papers hours ago and began to roll a fresh cigarette.

"They all done?" Jacob asked and yawned. His bloodshot eyes were rimmed by dark circles. He turned them back toward the feeds and giggled.

"Yep. They're done." Albin placed the cigarette between his lips and got up from the chair. He walked across the small office and stepped behind Jacob, looking over the man's shoulder. There were six feeds. One of them showed a children's cartoon cat chasing a mouse with an oversized ball-peen hammer. The cat tripped and fell in a dramatic tumble of fur and dust, sending the hammer skyward; it landed square on the cat's skull. Jacob erupted into laughter. Albin grimaced. The feed should've showed looped footage from an empty Hangar 19, not a damn cartoon. If any external monitoring stations accessed the loading dock feed, they should have seen a vacant concrete slab. With the cartoon running, the actual feed would be live.

"Jacob, what did I tell you about this shit?" Albin said and waved his hand through the cartoon. It disappeared in a burst of static and light.

"Aw, Albin. I got bored. At leas' I wasn't sleepin', right?"

"Jacob, of all the fuckin' feeds, why did you use our fuckin' decoy?"

"I did?" Jacob scratched his greasy head. Albin inhaled a lung full of smoke and let it out with a sigh.

"Jacob, you're getting careless on me. When's the last time you slept?"

"I don't know, Albin. Can't sleep. I hear things at night," Jacob said and glanced around the cramped office. Albin frowned and took another long drag on the cigarette. If Jacob mentioned the angels again, he'd stab the dim-wit.

"Did you take those pills I gave you?" Albin asked.

"Albin, the fuckin' pills don't work. I can hear them. I ain't crazy. It's not like I hear voices all the time. Only at night. When I'm in bed. I ain't crazy, Albin. Honest." Jacob was getting agitated and Albin held up a hand.

"Easy, Jacob. Go home. Take handful of those little red pills and sleep, got it? I'll be back around tomorrow afternoon. You just need sleep. You're fuckin' delirious. And that's no goddamn help to me or to anybody."

"Yeah, Albin. I know you're right. Just. It's this place…Crescent. I don't like it here."

"Well, better get used to it. We're gonna be here for a while."

Jacob moved toward the frosted glass exit door and spared Albin one last look. It was the kind of look a ten year old boy would give his parents right before asking, "Can I sleep with you tonight?" Fuck that, Albin thought. He was having a hard enough time sleeping himself. The door whispered open, Jacob stepped through, and the door whispered closed. There was a muted click as it locked.

[•••]

"That is asking a lot," Nigel said and folded his hands in his lap. He rolled back from a table that was buried in printouts and multiple glowing data pads, and turned to glance at the security monitors. A reflex, pure and simple—movement in one of the cycling feeds caught his eye. Swaren's first years in Core Sec had been spent staring at wall panels full of glowing security feeds. Old habits died hard. Something moved. He looked. Simple.

"Marisa…how long have I been on Crescent?" Nigel asked. As the words fell from his lips, he realized he couldn't exactly pinpoint how long he had been there. He thought it should've been a week, but it felt like he had been there for far less time. The only evidence of the length of his stay was the depth to which the table-turned-desk was inundated with audit materials. Marisa didn't answer him at first. She sighed and tugged her uniform jacket.

"I know you haven't been here that long and you hardly know me. And I know it's asking a lot, but I'm not sure how to proceed. Kendall is not someone to be fucked with," Marisa said.

"You don't know how to proceed? Look, Griffin. I like you a great deal. You've been nothing but accommodating. Thus far. You bring me the data I'm looking for when I ask for it. And you've respected my space.

But this is a bomb you've dropped in my lap. And it sounds like rubbish." Marisa frowned and glanced at her shoes.

Nigel took a deep breath. "I can't go to Crescent's mayor and accuse him of…" Nigel laughed. The notion was ridiculous. "There are certain routes to go through when leveling charges at any high ranking official. Besides, Marisa, this is all a little convoluted. This whole allegation about Mayor Kendall trying to blackmail you for letting illegal arms onto Crescent is, how shall I put it? Small potatoes, and not worth my time. Besides, I told you, your captain's mention of the event was a standard incident report. You were named as present at the time and place but not involved. That is not why I'm here. And this business about your friend Gerald Evans—I still need to question him myself. His records check out and so do this Dr. Donovan Cortez's, but I need to follow protocol—protocol based on what evidence shows. Tampering with ATC records *is* illegal. I have evidence that that occurred. Now, I have no evidence that Gerald Evans is running off-record jobs for the mayor. All of his ATC salvage records, in respect to his contract with Kendall, are legit. If Gerald states of his own volition that he is in cahoots with Kendall on something unsavory, then that's a different story." And, Nigel thought, a royal pain my ass.

"Don't you ever get frustrated with the red tape?" Marisa asked.

"If there was no red tape, guys like me wouldn't have a job." It was the truth. He was one of the tapers, more often than not.

"So, you said that your reason for being here had nothing to do with a security complaint. Can you tell me what it is that you're doing here, then?" If there was one thing that Nigel did like about Marisa Griffin, it was that she had the ability to ask the right questions. He applauded that ability and wished he could answer. But, orders were orders and his orders were to keep his lips sealed and get the job done.

"You know what I'm going to say, so spare me the breath and don't make me say it," Nigel said.

"You just wasted a lot of breath with that response, what's a little more?" Marisa countered and smiled. The smile was strained, though. He could tell she was not pleased that he wasn't going to look into her allegations.

He laughed and shook his head. She was persistent.

He thought on it a little more. Kendall didn't possess the trappings of an honest man. That much was apparent just by looking at the people he surrounded himself with. Walter Vegan made Nigel's skin crawl and Kendall's two roughnecks were perfect examples of the type of men capable of all manner of unsavory activities. But, Kendall's records were squeaky clean. All the i's were dotted, all the t's crossed. Too clean, maybe. But the only signs of tampering had to do with a salvage pilot and a neurosurgeon turned archaeologist. Nothing to do with the mayor or his strange bedfellows. Nigel was there to do a specific job. The whole ATC log tampering business would only slow him down. He didn't need to further complicate matters by pursuing Lt. Griffin's paranoia. It would only lengthen his stay on the station. And the less time he spent on Crescent, the better.

"I want to meet with Mr. Evans as soon as you can arrange it. I don't have time to spare on this nonsense. I'm not going to pursue your Kendall... situation." At that, Marisa seemed to deflate.

"It's just that... I'm so sure he's up to something. Why else would he ask me to keep an eye on you?" Marisa said. "Why? At least give me an answer to that."

"Lieutenant, do you think you're the first security officer a station mayor has asked to keep their eye on me?" Nigel chuckled and shook his head. For an instant, Griffin looked like she would cry. He realized he was probably pushing back too hard now.

He felt himself acquiesce, ever-so-slightly. He would keep his eyes open. Her desperation convinced him to do that much, at least. But Griffin didn't need to know he'd be doing that. It would only encourage her to stick her nose where it didn't belong. Nigel knew full-well that there was always a carpet that the dust was swept beneath, but he wasn't there for Kendall's rug of secrets. Now, if this Evans had anything of particular merit that would contribute to Marisa's case and anything that would make Nigel's goals easier to accomplish, that was another story. But Nigel wasn't going to go fishing.

"I can arrange the meeting, yes," Marisa said at long last.

"Good. Then I can continue to like you. A great deal." He gave her a winning smile. Marisa didn't return it; she left the office with out saying a word. Nigel turned back to the security monitors. There were over three hundred primary security feeds, with many more subfeeds. He began to cycle through them. He'd spend a little time looking in on Crescent's residents from above, so to speak. There was something centering about being able to change perspective with the wave of a hand. It helped him to think in different dimensions, to look at problems from various angles and attitudes. Despite his best efforts, Nigel's mind kept straying to Ezra Kendall. He was wading into some dark waters by letting his thoughts travel there—there was a drop-off in those waters, he was sure of it. And that drop-off would send him into an abyss. If the rip current didn't yank him out to sea first.

He stopped on a feed that caught his attention. The camera lens was dirty; grime partially obscured the view. But from what Nigel could see, it was a loading dock. He checked the address at the bottom of the display. It was one of the Farm's loading docks. Workers sealed off a large, long crate, and a pair of collector robots carried it off. Nigel shrugged and cycled past the image. Then he went back. It took him several minutes of scrolling to find it again, and when he did, the camera lens was clean and the view was clear. The dock was empty. The crate hadn't looked like a typical produce-bearing container. It had been too heavy-duty. It also struck Nigel as odd that there would be people working the Farm's loading docks well after hours—easily six hours into the station's night cycle.

Dark waters, Nigel thought. *Dark waters, indeed.*

[•••]

Bean was just ahead. Milky daylight oozed around the hauler and softened the ship's lines and contours. The cold rain fell more insistently; the wind lashed out with brutal intent, each gust the crack of an icy whip. The small portion of Gerald's face that was exposed had been rendered raw and numb. He looked back over his shoulder to see Ina shuffling along not far behind him. Her head was down and her gloved hands were stuffed into the parka's pockets. She hadn't slowed them down on their return trek. A good thing—their supplemental oxygen supply was nearly exhausted. Gerald felt like his knees were ready to give out. The goddamn gravity was really getting to him. He couldn't wait to get his tired ass into that control couch. He wanted to forget all about the geological station and its freak show. He couldn't help but wonder if the universe had gone mad while he was star-hopping his way to Crescent. There were no answers on Anrar III, as Marisa had hoped. Just more shit to pollute his dreams. He wasn't really sure what he'd tell Marisa about the visit to the planet. Would he tell her about the word—the name? Every time he thought the word Murhaté, it made his fillings ache. It was the name of the geological station—that was apparent. But somehow Gerald knew it was the name of something else. Something bad. But what?

He looked up at the dark, twisting clouds. Beyond them, Crescent circled countless kilometers above the rocky planet. Was this dead place—this former mining operation and the planet it had penetrated—the cause of all the weirdness on Crescent? Gerald had never cared about the station's earlier days. He had no cause to. But now that he was stuck on Crescent, he wanted to know.

Maybe staying on Crescent too long drove a man insane. Was that Marisa's issue? Had he missed earlier episodes of her madness due to his short stays? *Look at Naheela, for god's sake,* he thought. She was supposedly Crescent's longest resident and was clearly bat-crazy. On the other hand, Maerl seemed pretty well composed, and he had been on Crescent for years.

How well do you really know people? Gerald thought.

There was Ina—she seemed a little more than off at times, and she hadn't been on Crescent all that long. And he was having problems of his own. He cut off the rapid train of thought before it derailed.

Gerald was near enough to see the large drops of rain exploding on Bean's gray hull. *Thank god,* he thought. He couldn't feel his extremities. The rain had managed to work its way into his suit, chilling his entire being. He looked back to check on Ina's progress and didn't see her at first. Then he spotted her—she was laying face down in the wet grit. Gerald tried to run to her, but his legs were just too weary to manage more than a jerky amble. He dropped to his knees beside her and cried out from the pain of the impact. He caught his breath, then turned her over. Her eyes were open, but rolled back in her head. She was breathing, but her breath came in short and shallow respirations. Summoning the reserves of his strength, Gerald hefted Ina over his shoulder and began to make his way to Bean. His knees were white hot balls of pain. Every step burst through his bones like a nuclear explosion. The rain was coming down harder and it made the path slick. More than once, Gerald's booted feet nearly shot out from underneath him. The planet was trying to mock him. *No,* he thought, *this planet is trying to kill me.*

"What are you doing?" Ina's voice came muffled from his back. He instantly let her slide to the ground, where she settled on her hands and knees. She looked up at Gerald, her blue eyes piercing.

"You passed out," he said.

"I did?" She seemed entirely surprised. Her surprise grew when she saw noticed their proximity to Bean. "How far back did I pass out?"

"Just here," Gerald said.

"I don't remember walking this far," Ina said. Her voice quavered. She was about to freak out. That was one thing that Gerald definitely didn't want to happen.

"I wish I didn't remember either," he said and smiled beneath the tight wrap of his hood. She couldn't see it, he knew, but he hoped that it came through in his voice. "You're heavy as shit. Now, come on. Let's get off this rock."

She extended a gloved hand. Gerald took it and helped her to her feet.

[•••]

Gerald and Ina—both of them soaked to the bone—could not have stripped out of their excursion suits any faster. It was warm on Bean and the warmth felt good, but they both shivered despite the heat rising from the vents. Gerald looked to Ina. She sat on the control couch in her bra and underwear, with her thin, pale arms wrapped around herself. The clothing that she had been wearing beneath the excursion suit lay in a sopping pile at her bare feet. Gerald covered them both with a heavy wool blanket once they were harnessed in. Lightning lanced outside the front viewport in a long purple arc. Lift-off would be rough in this weather, but they couldn't wait for it to pass.

"About those other sites," she began.

"Entirely out of the question. You passed out, for god's sake."

"I feel okay," she persisted.

"Well, you're not okay. I don't think Papa Cortez would appreciate me leaving you to your death down there," Gerald replied.

"You wouldn't," Ina said, incredulous.

"Ina, you have no idea how hard you were to carry. And that was for, what, one freakin' meter? I'm not doing it again. So, your safest bet is to shut your mouth and let me get us out of here."

She had no response. Gerald was satisfied with her silence.

"Bean. Would you kindly get us out of this storm?" Gerald asked.

"And on to greener pastures," Bean replied. "It would be my pleasure, Captain. All this flying grit is bad for my hull."

"We wouldn't want to ruin that fine complexion of yours," Gerald said without humor. "Now, quit screwing around. Let's go."

Bean rumbled beneath them as the conventional engines fired, and then they rocketed skyward. The g-forces pressed the ship's occupants into the soft cushions of the control couch. They approached the wall of the storm at high speed. Angry clouds swirled with grey-black vortices, like the barrier between this mortal coil and hell itself. For a single, irrational instant, Gerald feared that the ship would explode when it hit the clouds. The heart of the storm pummeled the ship savagely. Lighting burst around them in blinding violet flashes. The turbulence was so intense, Gerald's eyes felt like they would rattle right out of his head.

They broke through the cloud deck and into sunlight. The bright orange-red orb of Anrar hung low, just above the fringe of the cloud line.

And then there were stars.

"Do you have any tea on this ship?" Ina said, fumbling at the buckles of the harnesses. "I feel so cold. It's deep. Really deep. Please, if you have anything. I need it." There was a queer desperation in her voice that made Gerald reach out and place a hand on shoulder. She was right. She was cold. He could feel it beneath the blanket. Ice cold. "Jesus, Ina. You're freezing. Do you feel okay otherwise?"

"Yes."

"You don't think that you're going hypothermic on me, do you?"

"I… I'm not sure what that would feel like. But I really don't think so. I just need some dry clothes and some tea. Please," she said.

"Okay. Bean, crank up the heat."

Gerald returned from the berthing quarters, dressed and feeling warmer. He carried a folded pile of clothing under one arm and a steaming cup of tea in his hand. Ina was no longer in the control couch. He heard her voice, though, thick and low. She was mumbling. He set the tea down on the deck and peered over the control couch to see Ina lying on her back. Her arms were folded across her chest; her fingers were curled into tight, white-knuckled fists. Ina's eyes were rolled back into her head. Her lips moved, but they were out of sync with her speaking. Gerald couldn't make any sense of what she was saying. It sounded like gibberish. But the more he listened to her, the less he believed she was speaking nonsense.

"Bean. Are you catching this… "

Her eyes went wide and blue. They fixed on him.

"The stone will be carved," she said before Bean had a chance to reply.

"The music will play. The vessel will be filled. The door will be young enough. We will be born complete. The Three will finally be whole. Unity." The voice was not Ina's. The sound of it made Gerald's blood run cold. Ina's eyes rolled back into her head and she began to mutter in the strange language once more.

It was going to be a long flight.

[•••]

Donovan Cortez crawled along the maintenance shaft. It was longer and far more cramped than he would've imagined. According to Ina, Gerald had lost his cool in this very passage. Donovan now understood why the salvage pilot had panicked so. The walls pressed against the elder Cortez's shoulders, and his fat belly seemed to get hung up on every junction that he crawled past. Donovan, who was not claustrophobic by nature, was finding it difficult not to panic each time he found himself momentarily stuck.

It was cold in the passage. The rest of the lifeboat had seemed to absorb the heat from Crescent's life support system eagerly, but not this place. It was cold enough that Donovan could see his breath.

He cursed at the hardhat he wore on his head. It was too big for him. It kept falling forward over his eyes, despite his thick coif of mad curls. He stopped for what felt like the nine-hundredth time and resituated the thing. First this way and then that; finally, he tried resting it further back on his head. That seemed better, and he started forward again. But after only a few paces of progress the helmet fell, rolled off his back, and hit the tunnel floor. The lamp shattered and he was in darkness.

He waited there on his hands and knees. His breathing was slow, measured, and deliberate. *Don't panic, Donovan,* he thought. He willed his pulse to stay even, though his cardiac muscle seemed to tremble with every beat. He would simply turn around and crawl back the way he had come. Piece of cake. He hadn't been traveling down the passage for all that long. Five minutes? Maybe less.

But he couldn't turn around. The space was too tight. And with that realization, his heart rate threatened to shoot through the roof. He took in several gulps of air. It was musty. Dank. Cold. Donovan squeezed his eyes shut against the darkness. The gulps retarded into more reasonable breaths. His pulse slowed. Donovan knew what he had to do. He had to press on until he reached the chamber where Gerald had ejected the reactor core. There would be enough room for him to turn around there.

His palms were clammy with sweat and he slipped frequently, but he crawled forward in the darkness. He wiped his hands dry on his shirt every few minutes to be sure that he didn't end up planting his face into channel floor.

Then Donovan stopped moving.

What is that? he thought. *Is that light?*

It was quite impossible that there was light up ahead. Yet, Donovan saw a vague, purplish glow. The violet luminance could have been his brain inventing light to cope with the complete blackness. Donovan started crawling again and as he moved forward, he knew the theory was wrong. He could see the outline of a circular junction—the hatch to the reactor chamber. But if there was light, where was it coming from?

Donovan went through the opening and the answer presented itself:

Everywhere.

The walls of the ovoid chamber were painted in a low, purplish glow. The light flowed along the curving wall panels like a viscous fluid. Donovan got to his feet, so enthralled by the living light that he didn't even notice the pile of corpses. When he did, he took several tottering steps backwards and landed on his rump. He was no stranger to cadavers, but the sheer volume of desiccated human remains was overwhelming. *You are a scientist, Donovan Cortez,* he thought, *and a doctor.* He took a slow and deep breath and reminded himself that he had seen plenty of bizarre things on the operating table, and he'd seen more than his fair share of death. But the stark and surreal quality of the scene made his chest feel compressed. Donovan continued to practice his measured breathing until calm returned to him. *Why had Gerald not said anything about this room?* Donovan wondered. The purplish light continued to ooze over the walls and floor. Tendrils of it curled around the soles of his white sneakers like smoke.

Donovan steeled himself and approached the mummified remains of what had been likely been the lifeboat's crew and passengers.

How did they get there? Donovan wondered. Were they already dead when they had been brought there? Some of the bodies were missing limbs. Some were even missing their heads: necks, ragged around the edges, jutted from sunken shoulders. Everything was lit in the ethereal purple light. Donovan felt like he was moving through a bad dream.

He found it hard to not stare into the lilac haze, swirling on the slanted walls. It was beautiful. Living. His eyes kept fixing on it. He settled onto the chamber floor and lay on his back. Now he could gaze up at the ceiling and watch the light. The old, dry corpses that surrounded him didn't matter. Nothing mattered but the magnificent light that moved in whirls and eddies above and around him. It seemed to take on shapes when he gazed at it long enough—spheres rose and sank back into the light. And those spheres were changing, too. He could hardly comprehend the beautiful wonder of it all. Faces. Yes! Faces emerged from the purple light; their mouths were stretched wide open. They were singing. Singing the glory of that wonderful light.

But they weren't singing.

They were screaming.

White hot, the sound of a thousand agonies reverberated in his head. He pressed his hands to his ears, but it didn't help. The faces continued to rise and wail. Their mouths were open so wide that the visages tore from ear to ear; the glowing flesh sloughed away to reveal skulls that were misshapen with bizarre protuberances. They didn't look like human skulls at all, but like the skulls of gargoyles and monsters. Donovan tried to stand, but the weight upon his chest had multiplied ten-fold. It was crushing him. He screamed; his voice joined the chorus in his head.

The light began to coalesce at the center of the curved ceiling into a single, undulating cloud of hateful faces and slowly began to descend. Donovan's heart jack-hammered in a chest that felt like it was about to burst into flames. *I'm having a heart attack,* he thought. *I'm going to die in here.* These were the only coherent thoughts he could manage through all the screaming.

The angel of death wore no black robes. Instead, he was a blaze of violet and agony.

[•••]

"What's the matter, Ezra?" the prostitute asked. Her clear eye blinked up at him. The milky eye stared off into nothing. She stroked Kendall's penis with a determination that was commendable. But he could not seem to get hard, despite her best ministrations and the pleasing swell of her bosom. He tried to focus on her breasts, which bounced with each pull of her soft hands. Nothing. His inability to perform was becoming a problem more and more lately. He had too much on his mind. Between Core Sec auditors, a halt in firearms production, and the station itself going crazy, Kendall was finding himself constantly preoccupied. At present, the bitch Griffin was to blame for his flaccid member. Griffin hadn't erased the security feed as he'd requested. She left the accursed footage on the hard drive. She left it there because she knew he would watch it again. And Kendall did watch it again. He couldn't help himself. He had to see it again to know for sure. And now he knew. The darkness on the station was getting restless—again.

The prostitute continued to stare at him. Her dark eye swam with frustration. Kendall brushed his long finger over her shoulder and smiled.

"Angela. That is your name, yes?" he said, and she nodded. "I have a terrible headache. It has been a long week for me. Why don't you leave and come back later tonight?"

"Are you sure?"

"Yes, dear. I'm sure."

Angela concealed her exposed breasts and began to cinch up her bodice. She spared him one last glance before leaving his bed chambers. Once she was gone, Kendall depressed a thumb behind his ear.

"Taylor. I would very much appreciate you arranging for Naheela to be at my office in thirty minutes."

Kendall went to his tall wardrobe and opened one of the double doors. The inside of the door had a polished mirror set into the wood, not the typical high-def liquid crystal displays favored for modern hygiene. Kendall always thought of himself as more of a classical man. There was someone standing behind him. It wasn't Taylor. It wasn't Angela. He turned. There was no one there.

Seein' shit, Ezra, he thought. *You better figure out how to get off before this stress kills you.*

Kendall straightened his shirt and ran a brush through the tangles in his thin hair until it was straight. He set the brush down and frowned. Someone was snooping around the Vault again. Had to be. The last time there had been a ruckus on Crescent—some fifteen years ago—people had been sniffing around where they didn't belong. Stupid little brats had been prying. Oh, the ends he had to go through to keep the peace. And yet, here he was again.

Kendall closed the wardrobe. He moved to the adjacent chest of drawers and chose a small bottle of cologne from the menagerie that sat atop the piece of furniture. He dabbed a tiny amount into his open palm. He clapped his hands together and then applied the smell-pretty to his cheeks with light pats.

Kendall did not want to talk to Naheela. Hell, it was the last thing he wanted to do. But, he needed to. The weird old bitch had guided him the first time. She *came* to him the first time. She'd help him again, no doubt. Who better to provide advice on a haunting than a witch? The thought made him laugh out loud. He pulled on his pants, fastened his belt, and then slipped his suit jacket on over his shoulders. Whatever spirits were restless on Crescent, he had best placate them off the radar. If it was a gaggle of virgins they wanted this time, or a basket of babies, those things would be delivered without Nigel Swaren getting wind of it.

The archaeologist. Kendall growled at the thought of soft and naive Donovan Cortez. If that damn doctor had gone sticking his nose where it didn't belong, Kendall would throw him and his young daughter into the meat grinder as a bonus.

Kendall found himself feeling much better. *The wonder of thinking things through and coming up with a course of action,* Kendall mused. His member twitched and he smiled. Angela would have better luck that evening.

[•••]

The crone traveled with a cloud of stink. Kendall found Naheela's smell unbearable, even with a lit cigar perched between his lips. The tang—an amalgam of spices, fetid breath, and body odor—was enough to make his nostrils sting and his eyes water. She sat across from him, on the other side of the big desk. Her gnarled hands were folded in the lap of the patched, brown skirt she wore. Her gray, greasy hair fell well past her shoulders in shiny clumps. She smiled through Kendall's cigar smoke, revealing her few remaining yellowed teeth. The deep wrinkles etched in her dark skin went to unfathomable depths. With all the technology that was available, why did this woman choose to look like she was holding hands with death himself? Kendall shook his head and took an exaggerated drag on the cigar.

"Naheela, do you know why I've invited you here today?" Kendall asked.

"I may be old, Ezra, but I'm no fool."

"Good, then. We are spared talking around the bush. I want know what is happening on my station, and I know you know."

Naheela snickered. A watery substance began to trickle from her nose. She wiped a hand across its bulbous end.

"You know," she said and pointed a finger at him.

"Why is Crescent doing this again? I followed your instructions the last time. You said that would be enough."

"Why do you think that is no longer enough, Ezra?"

"Crone, I did not ask you here so that you could ask me questions," Kendall snapped.

"The pact is broken, fool. Someone has found the Vault. Any deal you made with the Black is off," Naheela said.

"That is highly unlikely," Kendall said. "Even if someone was fooling around where they didn't belong, the deal you had me make..."

"A piece of chewin' gum will only keep the dam from breakin' for so long. Poke at the sore, and you hasten the flood."

Kendall sighed through his nose. He could think of only two people that would go down there. The milky depths of Naheela's eyes rested on him with a look of knowing.

"Very well, Naheela. Here I am again, looking for advice."

"I fear, Ezra, that it is not as simple as this time around," she said.

"What do you mean? How could it not be as simple. The same goddamn things are happening."

"Same? No. This is very different, Mayor. Much worse. The first time you only had the Black to contend with. A part of the whole. It wasn't worried about unity—only survival. Now the Three are nearly back together. The glass trembles. The Black gets stronger with each passing day. The same sacrifice will not suffice this time, Kendall. The Violet is here. We can only hope that the Red—the final piece of the trinity—does not show up, too. For if the Red does come, then it's too late."

Kendall couldn't fully grasp her message. Tangled in metaphor, her words rang like a steaming pile of shit to him. Even still, Kendall did not like the certainty in her voice. Naheela tested the bounds of his superstition. He drummed his fingers on the desk.

"I'm not going to ask what that means. But I will ask again. What can we do about it?"

"We? You mean you, Ezra. And I'm sure this time I don't know," Naheela said with a toothless grin. "You could destroy this place for good. That is always a possibility."

He laughed. The sound was bitter and harsh.

"Leave? No, Naheela. I won't leave. That is not an option."

"I didn't think it was." She folded her hands on his desk and raised her shoulders in a shrug. "I don't know what else you could do, Ezra. I may know soon enough. As for now, it is all too new. Things have not finished shapin' themselves. When they do—or when they get close—I'll know. Until then, there is nothing more I can tell you."

"I'll trust you'll get in touch with me as soon as… things have finished shapin' themselves," he said.

Naheela beamed. "I do so love our visits, and they are too far between." She laughed, and wiped her nose with her hand again. The hand, she wiped on the arm of Kendall's chair.

When Naheela took her leave, she left behind her stink and a growing sense of unease.

[•••]

Crescent floated black against the dissipating glare of Anrar. Its silhouette was a malignant hook, dark and terrible. Ina was slack in the harness of the control couch. Gerald leaned against the console, his hands in his pockets. He watched her chest rise and fall with slow breaths. Her eyes flitted back and forth beneath her lids as she lay in dreams. Ina's temperature had risen in the past several hours, but Gerald wasn't sure he was ready for her to wake up. Asleep, she was incapable of delivering more crazy talk. Gerald shook his head. The trip to Anrar III could be called any number of things, but a good idea was not one of them. Marisa had been so wrong. More bad things were going come of it—of that, Gerald was sure.

Ina began to stir.

Her blue eyes opened and fell on Gerald. He managed a weak smile as she sat up in the couch and undid the harness with slow moving fingers.

"How long was I out?" she asked.

"The better part of an hour," he replied. He waited for her to ask what happened, but she didn't.

"Okay. So, we're almost back?"

"Yeah, we're almost back."

"Good." She ran her fingers through the tangles of her blonde hair, piling it atop her head as she did so. "I need a shower. I feel so… dirty."

"Do you re—" Gerald began, but she cut him off.

"I don't want to talk about it. I don't think we need to talk about it. It's not for you and I to discuss."

She got to her feet and stretched. And suddenly, she was moving. Ina closed the space between them so fast that Gerald was nearly knocked off his feet, but her arms slithered around his neck before he could lose his balance. Her skin was cool and smelled of the rain. In the space of a single breath, her lips were on his, her mouth open, her tongue seeking his. Her kiss was cold, insistent, but not unpleasant. Gerald found himself unable to resist. The blind desire to lay with her overwhelmed him and he could think of nothing else. The lust filled his skull like the buzzing of a thousand wasps and consumed him. Even so, he gripped her by the shoulders and shook his head.

"No, Ina," he pleaded. "I can't. Not this time."

"It has to be *now,*" she said and broke his grip. And that was it—his resolve was gone.

He allowed Ina pull him down to the floor. He let her undress him. He let her put himself inside of her. There was nothing cold about her there. She was on fire; soon, his entire body crackled with it.

He closed his eyes and saw an ocean of surging red.

[Part XIV]

Nigel Swaren sat before the security monitors at HQ with his hands clasped behind his head. The air handling system murmured above him. He closed his eyes and took in a long, deep breath of recycled air, then exhaled just as slowly. He was done studying the security feeds from the Farm. Footage amounting to a month's worth of camera time had been under Nigel's close scrutiny for more hours than he cared to count. Nigel couldn't focus on it any longer—his eyes burned and all he saw were random pixels. But he had already seen plenty. His day had centered on studying regular outgoing shipments and his interest had been piqued by the occasional heavy-duty crate intermingled with the standard agricultural shipping containers. At first, the reinforced crates seemed to show up at random, but after tracking their appearance for hours on end, Nigel had noticed a pattern.

Now he cycled through feeds at random, watching as people came and went, carried by whatever force propels people from one location to another. Other screens were still, showing seldom-visited sections of Crescent—one snapshot after another showed cobwebs and flickering overhead light panels. Nigel dropped his eyes from the security feeds to the white mug that sat untouched on the control panel. The beverage had gone cold hours ago.

Nigel was annoyed—annoyed with himself for diving into the security feeds with such reckless abandon, because now he'd seen plenty to prove that Ezra Kendall was hiding something. *And this kind of dirt, I cannot wash off my hands.* Nigel hadn't been sent to Crescent to go fishing for corrupt politicians. Really, that was the last thing he'd wanted to get tangled up in. But now, a misbehaving mayor might be just what Nigel was looking for. He laughed at the irony. Salvation could be found in the most unlikely places.

A skinny, pallid kid in blues entered the monitoring station, rubbing eyes that were ringed with dark circles. He seemed surprised to see Nigel there.

"I... "

"You're late and you're sorry, right? Not my problem. Take it up with your captain if you're feeling guilty. And besides... you should be reporting to Temporary Monitoring Station 17—this is my office," Nigel said. *Not that I've seen Captain Benedict all that often since I've been here.* He walked past the kid without sparing him another glance.

[•••]

Nigel leaned against a bookshelf in Kendall's antechamber. He pretended to be examining the rows of neatly organized books. He pretended to be oblivious of the four eyes that burned holes in his back. Kendall's goons were just the sort of scum you'd find in a dark alley, at the other end the knife stuck in your side. The shorter one, with the slicked-back dark hair and the high forehead, appeared to be stupid as all sin. There was nothing going on in his dark eyes but a dose of the crazies. The taller of the pair, with the red hair and weathered features—he was no fool. He watched Nigel with a gaze that was as appraising as it was ice cold.

Taylor, gigantic and wearing cheap cologne, ushered Nigel into Kendall's office. Nigel spared Kendall's dogs one last look before the office door swung shut. The halo-globes in the spacious office were turned down low. A single lamp glowed on the large desk that dominated the room. Beyond the desk, the wide viewport that took up much of the anterior wall showed the night face of Anrar III, black and endless. Kendall sat behind the desk in a chair that Nigel found to be ridiculously oversized. His long fingers were twined together on the desktop. The mayor's gray hair hung to his shoulders in hastily combed rows. Kendall's thin lips curved up but never quite reached the altitude of a smile.

"I apologize that we have continued to miss each other until now, Lieutenant Swaren." Kendall's tone was honey sweet. "Mayor is a busy role, as I'm sure you can imagine. Were I not able to delegate, I might hang myself."

"That's Captain. And yes, I imagine it does keep you busy." Nigel spoke pleasantly enough. He looked around the office. More books. "The shelves are real wood?"

"Real down to the molecule." Kendall smiled. His lower lip stuck to his teeth for a brief second. “The books are real, as well. It’s taken me many years of collecting to fill these walls.”

“Do you go off-station often, then? To collect your books?”

Kendall laughed and shook his head. One of the strands of hair came free of its ordained row and fell into his face. He brushed it away.

“No, no. I never leave the station. Nexus auction, my friend.”

There was a strange tang in the office. Nigel inhaled through his nose. It was the smell of sex. He tried to not react to it, although his first instinct was to purse his lips. He matched gazes with Kendall. Nigel felt sorry for the poor girl, whoever she was. Kendall was not a picture of beauty.

“Can I interest you in a drink, Mr. Swaren.”

“I don’t drink,” Nigel said, matter-of-factly. “And besides, I’m on duty.”

“And here I was thinking this was a mere courtesy visit.” Kendall stood and made his way over to a slender bar set into one of the book-laden walls. Atop the bar sat multiple decanters filled with dark liquid. Kendall selected one and filled a crystal tumbler. Nigel had little doubt the bottles in Kendall’s bar were filled with genuine, non-synthetic liquor. There was a lot of money in the office. Kendall seemed to have acquired a lot more wealth than your typical fringe outpost mayor.

“The New Juno initiative seems to be favoring you, Mayor,” Nigel said as Kendall sat back down. Kendall looked around the office with a pleased glance.

“It certainly hasn’t hurt.”

Silence settled between them for several seconds. A leap of faith was not required here. Kendall was misbehaving himself into a fortune.

“What are you doing here, Swaren?” Kendall asked. His voice was even, almost indifferent. “And I’m not referring to your presence in my office. I want to know what you’re doing on *my* station.”

“I’m performing an audit, of course,” Nigel said.

“There is no reason for this audit. Crescent’s performance is with little flaw.” Kendall took a sip from the tumbler cradled in his hand. “This station has not been audited in some fifteen years.”

“Isn’t that reason enough for an audit?”

Kendall did not respond.

“At the risk of sounding disrespectful, Mayor Kendall, you don’t have the privilege to know my reasons for auditing this station. Your only role here is to comply with my needs,” Nigel said.

“Mr. Swaren. I’m going to remind you of somethin’. You are on my station. I run the show on Crescent and I run the show in a way that keeps things moving smoothly. You had best be careful where you stick your dirty little nose. It just might get bitten off. Do you understand what I'm sayin' here, son?" Kendall asked.

"I'm not quite sure I follow, Mayor. If I had to guess, I'd say you were threatening me." Nigel folded his hands in his lap and maintained eye contact with Kendall. For the first time during their meeting, Kendall's lips curved into a wide, Cheshire grin.

"What I'm sayin' is, you're a long way from any Core Sec hub. You don't have any friends here. I don't see that changin'. It'd be unadvisable to make enemies. Do your job and leave."

"I am doing my job, Mayor," Nigel said.

Kendall's grin turned into a smirk.

"Is there anything else I can help you with, Mr. Swaren?"

"I don't believe so, Mayor."

"Very well, then," Kendall replied and pressed a finger behind his ear. He muttered something and seconds later the door swung open. Nigel felt a large hand on his shoulder but did not bother looking up to see who it belonged to. He could smell the cologne just fine. "Thank you for your visit, *Mr.* Swaren. I trust if you need anything from me, you won't hesitate to ask. Taylor will show you the door."

[•••]

The man strode across the bar toward Nigel, rubbing his dirty face with a weary hand. Despite the slender and athletic build beneath his flight suit, his shoulders were slumped and his movements deliberate with exhaustion. His dark hair was in a mad tousle atop his head. Gerald Evans looked just as Lieutenant Griffin had described him: a mess. Nigel waved to him. Evans nodded and changed course. Once he was within range, Nigel stood and extended his hand.

"Nigel Swaren," Nigel said, and Gerald took his hand.

"I figured as much. I gotta sit down here, buddy. I'm dead on my legs."

"By all means." Nigel gestured to the open seat across from his own. Gerald seated himself with a long sigh of relief, and Nigel sat back down.

"Drink?" Nigel asked.

"Heavily and momentarily." Gerald managed a weak smile and waved to the girl tending the bar. She nodded back to him. Satisfied, Gerald returned his attention to Nigel. The salvage pilot's eyes were bloodshot. His lips were chapped and his cheeks looked either sun or wind burned. Strange. Not really the type of wear and tear you'd expect to see on a salvage pilot.

"You're the auditor," Gerald stated with casual indifference. It wasn't a question.

"I am."

"Funny. I expected someone older. Stauncher." Gerald paused and then added, "With less hair."

Nigel laughed. At face value, Gerald Evans did not seem to be a bad man—Evans and Kendall were a study in contrast.

"Mr. Evans, you're probably wondering why I asked you here," Nigel said.

"Wondering, yeah." He nodded to the serving girl as she set a bottle in front of him. "I've got all kinds of ideas. But, it'd probably be easier for the both of us if you got down to it."

"Very well, then. What is your employer up to? By employer, I mean Kendall." Gerald's drink halted mid-flight on its way to his lips. He set the bottle back down on the table and lit a cigarette. Smoke drifted past his dirty face in elongating wisps toward the sensors for the air handling system. The whirr of the fans kicked up a notch.

"Ah," was all that Evans said.

"I had the chance to meet with Mayor Kendall this morning," Nigel said.

"And he made you feel all creepy crawly, huh?"

"In a manner of speaking. He's up to no good, Gerald." As the words crossed Nigel's lips he realized how ridiculously obvious they sounded. "Certain members of his security team have alluded as much. I have seen enough to be convinced."

"What variety of no good?" Gerald asked.

"I was hoping you could help me with that. I always figure these things out eventually, Gerald, but I have no interest in prolonging my stay on your fine station," Nigel responded.

"Crescent isn't my home, buddy. Business keeps me here—that's all."

"Business with Kendall."

"Yes. Business with Kendall," Gerald said.

"Anything to do with heavy-duty shipping crates from the Farm?" Nigel asked. Gerald blinked, and shrugged. The look of recognition that Nigel had hoped for was not there.

"The Farm? No. Christ. I'm so tired." Gerald took a drink from the longnecked bottle of ale and then stabbed his cigarette out in the ashtray. The ashtray's top sealed with a click and when it opened again, the cigarette butt was gone. "I have to go," Gerald said.

"Gerald, you're at no risk, telling me about any of this. You have my word."

"There could be listener mites all over this place, Nigel. And it's like I said. I don't know jack about the Farm, okay?"

"The bar is clean, Gerald. No mites. You don't have to worry about Core Sec listening in on this conversation." From the look on Gerald's face, he did not appear to buy it.

"Nigel, I'm not worried about Core Sec listening in. I'm not worried about you. I'm worried about Kendall. If it's not mites, it'll be Catlier and Raney coming in at the wrong moment. The last place I want to end up is floating in deep space without a ship or suit," Gerald glanced around the bar.

"I see," Nigel said. *Catlier and Raney—the goons have names,* he thought.

"This is the part where you offer me protection, Swaren."

"Protection?" Nigel laughed again. He helped himself to one of Gerald's cigarettes and lit it with a lighter that was attached to their table by a plastic cord. "Gerald. I'm one man. One outsider. I can't protect you. I doubt I could protect myself."

"Nigel, you're not making me feel all warm and fuzzy about helping you," Gerald said.

"In the long run, I'll wager you'll be better off by helping me. Men like Kendall eat their slaves alive—it's just a matter of time."

Gerald shifted in his chair and lit another cigarette. "Yeah, yeah. I know. Believe me. I have regretted signing that contract with Crescent's benevolent mayor since day one. I regret a lot of shit. Top of the list: ever setting foot here." He took an exaggerated drag and exhaled the smoke in a sidelong plume. "Kendall's got me running salvage missions in Tireca. And let me say that there is something *all* wrong about these runs. Some of these so-called salvages are still hot. Sometimes, the raiders are only just leaving the scene. It's like Kendall—or his crony, Walter Vegan—have a sixth sense. They know where these ships are gonna to be. Which is fuckin' crazy, because, hell, I don't know how these miners could even know where they are. I keep being sent to the same field in Tireca. The fucker is dense."

"This wouldn't be in the vicinity of the fourth planet in the system, would it?" Nigel asked.

"It would be," Gerald confirmed.

"So, someone is informing the raiders where and when to attack, then?"

"You said it, pal. Not me," Gerald replied with a smirk.

"What kind of ships?"

"Mining. A few supply transports. There was one colony ship, way off course. I get this sinking feeling it was that same ship that showed up on the news feeds the other week. You know, now that I think of it, I was running a job right here in Anrar and saw a Crescent light cargo ship and an unmarked cargo ship—I thought it had been a raider—exchanging a heavy duty container."

Nigel sat back in his seat and examined his own cigarette. The end was smoldering and looked like a living thing. "Do know anything about Galatea?" Nigel asked.

"Galatea? Greek to me," Gerald said. Nigel laughed, not sure if the pun was intentional or not.

"Thank you, Gerald. You look tired. I think that'll be all. Go get some rest—you look like you're about to fall out of your chair. You've been extremely helpful," Nigel said.

"Can I ask why you came to Crescent in the first place? Was there a reason for this audit?" Gerald asked. He didn't get up.

"Crescent is being decommissioned. I'm here to make sure things go smoothly. And looking at the place, I'm just speeding up a preexisting necrosis."

"Wow," Gerald said. Nigel got to his feet and dropped the cigarette butt into the ashtray.

"Thanks again, Gerald. I trust you won't share the details of our talk with anyone. Being that your ass stands in to be in a precarious position for even talking to me."

"Yeah, that's right."

"Good," Nigel said.

"Nigel, you can help me with one thing," Gerald said.

"What's that?"

"You can help me up. I don't think I can stand on my own."

[•••]

"So, Kendall," Nigel said aloud as he made his way down the empty corridor." You're working with the local cutthroats to take out targets of opportunity." His voice and the sound of his boots hitting the deck were the only competition for the whispering air handlers and the occasional clicking of dying light panels. Nigel was well aware that ships went missing on the fringe of populated space all the time. There were ion storms, careless piloting, and of course raider attacks. But as far as Nigel was concerned, the ships that Gerald was hauling were the result of coordinated strikes—Kendall was in bed with Darros Stronghold, so to speak.

There was only one dense asteroid cluster in Tireca and that cluster orbited the fourth planet. That cluster hid Galatea. Security had been beefed up in Tireca to prevent attacks from Stronghold's clan so that the Galatea project could move ahead on schedule. Kendall might not know about Galatea but he would know about the new security patrol patterns and mining ops between Anrar, Tireca, and the New Juno gate. That was standard procedure. Ezra Kendall would know, along with his ATC controller—Vegan. Kendall was telling the raiders exactly where to hit and Evans was unknowingly helping Kendall hide the evidence.

He halted in front of the Core Sec HQ.

And there was the matter of the influx of guns to the colony on Habeos—the suspicious crates from the Farm could have easily been loaded with firearms. This was another dangerous lead to pursue for a Core Sec auditor working solo.

Nigel was close. He could feel the fact like heat on his face, but for now he was only playing the assumption game. He needed more evidence. Something concrete. He took a deep breath and let his head clear. He waited outside the door to HQ until his thoughts stopped racing.

[•••]

As far as Ina was concerned, her return trip to Crescent had been uneventful. She had slept for the duration of the flight, though she still awoke to a deep weariness when they landed. Gerald had been so exhausted as the pair climbed out of Bean that he hardly seemed to notice her milling about the flight deck. He was ignoring her. Eventually, she just left without saying goodbye. No more than a meter away from her apartment door, she was struck with the compulsion to go elsewhere.

She moved like a wraith down a cable-lined passageway that could only be described as forgotten. The few water-stained overhead light panels that still functioned flickered with a dull mustard-colored glow. There were cobwebs on the ventilation grates and the dust on the floor was thick. She left small footprints in her wake.

The musty air reminded her of the basement stacks in the library at the university on Caen. The smell was of spiders and old books; of things long untouched. There was something nostalgic about the odor, but it was so potent and cloying that it made her stomach feel queasy. She cursed her belly—it had been sensitive of late. Ina stopped and looked back the way she had come. The hallway extended well into the distance, in alternating plots of shadow and flickering yellow light. She turned back the way she was headed. The same indefinite distance extended before her.

She closed her eyes.

She had been there before, hadn't she? Ina took her next breath slowly and then held it. Her pulse drummed softly in her ears and her memories marched by as still frame images. It had been her idea to look for the area called *the Vault;* that was a long time ago, when she and her father had first arrived. She hadn't told him. She had crawled through the dust and spiderwebs, through the standing water, through the darkness. She remembered the fear. And when she had found the big door marked with the red X, her heart had hammered in her chest. There had been a moment of exhilaration. And then what? Darkness?

No. Not darkness.

I have to remember, she thought. *This is important.*

Her lungs burned, but she still held her breath.

The still frames quickened until the scenes she saw moved with life-like motion.

The door opens its eyes.

No, Ina thought, *I'm seeing this wrong.*

Something behind the door opens its eyes. Fissures appear—tears in space and time, behind which lies nothingness. The slits, they yawn wide and grow into a devilish darkness so thick she starts to drown in it. And then the other woman shows up and the Black stretches out and touches her as well. And when it pulls back—Ina thinks "this is just like the tide"—and the Black becomes a part of her and the dark-haired girl.

None of her actions since she had come to the station, she suddenly realized, had been of her own will.

There was a flash of red. Ina's eyes snapped open. She let out the breath with a gasp.

Another flash. She blinked.

Ina closed her eyes and all she could see was Red—a breathing wall of liquid garnet. It overwhelmed her with emotion. Hot tears filled her eyes and ran down her cheeks.

Keep the stone safe and hidden. Keep yourself safe and hidden. Keep the vessel safe and hidden. Your business is not here. Keep the vessel safe.

Vessel?

[•••]

Marisa punched in the entry code for her apartment. The door buzzed; the LED above the key pad cycled from red, to green, to yellow, and back to green again. The door was unlocked already. She hadn't remembered leaving it unlocked. But these days, she didn't really count on her memory as a reliable source of information. The door hissed open and she drew her stun rod.

"Come in, Lieutenant. No one is going to hurt you. Not in your home, of all places."

Kendall.

She stepped over the threshold. The door whined shut and she was promptly slammed against the wall by someone much larger, stronger, and less pleasant smelling than herself. The force of the impact knocked the stun rod from her hand.

"Christ!" she wailed. "Is this really necessary?"

"It might be. I heard that your friend Nigel Swaren was shooting the shit with Gerald Evans. Does any of this ring a bell?" Kendall asked. "This news came to me as quite the disappointment. We had a deal, Marisa… Nigel Swaren showed up in my office today. Un-ex-pected. Remember our little discussion about you being my eyes, ears, and hands. No? Perhaps I can refresh your memory."

Taylor slammed her against the wall again. Marisa studied his arms. The enhanced muscle moved beneath his hairless flesh like vipers.

"I'm neither Swaren's keeper nor Gerald's. Whatever Swaren wanted with him, I have no idea. And you know what, Mayor? I can't be on Swaren twenty-four seven. There's no fucking way." Marisa felt her cheeks getting hot.

"Taylor," Kendall said, and looked down at his well-groomed fingernails. Taylor slammed Marisa into the wall yet again, hard enough to knock the wind out of her.

Kill him, a voice whispered. She looked at Kendall and then up to Taylor's stupid, gleaming eyes. The walls moved behind the man—the shadows shifted and swirled, slowly at first and then with increasing speed.

"Swaren sends me off when he's about to get into something important. Has me check light fixtures." Marisa's tongue felt thick, but it wasn't the carthine.

"Taylor," Kendall said, and Taylor kneed her in the stomach before throttling her into the terminal. Something hard dug into her back. Was it the terminal's handset? She had no idea. She wondered, most absently, why the terminal even had a handset. Taylor held her firmly in place. Kendall got to his feet and began to remove his suit jacket.

Kill them both, the voice cooed in a honey tone. *Be rid of them.*

Before Marisa knew what was happening she had Taylor by the face. She pressed her fingers into his eyes. He screamed a high pitched wail—so high Marisa could hardly believe it—and batted at her hands like they were a swarm of angry bees. She pressed harder and felt one of his eyes burst.

"Enough!" Kendall shouted. She couldn't stop. Drool flowed warm out the corners of her mouth and down her chin. She began to laugh, her own voice ringing foreign to her ears. The shadows came to life; they spun around the room in a mad dervish. Marisa was transfixed for an instant and in her moment of hesitation, a stun rod—her stun rod—jabbed her directly in the ribs. A bolt of electricity rocketed through her nervous system. She relinquished her grip on Taylor and as the big man slid to the ground she whirled to face the source of the shock. Kendall stood in an awkward stance, legs spread apart and the stunner clutched in both trembling hands. He seemed positively surprised that the shock hadn't thrown her to the ground. In truth, she was surprised, herself.

"I'm only going to tell you this one time, Mayor," Marisa said. Rage, sheer and venomous, coursed through her veins. She was wildfire, ready to eat Taylor and Kendall alive like a pile of dry brush. *This is what it feels like to go mad,* she thought. "I don't know what Swaren wanted with Gerald Evans and I don't give a shit. I'm doing the best job I can for you. I'm about five seconds away from tearing your goddamn arms off, so why don't you take your piece of shit bodyguard and get out of here."

As if on cue, Taylor wailed, "I can't fucking see. The bitch blinded me."

"Shut up, you stupid cocksucker," Kendall hissed. "This was really inadvisable, Lieutenant. I just wanted to have a chat with you."

"Eat shit or get out. Or how about you get out and eat shit?" Laughter exploded past her lips, melodic and shrill. "And if you fuck with me, I'll start a shit storm between Crescent and Core Sec that will have you sucking vacuum before it's over."

Kendall averted his gaze and looked at his fallen bodyguard.

"Get up, you worthless son of a bitch." Kendall kicked Taylor in the side. The large man struggled to get to his feet. Taylor's right eye oozed thick, dark blood from between two swollen and bruised lids. The lids of the other eye were growing in size, but he was still able to open them.

"You're on your own now. I'm not your lackey anymore," Marisa spat.

"Very well," Kendall said. He straightened his suit jacket and walked out, the trembling man-mountain in tow. Marisa wondered if the big bastard had ever fought in his life—all brawn, no brain, no balls. The door slid shut and she activated the deadbolts. She leaned against the door and slid to the carpet. She felt exhausted to the very core of her being.

You should have killed them.

"I should have let you kill them." *I must really be losing it now,* she thought. Talking to one's self was not an attribute of the mentally sound. Neither was assault. Kendall would leave her alone now—she was sure of that, at least. She unbuttoned the top of her shirt past the line of her breasts and exposed one shoulder. There were two deep red spots where Taylor's ham hock of a hand had been. Marisa looked up at the terminal. The never-before-used handset still swung like a pendulum. The screen erupted with a burst of static and then filled with the glowing image of a long, darkened corridor and two figures—two women, one dark haired and dressed in the blues, one light haired and thin—walking hand-in-hand into the shadows. She would call Nigel. Yes. Soon. She closed her eyes.

Right after she took a little rest.

[•••]

Kendall wasn't sure if the sounds were of pleasure or of pain, but he was sure of one thing: He was enjoying Angela's pillow-muffled screams. He mustered a little more hatred with each thrust. He fucked Angela, his favorite little whore, but he saw Marisa the Core Sec Lieutenant bent over before him.

"I'm going to teach you a lesson," he said. "I'm going to teach it to you good. And you're going to learn it well."

Angela's voice doubled in octave as the violation continued. Kendall growled when he came. He withdrew and stood above her, panting. She rolled over on her back. The pillow she had been yelling into was stained dark with tears and saliva, and her eyes were ringed with red. Beneath the smeared makeup and snot, the girl looked shocked. She looked put in her place. That was well and good. He was able to picture Marisa's face easily—a translucent mask of imagination that highlighted the parade of tears that ran from Angela's eyes and the glisten of mucous that ran from her nose. Kendall lashed out with a backhand; the crack was loud and pleasing when his ring split her cheek wide open. He spit on her and left the bed chamber, closing the bathroom door behind him. Angela's sobs bled through the wall. The sound only fueled his anger. He turned on the shower—it almost drowned out the sound of her crying. But not quite.

If she wasn't gone when he stepped out of the shower, he would kill her.

Sheets stained with tears, sweat, and blood were all that was left of Angela by the time Kendall stepped back into the bed chamber. Also gone was the blind rage. Now all he felt was tired. He laid his sleep clothes out on the bed and began to dress himself slowly. His back ached from the pounding he had just delivered. Christ. Even his pelvis hurt.

The terminal in the bedside wall chimed. Kendall continued to button his night shirt, activating the terminal by voice command. Walter Vegan's horse face filled the screen.

"I hope I'm not interrupting," Vegan said.

"If there were anything going on worth interrupting, I would not have answered. What do you want?" Kendall asked.

"A ship just entered the docking perimeter."

"That's fucking wonderful, Vegan," Kendall paused. "When did you decide to start calling me every time a ship enters the docking perimeter?"

"It's him."

"Would you mind being more specific, Vegan?" Kendall's patience for bullshit was nil at the moment, but since he couldn't reach through the terminal screen to smack Vegan in the ugly mouth like wanted to. He'd have to tolerate the slow-wit.

"Stronghold. Either someone is faking or the raider warlord will be landing on Crescent in about," Vegan looked off-screen at a monitor and then returned his eyes to the camera, "fifteen minutes."

Kendall had expected to hear from Darros. It had been weeks since the last firearms shipment. *Had it really been that long?* Kendall thought. He was sure it wasn't any shorter than that.

"Vegan, contact Catlier. Have him and Raney escort Mr. Stronghold to my office. Make sure there is no reason for Nigel Swaren to show up. And make sure neither he nor that cunt Griffin are at the docks. Are my instructions clear?"

"Yes sir. Very clear."

Kendall disconnected. He got out of his sleep clothes and moved to the closet for a suit. Appearances must be maintained and Darros Stronghold surely had not come looking for slumber party.

[•••]

The curtains were drawn wide open and a bloody light filled the office—moonglow from Anrar III's largest satellite. Kendall had the halos turned down low; he quite liked the effect of the natural light. It wasn't often that station and moon were so well-aligned. Kendall surveyed the office—everything seemed in order.

He placed one crystal tumbler before Darros Stronghold's intended seat and filled the glass with two fingers of bourbon. Red moonlight glanced off a silver coaster and glowed elongated on the otherwise black ceiling. Kendall filled his own glass with twice the amount and seated himself in the wide-backed chair. He took a sip. It burned, and he allowed it to sit on his tongue for several seconds before letting it fall warmly down his throat. The mayor pressed his thumb behind his ear and instructed for Stronghold to be brought in.

The door swung open and Albin stepped in first. Taylor followed. The big man had a white med-pad taped over his bad eye. He looked like a fool. At the very least, he could have found a more menacing looking patch. Kendall pursed his lips and Taylor stepped aside.

The next individual to enter was garbed in an enormous fur cape with a hood pulled over its wearer's head so that all that was visible was the sharp point of a chin. It could have been any number of wealthy merchants.

"Like my jacket, Kendall?" the caped figure said in a rich, amused voice.

"Yes. It is quite nice."

"It's not safe for me out in public these days. You never know who has you in their sights."

"You're safe here, Darros. Guns, after all, are outlawed on my station," Kendall said.

"Right," Darros said. "Then how'd I get this one in here?" He waggled a snub nosed pistol—it looked like a needle gun, but Stronghold's hand disappeared back into the folds of the fur cape before Kendall could get a good look.

"We need to have a bit of chit chat, you and I. N'est que pas?" Stronghold said as he cast the hood off. The mass of fur that hung over his shoulders made his head appear small. He unclasped the chain at his neck and the fur cascaded down his legs to pool around his feet like a mammalian waterfall. Revealed was a tall and slender man—not slender in the same sense that Kendall was slender. Kendall was all skin and bone and he knew it. This man was sinew and muscle. He was lean and lethal. It appeared that the needle gun wasn't the only weapon that Darros had brought aboard. He had several large blades sheathed at his side and another gun holstered beneath his arm. Kendall tried to picture Vegan attempting to relieve the man of his weapons and laughed out loud.

"Then sit, if you feel we need to talk. I even poured you a drink. After all, how long has it been?"

"Not long enough, Ezra. You know I hate this place."

"My good Darros. You wound me," Kendall said and laid a hand across his chest. Stronghold ignored the comment. He seated himself across from Kendall and hoisted the glass of bourbon, downed the contents in one shot, and slammed the glass back onto Kendall's desk with a hearty bang. Stronghold leaned back in the chair and kicked his feet up.

"Take a seat, Kendall. I promise this'll be brief."

Kendall did as he was asked. He didn't like being told what to do, but Darros was impulsive, flighty, and well armed.

"Numbers and guns, Ezra. I'm missing both," Darros said. "I find it hard to believe that all that crazy mining activity in Tireca has stopped. And my little colonial rebel pups in Habeos are facing another Core Sec offensive."

"The problem is," Kendall folded his hands around the crystal tumbler. "The problem is Crescent operations are currently being audited by Core Sec."

"Kendall, I could care less about the Core Sec *merde* on your station." Darros smiled. "If you aren't covering your trail, it's up to you to be more careful. I'm paying you to provide a service and I'm respecting your space, so to speak. If I really wanted to, Ezra, I could pull this station out from under you faster than you could say 'Don't shoot me in the face, Darros.'"

"It's not that simple," Kendall objected.

"Oui?" Darros waggled his brows and patted the gun holstered under his shoulder.

"One of my people might be wise to our operation. My salvage man. He's been hauling your leavings. I have not quite decided how I will deal with him. I do know that I have to do something before he gives too much information to this auditor."

"No quite decided?" Darros rolled his eyes. "Getting soft on me, are you?"

"Not in the slightest, Darros. It's like I said. Matters are more complicated with Core Sec auditing my station," Kendall said.

"Ezra, I'll do you a solid. You send my people coordinates within the next forty-eight hours. You send your salvage boy out to pick up the scraps as usual, and we'll take care of the rest. Accidents happen in space all the time. I'm not so much concerned with getting free ore as I am with the guns."

Kendall nodded. Gerald would bite—he was almost sure of it. The mayor smiled and downed of the last of his bourbon.

"Very well, Darros. I appreciate your willingness to help."

"Good. I expect you to return the favor. Get me those guns soon." Darros got to his feet and strolled to the bar. "You wouldn't mind me leaving with that fine bottle of alcohol would you? Space gets so very cold."

"Of course not." Kendall gestured to the bottles lined up on his bar. "Consider it yours."

"Bien, Kendall." Darros picked a bottle at random. It was the most expensive one in Kendall's collection. "This it, then?" Kendall smiled and nodded. Darros pulled the thick fur cloak back over his shoulders. He drew the hood over his head. "Forty-eight hours, Kendall. I'm being reasonable. You figure out how to work around Core Sec. I don't care if he's monitoring every single transmission coming out of this station. Send it out your asshole for all I care."

"You'll get your coordinates," Kendall said. He found himself weary of Stronghold's attitude. "It's time you left, Darros."

"It's past time I left."

And like that, Darros Stronghold was gone.

[PART XV]

"L Deck is presently being drained, but is still under up to a meter of water in some locations. The housing authority has issued a public statement that indicates, 'things could have been far worse.' Loss of life has been categorized as minimal. Mayor Kendall could not be reached for a comment." The newsfeed showed a reporter standing in waist deep water with long, auburn hair wet and matted to her head and shoulders. She was wearing rubber overalls on top of her flashy red suit and looked quite ridiculous. Water rained down behind her from guttering ceiling light panels—there was an occasional burst of sparks as electronics shorted out. Collector robots trudged through the water, towing rafts and ferrying people off the flooded residential deck. "There was a similar scene here on L Deck some fifteen years ago. The flood occurred in the middle of the night, causing what can only be described as Crescent's single worst tragedy. Now back to Frank with an update on sports… "

Donovan Cortez clicked off the LCD and looked to his daughter. Ina sat beside his bed with her hands in her lap and her concerned eyes on his face. Donovan wondered how long she had been sitting there.

"You sure you feel okay, Dad?" Donovan had insisted he was fine each time Ina had asked the question. This was the fifth, not that anyone was keeping score. Truth be told, Donovan wasn't feeling all that good. He was coming down with a bug that was sure to be nasty. The headaches, joint aches, and occasional vomiting were the least of his worries. He certainly wasn't going to tell her about his blackout on the lifeboat. Or the visual and auditory hallucinations that preceded it. He smiled his best reassuring smile and patted her hand. "Yes. Quite well. I've been staying up late reviewing the photos from your initial survey of the geological outpost. Fascinating stuff, to say the very least. Occult phenomena. It will require some looking into. When will you and Gerald be going back to the surface to visit the remaining site?"

"I don't know," Ina said. "I haven't been able to get in touch with Gerald."

"I wish you'd had the opportunity to spend more time down there. At least, I wish you could have returned with something I could hold in my hands."

Ina's demeanor changed almost immediately. She sighed and looked away. It was the reaction Donovan had expected. He felt a twinge of guilt about having spied on her, but she needed to learn a lesson about keeping things from him. He knew she had hidden *something* in her dresser. The timer on the food processor unit chimed. Lunch was done. Ina started to stand but he took her hand.

"Are you telling me about everything?"

Her brow creased with fine lines.

"Well, Dad. I don't quite know how to say this… "

Good, he thought, *come clean with me. Tell me the truth.*

"I," she hesitated a moment longer. Donovan waved his hand—the gesture said *get on with it.* Ina sighed. "I'm pregnant."

Oh yes, she is, this is very good news, a cold whisper rose from the depths of his consciousness. The sound of the voice was distinctly *violet.* Yet, at the same time the thought occurred to him, he realized he didn't know what it meant.

"You're… pregnant?" Donovan's face twisted and his mouth fell open. He felt a tremor in the hand that held hers, but the sensation was distant. How was she pregnant? It didn't make sense. "How pregnant? Who is the father? The only many I've ever seen you with is… Is it Gerald? How… " Anger rose on a surge of stomach acid, filling his throat and igniting a firestorm in his chest. His head began to pound.

"Dad? Are you okay?" Ina grabbed his arm. There was an edge of panic to her voice.

"What. Yes. I'm fine. Why?"

"The color went right out of your face. You stopped mid-sentence and just started rubbing your temple and muttering."

"I did?" He couldn't remember what he'd been so angry about. He felt the emotion fading. "I've been having headaches from the lack of sleep. Maybe I had better lay down." Ina removed the pillows that had been propping him up on the bed and he reclined fully. "Ina," he asked, "who is the father?"

"Dad, it's not Gerald. I'm too… never mind. It's not Gerald. It might have happened before you and I even left the University. Do you remember Dimetrius Hyland?"

"Your lab assistant?" Donovan asked, flabbergasted. A bolt of pain lanced through his skull. He clenched his jaw and let out a groan.

"Should I call a doctor, Dad?" There was a quaver in Ina's voice, like she was about to break into tears.

"I *am* a doctor," he said with a weak smile. "How soon you forget that. I'm fine, Ina. This is just a lot to swallow."

"Please try not to worry about it, Dad. I'll figure it out. Remember, I am a grown woman. I'm almost thirty." She placed her hand atop his. "Get some rest. The food isn't going anywhere—and it's nothing exciting. Just some prefab lasagna I picked up in the bazaar. Heat it up when you're hungry. Go to sleep. I'm going to try and find Gerald and see when we can go planet-side again." Donovan appreciated the effort she was putting forth to sound strong, but he could see the concern swimming in her cerulean eyes.

A baby? *This is good news,* Donovan thought. But for some reason, the news terrified him. It terrified him because the part of him that was genuinely thrilled was the same deep-buried part of his mind that was making him feel sick and twitchy. Ina lingered; she studied his face closely. Donovan didn't like the sound of her going off in search of Gerald but he acquiesced and waved her off. "Go. I'll be fine."

And he was fine.

[•••]

At least for the first forty-five minutes after she was gone, he was fine. He had managed to fall asleep. He dreamed of great, rocky landscapes. Of shallow seas and of tall, craggy mountains. A thin violet light clung to the scenery before him like luminous fog, skewing his perception as if he were a passenger traveling in bubble of purple glass. Then it came to him—he was seeing through another set of eyes. Donovan licked lips that were not his own; they were salty and cold. He looked down at the hands that were not his hands—they were gloved in, was it leather? This other *self* was moving fast. Not walking, not running either. Wheels spun below him. He flew across the landscape at high speed now. Control did not belong to Donovan. *The other* was in control. The purple view showed ground racing by. The view shifted up to a long flat building.

Movement halted when he reached the building. Donovan watched as he entered the structure through a sliding glass door. The door slid closed, Donovan caught a glimpse of the letters. *Anrar III Outpost 13.*

"Is it ready yet?" a voice asked. It was a voice of a woman—lightly accented and sweet sounding. The eyes through which Donovan watched swung to the left, to a short woman with cropped red hair—Donovan knew it was red, even though it looked dark grey in the violet haze.

I'm experiencing someone else's memory, Donovan realized. *I'm dreaming someone else's life.*

The woman blinked up into the eyes of the other. An object was held up in front of the lady's face, a palm-sized carving—of what? A beetle? No. Not just an ordinary beetle. A scarab. Yes. It was a dagger shaped as a scarab.

"How did you manage to shape the sanguinite?" the woman asked. "That shit is harder than our diamond bits."

"Surgical lasers. Took forever. But I think the key is ready." This was the voice of the other. It was rough—the timbre of a smoker.

"Do you think that it will open her? First cut must be made with the stone."

"I know it will," the other said.

"So, then. It's sharp?" the female asked. She took an eager step forward. "Sharp enough to cut through flesh?"

"Of course."

The gloved hand holding the sanguinite scarab arced in a sudden path across the female's throat. She took a step back, blinking in surprise, but she was okay. Donovan thought it a feigned attack, but then a necklace of dark beads appeared around her throat. She opened her mouth and blood poured down over her chin. She tottered backwards; her head fell back and a blaze of violet light spilled from the ear-to-ear gash.

Donovan sat up in the bed. Sweat dribbled down his cheeks from hair that was plastered to his scalp. A raging fever had turned his body into a furnace. The wall clock was flashing eights; the power had gone out at some point. How long had he been sleeping? It didn't feel very long. A glance to his PDA told him it was 3:45 a.m. The apartment sounded empty. It felt empty. He called for Ina and there was no answer. Donovan got out of bed and started toward the bathroom, but instead he altered course and went to his dresser. There, he pulled open the underwear drawer and removed the palm-sized hunk of sanguinite. Donovan couldn't help but laugh at the foolishness of storing it there.

This is no laughing matter.

"Who said that?" Donovan whirled around.

You did, you old fool.

Yes. The voice belonged to him.

The realization caused him to startle. He fumbled the piece of sanguinite and it sailed through the air. He snatched out for the stone but it fell through his hands, clattered to the floor, and slid under the dresser. Donovan cursed at the rock and then at the dresser. He got onto his hands and knees and squinted so that he could see beneath the big piece of furniture. It was dark in the small space, but he could see the shape of the strange rock. He thought he could reach it—sure, it wasn't under there too far. It was just a question of whether or not he could get his hand into the tight space. Donovan wiggled his fingers into the thick carpet. The tips of his index and middle finger brushed against the cool, smooth stone. Almost got it.

Dry, leathery fingers wrapped around his wrist. The grip was cold and vise-tight, and yanked him forward with such force that the fake wood base of the dresser splintered and dug into his arm. He cried out and tried to crawl backwards but he was jerked forward again. The dresser tottered unsteadily. The phantom hand let go and Donovan rolled out of the way just in time. The dresser fell forward and slammed down hard, right where he had been. The slate top snapped off with a loud pop and the contents of the drawers spilled across the carpeted floor. Donovan lay panting for what felt like an eternity. The fever had fully consumed him now and his heart raced. His arm was bloodied and bruised. *I couldn't have been grabbed*, Donovan thought. *No way*. He had jammed his arm beneath the dresser out of eagerness. Or worse, maybe the spasm had been a seizure. He sat up as his breath returned to him and surveyed the scattered mess of trinkets and undergarments.

The small, black leather case containing his surgical implements sat amidst the disarray. He hadn't opened the case in years—it was a souvenir from his other life and he had no use for the set any longer, but sentimentality made it impossible for him to get rid of it. He crawled over to the monogrammed box and picked it up. The weight of the case felt good and familiar. Now, holding the surgical tools, Donovan felt the sudden urge to operate. But operate on what? As if to answer, a corona of violet light spread around his hand, numbing it slightly. Whispers circled his head like gnats.

The voices wanted him to act. They drew his attention to the spilled dresser. To the mess beyond it. The liquid purple light flowed up from his palm like a glowing tentacle and snaked its way across the floor, through the debris, and over the dresser to the other side. There was a flash and then the light was gone.

Donovan went to where the light had pointed and picked up the sanguinite with his uninjured left hand. The weight of the stone had a peculiar familiarity to it, familiar as the weight of the surgical tools. Now he had something to operate on. Something to sculpt.

He worked on the stone in near darkness. His expertise manipulated the delicate lasers of his surgical tools, but another power guided them—he was only watching them work. Violet haze blanketed everything Donovan looked at. Unlike in his dream, this time his own being was the source. The Violet wrapped him up in a shimmering blanket of fog. It was insane, but it felt wonderful. Donovan had never felt such a sense of purpose as he did watching the tiny lances of light cut away small bits of the hard, red stone. With each pass of the lasers, a new bit of detail was revealed—the curve of a wing, a pincer.

As he worked, his eyelids started to feel heavy. Each time they dropped, the purple light flared and he felt the urge to vomit. The sensation was fleeting, always quickly replaced by a burst of energy. This went on all night, until every muscle save those in his hands and arms twitched with exhaustion. Now the bursts of light did not make him feel exhilaration, only illness. He ran his thumb over the thin edge of the sculpture; the action drew a drop of blood. The scarab was sharp. The work was complete. Donovan collapsed from his office chair onto the floor, and vomited for the next twenty minutes. When the sickness subsided, he felt himself drifting toward unconsciousness. He hoped Ina wouldn't find him there. It wasn't that he didn't want her to seem him prone and covered in his own biofluids; he didn't want her to find the scarab.

[Part XVI]

Heathen's was the last place Gerald wanted to be, and Albin Catlier and Jacob Raney were the last people that Gerald wanted to be there with. Gerald was still water-logged and fatigued from the good times in the rain on Anrar III. The whole experience was already becoming hazy—like the border line between an alcohol blackout and memory. Sure, the recollections were there, but the pictures were fuzzy around the edges and Gerald didn't quite believe it had been him in the starring role. He couldn't. The air had been bad down there on Anrar III. That was all there was to it. It had to be why Core Sec never attempted to colonize the place—it was just a shitty rock in a shitty part of space.

Gerald tapped the beer bottle. It was an absent and impatient gesture. He had been sitting with Catlier and Raney for more than thirty minutes, and neither man had said more than two words. Raney spat out black tobacco spit on the floor and Catlier chain-smoked and stared off into the crowd. *They're trying to make me uncomfortable,* Gerald thought. *Kendall sent them here to make me squirm.* Gerald overcame the urge to roll his eyes. Instead, he tipped the dark bottle to his lips and drained the contents. A group of teenagers dressed in black entered through the batwing doors. From behind the bar, Maerl yelled at them to leave, shouting that they weren't old enough to come into the place. The kids tossed a stack of black flyers on one of the tables and ran out. Maerl shook his head and went back to tending bar. Gerald looked at his beer bottle.

"My beer is done. If you boys have nothing to say, I'm done here, too. Not much in the socializing mood." Gerald started to get to his feet. Catlier reached out and grabbed his wrist with a dry, calloused hand.

"We're not done here just yet, Mr. Evans." Albin flashed his teeth. Jacob Raney smiled as if on cue. Raney would still have been an ugly son of a bitch, even if his teeth weren't stained shit brown from all the tobacco chewing. Gerald slumped back into his seat. What was it with Kendall and ugly employees?

"In that case, I hope you're buying." Gerald signaled to the server for another beer.

Albin snorted and shrugged.

"The tab is on our good mayor," he said.

"Whatever you say, hombre." Gerald took one of Catlier's cigarettes and lit it casually.

"Kendall has work for you," Raney said at last. It was apparent that Raney's announcement had irritated his partner. Two small circles of red flared on Catlier's pale cheeks.

"Yeah? Been a little while," Gerald said. "I was starting to think I was fired."

"Well," Albin said. "That all depends."

"Depends on what?" Gerald raised a brow.

"Depends on what you told that Core Sec piggie," Raney said, and laughed. A trickle of tobacco spit ran down his chin. He wiped it away with the back of his hand.

"I had nothing to tell that guy," Gerald said. These two were boneheads. So long as Gerald kept his cool, they wouldn't be able to tell truth from lie and back around to the other side. His feet ached. He wanted to get out of his boots. That was his primary concern.

"You sure?" Catlier leaned forward, his lips pulling back in a snarl. "You real sure?"

"I'm real sure. I told him that I didn't know shit, which, really, is the truth. I want to pick up my paycheck at the end of the day, just like everyone else. I'm not going to rock the boat," Gerald said and wiggled his toes in his boots. Catlier looked over to Raney. Raney shrugged.

"Raney, there, he isn't the brightest globe in the chandelier, but he's got a sense about him. Like a human lie detector. Ain't that right, Raney?" Albin asked.

"Yep."

"He can sniff out a lie. What do you say about Gerald? He lyin', Jacob?"

"I don't think so, Albin. He's bein' straight with us," Raney hawked another glistening, brown glob of tobacco spit.

"Straight as can be, pal," Gerald affirmed.

Catlier's hand disappeared into the bulky, feathered jacket he wore; the ridiculous garment made him look like a big, black turkey. The hand returned with a data wafer which he slid across the table. Gerald placed his hand atop the wafer, palm down, and slid it the rest of the way across the tabletop and into his breast pocket. *Things have become awfully cloak and dagger,* Gerald mused.

"There are coordinates on that wafer. Upload'm to your ship's computer. Do this job and you're done. Kendall has decided you are a liability, but he's in a bind. And lucky for you, he can't kill you while Core Sec is here," Albin said, and winked. "Go to those coordinates and await further instruction. Once you finish the job, he wants you off Crescent in forty-eight hours. That is, unless you're spotted talking to the Core Sec auditor again. If that's the case, you'll be off the station when Raney and I find you."

Gerald patted his pocket and smiled. He would show up on time and as instructed. Bean's cameras would be rolling and the DVR would be recording. If proof was what Swaren needed to take Kendall out, Gerald would gladly hand over an optical disc chock full of evidence. Gerald would be flying free by that night, no doubt.

"All right, then." Catlier stood and dropped his eyes to his companion. Raney stood and spat a glistening wad of nastiness close to the toe of Gerald's boot.

"Tomorrow night, Mr. Evans. Seventeen-hundred hours. You be at those coordinates. Fuck it up and the next time Kendall sends us to you, it won't be a data wafer you'll be receiving."

"I'm sure not." Gerald said and tapped his pocket again. "Seventeen-hundred hours. I'll be there with bells on."

Raney's brow creased. He looked confused. Albin gestured to the exit with a cock of his head and Raney started obediently in that direction. Catlier followed, pausing briefly to add, "Thanks for the beers."

Gerald heard Raney asking the tall man, "*bells?*" as the pair stepped through the batwings.

"Ah shit," Gerald said, realizing that the drinks had been on his dime all along. *If I continue to be this sharp, I'm gonna find it harder to stay alive.*

A job, or a trap—either way, Gerald was getting tired of feeling out of control. If he was flying into a trap, at least it was his goddamn decision. Gerald approached the batwing doors and took one of the flyers the teens had left behind on his way. It said *Believe in the power of prayer. A change is coming!* An email address was printed on the back of the flyer, and that was it. The religious freaks seemed to be everywhere lately. Just the other day, Gerald had caught them trying to leave the flyers on Bean's viewports. A cult seemed to fit the times quite nicely. *Par for the fuckin' course,* Gerald thought.

[•••]

"I'm not even going to try and guess what you said to Kendall that got him so crazy. He wanted me to fire you, Griffin. I finally convinced him that taking you off active duty was a better idea. I told him there was too much going on here lately and that we might need you. He still wasn't happy, but he gave in." Captain Benedict frowned as they made their way down the corridor. He tapped the glowing screen of his data pad. "But, Marisa, it's your lucky day. Dock security is understaffed. Everyone is getting goddamned sick on me. I need to reinstate you in the same breath where I said I'd bench you."

Marisa didn't speak. She didn't know what to say about any of it. She knew there had been an altercation with Kendall, but the how and why of it remained a mystery to her. One minute, the mayor had been in her apartment; the next, he had been hurrying out the door and cursing her name. Taylor's face was bruised and bloodied. Both his eyes had been swollen shut. Did she hurt Taylor? She didn't know. The only clear memory Marisa had was of waking up on the floor to the sound of the wall terminal ringing. It had been HQ calling to let her know she was in deep shit. After that, she hadn't been able to make any outgoing calls or even leave her apartment. She was locked in. Her attempts to contact Nigel via PDA had been equally useless. It took Captain Benedict's housecall to prove to her that her door still opened.

"I know you're hot-blooded, Mari," Benedict said in his most fatherly of voices as they walked to security HQ side by side, "and I know Kendall can be a bit hands-on with the ladies." They stopped outside the bulkhead that led into HQ. Benedict crossed his arms over his chest and narrowed his eyes at her. "I know for a fact that he has taken a fancy to you. I have no doubt you set him straight." Benedict smiled his approval, even though he couldn't flat out say it. "But, that kind of behavior can't be encouraged. It'll be my head next." Benedict paused. "Have you been sleeping better lately?"

"Yes. Quite a bit, actually," she said, but she could see in his eyes that he didn't believe her. He shrugged as they stepped inside. Marisa followed Captain Benedict into the monitor station-turned-office.

"Report to the docks at fifteen-hundred hours. I've informed Captain Swaren that you will no longer be able to assist him, due to our staffing difficulties. You're all mine again, Mari."

"Really?"

"Captain Swaren had some very nice things to say about you. And because of your hard work, Marisa, I haven't had to have more than a single meeting with the man. Unfortunately, that's going to have to change," Benedict said.

"Do you think that Kendall didn't like the fact that someone who knows Crescent's idiosyncrasies was working with Swaren—that someone being me?" She suddenly wanted to tell Captain Benedict everything—Kendall's blackmail, the carthine habit, and all the other crazy shit. But her mouth stayed shut.

Benedict grunted. He stepped to the monitor displays and began to cycle through the various security feeds.

"Countless lives are on this station—residents and transients alike. They depend on *us*, Core Security, to make this a safe place. Kendall wants nothing more than to keep his record clean and keep his station running smoothly. Sure, some of his methods may be questionable—draconian, even—and yes, they may not follow Core Sec's standard operating procedures to a tee. But Crescent has been without major incident for more than fifteen years. And with the level of traffic that comes through here, that is a big accomplishment. Especially on the frontier. Kendall is old school, but the ship he runs is a tight one. He's got nothing to hide from Swaren and last I checked, womanizing wasn't a crime under Core Sec law."

Marisa nodded. She was happy to get back to dock rotation. She didn't want to be left to her own devices; not when she was dealing with blackouts and lost time. *That's what happens when you stare at a wall,* she thought. *You fall asleep and you end up in strange places.* Activity would help her as she eased off the carthine, too.

"All right, Lieutenant. That's all for now. Report to Walter Vegan at fifteen-hundred hours. Don't be late."

She nodded. "I won't be late."

"I know you won't be," he said and smiled. He waved her out and she took her leave.

Marisa passed Albin Catlier and Jacob Raney when she left HQ. Catlier watched her with his unnervingly blue eyes. He dipped his chin in salutation as she passed. She didn't acknowledge the greeting. Raney hawked a ball of blackish spit as she went by them. She continued on for a meter or so and then stopped and turned, preparing to deliver a scathing comment, but the pair stepped through the security office bulkhead before she had the chance. Raney's beat-up duster trailed behind him in a dark wake and almost got caught in the closing door.

Strange.

Marisa began to walk again, but her eyes were still on the door to HQ. She turned fully forward and ran right into a thin, pale woman. Wisps of blonde hair framed a delicate and surprised face. Time slammed to a standstill. Déjà vu, more consuming than she had ever experienced, gripped Marisa by the throat. She knew this girl. She'd seen her somewhere. Where? The same look of recognition was in the stranger's blue eyes. Marisa smiled uneasily.

"I'm… " she said.

"Sorry," the blonde girl replied.

"Should have watched… " Marisa began

"… where I was going. Right," the blonde finished. She smiled the same hesitant grin Marisa wore on her face and then went on her way. Marisa watched her go.

[•••]

Where do I know her from? Ina asked herself as she broke away from the dark haired woman. Her eyes had been like drops of jade. You don't forget eyes like that. Not for a second. You might forget a face, a name, but eyes like that—no way. Maybe they'd bumped into each other before. Ina shook her head as she hurried down the corridor. The medical parcel she clutched to her chest contained meds for her father and that was far more important than déjà vu. He had been sick for a few days now. The vomiting had stopped, thank god, but he still ran a fever. He was dehydrated. Donovan Cortez hadn't wanted to go to a doctor, so Ina went for him. He wouldn't be happy that she went to the clinic against his wishes, but hopefully he would take the meds that had been prescribed for him.

Ina stepped into the dim apartment. The halo-globes burned low, casting diffuse shadows between the pools of low yellow light. The air handlers hissed softly overhead. The music she had left playing—

something by Erick Haddyrein, the vatter—had been turned off in her absence. That meant Dad was out of bed. An encouraging sign. But, if Ina knew her father at all, he was already over-extending himself. She'd put an end to that right away.

Donovan's bed was empty. The bluish-green light cast by the bedside holoclock created dark valleys and bright peaks on the wrinkled and vacant sheets. She set the medicine on the nightstand and pulled the sheets neatly into place. Ina was about to leave the room when she heard a growl from above her. Ina lifted her eyes. What she saw made her take a step backwards. One hand went to her mouth; the other flailed out blindly for the light and, in the process, knocked the alarm clock off the night stand. The blue-green light danced across the ceiling's darkened light panels. There was her father, on the ceiling. His head lolled from side to side; his lips were peeled back. He growled again and Ina took another step back. This time she knocked a chair over. Her father's eyes shot open and locked with her own. The dilated pupils swam with a milky, violet glow. Something fluttered in Ina's skull. Red flashed across her vision and her heart murmured in her chest. Warmth rose in her mind and a sense of otherness began to peel away her consciousness like filmy sheets. Reality shifted and wavered as if she were viewing the room through a wall of water. Red water. Ina closed her eyes and willed the sensation to be gone.

"A weak vessel. Old," her father said in a voice that was not his own. "But the right knowledge. It won't be long now. Unity."

"No," she heard herself say, "it won't be long now."

"Not so long as we have waited," her father said.

Ina bit down hard on her tongue and the salty taste of blood filled her mouth. The pain cleared her head and she shrieked. Her father fell from the ceiling, bounced off the bed, and landed beside it on the floor. He moaned and retched. Ina hurried to him and fell to her knees at his side, her fear banished for the time being. She held his shoulders and could feel the heat of his skin through the thin nightshirt.

"So purple here, isn't it, Ina? So pretty. Your mother. Her favorite color was purple." He turned his face up to hers and smiled. His breath smelled like vomit.

Ina closed her eyes and behind her eyelids she saw a glass prism. Ribbons of violet, red, and black lanced through its center. The imagery halted and replayed itself in reverse. The colors went back through the prism to congeal into single, depthless shadow that glittered with distant lights.

[•••]

The familiar asteroid field was backlit by the blue glow of Tireca. The light of the swollen, azure star filtered through ice particles and refracted into a glittering rainbow of brilliance. Bean sailed through the rocky debris.

"Captain, I am reading ship signatures up ahead. Ore haulers, based on their transponder signatures. There is something else out there, well up ahead. Something big, but scans are fuzzy due to interference caused by the density of this field."

"No idea what's out there, Bean?"

"No, Captain. None whatsoever."

"Slow us down until we can confirm what it is. At the first sign of hostiles, you get us back to the jump gate. Got it?"

"It's my hull at risk here, Captain, so you won't need to tell me twice."

"Your hull and my hide, Bean," Gerald said.

"Captain. Raiders have entered the asteroid field." Gerald's eyes snapped to the radar. Six blips pulsed red and closed in on Bean's location.

"Spoke too damn soon. Bean, can we warp out of here?" Gerald stomach tied itself into a knot.

"Negative, Captain. The field is too dense. We need to find a clearing."

"Shit. Give me control of the ship," Gerald commanded. A panel in the floor whined open and Bean's seldom-used flight yoke ascended with a howling whine. Gerald took the wheel and they were off, sailing past freighter-sized ice hunks with speed that approached deadly. The raiders were in pursuit and coming in fast. There was no way Bean could outrun them.

"Captain, I have identified the ships as Class III spiders. They have armed their weapons. They are still out of range, but won't be for long. Six seconds. Hopefully, they will have a hard time getting a lock with all the interference." A cluster of fist-sized space rocks glanced off the viewport with a resounding series of bangs. "And Captain, please watch where you're going."

"I know, Bean!" Gerald snapped.

The comm system chimed.

"Incoming call, Captain. From Crescent."

"Put it through, Bean," Gerald said.

The comm squawked with a burst of static. "Gerald, this is Nigel

Swaren. Where are you going?"

"Nigel, I'm in Tireca... but this really isn't a good time." Gerald said.

"Did Kendall send you out there?"

"Yes, Nigel... .but I really can't talk right now," Gerald answered through clenched teeth.

An explosion throttled Bean. Gerald nearly lost control of the ship.

"Captain, we aren't being fired upon directly. They are targeting the asteroids around us." Bean said.

"So this will all look like a nasty accident. That is, if there is anything left. Bean, I hope you're rolling the cameras."

"Yes, Captain," Bean replied.

Bean shuddered violently and pulled hard to starboard. The ship began to spin and Gerald thought for a moment that it was all over, but he managed to pull them back on course. Asteroids detonated around them. The horrible sound of thousands of impacts—ranging in size from pebbles to small boulders—filled the bridge.

"Send me your exact coordinates ASAP!" Nigel shouted over the din.

"Bean, do it!"

"Done, Captain."

"Receiving," Nigel's voice replied.

Bean screamed out of the asteroid field's main body and into an open slice of space. Rock fragments, dust, sparks, and smoke trailed in their wake. Ahead of them a hulking structure laced with a lattice-work of construction scaffolding floated against the stars. Several smaller structures floated in orbit.

"Ore refineries and fabrication plants," Bean said. "The ships up ahead—those are ore haulers. The large structure is some kind of station, but nothing registered in the Core Sec database."

"Jesus Christ," Nigel said on the comm. "Gerald, get the fuck out of there."

"Sentry guns. Class VI Smart-auto cannons," Bean chimed in as the salvage hauler raced further into the clearing. "Big ones, and they are going online. Lock acquisition in progress. They are targeting the raiders. Sentry guns firing. Two of the raider ships destroyed."

Gerald cheered. "Ha ha. Eat that, you motherfuckers!"

"Captain. The sentry guns are now attempting to lock onto to us. Fifteen seconds to target acquisition. We are in a clear enough spot to warp out of here."

“Holy…” Gerald’s breath caught in his throat and he coughed. “Bean, get us out of here.” He could see one of the sentry guns clearly. It was mounted on a large, oblong asteroid. The turret end was glowing dull white, but that light was increasing as what Gerald assumed was an ion cannon prepared to launch super-excited death. Bean banked hard and began to pull away. Beads of sweat broke out on Gerald’s forehead. Bean’s near-light engines hummed as they wound themselves up to catapult the ship out of the area.

“Captain. The remaining spider has locked onto us.”

Bean raced toward the spider. Gerald could see the round ship growing in size in the viewport. Wisps of blue light arced between the glowing ends of the spider’s lethal plasmacasters.

“Get out of there now!” Nigel shouted.

“Sentry guns are firing,” Bean said.

The raider exploded.

Gerald closed his eyes.

[•••]

“Everything okay here, Captain Swaren?” Nigel pivoted on the stool. Captain Benedict stood in the open doorway to the communications station. His frame was a dark silhouette in the light falling from the main room of the security office.

“Everything is fine, Captain,” Nigel said.

“Really? I heard you shouting.”

“Bad connection. I had to raise my voice to be heard, that’s all,” Nigel lied.

“I see. That happens out here sometimes, yes. I know I’ve said this before, but should you need anything, don’t hesitate to find me,” Benedict said.

“Thank you, Captain. I appreciate that.” Nigel managed a smile. Benedict lingered in the doorway for a few seconds longer and then departed. The door slid shut. How long had Captain Benedict been there? Nigel hadn’t even heard him approach. There was something about Crescent that dulled the senses. He turned back to the comm terminal and spoke into the microphone, an archaic looking device enclosed in a wire mesh.

“Gerald. Are you there?”

Nothing but static came in response. Nigel sat back in his seat and cursed under his breath. He tapped the console with growing concern and impatience. Nigel contemplated standing up and pacing when a quavering voice came over the speaker.

"Fuck a duck. What was all that about?" It was Gerald.

"That was all about Galatea, Gerald," Nigel said and heaved a sigh of relief. "Are you okay?"

"I'm okay. My pants are not, if you catch my drift. Are you going to tell me what that was?"

"Yes. I have every intention of doing so. But not over the comm. Call me on my PDA when you arrive safely back at Crescent. And please do keep a low profile. It was no mistake that you ended up where you did. You were not supposed survive that."

"No shit. Kendall and his boys sent me out there to make sure those guns were working." Gerald's voice lost no sarcasm over the distance of the transmission. "They were fucking working," Gerald added.

"You knew it was a trap, but you went out there anyway?"

"Yeah. I went out there anyway. You needed evidence. And I needed my out. Catch my drift? And now that I've got some data to give you, I need to fuel up and get off the station as soon as I can."

"We'll talk when you get back," Nigel said, and ended the transmission. Kendall had the big secrets. Did the mayor know about Galatea and Nigel's mission on Crescent? Nigel was screwed if he did. After all, Crescent was Kendall's station.

And this was Kendall's piece of space.

[PART XVII]

Jacob Raney was not particularly smart. Nor was he particularly good looking. He didn't have all that much going for him, only that he was good at following orders and that he had fallen under the wing of Albin Catlier—his best friend and mentor. With Albin, Jacob had bounced from one system to another performing all sorts of jobs and meeting all sorts of folks. Jacob Raney wasn't spry or smart, but he was good with a gun, good with a knife, and really good with all shapes and sizes of metal pipes.

Jacob followed Albin down one of many identical residential corridors. Albin had his hands stuffed into the pockets of his long, leather coat. He seemed to be thinking. Albin was always thinking. Jacob figured that was why he was in charge of their little duo—and sometimes in charge of bigger groups, too. Albin stopped at door marked 16 B and held up a hand for Raney to stop, which he did immediately. Raney felt the first tingle of excitement blossom across his scrotum and shoot up his spine. The sensation caused the tiny hairs on the back of his neck to stand on end.

"This is it," Albin said as he lit a cigarette.

"Think he's expecting us, Albin?" Jacob asked.

"No. I don't. He's a dog. Stupid. Loyal. He won't see this coming."

"Yeah," Raney agreed. Albin was smart. He always said intelligent things. Albin thumbed he buzzer. The door slid open part way. Taylor's large, puggish face gazed out sheepishly, sporting a patch over one eye and a nasty bruise on his cheek. Like a sad dog.

"Albin. Jacob. What are you doing here?" he asked.

"We're here to talk to you, Taylor. I think it'd be wise to open that door all the way and let us in," Albin said, his voice undeniably sure.

"Okay." There was no menace in Taylor's face; it was odd to see him that way. All the girth and none of the mean. The door slid open and Taylor took a step back to allow them to enter. When the door closed, Raney clobbered Taylor over head with the titanium pipe that had been concealed in the folds of his duster. Taylor grunted and went down on his knees; he wrapped his hands around his head protectively.

"No. Please don't do this!" he begged.

"This is so unlike you, Taylor. Has it really come to this? Everyone used to be afraid of you. Once word gets out about what happened with Griffin… " Albin just shook his head. "The way I look at it—Kendall is my *investment.* You're not keeping him safe."

"I'll do better!" Taylor bellowed.

"I still feel my investment is at risk."

Fresh tears streamed out of Taylor's one semi-functioning eye. Raney gripped the pipe tighter.

"Please?" Taylor's eye blinked and Raney clubbed him over the head. Jacob's heart was pumping fast in his chest now. He hit Taylor in the side. There was a loud, satisfying crack as the former bodyguard's ribs broke.

"We're putting you out of your misery, Taylor. You've got no purpose now. Why suffer?" Albin said around the filter of his cigarette.

Taylor rolled on his back and began to shout. Jacob swung the wide end of the pipe in a devastating arc that slammed across Taylor's open mouth. The cries of protest became choked gurgles as Taylor's teeth and jaw shattered; tiny bits of enamel lodged themselves in his windpipe. Taylor clutched at his throat, gagged and sputtered. The man-mountain's constitution was impressive, but it was almost over now. Jacob looked over to Albin, who nodded, and Raney began to hammer Taylor's body with repeated blows, One. Two. Three. Four. Until the man lay twitching, the life pummeled out of him.

[•••]

The abandoned Belmont High School auditorium was quiet. Every so often, the rustle of some unseen, refuse-dwelling creature—the kind of voiceless animal that seeks out the rotted corpses of long abandoned spaces—broke the silence. The vacant floor sloped up to a row of poorly boarded doors. The seats had been ripped out many years ago. Gerald wondered why they had stopped at the seats instead of leveling the whole place.

"This is Galatea station," Nigel said and activated the holo-projector that sat atop the folding table. A shimmering star field blossomed above the round projector. Through the projection, Gerald watched Marisa at the opposite end of the table. The blue glow of the image made her look rather like a holograph, herself. The projector zoomed in on the 3D rendering of a big, circular space station. The hull, cream colored and pristine, was dotted with litany of glowing windows. Starships came and went from the slowly rotating station. "Galatea is the future waypoint between colonized Core Sec space and the frontier, including New Juno and beyond. She is to be a fully fitted outpost, complete with refineries, hydroponics and traditional agriculture, resorts, and a full marketplace. Galatea represents the next generation trading and supply conduit." Swaren leaned back in his chair and steepled his fingers. His hazel eyes moved from Gerald to Marisa. Gerald tapped his chin three times and looked at the floor. A yellowing flyer, curled at the edges, lay on the dirty stage planks. The fuzzy picture on the flyer showed two kids, one skinny and one round-faced. Time and mold had eaten away their features, but their names were clear—Brian Lavalle and William Mullen. The boys had been missing for, according to the flyer, some fifteen years. Marisa spoke.

"Why do we need two fully-fitted space stations within one jump of each other? Seems like Core Sec would be spreading its resources thin," Marisa said, and then paused and shook her head.

"You are correct." Swaren rocked forward; he placed his hands on the conference table. "There is no need for two space stations. That is why Crescent is to be decommissioned." Gerald nodded. In truth, he was surprised that Nigel had not yet told Marisa the news.

"Did you know about this, Gerry?" Marisa asked, and Gerald didn't answer. He clucked his tongue and looked at the glowing hologram that floated above the table, and then back at the flyer at his feet.

"There's more," Nigel said. "The Habeos jump gate, which is getting on in years, is to be decommissioned as well. This should eliminate most, if not all, of our current raider problems."

"If the Habeos jump gate is closed off, Habeos will be cut off from the seventeen systems. There's people on Habeos. Families," Marisa said.

"Habeos is militant and better armed with each passing month. That colony belongs more to Darros Stronghold than it does to Core Sec. Let him take care of them," Swaren stated matter-of-factly. "We close off the gates to Habeos and we're shutting the door in Stronghold's face. The loss is negligible to Core Sec and the colonization efforts. Now, let me show you something else." Swaren called up a new image—this one showed a sector map of the Tireca system. Asteroid fields were shaded in pulsing green. Brilliant azure, gold, and pink blobs of light floated amoeba-like in the green field. "The blue, gold, and pink areas are highly rich in the specific ore types used for fabricating Galatea's primary components. These asteroid fields are dense and debris-thick. High risk for any mining and hauling efforts. We've lost more than a few ships out there. But in the past three months, we've lost more ships than we have in the past year." Swaren waved his hand over the holo-projector's terminal and several red circles appeared throughout the ore rich sections of the asteroid field. "These are the last known contact points of several ships that have been lost in the last month. Lost without a trace. Core Sec figured they were obliterated by accidental collisions." Purple squares appeared beside the red circles. "These squares represent salvage runs that you were sent on, Gerald. What did you retrieve on these salvage runs?"

"Mining ships. Haulers. Drillers," Gerald replied.

Nigel smirked.

"Yes. I'm sure it will come to you as no surprise that these mining locations were secret," Nigel said to Marisa. "We—Core Sec—didn't want Stronghold's raiders getting wind of the mining locations and attacking our ships. It would have slowed down progress. And we didn't have the resources to pour into increased patrols. Not enough manpower out here. Now, about Galatea itself—it's far harder to mask the station's location. But there are sentry guns there that are programmed to destroy anything armed, and anything that gets too close without a pre-designated transponder signal."

"And Kendall knew all of this. He sent me out there to get blown away so I couldn't spill the beans to you," Gerald said.

"It certainly looks that way, doesn't it?" Nigel said.

"So, then, what's next? It's apparent Kendall has it out for all three of us, one way or another," Marisa said.

"The grand scheme is to remove Kendall from office before he can cause more damage. How we go about doing that is a different story. We've obtained enough legal proof that I can swing it. The Galatea project transcends almost all politics, so there is no problem going after Kendall directly. And on top of what Gerald has just provided, I have also uncovered substantial proof that weapons were being fabricated on Crescent as recently as last month. No number of connections will get Kendall's head off the chopping block now," Nigel said and laughed.

"What we need to do now is determine where the loyalty of the officers on this station lies." Swaren turned his eyes to Marisa. "That is where you come in. Do you think you can determine your comrades' willingness to take part in a coup?"

"I'll check it out, sure, but," Marisa hesitated and brushed a stray lock of dark hair from her forehead, "I think Captain Benedict will be on our side. I know him. He is a good man. And all the officers on the station look up to him."

"Well. Captain Benedict may be all we need. Find out where his heart lies," Swaren said.

"And what about me?" Gerald asked.

"I'd recommend you lay low for a while, Gerald. At least until we get the Kendall situation all wrapped up. You've done enough."

"I'd just as soon leave Crescent," Gerald said.

"We all would," Marisa said with conviction.

"Gerald, I suggest you keep yourself hidden until I can get you off the station safely," Nigel said and then stood up. "That's it. Marisa you know what to do."

Marisa and Gerald got to their feet and exchanged glances across the table.

[•••]

Main Street was nearly deserted, save for a few stray cult members placing flyers on the darkened windows of closed business. Sun globes oozed a low, azure light. The air was chilly. Heathen's lay up head of them, the neon sign flickering through a haze. A collector robot ambled down the boulevard, collecting trash as it went.

"What do you make of them?" Gerald asked, turning his head to watch a flyer flutter to the ground.

Marisa shrugged and sighed. "These freaks have been on Crescent for years. They call themselves the Aphotic. Some kind of church. Cult shit, if you ask me. But they haven't caused too many problems other than irritating people. They're brought into HQ every once in a while on solicitation charges. That's about it." She thought on it for another moment. "I've seen more of them lately." Marisa took Gerald's hand so suddenly that it startled him. She looked down the street to Heathen's.

"One more before you go into hiding?" she asked.

"I don't think that'd be such a good idea," he said reluctantly. A cold beer sounded like heaven.

"Okay," she said, the disappointment evident in her voice. She stood on her toes and brushed her lips across his. Gerald inhaled. She smelled good. Clean. Shampoo and soap. Her lips were cool and soft; soft as ever. He wrapped his arms around her waist. They kissed again, and this time the kiss was substantially deeper. Marisa grabbed him through his jeans and bit his earlobe. He let out a small gasp and worked his lips over her neck.

"My place... or yours," she said, her voice a breath.

"Yours, mine... " Gerald began to say, but was cut off.

"Yours is closer," Marisa whispered.

[•••]

They made love like feral cats—sensual and animalistic. Gerald explored her body, seeking out familiar sensitive spots with eager fingertips and lips. Her soft moans—and, later, full-throated cries—let him know that he hadn't forgotten a thing. She was wet and welcoming when he entered her. Climax came seconds later, for both of them. Afterwards, they lay in a tangle of limbs and sweat-soaked sheets, struggling for breath. Her head rested on the rise and fall of his chest; her green eyes blinked up at him.

The door buzzer cut through the post-sex haze like a hot and rusty razor. Gerald sat up and she grabbed his arm.

"We're not here," Marisa said.

The buzzer rang again.

"We're not here," he said. He lay back down and tried not to breathe. The buzzer didn't ring for several minutes and he heaved a long sigh. He looked to Marisa. "Maybe this isn't the best place for me to... "

The door whined open, and in came Albin Catlier and Jacob Raney. Gerald sat up with a jerk. Marisa scooted back and pulled the sheets up over her naked body.

"Looks like we picked a good time to stop in," Catlier said. Raney roared with jabbering, spittle-spraying laughter. He plucked the wad of tobacco out of his cheek and dropped it on the gray carpet, where it landed with a wet smack.

"We had no idea your tits were so nice, Griffin," Raney said with a wet, crooked-toothed grin. Gerald wanted to knock those teeth right out of his head.

"What the hell do you want?" Gerald asked.

"We're placing you under arrest, Mr. Evans," Catlier said in a calm voice. He struck a match on his boot heel and lit a cigarette.

"By what authority?" Marisa said. "You're not Core Sec. You're not shit."

Raney pulled a heavy pipe out from underneath his jacket and twirled it once. At the end of the pipe was a massive, octagonal joint, caked with blood. Some of it still looked wet. And was that hair sticking out of it? Gerald wasn't the first stop on their list. Had they already gone after Swaren? Gerald's stomach dropped.

"Mr. Evans, it'd be wise for you to get dressed and come with us. I'd be lying if I said we didn't want to hurt anyone. My associate here really enjoys hurting people. I can't say I blame him—when you're as good at it as he is," Catlier said. "So, what's it going to be? Come with us willing, or we bash in your pretty little girlfriend's head and *take* you with us."

"I get the point." Gerald climbed out of the bed. Marisa grabbed his wrist, almost savagely. "It's cool, baby. I'll be fine," he said. He wouldn't be fine for long—he knew that much. Gerald hoped she'd go to Swaren, if Swaren still lived, and rescue his salvage-hauling ass. He started mentally counting up his friends on the station, and wished suddenly that he'd made a lot more. How much force would it take to liberate him? Swaren, Marisa? Maerl? Cortez and Ina? Gerald pulled on his pants and shirt. He slipped into a pair of boots and stepped away from the bed. Raney leaned his pipe against the bed in a calm, deliberate movement. In the next second, he was slamming Gerald against the wall and slapping handcuffs around his wrists. *Please don't try anything, Mari,* Gerald thought. Marisa didn't throw herself at his captors as he was led out of the room; he was glad.

[•••]

Jacob Raney grabbed Gerald by the elbow and yanked him through the doorway. The salvage pilot tripped on the threshold and slammed against the opposite wall. The metal did not give, but Gerald's lip did—split right down the middle with a nice rush of blood. Raney found this all too amusing. He turned back to gauge the bitch's reaction, and froze. Griffin's head was surrounded by a corona of black—he had seen an octopus in a Gemar's Body Cream commercial, and he was suddenly reminded of the way it had thrown a cloud of ink. He blinked and the cloud was gone. She looked perfectly normal and perfectly pissed.

No.

She didn't look normal. Her eyes still looked like the ink.

"Come on, Jacob, quit gawking. Maybe Kendall will let you have her later. For now, his orders were specific," Albin said.

"What?" Jacob shook his head. "Yeah, okay. Right." He pushed Gerald down the corridor. "Start walking, Salvage Man."

It wasn't quite dawn as they led Gerald through the slumbering bazaar. All the storefronts were closed and pale violet light trickled down from the sun globes. The sulfur glow of the street lamps cast long fun-house shadows in their path. Jacob turned to look behind him and he saw movement in the shadows.

"Albin," he said, "I think we're being trailed."

"No, we're not," Albin said. His voice was sure and Jacob believed him right away. It was late, he was tired. That was all. It was like at the bar, when he saw that weird shit the night those gun-runner mercs were killed. Only, that night it had been worse, because not only was he tired, he had been drunk and on more than a few recreational drugs.

The feeling came back a few seconds later, though. Jacob was sure it was in his head, but that made it feel no less real. With every few steps he looked over his shoulder. Gerald took advantage of one such moment and bolted down an alley.

"Crap!" Jacob shouted as Gerald disappeared into the shadows. Albin, who was a good six meters ahead by now, turned and frowned.

"Go get him, Jacob. I'll wait here." Albin sounded pissed. Jacob felt himself getting upset. He hated disappointing Albin.

Jacob darted off after Gerald. The salvage man would pay for his bad behavior. If Jacob knew anything, he knew that much. The sneaky bastard couldn't have picked a darker, more narrow alley to flee down. Jacob's shoulders practically touched the walls as he ran in pursuit. Salvage Man couldn't have gotten far, though. As if in response to the thought, the sound of a garbage bin getting knocked over rang out from just ahead.

"Gotcha, fucker," Jacob said and quickened his pace. He came to a loading area behind a restaurant. The air was thick with spices and the smell of something that had recently gone bad in the trash. Jacob crept into the open space, metal pipe poised above his head. "Come on out and play, Salvage Man," Jacob called in a teasing voice. A cat screamed and Jacob turned. Blackness spread out in front of his face—it was like a sable blanket had been thrown at him, but it wasn't a blanket. It was shadow, pure and thick. For an instant, the darkness had a glittering maw filled with long, needle-like teeth. The darkness cried out, and its voice was hungry. Jacob staggered back as the Black wrapped around him, and then a burst of pleasure seized him. He fell over with a gasp. Jacob blinked, but the world remained without light.

[•••]

Gerald heard the trash can hit the deck. His pursuers were right on top of him. The next sound to roll down the alley was unexpected: a groan of pleasure bounced off the constrictive station walls, followed by maniacal giggling. Gerald skidded to a halt. His shoulders burned with his wrists bound so tight behind his back. More giggling and now a moan. Was that Jacob Raney? Gerald crept back the way he had come. He peered around the corner into the space behind the restaurant where he had first thought to hide. Jacob sat propped against one several refuse containers. His smallish member was clutched in one hand and he was working the thing as if he wanted to set it on fire. Raney picked up a shard of broken glass. It glittered in the dim alley light. Gerald hesitated only for a moment and then turned and ran hard. The sound of pleasure became a wail of terror that made Gerald pause. He looked back over his shoulder, but couldn't see what was going on. He turned forward to start off again and was greeted by a fist flying into his face. He saw stars and went down, cold.

(Part XVIII)

By the time Albin found him, Jacob had already done as much damage as he could do to himself. The man sat leaning against a stinking garbage bin with his cock in his hand—the sex organ was no longer attached to Jacob's body. He was screaming like a little girl—the pain was apparent on his red and scrunched face—yet he was making frantic masturbatory gestures all at same time. Blood pumped from the dark hole of his open fly. There was a piece of broken glass, the jagged edge bloodied, at Jacob's side. Albin's stomach did a somersault and his asshole clenched. He couldn't fathom what he was seeing. Jacob's spasmodic movements were as unreal as the sheer amount of blood pooling around him.

Albin snapped to.

"Jacob!" he shouted. Jacob's shrieking ceased. He looked at Albin with a befuddled and slack-jawed expression; his features were ashen in the alley's early morning light. Jacob's gaze turned toward his severed cock. He stared at the penis for a fleeting moment; then he looked at the glass. The deepening creases in Jacob's forehead made it apparent that his small brain was trying to make sense of it all and coming up empty. Finally, he looked up at Albin. Jacob opened his mouth to speak and promptly fell over.

"Mother fucking son of a goddamned bitch," Albin hissed through clenched teeth. He looked back at Gerald, who lay face down on the damp alley floor. He was beginning to stir. It seemed unlikely that the salvage pilot had chopped off Jacob's pecker, especially with his hands bound behind his back—meaning Jacob had to have done the gruesome deed himself. That explanation was more ridiculous by far. Albin activated his cochlear implant and called the emergency room.

"I need a med cart down here now," Albin said as he retrieved his cigarettes from his leather coat's inside pocket.

The dispatcher informed him the medical cart would arrive in a few minutes. Albin closed the connection, lit a cigarette, and went to Jacob.

He knelt beside the unconscious man. Albin watched as the wound continued to spew forth dark blood in rhythmic gushes. A few minutes would be pushing it. He averted his gaze. The sight was almost too much to handle, even for him.

"I'm sorry, Jacob," Albin said at last and then collected himself.

He left Jacob's side and went to the salvage pilot. It was time to get rolling. Jacob was well on his way to bleeding to death and there was nothing Albin could do about it. Either the medical cart would arrive on time or it wouldn't. He nudged Gerald with the tip of his boot. The action yielded a moan. Albin kicked Gerald with as much venom as he could muster. The savage blow woke the man up, complete with a full-bore yell. Albin grabbed Gerald's collar and yanked him to his feet.

"Did you cut him, you sick fuck?" Albin growled; his face was only centimeters from Gerald's.

"What?" Gerald attempted to wrest free of Albin's grip. It was apparent that the pilot had no idea what had just gone down. Albin let go of him with a shove and peered back into the alley. For an eye-blink, Albin saw a black shape, like a tendril of smoke, coiled around Jacob's throat. Albin narrowed his eyes and the phantasmal snake disappeared into a floor grate.

A warbling siren approached. Alternating blasts of red and white light filled the alley. Albin grabbed Gerald by the shoulder.

"Go." He gave Gerald a hard push.

[•••]

"They've taken Gerald." Marisa spoke into Gerald's apartment comm terminal. She hadn't bothered dressing; the bedsheet was still wrapped around her naked form as it had been when they hauled him away.

Her stomach churned.

"Marisa, that's the third time you've said that. You need to relax," Nigel said. His image frowned on the screen. He looked weary. Marisa recognized the look. Crescent was finally getting to him.

"Nigel, we have to go get him. They're gonna hurt him," she said. They were probably *already* hurting him. If they hurried, they could save Gerald from any permanent damage.

"No," Nigel said. "Not yet."

"What do you mean, not yet? They're probably beating Gerald to a bloody pulp as we speak." *Stupid horny assholes,* Marisa thought, *so stupid*. She wanted to puke.

"I agree we have to do something, but we're not prepared to go in there and grab him. Think about it for a second. We don't have any backup whatsoever."

She felt her cheeks flush.

"Waiting isn't going to change that. We'll be as outnumbered today as we'll be tomorrow. They're going… " A ball of hot grief choked her. Tears began to well up in her eyes.

"They're not going to kill him. Not while I'm around. In less than two days there will be a ship arriving. A colony ship. There are going to be undercover agents on that ship. That's when we'll make our move."

"Two days?" Marisa said couldn't believe what she was hearing. "In two fucking days do you think it's going to matter?" The thought made the nausea double.

"Don't do anything stupid, Marisa. You're no use to Gerald dead and he's going to need both of us to get him out of this mess. They are not going to kill him. Not yet. So don't be a bloody fool. Am I clear?"

"Yes. Infuriatingly fucking clear. Goddamn it, Nigel."

"I'm sorry, Marisa. I thought that Gerald would have gotten into hiding sooner."

"Yeah, we made a mistake. And now he's paying for it." And so was she. She clicked off the terminal and threw up.

[•••]

Gerald slept, and Gerald dreamed. He dreamed he was back on Anrar III. Above him the sky was striped with gray clouds and deep blue. A cold and familiar wind bit at his cheeks. He was barefoot and the ground was like ice beneath his bare feet; his calves clenched painfully with each step he took. *I know damn well this is a dream,* he thought, *but still I think I might freeze my balls off.* The wind howled as he walked through the grove of obsidian spires. And still, the rocky columns radiated a cold of their very own, so strong that their chill rivaled the wind.

Gerald came out on the other side of the grove. The gaping hole in the planet's surface was as dark and menacing as he remembered it.

Gerald felt something shift, all around him.

He couldn't quite define the sensation—it felt like something big, heavy, and alive was rolling over. Gerald then experienced a gripping instant of déjà vu. The air shimmered before his eyes; it looked like the very atmosphere had been turned to ice. Tiny particles captured the light for a glittering heartbeat and then the air cleared.

A spaceport and a mine/refinery stood where the hole had just been. A rover with a spherical, translucent glass cockpit left the structure on large, rubbery wheels, and another rover approached. Atop the spaceport was a squat, bulbous shuttle with *Murhaté 01* emblazoned in yellow across its starboard side. A lifeboat hovered above the shuttle. Steaming exhaust drifted upward from glowing vents at the ship's aft. The wind caught the wisps of white vapor, twisting them viciously before dissipating the tendrils.

Gerald approached a large window on the spaceport's face. Fresh grit and dust from one of the planet's frequent rain and wind storms covered the main viewport. Gerald was able to make out moving shapes through the grime. He considered entering the building, but knew his destination lay at the top of the slope—the geological outpost.

Gerald left the spaceport. He walked into the wind; every step was a little more painful than the last. Gravity licked at his knee and hip joints with invisible flames—unseen, but definitely felt. When he finally reached the top of the hill, he was breathless and on the verge of passing out. His clothes were drenched through with sweat.

Gerald stood outside Geological Outpost Murhaté and listened. There were muffled voices on the other side of the metal door; the sounds of their conversation were indiscernible. Apart from the voices and the wind, there were also whispers circled his head like flies; the disembodied voices zoomed in close and pulled away. It made Gerald feel dizzy. If he didn't get away from the disorienting whispers, he could envision himself losing his balance, falling over, and tumbling down the hill. The door opened and he tottered over the threshold.

It was dark inside the outpost. Gerald took several steps forward. A meager light leaked out from underneath the shelves with a yellowish glow that stretched and spread like sinews joining each dark, blotchy shadow. He walked into the clearing where the all shelves had been pushed back. The circle of stones he had witnessed on his visit to the outpost with Ina was illuminated by a concentric ring of candles. The flames shifted in the drafts that floated through the large, open space. Shadow moved across the walls and the ceiling like an undulating curtain of tar.

The metal ring was suspended in the center of the circle just as it had been on Gerald's previous visit to the surface. Instead of a barely identifiable corpse hanging at the heart of the ring, there was a woman hanging there. She was naked save for black cables that bound her to the metal piping. Her stomach was swollen with child. At least fifty people, all wearing dirty mining coveralls, stood around the circle. Some were chanting, some were whispering. All looked up at the woman. She was motionless save for the occasional lolling of her head to the left and right. She appeared to be drugged.

A female shouted from outside, accompanied by pounding on the entrance door. Although the voice was muffled, Gerald heard the word "stop" very clearly. But each time the woman yelled, the whispers that buzzed around his head increased in frequency and volume. Soon, Gerald could hear nothing else. Guttural, unintelligible sounds mingled with the whispers. Inhuman and terrifying, the sounds made him want to scream. The pregnant woman's head rose. She opened her eyes and began to cry out. A man walked through the circle. Dressed in black mining coveralls, he was surrounded by a dim corona of violet light. The gravity did not appear to bother the man.

And why would it? If he was a miner, he would've been acclimated to the higher gravity prior to assignment on the planet.

There was an A-frame ladder erected beneath the pregnant woman. She now struggled against the cords that bound her arms and wrists. The dark man climbed up the ladder and stopped when he was at the same level as her belly, raising an object above his head. The object was hard to identify from Gerald's vantage point, but it looked like to be some sort of crude tool, similar to a scraper used by humankind's prehistoric ancestors. The dark man dragged the tool across the woman's round stomach. The wound left in the object's wake was ragged and bloody. Gerald averted his gaze.

There was a woosh—like all the air had just been sucked out of the vast room. Everything went dead still. Then there was a flash red light. For an instant, crimson was all Gerald could see. When his vision returned, all that remained of the pregnant woman was a torso hanging from the metal ring. Her entire midsection was gone. Her innards hung out as glistening tatters. The fifty people that had been gathered around the base of the scaffolding were now laying one atop the other, completely motionless. Gerald turned and ran back the way he had come.

Something blasted by him—red, violet, and black—and the exit door flew open ahead of him. There was a cry on the outside. Gerald stumbled on the door's raised threshold and broke free of the outpost's shadows with a tumbling fall. He rolled onto his back and saw the shuttle, *Murhaté 01,* rising from the small spaceport. Three amorphous blobs of color—red, violet, and black—raced toward it. *The colors, trying to get off the planet,* Gerald thought. He could feel it now—a lifeforce's blind desire to be free of Anrar III. *It's too worked up,* Gerald thought, *it can't do it.*

Gerald clambered to his feet.

The red orb of light slammed into the shuttle. It exploded instantaneously; the resulting fireball crashed down into the spaceport. The structure buckled, collapsed, and then exploded itself. Gerald felt the anguish from the crimson thing. Glimmering, red blots of light like fireflies rained down around him. The light pooled around his feet and flowed like run-off back into the geological station. Another lifeboat screamed across the sky. The Violet and Black raced past in pursuit. He saw the Violet seep into the lifeboat. The Black continued to race toward the sky, closing in on the shuttle before both disappeared.

Reality trembled.

The air filled with glittering.

And then he was awake.

Slowly, he sat up on the metal cot. The strange dream seeped back into the darker reaches of his consciousness. His limbs were stiff and his lower back ached. Gerald looked to the confining bars of the cell. Bars. Simple and ridiculously effective. They were still firmly in place. He rubbed his forehead where Albin had clubbed him and then he hopped off the cot. Security had taken his boots when they booked him and the floor was cold.

And his feet were dirty.

He shook his head at the sight and took a deep, cleansing breath.

Gerald went to the bars and gave them a tug—because that's what you do when you're in jail: you tug at the bars and shout something like "Hey! Lemme outta here!" But Gerald didn't really feel like shouting, so he sat back down on the cot and placed his head in his hands. He was as good as dead now. *Marisa, don't you try and break me out of jail,* Gerald thought, and couldn't help but laugh. The situation defied logic.

"Gerald."

He lifted his eyes. Ina stood outside the cell. Her pretty fingers were wrapped around the bars.

"Are you okay?" she asked.

Gerald shrugged and stood back up. *Damn cold floor,* he thought. He walked over to the bars, stepping with the sides of his feet as he went, trying to limit contact with the cold floor panels. He put his hands over hers—once again, this seemed like the prison thing to do.

"I'm fine," Gerald said. "I have a headache and I'm a little stiff from sleeping on that cot." The response felt too matter-of-fact. He changed gears. "How'd you know I was here?"

"Heathen's… Maerl. I went looking for you. Maerl told me you were taken here. He overheard Albin Catlier talking to someone about you."

"Who was Albin talking to? Do you know—did Maerl say?" Gerald asked.

"No. Maerl just said Crescent security."

Gerald sighed. It could have been anyone from security.

"To be honest, Ina, you're the last person I thought I'd see here," Gerald admitted.

She smiled uneasily and glanced up the dark cellblock hallway as she did so.

"Gerald. My father is sick," Ina said.

"Sick? How?"

"I don't know. Whatever he has, he might have caught it on the lifeboat," Ina said.

"How do you figure?" Gerald asked.

"I don't know. He was fine and healthy before the lifeboat… " Her voice faltered. "There was something on that lifeboat, Gerald—you know as much. And Dad's body isn't strong enough for it. Whatever it is, it's changing him. Killing him. Eating him from the inside out. I know, it sounds crazy."

"I'm sorry," Gerald said. *What the fuck else am I going to say?* He thought. *Do I say, what's changing you, Ina? What is changing me?* Not that he felt all that different—he felt as fucked up as he did before he got involved with Ina, Donovan, or Crescent.

"At the risk of sounding insensitive," Gerald began, "why are you telling me this?"

"That's a fair question. I'm not looking for support or anything. We were all on that boat. You were on it *twice,* Gerald," Ina said. Gerald winced. "We may have been exposed to whatever it is he's got. I thought you should know."

"Thanks," Gerald said. In truth, he wasn't sure how much he appreciated the information. It was one of those things he'd really rather not have known. "It might be safest if you left now, Ina. I think I'm into some serious shit here."

"Did you get in trouble for helping us? For taking me down to that planet?" Her brow creased.

"I did a lot of things that got me in *trouble*. Taking you on your little field trips was probably the least of them. Let's just say, I tried to do the right thing and here I am." He spread his arms and smiled an exaggerated grin.

"There's something else…Something else you should know." she said. Gerald waited for her to go on. She inhaled sharply. "Gerald, I'm pregnant."

He let go of the bars and shook his head. *Why not,* he thought. *Why the fuck not?*

He opened his mouth. Closed it, and then opened it again, and spoke.

"Is it mine?" He tried to sound sensitive, but his tone sounded accusatory even to his own ears.

"I don't know. Maybe. Maybe not. I don't know for sure. You're…the most likely candidate…but…"

"I'm doing well in the race. Yeah. I get it," Even still, Gerald wondered just how many candidates there were.

[•••]

"I want to see him, Captain," Marisa said. Captain Benedict sat behind his nondescript desk in his nondescript office; he clutched his black mug between both hands. Two rosy spots stood out on his cheeks.

"That's fine, Mari. Someone's with him right now, actually," his words were slightly slurred. Marisa wondered what was in the cup today. The notion that the captain was drinking on the job made her feel a deep pang of sadness. She pushed it away.

"Who?"

Benedict shrugged.

"Marisa," he began tapping on a data pad, "I've got some files for you to go over. The big concert is coming up," he tapped several more times, "And as of now, you are in charge of the detail."

"Who, Captain? Who is in there?" Marisa didn't care about assignments or concerts.

"Some blonde girl."

All Marisa could think of was what Naheela had told her about Gerald sticking it in some other chick. She spared Benedict a fleeting glance and then left the office for the cells, intent on strangling the bitch, whoever she was.

The holding block was a single, narrow hallway consisting of sixteen barred cells. Most of the cells were empty that night. Or was it morning now? Marisa had no idea. Toward the end of the hallway she saw a tall, thin woman with cornsilk hair that fell damp to delicate shoulders. Marisa's gait slowed as she neared and the woman came into closer view. It was the woman she had run into outside of HQ.

But there was more to this woman. Marisa knew it right away. Hot jealously was doused in a flood of jarring memories.

A security alarm is going off. A trigger at Z-block. Z-block is off limits. It must be a rat? Marisa thinks. She glances around HQ; there is no one around. I better go check it out before I bother El Capitan, she thinks. This is against standard operating procedures in regard to Z-block alarms. SOP states the Captain must be informed of anything to do with Z-block. But there's never been an alarm triggered down there.

"You," Marisa said. Her voice was a nearly inaudible whisper as she stepped up to the cell.

The woman rolled her blue eyes over to Marisa and they locked stares.

More memories gushed into her head.

The service channel is as long as it is tight and Marisa thinks it is going to go on forever. She finally comes out the other side, but it is dark and dreary—there is little solace in the shadows. Only a few of the light panels are working. Marisa is surprised that any of them are working at all. Cobwebs drape every surface and Marisa chokes on air thick with must and the vague sent of decay. There are footprints in the dust. What fool is down here? Marisa thinks, but suddenly questions what she is doing down there. She wants to go back into the light and forget she ever noticed the alarm going off. But she can't do that. She's got a job to do. She follows the footprints in the dust and they take her to a large, windowless bulkhead with an X crudely painted over its surface. The Vault.

This can't be, Marisa thinks. This is all wrong.

Marisa sees her then—the woman with the waif-thin frame and the pretty hair. Her face is pressed against the bulkhead that seals the Vault and her eyes are closed. No Access. Authorized Personnel Only—the stenciled, yellow lettering seems to pulse. The woman has one hand up her shirt, rubbing her… breast? The fingers of her other hand are splayed out on the bulkhead's dark surface, just beside her cheek.

"Hey!" Marisa says, "You shouldn't be down here."

The woman does not answer. Marisa frowns and grabs the woman by the arm. That's when everything slows down. Black fills her field of view and she can no longer see the woman, but she feels the woman's fingers wrap around her wrist to pull her in close—into an embrace. They are both pressed against the bulkhead now. Marisa hears voices. Singing? Something touches her deeply—in a secret place. Marisa is struck and thinks, so long as this liquid shadow has a hold on me, I will never know loneliness again. Marisa will never be alone—ever—not now that she has come to this wonderful place. I have to share this. I have to set this free. For everyone's sake, she thinks. The other woman's lips are on hers now and they are kissing. And why shouldn't they be? They are liberated. They are free as many others shall soon be free. Freedom is the will of the Black.

"It's you," the woman replied in a similar hush.

"I… " Marisa inhaled through her nose. She was speechless.

"When I ran into you the other day I knew that I knew you from somewhere," the woman said, more strength behind her voice. She reached out a hand and touched Marisa's cheek. The woman's fingertips were soft and cold.

"Fuck me. It wasn't a dream," Marisa said, and she thought of the imagery she'd seen so many times on her apartment's comm terminal. Two women, hand in hand, walking into the shadows.

"Whoa, hey. Wait a goddamn minute." Gerald pressed his face between two of the cell's bars.

"You two *know* each other?"

"In a manner of speaking, though we've not been officially introduced." The woman extended her hand and Marisa took it. "I'm Ina Cortez. Dr. Ina Cortez."

"I know who you are. Gerald told me what you and your father have been getting into." Marisa shook her hand once. "I'm Lieutenant Marisa Griffin." Ina seemed nonplused.

"Good to meet you, Lieutenant. Marisa."

"Can I ask—what are you doing here? Obviously, I know Gerald ran some salvage for you and your… " Marisa began, but was cut off.

"Father, yes. And now my father is sick and I thought that Gerald should know." Ina's voice rang with defensiveness. The sound set Marisa on edge. She glanced over to Gerald, who was busy counting dust particles on the floor. He looked miserable. She felt bad for him, even though she knew beyond the shadow of a doubt that he had fucked Ina Cortez.

"I should leave you two alone," Marisa said, turning to leave the cell block. The way Ina was looking at Gerald made her uncomfortable. "I didn't mean to interrupt. I just wanted to check on Gerald."

"No," Ina said. "I should be the one leaving the two of you." Ina began to move down the hall and paused beside Marisa. She placed a hand on her shoulder and Marisa felt the familiar sense of otherness swimming in the back of her mind. "I think you and I should talk soon."

"Yes," Marisa agreed. "Tonight."

"Tonight," Ina echoed.

Ina Cortez disappeared down the corridor leaving Marisa and Gerald alone. Marisa leaned against the bars with a heavy sigh and let exhaustion run over her.

"Did you screw her, Gerald?" she asked, not really caring for an answer.

"Yes," he said.

"More than once?"

"I did. I tried...to use control. I'm sorry, Mari. I'm really..." Gerald said and continued to stare at the floor panels.

"Why are you sorry? You're not obligated to me anymore than I'm obligated to you. We're nothing to each other." Gerald frowned from behind the bars and she could see that her words had stung him. If Marisa was honest with herself, she had little reason to feel jealous. *Maybe I'm entitled to feel a little bit jealous.* Even still, she had thrown him the cold shoulder as she spiraled further into her neuroses, so what did she expect would happen? Gerald Evans was human and male, and loneliness was only exacerbated by deep space. Besides, she hadn't gone to him in the holding block to begrudge him anything. Minutes ago she was worried for his life.

"Okay. I guess that wasn't really called for, was it?" Marisa said. "Look. It's not like we were ever officially together." She paused and weighed her thoughts. "For more than a little while, it's been like quite the opposite, you know? And I don't blame you. A man has his needs, right? She's pretty."

Gerald didn't answer, and she shrugged.

"I'm not here to talk about our relationship. I'm here to talk about getting you out of here."

"Do you have a plan?" Gerald looked up, his eyes bright.

"No. I don't," she admitted. His forlorn expression returned.

"I'm pretty much fucked then, don't you think?" Gerald said.

"There's something in the works, Gerry. If you can hold out a few days… " Marisa tried to sound as reassuring as she could.

"Is Nigel captured? Dead?" He asked without looking at her.

"Nigel is fine, Gerry," she said.

"Well, then get me out of here now." His words were insistent, but he wasn't pleading yet. Marisa was glad; she didn't want to hear him beg. Although, were she on the other side of those bars with nothing more to look forward to than an up-close-and-personal with Kendall and the boys, she'd already be begging.

"We can't, Gerry. We have to hold out just a little longer. There are plans in the works. There are people coming. We *will* get you out of here."

"Holding out isn't up to me. It's up to Kendall and his posse."

"Look. Kendall and his boys are going to ask what you've told Swaren. They're going want to know how you side-stepped that ambush. Don't tell them, Gerry. Hold out. You are the only witness that can incriminate *or* protect them." A look of recognition dawned on his face. Marisa saw that he knew Kendall was going to come as close to killing him as possible without actually ending his life. Kendall *would* get his point across. Gerald suddenly looked very sad. Sad and scared.

"I'm really going to get my ass kicked before this all said and done, aren't I?" he said at last.

"Probably. I'm sorry."

Gerald gestured with his head in the direction that Ina had departed.

"How do you know her?" Gerald asked.

"It's more than a little complicated."

Gerald just looked at her with an expression that said *it doesn't get much more complicated than this.*

"She was there when everything changed. We were there together. The fucking Vault, Gerry. It's real. All the stories… " Marisa looked first up and then down the hall. She didn't want the Captain to hear her talking like this. She went on: "Your little friend there, she triggered an alarm on Z. I thought it was a rat or a glitch. We never hear a peep out of Z. So, I checked it out. Only, I had no recollection of being down there until I saw her. But, I know that's where it all started. That's when the station woke up. We were there, Gerry."

"I'm going to be perfectly honest with you, Marisa," Gerald said. "The hoodoo voodoo shit you and I chatted about in the auditorium is the furthest thing from my mind right now. Right now, I'm wondering what's going to be clamped to my nipples in the near future and how many volts of electricity will be coursing through my body," Gerald said.

"We're gonna get you outta that cell. I promise."

"I just hope it's not in a body bag… Or in little pieces." He looked at her, then turned and reclined on the cot. "You probably shouldn't stick around here when Kendall and his boys show back up. You just might end up in here with me."

She knew he was right.

"Take care of yourself, Ger. Hold out. You have to."

He closed his eyes. Marisa spared him one last look, and then left.

[•••]

Marisa stood outside of Heathen's. The neon sign above the batwings flickered tremulously; its glow looked like it would go dark at any second. Marisa's had her arms wrapped tight around herself. The massive air handlers on either side of Main Street puffed out big blasts of cold air that moved like wind. The handling system throughout the station was way out of whack. The sun globes were at their lowest level of illumination, but she wasn't convinced that it was really night.

Marisa thought of Gerald, laying in darkness of the small cell. Even worse, she thought of him in a room somewhere, strapped to a table and having god knows what done to him. She stopped herself before she could think of him screaming. Marisa thought of Ina then. Their brief conversation outside of Gerald's cell earlier that day had been surreal enough—Marisa wasn't really sure she needed to remember anything else about the Vault. The hoodoo voodoo shit, as Gerald had put it, was pretty far from her mind, too. She feared for her life and she feared for Gerald's. She was even afraid for Swaren, who was partially to blame for stirring up the wasp's nest.

"Fuck it," she said. "Things can't get worse than they already are." She silently chided herself for even thinking it, and pushed through the batwing doors.

The familiar and pleasing stench of tobacco smoke and beer assaulted Marisa as she stepped through the doors. The bar was busy, the conversations a din of drunk and excited babble. Everyone looked strung out—all dark circles and pale complexions. The bar was jammed with people drinking themselves to the point of forgetting that it was too hot one day and too cold the next. The wind was strangest of all. It made you wonder if Crescent wasn't really decompressing. Yeah. Weird weather for a space station.

Ina sat a table at the far end of the dance floor. Some tall, homely son of a bitch was attempting to hit on her. Even from afar, Marisa could see his advances were amounting to nothing. The guy was annoyed; his gestures became more and more animated with each failed pickup line. Marisa forced her way through a crowd of half-hearted people dancing in the center pit of the club, bouncing off one another of one another in blasts of colored light. She stepped up a short flight of stairs and moved to Ina's table.

"Take a hike, pal," Marisa said.

"What? Fuck you, bitch." Without a moment of hesitation, Marisa grabbed him by the ear and slammed his head into a nearby handrail. He cried out. Marisa twisted his ear and he cried out again. She shoved him down the short flight of stairs. He fell onto the dance floor and struggled back to his feet. The man was wasted. "You are a crazy bitch," he growled and shuffled away.

"Thanks," Ina said, not visibly swayed by the scene either way. "Won't you sit down?"

"Yeah. Why not," Marisa replied and seated herself across from the wisp of a girl. There were several beats of silence. "So… " Marisa said.

"I know this is awkward," Ina said. *No shit, it was awkward,* Marisa mused as she shifted in her seat. "But I know you feel it," Ina went on and glanced around the bar. She then returned her eyes to Marisa's. "Everything changed after you and I met at that bulkhead at the… "

"Don't say it," Marisa said, cutting Ina off. She didn't want to hear the word.

"It's hard to talk about." Ina smiled softly. "Believe me, I know. There is so little logic to any of it. And the periods of not being in control of ourselves. That's the most difficult. I've acted in ways… that… I," Ina shook her head. "Regardless. Right now, Marisa. Right now I feel in control, which is why I wanted to talk to you. I'm worried about my father. He's wrapped up in all this and is not in control at all. And whatever it is that is happening, it's killing him."

"Is that why you had me meet you? So you could tell me we've bonded? That we're blood sisters or some shit? And that I should be inspired to help your sick dad? Look Ms. Cortez. Ina. I've got enough to worry about."

"Things are happening here, Marisa. Big things. Look—Dad's not the only reason I wanted to meet with you. I just needed to not feel alone in this anymore. I know you've felt that same bitter isolation. You can't tell me that you haven't."

Marisa sighed.

"Okay. Tell me, then," Marisa said. "What happening on Crescent, Doctor Cortez?" *Aside from corrupt mayors, gun running, and secret plans to decommission the whole works.*

"It's life that's happening on Crescent, Marisa. I'm sure of it. A life that has always been here, long before Crescent was even a thought in an engineer's head. Existing just on the other side of," Ina looked down at the table for several seconds and then looked back up. "Just on the other side of the glass. Maybe it had always been aware of our side, but when people first came to Anrar it began to care." Marisa could tell Ina was working things out as she spoke. "And then… sensing human life, it wanted to come through, to say hello—to make contact. But things went wrong when it tried to come through. It became… split up. Dissociated. Like light through a prism. The *Three* were born. The Violet, the Red, and the Black. Now it's stuck. Halfway here, halfway there. Three pieces. It craves unity," Ina's voice trailed off and Marisa took the opportunity to interject.

"That makes little sense," Marisa said, but she knew she understood.

Ina groaned. "Does it really? Are you that limited by a standard notion of life that it's beyond you to grasp that we might be dealing with some completely new form of life?"

Marisa wasn't limited in her thinking. And putting a scientific spin on things made her feel a little bit better. Saner. Marisa thought on it for several seconds. The academic approach seemed to bring the pieces a little closer together—a little nearer to forming a whole picture. Whatever this force was, maybe it *was* using them to communicate its wishes? To fulfill its wishes.

"You've been blacking out. You've been having strange dreams. This thing talks to you as much as it talks to me. And whenever it communicates it sucks the life right out of you, right? We're not wired for this. You're probably more tired than you've ever been."

Marisa was tired. That was no secret.

"Why are you telling me all this?" Marisa said. She wanted a drink. She looked around for a server.

"I want you to help me help my father. Like I said. He's been… contacted, too. But his body can't handle it. It's killing him," Ina said. Suddenly, the blonde's eyes glistened with unshed tears.

"You're a smart girl. A doctor to boot, right? I'm sure you can figure it out on your own," Marisa replied.

"I can't help him alone," Ina said.

"Why the hell not?"

"Because all three of us are involved. We are part of the whole now. And we have to make sure whatever needs to be finished here is finished here. And then my dad'll be set free, along with us."

"Last I checked, I wasn't trapped, honey."

Ina laughed.

"You're wrong. You couldn't leave this sector of space, even if you wanted to," Ina said.

"So, what the hell do you want me to do about this?"

"I want you to stop fighting it. The sooner it can accomplish what it needs to accomplish, the sooner we're done, too. Don't you see? Resisting only slows it down," Ina said.

"I'll be perfectly honest with you," Marisa said. "I showed up tonight expecting not to like you. And now that I've sat down and chatted with you a little bit, I'm not surprised in the least to discover that I don't like you. With all due respect, I'm done here."

"Is this because I slept with Gerald?"

Marisa sat back in her chair. Now she was surprised. It was stated so matter-of-factly, with the batting of innocent lashes, no less.

"Lady, you're crazy. And I'm done."

[•••]

Albin sat at the corner of the bar in Heathen's nursing his third glass of scotch. The corner seat was the best seat in the house, as far as he was concerned. The scowl Albin wore on his weathered features was nothing short of menacing.

Albin couldn't help but think of Jacob, and every time he did, Albin shuddered. Chopped his own cock right off. When Albin had gone to visit Jacob, his friend had been a babbling fool. Jacob had gone on and on about shadows with teeth and the black. Jacob had also said something about Marisa Griffin in his ramblings. That she had been there in the alley. That he had seen her, or some nonsense. Albin didn't know for sure. What he did know was that Griffin had kicked Taylor's ass and that she was a loon. Anything was possible. So, Albin now watched her guardedly as she had her little chat with Ina Cortez on the opposite end of Heathen's. He knew those two bitches were up to no good. He took another swill of the scotch and as it went down his throat he recognized his own paranoia. He'd been feeling that way a lot lately. The messed up systems on the stations—the screwy light cycles and the confused environmental zones—it was fucking with everyone's heads. His included.

As if to prove the point, two men were busy getting into an excited verbal altercation several tables over from the bar. One guy, a fat man with two small puffs of hair on either side of his bald head, was yelling with such ferocity that the vein that ran across his polished dome was bulging. Bulging so dramatically that Albin thought it would burst.

And it did actually burst. Right when another bar-goer broke a bottle over the man's shiny scalp. From the point of impact, fighting surged out across the bar like a tsunami. The brawl spread as fast as wildfire and was quite unlike anything Albin had seen in his life. Albin emptied the last of the scotch down his throat and slid off his stool. The fighting rippled down the bar toward him, a frothing mix of flying fists, shouts, and broken glass. Albin was too drunk for dodging punches and pool cues, but he wasn't too drunk to shoot his way out. He slipped the needle gun out from under his armpit and let death fly. A different body fell with each concussive thwap. Albin began to move toward the batwing doors; he fired as he went and felt a bit more sober with each step. Killing had that effect. No one seemed to notice the gunfire. They were too busy beating the shit out of each other. A chair sailed over his head, almost braining him. Something wet hit him in the cheek. He touched the spot and his hand came away bloody. A palm sized hunk of flesh—it looked like rare roast beef—hung from the lapel of his jacket. He brushed it off and picked up the pace. People were literally tearing each other apart and he only had so much ammo on him.

[•••]

Marisa got up from the table and contemplated giving Ina the finger. Instead, she decided to walk away in her best indignant swagger, but the fighting stopped her dead in her tracks. It was like someone had dropped a rock of aggression into the pool of drinkers and the brawl extended outward in sustained waves of violence. The frenzy was a spectacle both horrible and mesmerizing. Marisa knew there was no way she could make to the exit. She looked back toward Ina—her palms were splayed out on the table and her eyes were wide with panic. Her mouth gaped stupidly. *Goddamnit,* Marisa thought, *can't this shit ever be simple?*

Marisa grabbed Ina by the wrist and yanked her out of her seat. Ina yelped but protested no further. They hustled past a small sidebar, ducking as debris flew overhead. Behind the sidebar, a female bartender was being savagely raped by two male assailants. Ina hesitated and pulled free of Marisa's grip. Marisa knew they couldn't help the girl, so she regained her hold on Ina and continued to pull her along until they came to a storage closet door. *What is it with fucking storage closets?* Marisa thought as she checked the access handle. It turned, and Marisa threw the door open, slamming it against the wall with a crack. She pushed Ina into the small space with both hands. The blonde stumbled across the threshold and Marisa dashed in behind her. She pulled the door shut and looked around for something—anything—to brace it.

A metal shelf stacked with cans of condensed foods stood adjacent to the door, tall enough to nearly reach the light panels in the ceiling. All those cans meant it'd be heavy. Too heavy for only the two of them to slide it in front of the door, and it'd take way too long to get all the goods cleared off. Marisa thought she might be able to topple the thing over so that it blocked the door. She climbed up the shelf to the top, squirming herself into the small space between shelf and ceiling. She pushed at the wall with her feet and the shelf started to totter. An instant later, she was riding it to the ground. She crouched and covered her head with her arms as it slammed into the opposite wall. Cans rained down around her, bouncing off her body with stinging, bruising blows. She crawled out from underneath the mess, dazed but as far as she knew, unharmed. Ina sat against the far wall, her hands over her abdomen protectively.

"Are you okay?" Ina asked, although she didn't sound all too concerned.

Screams came from the other side of the door. People began to hammer at the barrier and the door rattled in its frame, but it did not give.

"Yeah," Marisa said and touched the back of her head with hesitant fingers. She found her hair a tangled and tacky mess. She wiped the hand clean on her pants.

There was more screaming—bloodthirsty cries that sounded more like a pack of animals than anything human. The pounding had taken on a wet sound, each impact a crunching slap. Marisa didn't want to know why it sounded that way.

"You're bleeding," Ina said over the racket.

"I'm fine."

"Good. When we get out of here, we're going to have to work fast. I'm sure of it." Ina closed her eyes.

The beating on the door stopped, and the screaming really picked up. The wails were like nothing Marisa had ever heard. And judging from the lack of color in Ina's face, she was scared, too. Marisa sat down on the floor beside her. They both put their hands over their ears and Marisa closed her eyes. *This station has been hungry for so long,* Marisa thought, *and now it's feeding time. Sweet Christ. Let this be over soon.*

(Part XIX)

The brawl began as a single bottle impact, but the fighting birthed out of Heathen's and onto Main Street like a living thing. The batwing doors spewed forth a giant serpent with hundreds of punching, kicking, and tearing limbs and hundreds of howling mouths. The beast flowed over the innocent and unsuspecting, leaving twisted, bloodied bodies in its wake. Crescent security arrived just as the rioters began smashing storefronts and destroying anything they could get their hands on. The serpent was clubbed and gassed. Repeated gunfire picked away at the rioters; it wasn't Core Sec doing the shooting. It finally took an army of collector robots to subdue the man-snake.

Nigel's heart skipped several beats when he stepped through the brushed chrome batwing doors and into Heathen's. It looked like a bomb had been set off. Concentrated death—there were bodies everywhere. Some were missing ears, others noses, and eyes. Some of the bodies were even missing limbs. Still others had holes in their torsos—fist-sized and bigger. There was blood everywhere. It fell in droplets from tables and from the bar.

Nothing stirred.

Nigel lifted his camera, placing its lens between his eye and the grisly scene—a necessary buffer between reality and emotion—and began taking pictures of the carnage. Movement from above caught his eye; the camera fell to his side to dangle from its strap while he reached for his sidearm. A closet door on the bar's second tier opened and Nigel raised the weapon and took aim. A dazed Lieutenant Griffin stumbled from the closet followed by a waif-thin blonde woman. Nigel sighed relief, lowering his weapon, and ran to them, careful to avoid the carnage. Marisa's face was devoid of color. Her green eyes went wide at the devastation as they swept across the macabre scene, first to the left, then to the right.

"Marisa," Nigel grabbed her by both arms. She hardly responded.

Lost in shock, she seemed unable to make eye contact, staring instead at the bodies sprawled one atop the other.

"God, Nigel," she said at last. "The screaming. The sounds they made killing each other. It was horrible."

Nigel couldn't imagine. He didn't even want to try. He let go of her arms and nodded once.

"I'm sure it was heinous. Security arrived in time to keep the riot from making its way down Main Street. It's over now. The whole level is closed."

"Riot? Main Street?" Marisa looked over Nigel's shoulder to the club's exit.

"Yes, Marisa. The violence didn't stay confined to Heathen's. But, it's over. All of it. You're okay?"

"I hit my head … " She probed the back of her skull and winced. Her fingertips came back with fresh blood on them. "Otherwise, I'm fine."

"Get that checked out. There are medics out on the street. Is your friend all right?"

"Yeah," Marisa said, glancing behind her before adding, "she's not my friend, but she's fine. This is all you needed, isn't it? You're happy about this," Marisa said. Her cheeks flushed. The violence was another nail in Crescent's coffin, but Nigel felt little cheer. He was surprised to actually find himself insulted by her words.

"This is a tragedy. I'm not happy about it at all. Now, go on. I'll join you in a moment. I need to take a few more pictures."

Marisa brushed past without sparing him another glance; the blonde woman followed her wordlessly. Nigel examined the door of the women's hiding place. Bloody handprints and fist marks smeared the gray metal exterior. He shook his head and turned around to face the barroom. Close by, a young woman lay on her stomach behind a small side bar. A mosaic of broken glass surrounded her contorted limbs. Ruined black underpants had been pulled down around ankles that were mottled with fresh bruises. Her neck was twisted at an unnatural angle so that her bloodied face looked at Nigel. He raised his camera to take a final photo.

"The glass shudders … unity is almost here," the girl said. As she spoke, a fresh stream of blood flowed down and over her chin. "You will join us soon."

Nigel stumbled backwards, dread overcoming him completely. The sea of corpses stared at him, their unblinking eyes peering out from gore covered faces. The dead seemed poised to rise at any second. The air grew heavy and all the hairs on Nigel's body stood on end, as if each individual molecule around him trembled with energy. He took another jerking step back and stumbled over his own foot, losing hold of the camera in the process. Nigel managed to catch himself by grabbing the closet doorframe, but the device dropped to the floor with an unpleasant crack of glass and plastic.

The atmosphere went still and Nigel scanned the room, refusing to give up his hold on the frame for fear his legs would turn to water. The corpses had regained their blank, death stares, their eyes no longer focused on him. He looked back to the sidebar; the serving girl's head faced the other way now.

Nigel swallowed hard and retrieved the now-worthless camera. *The sooner I get off this god forsaken station, the bloody better.*

[•••]

Maerl sat on the opposite side of the street from the club that had been his life for more than ten years. Heathen's had been the promise of a bright future. Bodies and broken glass now littered that promise. Wide, angry brushstrokes of spilled alcohol and spilled blood sullied its face. The end had brought horrifying things—unreal things. Maerl had watched as people beat each other to a pulp, and then the colors had come: the Black, the Red, the Violet. The walls had come to life then—gleaming, razor sharp, and hungry. People had been maimed or cut clear in two. And what the station hadn't taken, the brawlers took from each other. While the victims screamed, Maerl had cowered. When someone came too close, he had thrown bottles of alcohol at them. Cuts from broken glass marked his hands. He was covered in blood up to the elbows. How much of it was his blood and how much of it was his customers' blood? He didn't really know. It all amounted to the same.

Now he sat with his hands between his legs and watched the medics cart body after body out of his place. He wondered how many of his staff had been loaded into those carts. A sob rose in his throat along with the urge to vomit. What was left for him to do now?

"Sir." A security officer stood above him, arms crossed over the chest of a too-tight uniform. "I'm going ask you again. Please, leave. You can't be here anymore. This portion of the station has been closed off."

"This is *my* portion of the station," Maerl said, and pointed. "That is my place. My lady. You expect me to walk away while you pick over her remains? No way, Jose. Not if this is the last time I'm going to see those neon letters. No fucking way, man. I'm not going anywhere."

"Sir, if you stay here much longer, we're going to arrest you."

Maerl stuck his tongue out at the security officer; he didn't know what else to do. The officer shrugged and walked away, leaving the man squinting into the heart of the destruction again.

White light, cast by portable floodlamps, washed over the epicenter—a circle of blood, bodies, and smoking debris. Uniformed men and women prowled the scene casting long, exaggerated shadows. He wanted to leave; he'd seen enough. Maerl just didn't know where he'd go. Not only was Heathen's his business, it had been his home. *Where do I go from here?* Maerl thought again.

Fresh tears stung his eyes.

A girl with long black hair sat down next to him. Thick, brownish-red smears covered her slender arms. Maerl stared.

"The blood—it's not mine," the girl said, and offered him a cigarette from a steel case. Maerl blinked and shook his head before taking one of the smokes gratefully. She lit it for him and then did the same for herself. Eyes as dark as her hair looked him up and down as she took a drag.

"You look tired," she said, and then exhaled the smoke in a sidelong plume.

"I have nowhere to go," he responded dumbly.

She cocked her head in the direction of Heathen's. "I've seen you working in there a lot. That your place, then?"

"It was. So much time… so much of my life poured into that bar… just so I'd have somewhere to go. And now… " The threat of a fresh sob silenced him. His vision blurred with tears. The girl placed a hand on his knee.

"Hey man, I'm really sorry about your place," she said. He looked up at her. Beneath all the dried blood, there was a pretty girl. She stood and extended her hand. A small, azure beetle tattoo decorated the back of it, between her thumb and forefinger.

"My name is Dhalia," she said. "Come with me. I know a place you can go."

[•••]

Dhalia led Maerl through one of Crescent's storage levels. Dark corridors went on and on with no seeming end. They turned a different direction at each junction. Maerl was positive they were lost by the time she finally stopped their trek at a rusty bulkhead. She tapped in an entry code on the keypad beside the door. Locking mechanisms released with a clank. She pushed the door open and took Maerl's hand.

Dahlia guided Maerl into a warehouse. A thick layer of dust covered a handful of empty and scattered shipping containers. The warehouse hadn't been used for storage in a long time, that much was apparent. The shipping containers shared the largely empty floor space with big and unidentifiable objects that were draped in moldering canvas tarps. Dahlia led Maerl to the far end of the warehouse to where a handful of black-garbed men and women lounged on mismatched furniture. The furniture rested on equally clashing swatches of carpet. Black leaflets were piled atop several, rickety tables.

The strange den glowed with hundreds of candles. The warehouse smelled of wax, matches, and dust. As they neared the group of people, Maerl could see they wore the same tattoo as Dahlia. Some had the design on their hands; others had it on their necks or arms.

"Everyone. this is Maerl. He has nowhere to go."

The group welcomed him with soft greetings.

"What is this?" Maerl asked.

Dahlia giggled softy and stroked his arm with her blood-stained fingertips.

"We are the children of a new beginning, Maerl. The Aphotic, you silly man. I know you've seen us around," Dhalia said and winked. A shirtless man, his wiry frame covered in ink, stood and approached Maerl. He clapped him on the shoulder with a strong hand and grinned.

"Welcome, my man. Welcome. Drink?"

[•••]

"A mess. In the truest sense of the word," Captain Benedict said and tossed a data pad onto Kendall's desk. The data pad's viewscreen rotated with glowing scenes of the inside of Heathen's and the section of Main Street. Kendall hardly glanced at the images. You didn't need to stare long to know the term "mess" was a grave understatement. The timing could not have been worse.

He looked to Albin, who leaned against the closed office door with his arms crossed over his chest. A cigarette hung from his lips, the thin trail of smoke drifting up past the tall man's unshaven, freckled face.

"Youwereshootingpeople?" KendallaskedAlbin. "Ismyunderstanding correct? Shooting like you were in some carnival gallery?"

"Fuck, Kendall. That's the only way I could get out of there." Albin's words were more than a little slurred. The son of a bitch was still drunk.

"I've got Jacob Raney cutting his own cock off. I've got you drunk, shooting up Heathen's." Kendall growled and turned his eyes on Benedict. "Captain, are you about to tell me you fucked my dear, dead mother?"

"I've reviewed the feeds," Benedict said. "Things had gone to hell even before your man started shooting." Benedict looked at Albin and scowled. "I should have him booted off the station, but right now the flaunting of his firearm is the least of my worries. When things got really nasty in Heathen's is when all the cameras cut."

"Maybe for the better," Albin said. "You really want to see people choppin' each other up?"

Benedict grunted.

"I have a meeting with Captain Swaren later this afternoon," Benedict said and got to his feet. "I didn't sleep for more than a goddamn hour last night. FYI, the vatter's tour ship arrives tonight. The concert is tomorrow evening."

"Concert?" Kendall asked. "What concert?"

"Erick Haddyrein, Mayor." Benedict said.

Kendall had all but forgotten about the rockstar's upcoming concert on Crescent. Kendall had agreed to host the final performance of Haddyrein's outer rim tour months ago. It was to be good publicity for Crescent—a revitalization of the station's image. Kendall didn't realize the date had almost arrived. *You can't pay for timing like this,* Kendall thought. The station's complete disarray would be broadcast across all the seventeen systems. Kendall took a deep breath. It would be far worse to cancel the concert.

"The concert will go on. You get the station running in top shape again. Do you hear me? Work with Vegan. Pool any and all resources you need to. And make sure we have more than enough security at that concert. I don't care if you get people from off the streets."

"Yes, Mayor."

"Clean up this fucking mess," Kendall commanded.

Albin stepped aside and opened the door for the security captain. After Benedict took his leave, Albin closed the door and resumed his casual lean. He dropped the cigarette he had been smoking and crushed it out beneath his boot.

"What did I tell you about that?" Kendall said. He was not in the mood. A small, flat circular robot exited a mouse-hole in the wall and scooped up the discarded cigarette butt. It vacuumed the portion of the floor where the cigarette had been extinguished and then disappeared back into the wall.

"Things are falling apart around our ears, Albin," Kendall said and slammed his fist down on desk's dark surface. The LCDs were blank; Kendall had disabled the feeds as soon as he heard about the riot and ensuing bloodshed. "Swaren is comin' after me. By now, he's ready to make his move. You keep a close eye on him. That means, don't get drunk, you fool. We need our wits about us. We are at a crucial time here."

"Why don't we just get rid of him, Ezra?" Albin lit another cigarette.

"It's not easy to make a Core Sec auditor disappear."

Albin shrugged and said, "Matter of opinion."

"Go drink some coffee or something. Sober up, for god's sake." Albin smiled around the filter of his cigarette and left the room.

Kendall was alone.

"We had a deal," he hissed through clenched teeth. "You're *my* fucking station and we had a deal."

The office was dead silent.

"You still have no words for me? After all these years?" The mayor activated the door lock; the bolts clacked into place. He leaned back in the consuming leather chair and closed his eyes.

"Then perhaps," Kendall said, "I still have a chance."

[•••]

The conical speakers in the cell block screamed for two straight hours. When the alarm finally stopped, Gerald's ears rang with a persistence that was almost as bad as the sirens. Almost. Gerald stopped combing the cell for sharp objects to shove in his ears, and thanked every god he could think of for the silence. He even made up some gods to thank. Whatever the hell was going on in the outside world, it must have been a big deal.

Not long after blessed silence had fallen, people were deposited into the holding cells around him. Shredded clothing hung on bodies that had clearly been involved in some brand of violence. If his new neighbors had been a fighting bunch earlier, all the fight had gone out of them now. Gerald wasn't sure if he was glad to have the company. It had been quiet earlier when he was all alone—that silence had been unsettling. Now, Gerald was surrounded by people and it was still dead quiet. The variety of silence freaked him out even more.

"Hey," Gerald said in an attempt to get the attention of the opposite cell's occupant. A fat man in a stained shirt—it had to be blood—and torn khaki pants lay on his side on the cell's metal cot. The bed was far too narrow for the man's substantial girth. He didn't respond, so Gerald called him again.

"Shut the fuck up!" someone shouted from down the row.

"Mister," Gerald called, a little softer this time.

"Please. Leave me alone," the fat man said. "I just want to sleep and forget that anything happened. They promised me they'd let me go tomorrow if I kept my mouth shut. I just want to get home to my family. I just want to make sure everyone is okay."

Gerald leaned against the bars and remained silent. He looked down at his bare feet. Suddenly, the floor didn't seem so cold. Or rather, Gerald just didn't care anymore. He felt bad for the guy. The sound of defeat was thick in his voice. But, Gerald couldn't keep his curiosity at bay any longer.

"Look. I'm not trying to be insensitive. I can tell you've had it rough. I've been in here all night. Do you think you could tell me what happened out there?" Gerald asked.

"What's your name?" the fat man said, but didn't change positions.

"Gerald."

"Gerald. I'm Bob Parks."

"Nice to meet you, Mr. Parks."

"Gerald. Do you have a family?" Bob asked.

Gerald thought of Liam then. He tried to picture his older brother in the same situation, and could not.

"Not really, no," Gerald answered.

"Consider yourself lucky. Something really bad is going on around here. No one is safe anymore," Bob said.

Gerald didn't have the stomach for anything cryptic. He grimaced, but bit his tongue before he could lash out at his neighbor. The pilot took a deep, measured breath before he spoke.

"Bob. Mr. Parks. With all due respect, please don't get all preachy-creepy on me, here. I've got people that I care about on this station too, and I want to make sure they're okay. So, please. Cut to it. What the fuck happened out there?"

Silence grew between them. Gerald had all but given up on Bob Parks when the man finally started speaking.

"There was a fight in Heathen's. Turned into a brawl. Turned into a riot. And then… it happened."

"What happened, Bob?" Gerald insisted.

"I… I don't know. Horrible colors… a lot of blood and a lot of screaming. I hit the floor and started crawling. I remembered something I had learned once, in an emergency, you should crawl to safety," Bob said.

"That's if there's a fire, Bob."

"Right. Yeah. Okay. I'm lucky I didn't get trampled. But people… " Bob's voice trembled with a sob. "They were getting torn apart in there."

"It's okay, Bob. I think I've heard enough." Gerald sat down on the cold slab of a bed. He propped his chin on his hand. He was sure Bob was exaggerating a little bit, but judging by the man's appearance and the quaver in his voice, Bob wasn't exaggerating by much. No doubt Nigel was having a field day. Gerald looked at his toes and wiggled them. He told himself the riot had nothing to do with all the other weird shit that had been happening. The wrong combination of people in the wrong place at the wrong time, that was all. But that wasn't all, and he knew it.

A prisoner several cells down started muttering. The *piss off* guy yelled at him to shut the fuck up and he went silent. Gerald stretched out on his cot and yawned. Now that the alarm was silent maybe he'd get some sleep. The muttering started again. The pissed off guy was screaming for quiet again.

Maybe he wouldn't get any sleep after all, but he was damned if he wasn't going to try. What the hell else was he going to do?

[•••]

"Dad?" Ina stepped into the apartment and the door whispered shut behind her. The unmistakable thundering bass lines and enthusiastic

"Uh huhs" of Charles Mingus's Old Earth Jazz drifted from the back of the three bedroom flat. Dimmed halo-globes rendered the lines and contours of the living room furniture soft. Ina pulled off her shoes. The white soles of her sneakers were caked with dried blood. She tossed them aside. Exhaustion came over her in waves. The thick carpet pushed between her toes as she walked. If she stepped hard enough, maybe she could sink into the material and melt away. At that moment, that was what she needed—all she needed.

She found her father sitting up in bed. Donovan's features were still ashen, but there were two rosy circles of color on his cheeks. He had a plastic tray folded out over his blanket-covered legs, holding a steaming bowl of soup and a portable terminal. He studied the terminal screen and adjusted his glasses. The frames had become slightly bent and refused to sit straight.

"Hi dear," he said, and smiled, but did not look up at her.

Ina echoed the smile. Her already fragile mind had been stretched to the breaking point, and while the term of endearment from her father made the tension scale back some, she still trembled in the aftermath of the violence she had witnessed. The small taste of affection had her suddenly starving for more. The realization of it—of just how unloved she had been feeling lately—made her want to cry. She placed a hand on her stomach and wondered if it was hormones making her feel that way. Hormones, and exhaustion.

"Feeling better, Dad?" Ina asked, forcing the wave of emotions back.

"I'm feeling much better. It's amazing, really. I feel more myself than I have in days." Donovan took a big swallow of soup. Ina wondered if the riot had been the space station's way of feeding—the underlying form of life gathering strength for its final push to freedom. That the force was getting stronger could not be denied. Crescent was unstable and changing, and with each catastrophe—the floods on L Deck, and now the riots—the Three needed Ina and Marisa less to exhibit its presence. Maybe it was almost done with them.

"Something happened tonight, Dad."

"What something?" Donovan asked.

"Did you watch the news at all?"

"No. I did not," Donovan returned his focus to the terminal. "There's been nothing but bad news lately. Murders. Abductions. Fighting in the colonies… All hard to stomach when you're not feeling well. Do you want to know what Murhaté means?"

"There was a brawl at Heathen's and I was there to see it. It got out of control fast. The fighting spread out to Main Street. There was a riot," Ina said.

"Are you okay?" He asked and finally looked up at her. He didn't react to the blood stains on her clothing and Ina was taken aback. She had to gather herself before she started speaking again.

"Yes. I'm fine," she said at last and then added, "A lot of people are not."

He smiled then, and she wasn't sure if he was smiling at her reassurance or at the fact that a lot of people were hurt. Either way, his response to the news that his daughter had been caught in the middle of murder and violence was lacking. Ina wondered much of her father was present behind that familiar face. She couldn't see the purple light swimming in his eyes like she had before, but that didn't mean it wasn't there. She knew it was.

"I'm glad you're okay, Ina. It's not safe out there," Donovan said, though his words carried like an after thought. There were several seconds of quiet as Donovan returned his eyes to his terminal screen.

"Do you want to talk about what I told you yesterday?" she asked, breaking the silence with the sudden impulse to get an emotional response out of him.

"About..." he hesitated and looked up at her. His eyes flitted to her belly before returning to the terminal's display. "No."

Ina was disappointed, and a little relieved. She was physically and mentally unable to have a discussion about the tiny life growing inside of her. She was quick to change the subject.

"What are you doing, Dad?" She sat at the foot of the bed.

"A bit of research on the Anrar III mining colony. Formerly dubbed Outpost 13—the residents renamed it Outpost *Murhaté*."

"Oh." She glanced at the open bedroom door.

"As far as I can tell, Murhaté is the name of the *final* home. According to one line I read in some fragmented correspondence between miners," Donovan read directly from the terminal screen, "*There can be many vessels, but Murhaté is the omega*."

Ina nodded and studied his face. *Vessel,* she thought. Another conversation she didn't want to have. She kissed her father on the forehead and left him there.

Ina took a long, hot shower, wary that at any moment the water pressure would drop or the temperature would flare too hot or cold. She couldn't remember the last uninterrupted shower she had taken. Nothing was constant on Crescent anymore. But water pressure and temperature remained steady for the duration, and she was thankful.

After, Ina padded barefoot across her bedroom floor, slipping out her robe as she went. Naked, she crawled beneath the bedsheets. The light panes on the walls, fashioned to look like frosted windows, began to blanch with daylight. Was it really only morning? Nausea fluttered in her belly.

The fingertips of one hand trailed down between her breasts, across her flat stomach, and found the tender spot between her legs. She closed her eyes and applied the slightest bit of pressure. Ina wasn't in the mood, but the slow crimson that pulsed behind her eyes was insistent. The Red had surfaced just enough to urge her on. It allowed her to do the driving, but would not let her stop until she climaxed. When Ina came, the Red slinked back into murky depths of her subconscious, taking the nausea away with it.

She tried to sleep. She begged for sleep, but no matter how Ina tossed and turned, sleep would not come.

Finally giving up on rest, she climbed out of bed and began to dress. The window panels glowed a warm orange. *Sunrise,* she mused. Once she was clothed, she crept into her father's room. He was sound asleep. The tray was still on his lap, although it was now balanced at a precarious angle that threatened to spill both the terminal and the cold bowl of soup onto the duvet. She removed the tray delicately, careful not to wake him. Ina drew the shades down, obscuring the wall panels completely, and then clicked off the bedside lamp, setting the room to darkness fit for sleeping. She kissed her father's forehead. It was cool. His fever was finally gone.

The bazaar was quiet. Everyone Ina passed looked deeply weary. Even the children moved in listless packs. Ina looked up at sun globes that shone a fierce orange. She should have felt warmth on her face, but it was as cool as it had been for days. Her gaze dropped from the globes to a group of five or six men and women dressed in matching black tee shirts, cargo pants, and boots. Ina knew who they were: the Aphotic.

Ina thought she recognized the owner of Heathen's in their midst.

She turned down an alley to avoid them, glancing behind her several times as she went to be sure she wasn't followed. She continued on, and soon the air became heavy with the scents of cooking. Grease and spices—the odor made her mouth water and her stomach growl. She let her nose lead the way to a dwelling that seemed to have grown out of a tarnished and charcoal stained back alley wall. The bulkhead was opened wide. Ina stepped over the threshold without even thinking.

"Hello, young lady." The voice was like sandpaper. An old woman stood at the stove and monitored the steaming contents of a big, metal pot.

"I'm so very hungry and whatever you're cooking smells delicious. You must share it with me," Ina said, a bit shocked by her own brazenness.

"If you like cat, then by all means," the old woman cooed.

Ina took a step back and placed a hand over her mouth. The crone cackled. She turned then, showing a face that was older than the void itself. The old woman's wrinkles were set so deep that they appeared to go right through her head. Her mouth was an 'o' of laughter, showing a few rotting stubs of teeth.

"I'm only kiddin' dearest. No cats. Pork. Not fresh. They're not sellin' fresh pork this week. Apparently, the livestock down at the Farm is getting sick. And I ain't surprised. They gonna be dead soon, the whole lot of'm."

Though Ina was relieved the pot's contents were not feline, she was so hungry she might have considered eating cat all the same. She glanced about at the antiques that filled the home. Trinkets spilled out of crates and were stacked on just about every surface, save for an old table with a big and rusted metal base. She reached into a nearby crate and retrieved a replica of a pointy looking spaceship—wiping away some of the dust that covered it revealed the word 'Viper'. Ina tossed the Viper back in the crate. In another box she spied an old fashioned holo-projector and something called an 8-track cassette player. A fortune lay in the small space.

"Don't mind all that junk. Jus' things I've picked up along the way. I don't have the heart to get rid of'm. Now, sit my dear. It's almost done." The old woman gestured to the table. "My name is Naheela."

"I know who you are," Ina said.

"And I know you are Ina," Naheela paused, "of the Red." The crone looked back over her shoulder at the girl, and winked one cataract-milky eye.

Ina sat and contemplated the title. *Ina of the Red,* she thought, and chuckled. *Makes me sound like a Viking.* Naheela filled a plastic bowl to overflowing with thick, brown stew. Some of the liquid splashed out as she set the bowl down on the table in front of Ina, but Naheela didn't seem to mind. Judging from old stains on the table and floor, spills probably happened often in this home and were just as often ignored.

"Eat while it's hot. It's best while it's hot," Naheela said.

Ina believed her without question and took the spoon that stuck out of the steaming broth. She began to suck the stuff down. It was delicious. A plethora of spices, only a handful that she could identify, made her mouth sing. Ina looked up and smiled as she chewed. A trickle of stew ran out of the corner of her mouth when she grinned, but she didn't care. She returned her attention to the bowl, and it was soon half empty. She continued to eat.

"I know you didn't come here for stew. But you wouldn't have even spared my humble home a glance if you hadn't smelled the spices. And aren't you a lucky lil' thing that I happened to be making it."

Ina nodded. She wished she had a piece of bread. She was already foreseeing the need to clean the bowl entirely. Would it be out of line to lick it? She glanced around the disheveled living area. It probably wouldn't matter if Ina licked the bowl; she certainly questioned the receptacle's cleanliness, but she found she didn't care. *What bliss*! Ina thought. *Not to care about anything.*

"You want to know, eh? Old Naheela, she knows the way of things. She always does and always has," Naheela said. She sounded sad. "The life that stirs here. You call it the *other.* Some call it the Three. I call it the clusterfuck of the universe." Naheela laughed; there was no humor in the sound. "You're not the first to be touched." The crone shook her head and clucked her tongue against the roof of her mouth. Stray strands of greasy gray hair fell across her ruddy cheeks. "It's been right here a long time, Ina. Longer than this station. Longer than that planet out there and longer than that star. So, the knowing of one little girl doesn't really amount to that much in the grand scheme of things. But yes, it's been here all along."

"Right here?" Ina asked and looked around. Her head became foggier with each spoonful she took, but she couldn't stop eating.

"Not right here, ya fool. Just on the other side of the glass."

"The other side of the glass," Ina said.

"You think this is all there is?" Naheela spread her hands out. "The void and crap that fills it?"

"No. I know what you're saying," Ina set the spoon down as she spoke. "There could be an infinite number of dimensions in our universe. Parallel universes, even. I took more than one quantum philosophy class in my time."

"Blah blah blah. Can your smart-talk, girlie. It only makes ye sound daft. There ain't nothin' parallel about it." Naheela reached into the pocket at the front of her ratty dress and revealed two scraps of paper: one brown and one white. She held them up. "Ye see? Ye see these pieces of paper?"

Ina nodded.

Naheela crumpled them together and tossed them on the table. She smiled a satisfied grin. "Lookit that for a bit. *Really* look at it. So you understand what you're lookin' at." Naheela got up from the table; her joints popped as she moved. The old woman shuffled away and soon Ina heard her rummaging through some mess or another. Ina eyed the crumpled ball of brown and white paper. Two separate pieces of paper. One ball of crumpled paper. The folds and creases overlapped in places. She poked at it with a fingertip and wished she had more stew. Naheela returned and watched her for a moment before speaking.

"You'll get more stew in good time." Naheela shuffled away again. When she came back with no stew, Ina was deeply disappointed. The crone tossed a shard of deep red stone onto the table, so dark it was almost black. Sanguinite. The muted light reflected in a trail along the curve of the polished piece. The stone had been carved into a dagger—a beetle-shaped dagger. Ina felt her senses clear at the sight of the object.

"Ye know what that is?"

"Sanguinite. Yes. We found some … "

"On the planet. Three-quarters of that rock is full of the shit. Maybe the whole planet is made of it," Naheela said. She was slurping on something now. Ina smelled menthol. "Did ye study that piece of garbage?"

"Yes. I understand what you are trying to explain to me."

"If ye understan' so well, then tell me."

"You're saying the universe—*existence*, maybe—is different dimensions all crumpled up on top of one another. No uniformity, no pattern."

"Existence. Very good. You're smarter than you look, then," Naheela beamed. "I'm old, girl. Older than you think. I ain't wastin' my breath to tell you something you've figured out on yer own. This is the way of things. Do you believe it?"

"I believe that anything is possible," Ina said. Naheela nodded approvingly.

"Between the folds, where worlds come close together, the boundary is like glass. In some places you can see through to the other side; in some places, you can only see through one way, and in most places, you can't see nothin' at all. Ages of friction have made some spots weak. And in the weak places there is always this." Naheela held up the smooth sanguinite carving.

"What happens at the weak spots?" Ina asked.

"The life on the other side can touch us. These things can influence us in small ways." Naheela nodded.

"Life?" Ina asked.

"Not like you know it, but yes, for lack of a better word. Life."

"Can this weak glass break?" Ina asked.

"It'd be bad for the likes of you and I if that ever happened. Damn bad for sure."

"This life, from the other side. Can it ever come through without the glass breaking?"

"There are ways," Naheela said and clicked her long, curled fingernails on the tabletop. "Foolish ways."

"How?"

Naheela glanced around with a frown. She raised her gaunt shoulders in a shrug and stared at Ina's stomach for an instant. Then Naheela folded her hands over the sanguinite—when she opened them again, it was gone.

"More stew now?" Naheela asked.

"How can they come through?" Ina didn't want the stew anymore. Not now that her head was clear. She leaned forward in her chair. It creaked beneath her. "Please."

"You are a stubborn girl," Naheela said and sighed through her nose. She left the table and came back with a handheld video recorder. The thing looked as if it had been thrown down a flight of stairs, submerged in water, and then buried for a century. Naheela cleaned off the small LCD with the hem of her ratty sweater and then handed the device over to Ina.

Footage played in the small window. Ina held it close to her face. Right away she knew she was looking at the geological storehouse down on Anrar III. The footage appeared to be slowed down—people hardly moved. Ina was unable to take her eyes of the pregnant woman's swollen belly.

"The vessel was too mature," Naheela commented as Ina watched.

On the screen, a fissure opened in the woman's flesh and red and violet light poured out of her in twisting streams. Next, came a living shadow—a serpent of pure night.

"The *Other* became Three," Naheela went on. "And those very Three are now here on Crescent. Back then in that damned colony, essence already filled the intended vessel. It had a soul. The Other couldn't rest there and became stuck, halfway here and halfway there. A painful state of being. It killed all of those poor people who tried to help it. That was a long time ago. Crescent was just a babe, and was left unfinished. The science crew on Crescent *trapped* the Black in the part of the station you know as the Vault, and there it slept." Naheela thrust a finger in Ina's direction. "*Until* you woke it again. You and the other girl." Naheela shook her head. "And you now you and your belly have given it its best chance." Ina covered her stomach protectively. *The fetus growing in her womb; it was the new vessel.*

"No," Ina said. "This is too much."

"Your baby has yet to quicken, dearest. And the Other knows it. It's a cup waitin' for drink," Naheela said.

"My child has a soul," Ina spat and got to her feet. She took a deep breath and calmed herself. "What can I do? The Three are killing my father."

"He's old," Naheela nodded, as if that were all that was important about the situation.

"Please."

"The Red and the Violet. You were responsible for bringing them back here. There is only one way, now."

"What is it?" Ina asked.

The hut shuddered around them. Ina gripped the sides of her chair, but Naheela did not seem to notice or care that the walls trembled. Objects clattered to the floor, and then things grew still. Naheela clicked her long, yellowed nails on the tabletop.

"Sit, and I will show you," Naheela said.

Ina did as she was told, and no sooner than she was seated, Naheela was across the table. The crone's dry, calloused hands wrapped around Ina's throat and began to squeeze. For an instant, this seemed right to Ina. This was the way. But then, she thought of the tiny life within her and she wanted to breathe. She batted at the hands that choked her. Naheela was breathing hard through her nose. Ina could hear each respiration through the sound of her own heart pounding in her ears, along with the dull, metallic sound of her shoes kicking the table's metal base. Ina beat at Naheela's arms and face as spots began to fill her field of view. Suddenly, the grip eased and Naheela was off her. Ina fell out of the chair and onto her hands and knees. She coughed and gasped for air. Streamers of snot trailed down from her nose.

"You're crazy," Ina said, once the breath had returned to her.

"Things have gone too far. Death is the only way out that I can see. If you don't want to die, then I can't help you," Naheela said. "Let the colors do their work, and your father may be set free. But there'll be unity and the Black will be whole. What is worse? The death of your dad, or hell leaking into our side of existence? You should launch your father into the void and do the same with yourself. Now git gone."

"Wait. I have more questions," Ina protested.

"I don't give a mother-fuck about your questions, girlie. Get out of my home while you're still young and pretty." Naheela thrust an arthritic finger toward the door. "Go!"

Ina got to her feet, standing so quickly that she knocked her chair over in the process. She bent to pick it up and Naheela screeched at her.

"Leave it be, girl. Outta my sight!"

Hot tears streamed down Ina's face. She wrapped her arms around herself and darted out of the hut. She was crying hard as she stumbled back out onto Main Street but no one seemed to pay her any notice. The reality of things was far bigger than she had realized. Scientific rationale no longer applied. She had to find Marisa and tell her—tell her that she had been so wrong.

But the Red began clawing its way to the surface. It swelled forth from the back of Ina's mind and filled her insides with molten heat. She swooned and placed her hand on a lightpost to keep from falling over. Her heart pounded in her chest and she felt a warm moisture blossom between her legs. Her mind—her very will—was being peeled away, tugged back by the insistent fingers of a consuming red tide. She careened down Main Street. The world was full of colors, lights, and faces, all spinning around her. She tripped over her own feet and was falling. A set of strong arms caught her and gently lowered her to the ground. A sea of black boots and black pants closed in around her.

(Part XX)

A single whisper—that's what started it all. The first voice had been so quiet that Gerald wasn't really sure he'd heard anything. Then the solitary voice was joined by others and the whispering rose in volume. Soon, the holding area sang with full-throated and nonsensical babble. Gerald climbed off the cot and went to the bars. He wrapped his fingers around the cool, metal shafts and peered into the shadows in the cell across from his own. Bob Parks sat on his own cot, his back to Gerald. He swayed back and forth, his voice joined with the others in gibberish. Bob raised his hands above his head and then lowered them. He continued making the jerky movement while his head rose and fell in sync with his pudgy limbs. The man looked like a marionette.

"Hey, Bob?" Gerald said. Bob did not answer. *Of course he's not answering, he's busy going completely fucking crazy over there.* "Hey, um, Bob? Are you all right?"

The prisoners continued to ramble away around him. Their clipped consonants, syllables, and elongated vowels were nearly in unison, with a sing-song meter that was mesmerizing. Gerald wondered if it was babble at all. Maybe they were saying *something.* He just didn't understand a single word of it. The song spread across all the cells in the block. The sound of it made every hair on Gerald's body stand on end. He half expected—and all-feared—that the strange sing-along nonsense would start flowing out of his own dry mouth. But, thus far, no such bad luck.

"Hello!?" he shouted. "Guard? Guard?!" Gerald didn't think the guard could do anything for him, but he was getting to be genuinely afraid. He suppressed a shudder. "Fucking guard!?" he shouted again—this time, his voice cracked. *I sound crazy in my own way,* Gerald thought. *Great.* But the door to the cell block chimed as it unlocked. Footsteps sounded down the corridor, first quick and then slowing to an uneven click clack. Gerald was about to call out again when the footfalls picked up once more. "Over here!" The guard stood in front of his cell a few seconds later.

"What the hell is all this?" The guard scratched a freshly shaven scalp.

"I have no idea," Gerald said. "I just wanted to make sure that every single person on this station hadn't lost their mind."

"Why would you say a thing like that?" The guard looked up and down the corridor with wide, feverish eyes. Beads of sweat stood out on his flushed skin. "I decided to give myself a haircut." He rubbed his shaven head. "I think I'll do my eyebrows next."

The sound of glass shattering made the guard go silent. Bob Parks had put his fist through the washbasin mirror. He removed a hand now bloodied and dripping. Bob bent over and picked up a jagged piece of glass from the floor.

"He's going to hurt himself," Gerald said. His voice quavered with urgency. "Stop him!"

The guard stood frozen from the neck down. Only his head moved, twisting back and forth, birdlike, between Gerald and Bob. Gerald and the guard watched Bob lie down on his cot and rake the sharp bit of glass across his jugular. Dark liquid erupted from the wound.

"Jesus god!" the guard gasped, and bolted for the exit.

"Hey, you son of a bitch!" Gerald shouted after him. "Don't you fucking leave me in here!"

One by one, the voices dropped out of the choir until Gerald was once again surrounded by complete silence.

Silence, and fresh death.

[•••]

"Have I wronged god himself?" Captain Benedict asked as he looked up from a scatter of papers on his desk. He gaped at the mess as if he didn't know where it had come from or what in the hell he was going to do with it. He laid a finger on one page. "That—that's from Kendall's office. It says that now that Main Street is opened, security needs to be tripled over the next twenty-four hours." He laid a finger on a document that poked out from underneath the first. "This one is from that damn vatter's concert promoter. Mr. Haddyrein will be arriving with his tour in *thirty-six* hours. Oh, and this, last night… " he hoisted a thin piece of paper. "This is the notice from Nigel Swaren saying that every report, every communiqué, every goddamn thing is to be printed out from this point forward. So I'll ask you again—" Marisa stood forward, ready to answer. "No. Not you, Griffin." Benedict's tired eyes looked ceilingward. "*You*. I ask you, what have I done to thee?" He barked a laugh that sounded more weary than amused. "Paper," Captain Benedict grumbled. "When have *I* ever used paper?"

"I'm sorry, Captain," Marisa said and placed a hand on his shoulder. He patted it, then heaved a sigh and slumped in further into his chair.

"This too shall pass," he said in a most unconvincing tone, but she forced herself to nod her head in agreement. The captain glanced around the room. "At least there have been no power fluctuations in the past twenty-four hours, and the environmental grid seems to be cooperating on all decks. According to Vegan, whatever was wrong is no longer wrong."

"Does that mean he fixed it?" Marisa asked.

"I didn't ask. I didn't want to know. We're stretched too thin, Marisa, with the added security on Main Street, the arrival of this colony ship, and this goddamned concert. I've got a lot of sick officers—some bed-ridden, and some that have not showed up to work in days with no word. It's like my men are vanishing, here. If another riot happens—say, at the concert—there'd be no stopping it."

"Well, who ever heard of a riot happening at a rock concert?" Marisa said, and flashed her teeth in a bright grin.

There was a moment of silence, and then both she and the captain were laughing. It felt good to laugh, but it was short lived. A young officer burst into the office. Beads of sweat glistened across his clean-shaven scalp.

"What is it, Jenkins?" Benedict sounded both irritated and disinterested.

"Holding cells. The rioters. You should… they… " He bent over and vomited all over his boots. The thick, pungent odor made Marisa want to toss her own cookies.

Benedict was on his feet immediately and heading toward the holding cells. Marisa followed close behind.

Silence greeted them when they entered the cell block. *It's too quiet,* Marisa thought. *Oh, Gerald.* Her stomach did a somersault.

"Hello?" She heard the salvage pilot's voice clear as day, and thought she would melt through the floor with relief. "Please, are any of you still… .okay?"

"Gerald… Mr. Evans. Please remain calm," Marisa said. Benedict shot her a sidelong glance as they moved down the narrow corridor with slow steps. The rioters lay on their cots, not moving.

"They all slit their throats. At least, I'm assuming they all did." Gerald said from down the hall. "The glass from the mirrors. They broke the mirrors above the sink. They used the glass and cut their own throats. Just like that. Man, what the fuck?"

"Mr. Evans," Captain Benedict said, "please relax. We're checking it out."

But Marisa didn't need to do all that much checking out to know that it was true. Shards of glass lay on the floor of each the cells. Light reflected dully off the bits of mirror and the spreading pools of blood beneath each prisoner's cot. Things were getting worse, fast. With each death on the station, she knew the Beast in the Vault grew stronger. She looked to the captain.

Captain Benedict rubbed his temple, then activated his cochlear. He frowned and spoke softly, requesting a coroner and a meat wagon.

"Yes. That's right. At security HQ." Benedict paused and listened. "No, we're fine. Some of the rioters from last night are dead." Another pause. "No, suicide. Cut their throats. Just hurry it up," he paused and listened. "The rioters at the penitentiary, too?" He turned to Gerald. "Mr. Evans. Are you feeling any... unnatural urges?"

"I thought I wanted to take a shit a little while ago," Gerald called, "and considering the lack of privacy and good reading material, I thought that was pretty unnatural. Now I just want to get out of here. Can you at least let me out until these goddamned bodies are gone?"

"I'm afraid not, Mr. Evans," Benedict responded.

"Captain. What's the harm? It's not like Gerald Evans is a hardened criminal. As far as we know, he hasn't hurt a fly."

"As far as we know," Benedict said. "Well put. He stays in the cell. We go back to the office and wait for the meat wagon. Clearly, this was some sort of post-traumatic stress incident. We'll start filling out the reports that Swaren will most certainly be asking for. That little bastard is becoming quite the pain in the ass, isn't he." Benedict made it a statement, not a question.

Marisa nodded. She wanted desperately to go to Gerald's cell and look at his face. To see him for a second, that's all she needed. Instead, she followed the already-exiting Captain Benedict. *Don't you go and do anything stupid,* she thought with all her will. *Please hear this, Gerald. Please hear this, you son of a bitch.*

[•••]

"What do you mean, she won't see me? She doesn't make those decisions—she's a whore!" Kendall all but screamed.

Albin shrugged and focused on rolling a cigarette, his long fingers working with delicacy. He licked the seam of the smoke and inspected it. It was a fine rolling job, if he did say so himself.

"I'm just repeating what the girl at the brothel said." Albin perched the smoke between his lips and lit it. Kendall had the curtains open behind his desk. Anrar III's gray, cloud draped surface rolled by beneath them.

"And why didn't you kick in the fucking door, good Albin?" Kendall asked. "Isn't that just your style?"

Albin took a drag. He hadn't even considered kicking in the door. The errand wasn't one that struck him as pressing. He was no pimp. That was not why Kendall had hired him.

"I didn't think it was that important, Ezra."

"Listen, you redneck piece of shit," Kendall stood from the big desk chair and leaned so far over the glowing glass surface that Albin wasn't sure how the mayor was keeping his balance. He looked like a character out of one of Jacob's goddamn cartoons. "I decide what is important and what is not important. Don't get any delusions of grandeur. You're not much smarter than your little friend, Raney."

"Maybe so. But I still have a cock."

To this, Kendall had no response. Albin led into the next topic of import.

"The *Odessa,* a colony ship, is coming to Crescent for emergency maintenance. Vegan tells me it'll be here in less than twenty-four hours. What do you want me to do about that?"

"Two things. One—I don't want anyone from that ship leaving the hangar. They land, receive repairs, and then are off this station," Kendall said. A smile spread across the mayor's tired features. "Two—Make sure Nigel Swaren leaves on that ship, one way or another."

"Likely," Albin said, "it will come to another."

"Drug him, Albin—do not kill him, do you understand?—but make sure that he doesn't wake up until he's many jumps away. Use that... what do they call it?" Kendall paused for several seconds. Albin could see him thinking it out. "You know what I'm talking about. The retard powder."

"Fractum," Albin supplied.

"Yes. Fractum. I want him to be crazy when he comes out of it. We will report him missing to Core Sec the following day. They'll think their man went AWOL. Meantime, we'll clean up his reports as necessary."

"How do we get to his reports?" Albin asked. He hoped Kendall wasn't planning on having him mess with the paperwork. Albin was also not a secretary, that was for goddamned sure.

"Not to worry, Albin. You just leave that to me." Kendall slid back into the consuming chair and seemed to be lost in thought. "Also, bring Gerald Evans to me tomorrow morning—first thing," he said. "I'd like to speak with him one last time."

[•••]

It had been a long time since Kendall had walked through Crescent's corridors unescorted. It had been even longer since he had used the secret by-ways. Few knew of their existence—most of those who had were dead and gone. The solitude was a strange feeling. It made him feel like a ghost. He passed silent maintenance robots docked into their small charge ports. Lights flashed on their domed hulls as they took in life from the station. Most of these critters had been on the station since she was built. There was no saying how long their batteries would hold a charge. For the moment, Kendall and the robots alone shared the spaces behind the walls.

The corridor ended at a small, octagonal room bisected by another passage that disappeared into darkness on either side. Above him, a circulation fan whoomped and squeaked. A lift lay directly ahead of him. He pulled back the metal gate, collapsing it like an accordion, then stepped in and selected the appropriate level. His angular features were a mask of determination. The lift began to descend slowly at first, but then it picked up speed. Cool, stale air rushed up past his face, lifting the thin hair from his forehead. He wondered if the lift would continue to accelerate and smash him to pieces when it hit the end of the line.

It began to slow, and finally it stopped.

He pulled back the gate and stepped into another round chamber, identical to the one he had left many levels above. The large duct fan set into the low ceiling was long dead. The air was cold, very still, and smelled of dust and mildew. He could hear water dripping somewhere not far off. He was below L Deck by several wide station levels, but some runoff from the recent floods was still trapped between decks.

Kendall made his way down a lightless corridor. The very walls seemed to drain away the beam from the flashlight he held in front of him with a rigid arm. The light's meager radiance was no talisman—it wouldn't protect him from whatever lived deep in the station—but he held it poised ahead of him with a conviction as if he thought it just might. After wandering in the darkness, he finally spotted a sliver of light ahead. Approaching it, the mayor slipped his fingers into the crack. He pulled, and a panel came away, falling to the floor with a clatter. Silence amplified the sound, and the mayor cringed. He stepped through the hole he had made, out of the darkness and into jaundiced illumination.

Kendall knew he should have been thankful for the light, but something about the quality of the glow made him feel sick. The temperature in the passageway was cold. The air hung around naked halo-globes in a hazy aura, thick with moisture. It had been years since he'd been down here, and the place hadn't changed at all. Each step brought him a little closer to hell's doorstep.

The air felt electrified, like it could catch fire at any second and burn him alive. *You're just being dramatic,* Kendall told himself. *This is a superstitious trek and nothing more.* But it felt the same as it had felt fifteen years ago.

Not the same. The air felt heavier now than it had fifteen years ago—fifteen years ago, when those brats had started something *unnatural* and Kendall had been forced to fix it.

He walked on, into the depths of the unnerving silence.

Cables bound to the corridor walls looked like slumbering obsidian snakes. If he were to stumble, would they hear him and wake? As if in response, there was a rustle from deep in the shadows, like a dry whisper. Kendall stopped, turning in the direction of the sound. He squinted into the shadows, but could see nothing.

A hard shove hit Kendall from behind, sending him falling face first onto the dirty floor. He rolled onto his back and scuttled back several paces, swallowing hard and willing his gut to slow its nervous churning. The unmistakable sound of a young boy's laughter reverberated in the shadows. Maybe two boys.

"Come on, Brian..." a distant voice called. Kendall squeezed his eyes shut and the silence returned.

He got to his feet and brushed himself off. *It doesn't welcome my visit this time. It doesn't need me,* Kendall thought. *Just turn around and run. Get out of here. Get off the station. It's over.*

"It's not over," he growled to himself. "Not at all."

He arrived at the Vault several minutes later. The overhead light panels were nearly burned out there. They guttered amber. The Vault bulkhead was bigger than Kendall recalled, and its red X—a mark Kendall remembered more clearly, and dreamed about more often, than he would ever admit—was gone. The door was black as pitch and it shimmered occasionally with points of weak light, as if tiny flecks of glitter were set in the surface.

"I know you know that I'm here," Kendall said. He didn't expect a response, so he wasn't disappointed when none came. "I don't know what you want this time. I will find you another woman with child. I can do that. The child in-utero will be just as young and fresh as last time. But you have to stop this nonsense."

A low sound came from behind the door, a *woomp woomp* that Kendall felt in the cavity of his chest, more than he actually heard it with his ears. The pulsing sound persisted, growing louder with each trembling breath he took. His mouth went dry. The light globes that ran down the corridor even pulsed in time with it. *God,* Kendall thought, *it's a heartbeat.* The Beast was fully awake now.

[•••]

Nigel's instructions had been specific. Griffin could hear the auditor's voice in her head: *Wait for the signal, Marisa—no cowboy shit.* She didn't have to be told twice. The plan was risky. Hell, the risk was incalculable. Marisa didn't care. She just wanted to get on with it.

A sleek, three-leveled passenger liner glided into the hangar—the *Odessa.*

"It's a big one," Walter Vegan said past her to Albin Catlier.

"What are you doin' here, Griffin?" Albin said to Marisa, ignoring Vegan.

"My job. What are you doing here, Albin?"

"The same, Miss," Albin said, and lit a cigarette. Marisa hated the smell of the self-rolled things. The tobacco didn't smell right to her, like it was always on the verge of going bad. She looked between Catlier and Vegan, and thought the men couldn't be more different from one another. Vegan was slow; Albin was lethal. Watching him, Marisa knew that laying off the carthine had been the best thing she'd ever done.

Hissing geysers of steam pumped out of ports on the *Odessa's* side as the large ship matched pressures with Crescent. The pounding in Marisa's chest rose in tempo. She had never been as aware of its beating as she was now. Even before the steam had dissipated, a gleaming docking ramp folded out from the ship's starboard side to rest upon the deck with a loud clank. The sound of metal scraping against metal floated down to them as an oculus hatch swished open. A group of four people descended the ramp: two men and two women. One man was tall as a rod, and just about as thin. He had close-cropped black hair that was just beginning to gray at the temples. Beside him was a short, stocky woman with red hair piled atop her head. She had a pretty, if not slightly plump, face. Behind her walked a lithe, dark-skinned woman, with almond-shaped eyes and sleek black hair that was braided and fell well past her waist. Next to her walked a man of average height and build with gold-rimmed glasses. With the exception of the dark-skinned girl, Marisa didn't think any of them looked capable of staging a coup. Her palms began to sweat.

She glanced back around at their own Crescent greeting party. There was horse-face and Albin, plus five security guards who had been assigned to the detail, a last minute decision handed down from the mayor's office. No doubt, Kendall was beginning to feel concerned. Marisa didn't blame him. He had every right to be paranoid. She could almost sympathize.

The group from the colony ship halted at the foot of the ramp. The stocky woman smiled, revealing perfect teeth.

"Hello! It's lovely to be here!" she beamed. The signal.

Marisa's hand disappeared into her Core Sec jacket and came out with the gauss pistol that she had taken from the dock's confiscated weapons area. She leveled it at Albin. Beside Albin, Vegan's eyes went wide in both misunderstanding and abrupt fear. He opened his mouth as if to speak. Out of the corner of her eye she could see Vegan reaching for something. She turned the gun on him and pulled the trigger, putting a lead slug right between his eyes. He made a mewing sound, a stream of blood trickled out of the smoldering hole in his head, and then Vegan toppled face down onto the deck. Before Albin could draw his own weapon, the new arrivals had their guns trained on him. The group from the colony ship was packing heat, as promised. A second group descended the ramp. The approaching five men and women wore shiny black body-armor over their Core Sec uniforms, *and* they were heavily armed. The Crescent security team had their weapons drawn and leveled at Albin as well. The thug shook his head and thrust his hands skyward. The cigarette still dangled from a smirking set of lips.

Marisa led the strike force through a maze of maintenance corridors with practiced ease. She knew the passages well—she had spent the previous eight hours rehearsing the route so that every step she took would be quick and unthinking. There could be no hesitation now. The group came to a ladder at the end of the hallway; the worn metal rungs reflected the red glare of maintenance globes set amongst thick cables on the walls. She holstered her gun and ascended. When she finally reached C Deck, her arms trembled from the strain. If Kendall wasn't in his private quarters as Nigel had promised he would be, the plan was done.

The team's boots clanked on the narrow service walkway as they headed down another tight passage. The corridor widened where it terminated. A false panel leaked light at the end of the channel. Marisa kicked the thin, metal square in. It was a foolish and impulsive move, and she regretted it the instant bullets and needles rained into the passageway. The projectiles sang as they glanced off the walls and floor. Someone cried out behind her, and everyone hit the deck.

"Fuck," Marisa gasped. Another member of the team cried out, hit. The hallway had become a shooting gallery—there was no cover. *One, two, three, goodbye to you and goodbye to me,* Marisa thought, and an object whistled past her head from behind. She closed her eyes. A second later a flash grenade went off with an enormous bang. There was a cry from the other side of the open panel. The *Odessa* strike force pushed past her and into the other room. A couple fleeting bursts of gunfire sounded, and then there was blessed silence. Marisa's ears rang painfully. She pressed the heels of her hands to them as she got back to her feet.

She found three Crescent security officers handcuffed and sitting against a far wall when she stepped out of the tunnel. Their heads were hung low, like they had just lost a soccer game. A Crescent security officer lay in the middle of the room in a spreading pool of blood. The *Odessa's* medic tended to the fallen woman, whose chest rose in quick, labored breaths. Marisa looked back out into the hallway. One of the *Odessa's* officers was bandaging up his own leg.

[•••]

Kendall sat grim-faced in his bed chamber, his body wrapped in a thick terry robe. A nude woman occupied his bed. The sheets were pulled up to her chin with one hand and she had a needle gun leveled at Kendall with the other.

As the security team put handcuffs around his bony wrists, Kendall looked at the girl in his bed in a way that turned Marisa's blood to ice. It was a look that said, *If I get out of this situation, you'll be worse than dead.* When Kendall turned the same look to Marisa, she gave him her best shit-eating grin. She expected a speech out of the typically gregarious man, but he remained silent as he was led out of the room in his robe and slippers. For once, Ezra Kendall had nothing to say. He had fallen into their trap, hook, line, and sinker. Had the hooker been Nigel's plan? Well played, indeed.

"Good work," the stocky redhead said to Marisa and extended a hand. "I'm Captain Judy Rosenthal."

Marisa took the hand; it was warm, the skin soft. The grip, however, was anything but weak.

"Lieutenant Marisa Griffin," Marisa said with an easy smile. "But you knew that."

"Yes. You did extremely well here, Marisa."

"I didn't know Kendall would have a compliment of officers in his personal chambers. I'm sorry." Marisa paused and then added, "Is your boy okay?"

"Mitchie? Yeah. He'll be fine. Bullet went right through his calf. It missed the bone and any major blood vessels as far as he can tell. A quick patch-up and he'll be playing basketball in no time. As for Geiden, she's on her way to the *Odessa's* sick bay. We'll do everything we can for her."

"What's next?" Marisa asked.

"Who can say? Certainly not me. Not my job. I perform the coup, I don't follow up. There are administrators aboard the *Odessa* that will be taking over the operations here. Better them than me." Captain Rosenthal winked a hazel eye and left the room.

"Are you okay?" Marisa asked the prostitute.

"I said I'd never let his shriveled old prick near me again. And he still had time to fuck me before you all showed up." Her words were caustic as she turned her head up toward Marisa. One of her eyes was milky and blindly stared off to one side, the other eye was dark and swam with tears. Marisa didn't know what to say.

"I'm… sorry."

"Whatever," the prostitute sighed. "We get to choose our clients most times. Most, but not all. Men like Ezra Kendall… they choose you."

The prostitute slid off the bed and began to dress quickly. Once she was mostly clothed, she gathered her shoes and her bag and held them close to her chest, making for the door.

She paused only for an instant. "I'm done here, right?"

"As far as I know, you are," Marisa said.

"Good." The dark-haired girl left without another word.

Marisa sat at the edge of Kendall's big sleigh bed. She was alone now. The coup was over, but the uneasy flitter of butterfly wings had yet to leave her stomach in peace.

[•••]

Marisa found Gerald asleep in his cell. She envied the near peaceful quality of his slack features—she almost didn't want to wake him. The ridiculously old-fashioned lock on the cell door turned over with a clank. His features went rigid and he sat upright so abruptly that he came close to falling right off the sorry excuse for a bed. He rubbed at his neck and blinked up at her. She sat down beside him and placed a hand on his knee.

"It's over, Gerry."

"It's… over?" He cocked his head; he didn't understand.

"Kendall. We arrested him an hour ago," she said.

"And it took you an hour to come over here and get me out? Shit." But he smiled. He leaned over and kissed her on the lips. "I have no speech prepared. I'm ready to get the hell out of here."

[•••]

"We've got a ride away from here, you know," Marisa said as Gerald punched in the access code for his apartment. He looked at her as the door chimed that it was unlocked.

"I've got a ride," Gerald said, "named Bean, who I think would be extremely upset were I to leave him behind." He stepped into the apartment and she followed. The door hissed shut behind them.

A woman stood in the center of Gerald's apartment.

She screamed.

Three long, grievous wounds ran from her left shoulder to her right hip, as if she had been brutally raked with some crude weapon. The wounds oozed blood and were laced with what looked like black oil. Wide and bloodshot eyes stared out from her dirty face. Her hair clung to her skull in bloody mattes. She screamed again. Gerald grabbed Marisa's arm.

He was seeing it, too.

"No!" the girl cried. "You can't let them take it from her! Unity! It will bring unity!" She bolted at them and both Marisa and Gerald took a step back, relinquishing their grip on one another. The girl disappeared through the closed door. Marisa looked at Gerald and he frowned.

"Marisa," he said, "I don't think anything is over yet."

(Part XXI)

The Crescent security roster floated above the long, gray conference room table. A handful of names had been lined-through with glowing red—officers who were off duty on account of illness; or, worse, officers who had disappeared. The remainder of the list shimmered in green and showed an active Crescent security force far more robust that Nigel Swaren had hoped for. The text winked out and the lights came up.

"All are committed to this transition, Captain Swaren, unless otherwise indicated. You have a hard copy of the report, as requested," Captain Benedict said.

"Thank you, Captain," Nigel said, and smiled. His doubts about Benedict had been ill-founded.

"I would like to backtrack a moment here," Belinda Michaels spoke up. She had arrived with the *Odessa,* and would be running the show on Crescent until the approaching decommission—an event that would remain unannounced until Crescent had sufficient time to recover from its more recent catastrophes. Nigel nodded for her to go on. The crow's feet around her eyes deepened as she smiled. "I don't think it is necessary to keep the colonists confined to the *Odessa* any longer. She'll remain here for another day or two as final details of the transition are ironed out. Why not let them stretch their legs and see the sights? After all, this may be the last time they get a chance to see Crescent."

"With all due respect, Ms. Michaels. Ma'am. In light of the recent riots and the general sense of unrest that has plagued this station for weeks, I'm not sure that's in the best interest of the colonists," Captain Benedict objected.

"Captain Swaren?" She looked to Nigel for his opinion.

"I have to side with Captain Benedict. At least until we get things stabilized, I don't think it would be wise to introduce tourists into the population. Most of Crescent's residents are pleased with Kendall's arrest. However, there are always a few bad eggs in the bunch. Tourists are a favorite target of dissidents. At least in my experience."

"And this vatter concert—are you still planning on letting that occur?" Ms. Michaels asked. She glanced down at her personal terminal before looking from Swaren to Benedict.

"I am," Captain Benedict said. "Again, the decision is ultimately yours, Ms. Michaels, but I think the event will aid in expediting the... healing process. Renew the sense of community. A positive event after a streak of tragedies."

Belinda Michaels dipped her sharp chin in a nod.

"Very good then, Captain Benedict. You know your people better than I." She stood and straightened the small, dark suit jacket that hung from her thin shoulders, then bowed to Nigel and then to Captain Benedict. "I thank you both for your time. I have other responsibilities to attend to."

Belinda Michaels left with an armed security officer at her side. Benedict folded his personal terminal, placed it under his arm, and departed. Nigel was left in the silence of the large conference room. He suppressed a grin, but was having a harder time keeping his giddiness at bay. Kendall and his loyalists were locked up in a secret location and they'd be off the station in less than a week. A fleet of Core Sec boats was nearing Tireca and would be permanently shutting down the jump gate into Habeos. Darros Stronghold would be cut off, and the raider clans did not posses the resources to create another way around.

Vacation was blissfully close.

[•••]

Ina Cortez murmured and pulled a blanket over her naked body. She shoved a large arm away from where it was pressing uncomfortably on her breasts. The limb belonged to the stranger that lay beside her. She rolled onto her back and the man on her other side came into view; he lay with his back to her, the flesh there a canvas of so many tattoos it was hard to discern any one shape. She sat up and pulled the sheets close around her. A woman lay curled feline-like at the foot of the bed, naked save for a single black stocking. Her buttocks were pink with handprints. Ina closed her eyes and inhaled through her mouth. She exhaled through her nose and then climbed over the human mural, careful not to wake him. Black leaflets were scattered everywhere, along with sheets, pillows, and clothing. Ina tiptoed into the bathroom. The tile floor was cold beneath her feet. She closed the door, sat on the toilet, and thought one very clear and very unsettling thought.

Where am I?

Ina refused to ask *what* she as doing there. She knew. Ina felt it in the aches and pains that came each time she moved. She looked at the floor and closed her eyes. The Red had gone for now, but it had consumed her completely the night before. Without the Red, she felt empty and ashamed of the depraved things it had allowed her to do in the other room. Ina called to it. She wanted it to come back because she couldn't face reality without it.

Ina stayed locked in the bathroom for the better part of an hour and waited, but the Red didn't come. Gathering the will to stand, she climbed into shower. She set the water temperature high enough that she nearly scalded herself, but she didn't care—it was making her feel clean, and the memories of what had happened in the room outside were falling deeper into her subconscious.

Good, she thought, *The Red couldn't hold onto me for long enough. It tried, but it couldn't. I know what I have to do.* The small victory made her feel a rush of motivation.

There was still hope, but that meant she had to find Marisa before it was too late. Ina got out of the shower. After she dried off, she wrapped the thick, cotton towel around herself and unlocked the bathroom door. She would look for her clothes, but only for a minute. If she couldn't find them, she would leave in the towel. The desire for flight far exceeded any sense of modesty. She wanted to get out of there. That was all that was important. Let the people in the corridors of the station call her crazy. It was not far from the truth, after all. Ina stepped back out into the bedroom.

The human mural stood a meter or so from the bathroom door. His wiry arms were crossed over his chest. The woman who had been slumbering at the foot of the bed was not far behind him. The lone, black stocking still clung to her calf; her dark hair was a rat's nest atop her head. The man with the big arms stood next to the dark haired girl. His arms hung at his side, fists clenching and unclenching. The owner of Heathen's—Maerl—she recognized him clearly now, stood at the rear of the pack.

There was something behind their eyes; something that glowed a low but wild red.

They were not going to let her leave.

"What do you want from me?" Ina asked.

"You're very special, Ina," the human mural told her. "You have a job to finish."

"I just want to go home," Ina said. "Please."

"You must anoint the vatter—open his eyes to the Red. His will shall become," the human mural gestured to the others, "our will. The will of the Three. He will play the music that will open the gateway."

"I don't want anything more to do with this," Ina said and looked toward the door. She didn't think there was any way she could make it there.

"We have your father, Ina," the human mural said, and that changed everything.

"What do I have to do?" Ina asked.

"We will show you," he replied.

The human mural walked up to her, so close she could feel the heat of his body; his scent was powerful. She felt a flutter between her legs. She had no doubt that the same red that glowed behind her their eyes glowed behind hers now. Had she infected them? Or was it the other way around? She leaned into the mural's lithe frame and his arms slid around her. She began to cry. Ina closed her eyes and felt lips on her neck. The mural's cheeks were rough and unshaven. It hurt just a little bit, and the hurt began to fuel the Red. She felt more lips on her shoulders. They were soft and feminine. The towel was undone and it fell to her feet. Delicate fingers slipped up along the inside her of her thigh and touched her where she tingled.

There was no way out now. There was only Red.

[•••]

Gerald sat in the control couch with a bottle of 100% real, no-derivative Kentucky Bourbon resting on his knee. He uncorked the bottle and inhaled deeply. The potent aroma made his eyes water. Gerald had saved the liquor for a special occasion. What sort of occasion, he had never really been sure. Up to that point, Gerald's life had been a string of random and sometimes unsatisfying events that he followed from one star system to another. He had kept the bottle onboard Bean for almost seven years, convinced that one day, there would be a special occasion.

A thick layer of dust had accumulated on the bottle. He drew a smiley face on its side with his index finger. That made him laugh. He poured three fingers of the liquid into a highball glass and set the bottle down on the control console. Gerald put his nose of the rim of the glass and inhaled again, with a little bravado, even. *Good shit, yes-goddamn-sir.*

"Bean. It's a damn shame that you have no mouth, let alone a tongue or taste buds."

"A minor shortcoming, Captain," Bean said. "If I had a mouth and a tongue with taste buds, I hazard I'd not be dulling said taste buds with alcohol."

"You say that now, but you have no idea." Gerald hoisted the glass in the direction of one of the bug-eye cameras set across the fore of the bridge. "To you and I, buddy."

"Thank you, Captain."

"No. You're supposed to say cheers. How many times do we have to go through this?"

"Right. Cheers. Why are we toasting, Captain?"

"Because we're leaving this hunk of metal in two days. No more bad mojo. No more seeing ghosts. No more salvage. No more Kendall. Swaren deposited a hunk of change in the account for assisting Core Sec… "

"By assisting, do you mean how you got taken into custody—with your pants down, no less?"

"Forget it, Bean. We're done. Retired."

"That's good news, Captain. But I'm much too young retire," Bean responded in a tone of amusement.

"Bean, you were an old man when I bought you."

"Touché, Captain. Where will we go?"

"We've got free escort to New Juno with the *Odessa* once the Core Sec fleet arrives. I'm inclined to see what New Juno has to offer."

"I see. Very upper-crust, Captain. Will we need to begin elocution lessons en route?"

"Nope. I'm going to find a nice spot of land, away from everyone else and set up a little house there… " Gerald thought of poor Maerl—Maerl, who had lost everything in the wake of the riots. He felt a pang of guilt. Compared to Maerl, Gerald had not earned the retirement. He reached out and removed the photo of his brother from the control console. Liam's smile was still bright, Liam's wife was still beautiful, and Gerald's haircut still remained as tragic as when the photo had been taken. *I'm gonna make it count,* Gerald thought, *and then I'll have earned it. I won't take a second of it for granted, that's for damn sure.*

"Cheers, Bean."

"Cheers, Captain."

Through Bean's front viewport, Gerald saw a ship permeate the hangar's ion membrane. The long, polished Mira class cruiser was hard to mistake for any other ship. The discriminating rock star always traveled the stars in a Mira. So, Erick Haddyrein had come to Crescent Station after all. Gerald didn't think it would really happen. Erick Haddyrein was big shit—one of the music industry's biggest product pushers. Gerald couldn't quite figure out why he would choose Crescent for the last stop on his tour. But, famous people were eccentric and he was sure that Haddyrein was no exception to that rule. Gerald laughed and polished off the bourbon. He set the glass aside in favor of going straight for the teat. Maybe he'd check out the concert, for one reason and one reason alone: with Heathen's shut down for good, he had nothing better to do.

[•••]

The Mira came to a halt in a roped-off landing area. Two rows of security officers flanked the vessel. Some of the officers had just come back to duty from sick leave; Marisa couldn't help but notice that most of them still looked ill. The nose cone of the Mira lifted open and a docking ramp extended like a silver tongue. A plastic surgery job wearing a shiny chrome suit and matching tie walked down the ramp with an obvious swagger. Unnaturally blue eyes swept back and forth over the deck from beneath a shock of bleached blond hair. Marisa had almost forgotten just how fake civilized folk could look. The man smirked and halted when he reached Marisa and her security team.

"I'm Peter Trappe. Mr. Haddyrein's manager."

"I'm Lieutenant Marisa Griffin. I'm in charge of Mr. Haddyrein's security detail. As you know, we've had some recent activity on Crescent and request that Mr. Haddyrein be under guard at all times. He is to stay on his tour ship until the concert. For his safety, of course."

"That is understood very clearly." Trappe looked around the deck. "And if your main hangar is any indication, I can't see why he'd want to go anywhere else on this … station."

Marisa smiled.

"We call it Crescent, Mr. Trappe. Home," Marisa said. A figure standing just inside the nose cone of the Mira caught her attention. She wouldn't have even registered the presence had she not seen the red tip of a cigarette flaring in the shadows. She could make out the bald head of Erick Haddyrein. Trode points on the back of his hand caught stray light off the deck floodlamps and glittered diamond-like for an instant. Marisa had to work to pull her eyes away. Trappe had his hands on his hips and he eyed her with growing impatience.

"Anything else we should be aware of? Perhaps there were details omitted from your initial and wordy email communiqué?" he said.

"No," she replied and handed Trappe a small data flimsy. "My contact information. You need anything, please don't hesitate to call. Everything else should be handled by Crescent's concert promoter."

After the meeting with Peter Trappe, Marisa returned home. She locked the door to her apartment and turned the lights down low. She slipped out of her uniform and sat cross-legged on the floor. The short, bristled carpet pinched the bare flesh of her thighs and ankles. The air that hissed from the overhead vent was cool and brought goose bumps to her bare skin. The ratty armchair sat across from her—it was mostly a skeleton now, with just a few tattered shreds of fabric hanging from its black plastic frame.

Marisa stared at the towel-wrapped package beneath the piece of furniture. *Light the chair on fire. Burn this whole apartment. Get rid of that... that thing,* her mind commanded her. It wasn't too late. If only she could find a way to destroy the optical disc.

Despite her desire to end things with fire and obscenities, she crawled across the floor on her hands and knees toward the chair, her dark hair spilling over her face. She lay on her stomach and reached underneath the chair, almost expecting something to grab her and pull her under. Her fingertips brushed the towel and even through the thick cotton she could feel the concealed object's power. *If someone else touched it, would they feel it, too? If Gerald were to handle it, would every hair on his body stand on end as mine are now?* She tugged the bundle free from where it was nestled. It felt good to hold it again.

When she had sent the strange, singing hammer down garbage shaft, she had sent with it any chance of destroying the object.

Marisa sat with her back against the wall and the package resting in her lap. She unwrapped the towel slowly—not because she was afraid, but because she wanted to make each moment last. Soon, the towel was spread open on her thighs. Her face was reflected in the dark, polished surface of the optical disc. The towel was stained with a rust colored ring, as if the disc had bled while it hid under the chair. She ran her fingertip around the edge of the disc. It was cold.

The vatter would ask for it soon, Marisa knew, and when he did she would give it to him. But only when he asked. He would know what to do with it. She would wait. The Black would wait—a handful of hours was nothing.

[•••]

The hush of evening shrouded Crescent Station's main hangar. A slender woman with cornsilk hair that fell past her shoulders led a handful of black-clad men and women across the flight deck, toward the sleek Mira class starship. The four officers stationed at the foot of the vessel's docking ramp did not move to intercept the posse—they joined the Aphotic as the group passed by. The motley bunch led by the pretty girl entered the Mira with no resistance.

Even in the dark, the vatter's quarters were not difficult to locate. The blonde woman left her friends outside the narrow door behind which lay the final key to unity.

She found the vatter asleep. The bedsheets were half cast off his body. He had an erection. She slipped the paper-thin dress from her shoulders and it fell toward the ground. Time seemed to slow with the garment's descent. The blonde woman mounted the vatter. He didn't wake, but a quiet moan slipped past his lips as he entered her. She rocked atop him until he released. Even then, he did not wake, but dreamed only of red.

The air shimmered.

The dress hit the floor.

[•••]

The door buzzer rang with a sound distant and murky, as if Marisa had heard it from under water. Slowly, she clawed her way back to the shore of consciousness. She flipped on the bed side lamp. The clock told her it was 3:45 a.m. She rubbed her eyes with the heels of her hands and swung her feet out over the floor. The door chimed again.

"Jesus. I'm coming," she said.

She slipped into her pants and padded across the carpet. Movement ceased when she saw the towel open on the floor. The optical disc sat there, gleaming up at her. It grinned in a way that only a razor can smile. Marisa opened the apartment door without bothering to see who was on the other side. A man stood in the corridor. He wore a thick, hooded sweatshirt, and the hood was drawn up over his head. She didn't need to see his face to know his identity.

"Come in," Marisa said.

He entered stiffly and the door slid shut behind him.

"I've come here for something… " His voice trailed off. She put a hand on his shoulder, a gesture of reassurance. He cringed away from her. "I've come here for something… ." he repeated in the same unsure voice. Marisa knelt before the optical disc and wrapped it back up in the towel. She held it out to him and he looked at it stupidly.

"This is what you've come for. Take it."

He stood there gaping at her like an idiot. He probably wouldn't remember any of this come morning. He wouldn't remember until it counted.

Marisa grabbed his hand and thrust the bundle to it. She grabbed his other hand and clasped it around the thing. He drew it to his chest and took a step back.

"There is music on this disc?" he asked her.

"… The fuck should I know? Take it. I don't want to see it ever again." She opened the door and pushed him back out into the hallway. The door slid closed with him still looking in at her.

A pressure eased from her chest. Her head cleared and she became suddenly weak. She knew the musician had departed, and he had taken with him something far heavier than the optical disc: he had relieved her of her phantasmal chains. For the first time in as long as she could remember, she felt alone. Completely and utterly alone. Marisa began to weep. She wondered why she cried. Was it relief? She felt like she had been let go. *I can leave now.* She could leave that very instant. Her will was her own again. She was sure of it. The Black had left her. She could no longer sense it. It had slipped away to wherever it slept. The Black was resting for the final thrust.

For the end game.

[•••]

Donovan Cortez was dying. Crescent was killing him faster with each passing day. Ina had not come home to him since the terrible riots. He was frightened for her, and even more frightened for himself. He drifted in and out of consciousness so frequently that he could no longer discern waking from sleeping. The purple glow was all he could see, living and anxious. The Violet was disappointed with Donovan Cortez. It had not anticipated the man's frailty.

But if Donovan Cortez died, the Violet would be cast out, and there would not be enough time to find another with the right skills.

The bedroom door creaked opened. A figure stood there, backlit by the milky light of the hallway—a black shadow with features unidentifiable.

"Ina?" Donovan croaked. His throat felt like it was full of broken glass. The figure stood silently a moment longer, then moved out through the open door. Shadows pooled like water around its feet. "Wait." Donovan whispered. He struggled out of bed, tumbling off the edge of the mattress. His wrist gave way with a dull snap when he hit the floor—he heard it, but he righted himself and crawled toward the living room, only distantly aware of the pain that radiated up his arm. The shadow stood in the apartment's open doorway. It wanted him to follow. It had come to help him—Donovan knew it with a certainty. The walking shadow would prolong his life until he could say goodbye to his daughter. Donovan found a flashlight—he had a feeling he would be needing it—and pulled himself out of the apartment and into the corridor. It was empty, save for himself and the creature that his eyes seemed unable to focus upon.

Donovan crawled after the shadow-man for what felt like an eternity, following him through corridor after corridor until consciousness fled from him. When he came to, it was to the sensation of motion. He was lying on his back in a slowly descending service elevator. The deeper into the station the elevator traveled, the more laden with moisture the air became. When the lift door finally slid open, cold water spilled out onto the floor panels. Donovan rolled over and pulled himself out of the elevator, crawling onward through a thin layer of stinking water. *L Deck,* he thought—why else would the panels be covered in water?

The entire level was a ghost town. The corridors were lined with the mildew covered luggage, toys, and appliances the residents had been forced to leave behind when the residential level had flooded. Donovan crawled past abandoned apartments with doors that stood open. It seemed vulgar that the former homes were so exposed. Weak dregs of starlight bled through dirty viewports to show the insides of the vacant, water-damaged living spaces.

The corridor led to a dead end alley where a dark hole marred the otherwise featureless far wall; a metal grating lay cast aside in a pool of standing water. Donovan pressed his cheek to the damp floor panel, catching his breath. The walking shadow was nowhere in sight.

"Geez. I dunno, man. We probably shouldn't do this. What if we get lost?" a young boy's voice echoed from the shadows.

Donovan gathered his strength and pulled himself through opening.

It was tight in the maintenance shaft and Donovan found that he had to rely on his legs and elbows to move forward. His broken wrist was all but useless and he had cut his other hand badly at some point in the trek. Fortunately, water and grime had turned the channel's surfaces slick, making the travel easier. Donovan crawled below L Deck and the shaft began to descend sharply. His descent continued for almost thirty minutes. The small flashlight he had clutched between his teeth was useless against the shadows.

Donovan came out into a chamber where two rusted collector robots leaned against one another in awkward pose. A sneaker—a child's sneaker—and a couple of flashlights lay covered in mold and muck just beyond the robots. An exit stood at waist height on the other side of the chamber. A child's face appeared in the opening. The boy's skin was so pale, it was nearly translucent.

"What are you waiting for? Come on, scaredy cat," the boy said, and his face disappeared back into the dark.

Donovan ducked through the opening unthinkingly. A will that was not his own moved his limbs. For that, Donovan was grateful. He was so tired now.

On the other side, Donovan found dust, spiderwebs, and dying light panels. A steady drip-drop of water could be heard not far off.

He crawled past a bulkhead that looked like it had been sealed shut with a plasma caster; the seams were bloated with brownish, oxidized chrome.

A massive, black bulkhead marked the end of the line. The door pulsed and glittered. It was quite possibly the most beautiful site Donovan had ever set his eyes upon. Between the pulses of shimmering black, Donovan could make out a crude red X. He reached out for the door. Contact was the only thing that could save him now. His fingers brushed against its ice-cold surface.

"Brian, let's go. I don't like it here," a voice in the shadows said.

"Wanna run home to mommy? Go, run home, then. I'm gonna touch it," another voice replied.

"No, Brian. Come on. This isn't cool. Let's go."

Donovan's hand fell away. Even that brief touch had started his heart pounding with a renewed surge of energy. He got up on his knees and placed both hands on the door. The cold hurt. It made the muscles in his forearms spasm and cramp. He was sure he'd lose the first few layers of skin when he took his hands away—possibly a finger or two.

But Donovan didn't want to take his hands away. Ever.

It was the last thing in the world that he wanted to do.

(Part XXII)

The cavernous room rumbled with the sounds of the eager crowd even before Erick Haddyrein's fans were admitted to the auditorium. Shapes could be seen moving on just the other side of the opaque flexi-glass scrim. The concert atrium and adjoining foyer were packed to capacity with Crescent residents. The corridors that fed the atrium were equally filled. Marisa watched the crowds on a security monitor. She felt measured doses of both good cheer and unease. This was a good event for the station, so long as those in attendance behaved themselves. Things had finally begun to stabilize after being out of whack for so long. Crescent's citizens needed something good, something from the outside the station. Haddyrein was well-loved across the seventeen systems, and judging from the crowded concert area and the lines that marched to the auditorium, Crescent was no exception. Marisa herself enjoyed his music. Maybe not enough to have camped outside the box office months ago, but she was more than happy to check out the concert for free.

The free concert came at the cost of vigilance.

Marisa was on the clock, but she had a feeling that the evening would go smoothly enough that she could hazard to enjoy herself just a little bit. Security was thick. Haddyrein's personal muscle detail supported Crescent's staff. There was more than enough manpower to deal with anything that might happen. She rapped the faux-wooden railing with her knuckles and then looked out over the concert hall. Music thumped from massive honeycomb speakers embedded in the walls. A waving curtain of blue-green light obscured the stage from view. The shifting luminance was hypnotic. She smiled.

Marisa wouldn't deny that she was feeling better. Her head was clear, maybe clearer than it had ever been. All the strangeness that had plagued her recently was fading fast from her memory. It all seemed like a bad acid trip. Things that had seemed so dire, almost seemed foolish now.

But regardless of the attitude adjustment and the improved outlook, her plan was still to put Crescent behind her. She need a change, and would be off-station in two days. Gerald was leaving Crescent, too. They weren't headed out together; per se. Shit had to be worked out in that department. But, there could be a future there. Core Sec had paid him a big chunk of change for his involvement in the successful coup, so Gerald was going to retire; hang up his wings. Good for him. Gerald had never liked space. With his bank account showing lots of zeros, he would never have to fly salvage again.

A security officer entered the auditorium through a red-lacquered door. Marisa remembered having gone through that same door not so long ago. She marveled at the distance of the memory. *It almost seems like it didn't happen—at least, like it didn't happen to me.*

She activated her headset.

"Okay, Miguel, open the doors. Let's let these people in before they flatten themselves."

The man on the dance floor gave her an enthusiastic thumb up and ducked into a control booth. The big partition ascended with a whine of motors and disappeared into the ceiling, and the people began to file into the auditorium. Security checks and spinning turnstiles made the march an orderly one. Soon, the room echoed with thousands of voices. The space filled with an acrid haze of booze and cigarette smoke. Marisa glanced down at the bar that stood five meters below her monitoring platform. She would've killed for a drink in the name of good times and new beginnings. She couldn't really recall the last time she had drank for pleasure. Perhaps at the end of the night, she and Gerald could find a place to grab a cocktail or two.

Yeah, she thought, and smirked to herself, *that'd be really nice. So long as he doesn't get too bombed beforehand.*

It took more than an hour to fill the entire auditorium. So many people had showed up for the concert, some were forced to watch it on the big holo-projector out in the atrium. As far as she was concerned, Marisa had the best view in the house. The anticipation in the air was palpable—as if electricity arced from air molecule to air molecule, causing the whole room to buzz. She closed her eyes for a moment and savored every sound and smell. It was life. The crowd began to cheer and she opened her eyes just as the house lights darkened, filling the room with the stage curtain's ever-changing light. The blue-green radiance bounced off thousands of glittering mirrors embedded at random in the floors, walls, and ceilings, and danced upon every surface. The photosensitive flooring swirled beneath the crowd's feet.

The curtain shimmered out of existence.

A vaguely glowing fog-like haze filled the stage. The vatter's equipment looked like dark, hulking beasts hiding in the murk. A green light grew from panels set in the platform, and as it brightened, a large, glass vat became apparent as the heart of the flaring beacon. The glittering liquid inside the crystal chamber scattered the light and shot it back in a thousand different directions. A beat began to pulse. More than pulse, it began to throb. The crowd swayed to the rhythm, wrapped in shifting shadows and bursts of colorful effulgence.

A shape plunged into the liquid with a mighty splash. Purple, red, and green light flared in a blinding explosion and the opening song roared across the room like a helium flash.

[•••]

"I hope this isn't a bad time, Captain." Crescent's head of security stood in the open doorway to Nigel's temporary apartment. Nigel folded the last of the few articles of clothing he had on the station and placed them in a suitcase. He looked up and smiled.

"Not at all, Captain Benedict," Nigel said.

"I'm surprised you're not at the concert."

"I could say the same for you."

"A security captain is never off duty, it would seem," Benedict said. "There are still some matters. How do I put this? Delicate matters, pertaining to our Mayor Kendall… "

"Former mayor," Nigel interjected.

"Yes, *former* mayor. There are final matters that need to be dealt with. Ezra Kendall is not your typical prisoner, Swaren, and there are some things you should know. Some things you should *see* with your own eyes if you're going to call your job here complete."

"Things such as?" Nigel asked, his curiosity piqued. He stopped packing and stood, hands on his hips. Benedict shrugged and smiled.

"Not here. There is still some loyalty to Kendall in the ranks. It's not safe to do this here."

"Okay, Captain." He paused. "Should we notify Belinda Michaels?"

"I've got someone on their way to her office," Benedict said.

"Fair enough. Let's go, then."

[•••]

Belinda Michaels sat behind the former mayor's large desk. She had disabled the desk-embedded security feeds. The crazy, ever changing cross-hatch of images and video made her head spin. She had plenty to think about for this interim rule. Crescent had a security force; let them monitor the feeds. After all, that was their job. *Mayor Kendall must have been over the top with his paranoia,* she thought with a smirk. She fingered a control on the arm of the chair and it rotated to face the large viewport. The curtains hummed open to reveal a dense starfield laced with glowing, orange-red nebulosity. She couldn't argue with the view. For the time being, it was better than Galatea's view of the hand toss of dead rocks. With the Habeos gate being closed, the sentry guns would be dismantled. The asteroid field would be harvested and cleared in due time.

The door chimed, and she rotated the chair to face it.

"Come," she said. It then struck her as strange that her personal guard hadn't notified her of a visitor. But at that point, it was already too late. The door was swinging open.

Belinda Michaels only had time to register two things:

The way the man's stubble looked like rust in the orange light cast by the nebula and the flare of equally orange light that sprayed from the barrel of the needle gun.

[•••]

The pounding bass tones were going to crush his heart at any moment, Gerald was convinced, but he didn't care. He danced like a drunken idiot and loved every second of it. From his location in the auditorium, he could see Marisa on her balcony. He respected that she was on duty, so he wouldn't bother her just yet. *Maybe after a few more frosty ones,* he thought, *I won't have so much respect for her duty.* Until then, he was content to enjoy the pure sensory overload that was a vatter concert. Erick Haddyrein twisted and spun in the viscous liquid that filled the vat. Light poured through the chamber's thick, clear walls in a dizzying spasm of color. Rainbow lances of photons, beginning as pinpricks, exploded from the sparkling trodes attached in multitude to Haddyrein's nearly naked form. The beams cleaved the smoky darkness.

Thick fiber optic tentacles slithered and curled on the stage like great, glowing serpents. Liquid-filled orbs attached to their lengths pulsed in sequence. At times, the long structures would roar out from the stage to circle above the audience. If Gerald were on anything hallucinatory, he was sure he would have lost his mind by then.

The lights went dim and the sound died.

A muted click came from the speaker system and then the music started again. Notes screamed from the speakers, the pitches high and ugly. Gerald pressed his hands against his ears. Something had gone wrong with Haddyrein's gear. The vatter himself looked panicked inside his glass chamber.

The trodes on his body began to pulse madly.

And then Haddyrein writhed as if he was in pain. The speakers howled. The bass notes were a low rumble that sounded like the very end of the world and the auditorium shuddered with each thunderous pulse. Gerald turned to move for the doors, but the rest of the concert goers, stricken with panic, had the same idea. The crowd ripped down the security check points as if they were made out of cardboard. As unpleasant as the sounds coming from the speakers were, Gerald figured getting trampled to death would be even worse. He jumped behind one of the sidebars for cover. A bartender crouched there, her arms over her head protectively. Black mascara streaked her powder-white cheeks. She stared at him wide-eyed. He put a hand on her leg and mouthed *everything is going to be all right.* If he believed that, though, he wouldn't have been cursing himself for not having left Crescent that morning. She held out her hand to him; a set of earplugs sat on her open palm. He took them gratefully.

[•••]

"This way, Captain Swaren." Benedict opened a narrow bulkhead that marked the end of an even narrower passage. Nigel looked at Benedict uneasily. Three officers from Captain Benedict's own personal company had escorted them to the remote location. The officers stepped through the bulkhead first. Nigel took that as an encouraging sign that nothing deadly lay in wait on the other side. *No need to continue your paranoia, Swaren,* he thought to himself.

"After you, Captain Benedict," Nigel said, turning to face Crescent's head of security, only to be caught square in the chest by Benedict's outthrust hands. Nigel tripped on the door's raised threshold and he fell through, landing on his back with a jolt, his chest still stinging from the blow. He scrambled to his feet and lunged for the door as it swung shut, but was rewarded only with cold metal on his palms. Nigel stepped away and unholstered his sidearm. Around him, the Crescent security officers had their weapons out and were speaking to one another in clipped, nervous chatter. The officers had no idea what was going on, either.

Nigel surveyed the cavernous hangar. Large, metallic cargo crates were stacked one atop the other. Benedict was watching them through the small glass porthole in the bulkhead, but he would not make eye contact.

A light came on up above and Nigel lifted his eyes to see people filing onto a glass-enclosed observation deck. The lanky shape of Crescent's former Mayor Kendall was unmistakable. Kendall approached the glass and waved. His voice echoed from the hangar's PA system.

"I was afraid we wouldn't get the chance to say good bye, Mr. Swaren," Kendall said. "After all we've been through during the course of your visit, that would have been a damn shame."

Nigel said nothing.

Kendall sighed. "Swaren, I know about your little station in Tireca. It will never replace Crescent. You and I both know that asteroid field will never be safe to mine. And without precious minerals, that station will never get finished."

"Where is Belinda Michaels? Is she safe?"

"She is in good hands, Mr. Swaren," Kendall said. "Is she safe? Not likely. Goodbye, Mr. Swaren."

A klaxon filled the chamber.

The hangar doors rolled away on their tracks and air began to roar out into space. The vacuum plucked away cargo containers like they were pills in a pillbox. Nigel skidded along the floor on his back. Two of the officers were sucked, flailing, out of the station. The remaining officer was gripping a handrail and screaming in terror. She had the prettiest auburn hair Nigel had ever seen. Nigel continued to slide. He managed to roll over onto his stomach and tried to clutch at the deck grating as it blurred past him. Several of his fingernails tore free and he cried out. Nigel knew he was moving too fast to get any kind of purchase—he was more likely to lose his fingers entirely. His shoes were pulled right off his feet. It struck him as both absurd and mortifying. The officer with the pretty hair was brained by an untethered storage crate. Her grip fell slack and she slid past him.

A big container, painted a shade of baby blue—the color of childhood toys, of teddy bears and footed pajamas—rocketed toward him like a freight train. Sparks flew out around its belly like luminescent sea foam churning at the bow of a ship. Nigel could feel the cold of space on his bare feet as he neared the open hangar bay doors.

He could smell the cargo container's burning paint.

There was no way out of this one.

He closed his eyes.

[•••]

It takes .36 seconds for an average human being, under relaxed conditions, to take in a single breath.

A single inhalation.

It took Marisa the span of a single breath to become fully cognizant of what was going on. A black, multi-fingered crane lifted Haddyrein out of the shining goo. Half-submerged, he swished his arms in chaotic arcs, streaming the viscous material over his head in sticky flashes of glare. The large speakers vibrated in their casings with hellish sounds. The question of what had been on the optical disc from the cistern had been answered. It was music—but not the sort intended for human ears. Marisa was thankful to be wearing earplugs, but even the ceramic plugs were not enough to dull the sound.

Below her, the less fortunate were on bent knees with their hands over their ears. Blood gushed out between splayed fingers and ran down their arms. The poor bastards had likely been pumping the concert through cochlear implants when everything went to shit. She looked back to Erick Haddyrein. The vatter now hung limply from the retrieval crane. The trodes attached to his wet flesh pulsed dimly. Marisa didn't think Haddyrein was dead, but she was pretty sure he'd be a vegetable for the rest of his life—however long that might be. The entire station seemed to tremble with the sounds screaming out of the speaker system. The stench of melting plastic soon overcame the concert smells. The speakers were burning.

Marisa put one foot over the edge of the balcony, followed it with the other, and climbed down a trellis decorated with glowing vines of blue fiber optics. She nearly fell several times before she reached the floor. She ran across the center of the dance pit. Most of the people in attendance had already fled, leaving the trampled behind. Motionless, with limbs at awkward angles, the forsaken all looked dead. She was sure some of them *were* dead, but she was also sure that some were just knocked out cold. That was for the medics to deal with when they arrived. If they arrived. For now, she had to stop the noise. She climbed onto the stage and gawked at all the gear up there. Interlocking cables as thick as her arm connected the equipment. She picked a cable at random and tugged, then moved to another, pulling them free from their large, gold input jacks. The cables gave way grudgingly. If she made it through the ordeal alive, she would have one hell of backache. Despite her efforts, the speakers' demonic chorus did not abate. Marisa gave up on unplugging gear. Casting about for another solution, she found a stray microphone stand with a heavy metal base. She hefted it, then swung it at a delicate-looking array of computer equipment. Colorful flashes of sparks and choking smoke rewarded each downward stroke. She smashed one throbbing unit after another.

And then there was stillness.

An instant later, a loud splash made her turn on her heels. Haddyrein's crane had released him and he was sinking toward the bottom of the liquid filled chamber. A slow trail of bubbles rose from his lips and nostrils. She made a hasty path toward him and had almost reached the vat when the floor came alive.

[•••]

Gerald lifted his head to peer over the sea of broken, multicolored glass that covered the bartop. He saw Marisa as she raced across the floor. She leapt over the prone bodies of concert goers and clambered onto a stage that was pulsing with so many different colors, he thought he might seize just by looking at it.

But Gerald didn't seize. He looked to his mate-in-hiding and mouthed the words 'stay put'. At her nod, he clambered over the top of the bar, cutting himself in the process, and half crawled and half rolled off the other side onto a sprawl of fallen stools. He groaned as he got to his feet.

On the stage, Marisa was beating the ever-living crap out of the vatter's multi-million credit gear. She had the right idea, and Gerald hoisted one of the stools and ran toward the stage to help her. Suddenly, the music stopped, but Gerald's ears continued to ring in retaliation. He watched with growing alarm as the black digits of Haddyrein's crane disengaged one by one. Haddyrein seemed suspended in midair, like a character out of an old fashioned cartoon, and then he splashed into his light-goo.

It was as if the vatter's impact was the trigger, tugging the floor right out from underneath Gerald just like the old tablecloth trick. *And the flowers are no longer standing!* Gerald would have laughed at the comedy of it, were he not sailing through the air. He landed hard on floor's rebar support structure. The bar stool clattered onto its side a meter or so away from him. The now-black dance floor moved like a tidal wave with bits and pieces of photosensitive tile flying off in its wake. Something big beneath the floor was moving, roaring toward the stage. Marisa screamed and darted for the rear of the platform. The floor-wave slammed into the stage; the vat shattered in a cloud of diamond-glass and glowing liquid.

The auditorium was mostly dark as the dust settled, lit only by a few sputtering electrical fires. Hunks of debris crashed to the ruined floor, punctuating the stillness like afterthoughts. Gerald limped to the stage on the crosshatched metal supports. A pile of rubble and sticky liquid was all that remained of the structure. Gerald dug through it as best he could, but after just a few minutes he had already worked his hands raw.

Marisa was gone.

"Down here!" Marisa's voice called from below. A hallucination brought on by impending grief? He hobbled around the rubble pile. The floor had been peeled away from behind the stage thanks to the tidal force of the wave. Marisa lay on her back about three meters below the auditorium, covered in thick, white dust. It looked like someone had thrown a bag of flour at her and scored a direct hit.

"I thought I lost you." Out of breath and choked by emotion, he asked, "Are you okay?"

"Now sure as shit isn't the time to get sentimental, Gerry." She stood and grimaced. "Ankle is mildly fucked," she said. "But yeah. I think I'm okay, otherwise. Are you?"

"I'll be all right as soon as my heart slows the hell down and my ears stop ringing from the aural ass-fucking," he said. "Can you walk?"

[•••]

Donovan's ears filled with a chorus of whispers and dry rustles, rising in pitch and intensity—the sound of dead leaves blowing across concrete. The lights in the tunnel flared. Old ceiling mounted speakers spewed forth an awful sound along with big, dark clouds of dust. The sheer pain of the noise almost brought Donovan back around. For a split second, he felt rationality return; in the next, he thought his skull would split down the middle. The Vault's massive bulkhead trembled beneath his frozen hands.

A banshee's wail rolled down the corridor toward him and then the shuddering door ground open. Its old mechanics cried mournfully after hundreds of years of disuse. Donovan stood with creaking, trembling knees and stumbled over the threshold into the corridor beyond, into darkness. Light panels set in the ceiling of the revealed passage flickered an azure so deep it was almost black. The walls glittered as if painted with the very stars that Crescent floated through.

The air was cold and Donovan could see his breath. Each inhalation made his lungs burn. He walked down the corridor, letting his feet take him where they would.

He passed two motionless collector robots. These models were black metal creations that rested on curved, many-jointed legs—different from the typical units that were on the station. Their standard arm attachments had been replaced with long, rusted tethers that looked like tentacles. Multiple sensors dotted the automatons' heads, glowing like hot embers. Donovan approached one of the robots for closer inspection. The big machine raised itself on its curved legs and stood to its full height. It was easily three meters tall. Then the robot bent back down, leaning over Donovan to examine him closely. Servos whirred somewhere deep within its metal body. The collector straightened and moved away with loud, shuffling clanks. It was joined by the other big robot. Donovan looked over his shoulder and watched the things disappear through the open Vault door.

The robots are part of this station—and this station is inextricably part of the Three now, Donovan thought distantly.

He traveled down the corridor, feeling like he was not covering any distance. There were more collector robots here; each activated with his passing and moved down the passage in the way he had come. At times, the tunnel submerged into inky blankness so complete that the collectors appeared only as floating orange lights. The smoldering eye nodes would swing in close to Donovan and then move away behind him, carried by invisible, clanking limbs. Creatures that defied identification dwelled in the patches of darkness. Shifting, amorphous forms drifted past, glowing like afterimages. Faces lurked in these changing shapes, their mouths stretched wide in silent screams.

His flashlight was worthless against the unnatural darkness, so he cast it aside.

Pleas echoed around him—long-forgotten cries for help, trapped for centuries between bulbs of the hourglass. Something very bad had happened down here in the dark. He trailed his fingers along sealed bulkheads. The doors were welded shut. Some of the bulkheads had dusty viewports. Backlit, the windows in the sealed doors were like blue disks suspended in the murk. Donovan peered through one. Corpses lay one over the other behind the door. He was in a crypt.

He could feel the fever creeping back up behind his eyes. He was weary and wanted to stop, but the Violet pushed him on.

At last, Donovan left the darkness behind him. He came to a well-lit intersection where the corridor split in two. He chose the passage to his left and followed it a short distance to where it ended at a glass door. The door was labeled *Infirmary* in yellow block letters. The door slid open, squeaking and rattling in its track. Donovan stepped into the flickering light of a medical suite.

The room was in perfect order. Neat vials stood on countertops that had likely been well-polished once. Long-expired medications lined glass-faced freezer units. Rows of surgical tables stood vacant. Tool carts stood beside the tables, meant for surgeries that would never happen. The same dust that seemed to permeate the entirety of Crescent covered everything in the infirmary in a thin, fuzzy layer. Donovan ambled past each surgical station and stopped at the last table. The tools on this cart had been removed from their sterile cases, and a scattering of photographs sat on the surgical tray. The instruments were covered in dark flakes. Donovan took the pictures and blew the dust off them.

The first photograph—tiny stains spattered its once-glossy surface—showed a pretty woman with long, dark hair. Pretty was an understatement. Whoever the girl had been, she was beautiful. She posed in the photo with her delicate fingers framing a milk-white abdomen.

A proud smile graced her elegant features. The next photograph was an ultrasound image. It showed a small fetus, thumb in its mouth. The following image showed the woman on an operating table. A figure in scrubs, back to the camera, made a crude abdominal incision with a dark, rounded object. Donovan was suddenly aware of the carving in his pocket. Dark, rounded. And sharp enough to cut flesh.

The last photograph showed a team of surgeons removing the woman's uterus. Donovan couldn't tell for sure, but he thought the patient looked awake.

The door rattled open behind him. He turned so quickly that he lost his balance and fell into the surgical cart, knocking it to the floor. Unable to stand, he lay tangled in the cart, vulnerable. A group of men and women, all dressed in black, filed through the room and approached him slowly. Their complexions were porcelain and their features were slack. He recognized these people. He had seen them all over the station handing out their black flyers and antagonizing people.

And now they were here.

"Dude. You don't look so good." A young boy approached Donovan and helped him to his feet. The boy reached into the breast pocket of Donovan's nightshirt.

"Wow. This is really good, man. And it looks nice and sharp," the boy said. He handed the sanguinite carving to a freckle-faced girl who stood behind him. She moved to the surgical table and cleared it. Righting the fallen cart, she began to pick up the scattered tools.

"Look, pops. You did really good. But you're not done yet. The Other is dying right now. It can't sustain itself on its own anymore. You gotta give it whatever you have left. Do you dig?"

"I don't understand," Donovan said. He felt very upset and very much like a child. He wanted to see his daughter desperately.

"Go down the hallway and you will understand." The boy clapped Donovan on the shoulder and gently guided him out of the room. "The Other—the Three-to-be—is counting on you to hold it over until its chosen vessel can get down here." The boy looked at his watch. "I sure hope they hurry!" He flashed Donovan a grin and joined the freckle-faced girl at the surgical table.

[•••]

Donovan traveled back the way he had come. A man covered in tattoos waited at the intersecting corridors. Without a word, he led Donovan to another glass door.

"Ina?" Donovan whispered.

The door opened, and the tattooed man nodded and indicated for Donovan to enter. Donovan stepped over the threshold and the door slid closed behind him. In the room beyond, several open crates were scattered about on the floor with large black rocks nestled inside. Each chamber wall had a door. Light bled from beneath one of the exits. Donovan took a breath and placed his hands on its surface. The door slid into the ceiling.

He found a circle of black stones in the next room. In the space between each pair of stones was a flickering candle. A metal pedestal was at the center of the circle, with a cylindrical glass aquarium atop it. Cables ran from the base of the pedestal and into the walls. The Other was close. Donovan could feel it. The presence reached out and caressed him. It was dying, but Donovan was not too late to save it.

He approached the center of the room. There was a metal ring around the pedestal with tiny rock fragments set into it—a smaller version of what Donovan had seen in the Anrar III photographs.

Donovan looked in to the glass cylinder. Something small and pink swam in the liquid. It looked like a tiny fetus with ridges on its back that tapered at a curling tail. The small creature swam in lazy somersaults, trailing threads of color—violet, red, and black—behind it. The fetus-thing stopped moving when Donovan put his face close to the glass, and it opened its eyes. Black eyes. Donovan looked into them and saw a thousand stars being born and saw a thousand stars die. He saw universes writhe and fold in on one another like they were living masses of dark and light. Donovan grabbed the sides of the large tube with the intention of setting it down on the floor, but instead, it tipped off its stand and he was too weak to hold onto it. The cylinder tumbled and shattered.

The creature wriggled in a steadily evaporating puddle of liquid. Donovan picked the thing up and cradled it in his hand. Its flesh was painfully cold to the touch. Donovan raised his cupped hands to his lips and opened his mouth. Something sharp anchored itself into the back of his throat. His eyes went wide with the pain of it. The fetus-thing snapped from his hand and into his mouth.

Before Donovan's eyes, he saw a flash of violet.

A flash of red.

And then the shadows began to flow off the walls, flooding the room in devil darkness. He was consumed by the Black. It devoured what was left of his mind, suckling at the last few shreds of Donovan Cortez's being so that it could sustain itself until the true vessel arrived.

The last thing Donovan saw in his mind's eye was his daughter. And right before he ceased to exist, it all made sense.

[•••]

The floor rocked beneath Ina's feet. The station corridor tilted one way and then the other, throwing her into the walls with enough ferocity to rattle her teeth. She burst into the apartment and ran to the bedroom. It stank of urine, feces, and vomit, but it was empty. She began to cry and scream uncontrollably.

"Dad?" she yelled. There was no response. She looked in the bathroom. He was not there. She went to the study. The light was on above the desk. His surgical implements were scattered about, along with tiny red shards of sanguinite.

Oh, Dad, no.

There was a pad of paper beside his surgical tools and she flipped through the pages rapidly. A sketch showed a crude map of the station—the forgotten tunnels and crawl-spaces she herself had once crept down. She stared at the map with the sinking realization that her father's part in things was not yet done. She began to tremble. *Get it together.* She forced herself to take a deep breath but still, her body shook. *Get it together, damn you.* She repeated the deep breaths, one slow inhalation and exhalation after the other, until she felt some semblance of composure return.

She would find her father and get him to safety, but by that time surely all the station's lifeboats would be gone.

"Gerald," she said aloud. The salvage pilot might already have fled the station. Or maybe he'd just laugh in her face. But really, Gerald Evans was her only hope. She went to the terminal and called up his PDA. "Please pick up," she said. "Please. Pick up."

[•••]

Ina's distraught face appeared on the small LCD screen of Gerald's PDA.

"Gerald, please, in the name of all that is holy, tell me you're still on the station," she said.

"So glad you're concerned about my well being, Ina. I'm still here." He looked around the auditorium and then back to the pile of smoking metal and concrete that had once been the stage. "For how much longer, remains to be seen. But I'll make a bet and say it won't be any longer than it'll take to fire up Bean's engines."

"I need you to wait for me, Gerald."

"Wait for you? For all I know, you brought this shitstorm on us," he said.

From below, Marisa groaned.

"We all did," Ina said. "I'm sorry… is Marisa okay?"

"No," he said, clipping the word short. "I'll get you off this falling-apart hunk of metal, but I'm not willing to wait to do it. Why do you need me to wait?"

"My father is gone, Gerald. I need to find him. I know he's still alive." The desperation was apparent in her voice. She was crying now. "He went down… there."

Gerald didn't need to ask. "If he went down there, he's a goner by now. Sorry, Ina."

"No. I need to get him, Gerald. He'd do the same for me. I'm going, but I know the lifeboats will all be gone by the time I find him and get back."

"You're right about that, Ina. No one is sticking around here for much longer. And those that get stuck here—and there will be a lot of them—will rip apart any ship that was stupid enough not to launch ten minutes ago. I don't want to be on the receiving end of that."

"It won't take long, Gerald. I promise. He couldn't have gotten too far. He's very sick."

Gerald hesitated and shook his head. He didn't couldn't believe what he was about to say next.

"Fine, goddamn it. I'm going with you, then."

"You're what?" Ina said. He heard an equally incredulous sound from Marisa down below.

"You heard me. If I'm gonna wait, I might as well make sure the job gets done right. Now, where the hell are you?"

"My apartment," she said.

"I'll be there soon. Don't you do anything until I get there. Understand?"

"Yes. Thank you, Gerald."

He snapped the phone shut, grimaced, and let loose a string of obscenities. He was no hero, that was for damned sure. And apparently, he also wasn't very goddamned bright. He snapped his PDA open and hit another number. The device chimed.

"Captain," Bean's voice came from the small speaker.

"Bean, initiate prelaunch. We're going to have to get out of here quickly."

"That, Captain, is one of many understatements you've made since we've known each other. Please do not allow it to be your last. Initiating prelaunch. Hurry, Gerald."

"I think I've lost my good judgment altogether," he called down to Marisa as he snapped the PDA shut.

"When did you ever possess it?" He could hear her moving around.

"Can you get to Bean on your own?" he asked. Shouting echoed in from the atrium. Something new was going on now. He turned his head toward the sound. People were fighting out there, fighting and moving back toward the auditorium in feral packs that lashed out at any vulnerable living thing in their paths.

"What's going on up there?"

"Killing. I'm going to have to find another way to get to Ina."

"Leave her, Gerry," Marisa said.

"I can't, Marisa. Not in good conscience."

"It's your funeral, Gerry. But, I'll upload something to your PDA that'll help. A map of the back channels. It'll get you around with out having travel the main drags. Make sure you lock the hatches behind you. It's close quarters and you don't want to be followed." She hesitated a moment before speaking again. "Gerry, if you don't make it, you better make sure that Bean is prepared to get my ass out of here. I'm not going to die because you decided get chivalrous in the last few hours of your selfish life."

"Thanks," he said.

"Yeah, well. You better fucking make it, okay?"

There was a scream. A body went sailing through the air and hit the ruined floor just meters away from where Gerald stood—it was the young girl who had given him the ear plugs.

"Holy shit," he managed.

Two hulking collector robots careened into the chamber. Long, articulated limbs—they looked like docking tethers—snagged a woman and lifted her in the air. The machine held her there for a long, agonizing second, then slammed her into the ground with one quick swoop. The pack of wild humans scattered. Robots pummeled those who weren't fast enough to get away, stacking the bodies in a crude pile. One robot swiveled its head. Six orange eye nodes looked directly at Gerald.

It was time to move.

[•••]

Kendall watched the pandemonium on the desk LCDs. If his mouth could have opened any wider, his jaw would have hit the floor minutes ago. It was happening. The worst case scenario was now in full tilt. There were riots everywhere. People were killing each other brutally. Even with the cameras zoomed out fully, he could see the heinous acts in far too much detail. The Beast was coming up from the depths of the station. It would devour everyone and save him—the best—for last.

Unless…

"You look like you finally have a plan, Kendall," Albin said, and leaned forward in his chair. He had been prodding Kendall for the past three hours, and the former mayor's patience for it was slipping. "Kendall. Do you have a plan? Tell me. What is it?"

"Albin, shut the fuck up." The bullet that flew from Kendall's revolver took off the top of Albin's head in a burst of hair, skull, and brain. Albin's chair went over and all Kendall regarded now were the bottoms of the dead man's twitching boots. Calmly, Kendall set the revolver down and drummed his fingers on the desk. A plan. He needed a plan. He knew that. A decompression of the station would take far too long—air had to be purged deck by deck because of hard-wired failsafes and by that time, the rioters would be banging on his door. All that was left was to gas the station. He entered the commands on his desk terminal for that final contingency plan. Paranoia had prepared him for the worst. In the end, Kendall supposed he hadn't been paranoid after all. He hesitated with his finger above the execute key. He would be helpless, with everyone dead on the station. When Core Sec came to investigate, he'd be arrested all over again. He needed a lift.

He activated the comm terminal and recorded a message for Darros Stronghold.

"Darros, this is Kendall. The situation at Crescent has become critical. Send ships to come get your guns and that'll be the end of it. There are twelve hundred cases of firearms. They are yours for free if you come rescue me."

Kendall hit send.

And then he hit execute.

Crescent would be flooded with poison gas, and that would be that. No more rioters. No more monster. Just freedom. Kendall would fade into obscurity in the frozen wilderness of Habeos.

The station shuddered beneath him and he toppled out of his big chair. Kendall growled and got to his feet. *It will all be over in less than an hour,* he told himself. He flipped a toggle on the desk's surface and one of the bookcases slid into the floor. He darted into the revealed tunnel as fast as his old knees would carry him.

[•••]

Ina hugged him so tightly, Gerald thought his eyes were going to bust right out his skull. He held her back at arms length. Tears were streaming down her face and she was shaking her head back and forth. He thought he was going to have to slap her, but she came around an instant later.

"Thank you, Gerald. You're all I… "

"Can it," he interrupted. "If you know how to get where we're going, lead the way. We don't have a lot of time to waste."

The modified collectors ambled around on their strange, curved legs. The machines were joined by Crescent's standard complement of robots as they collected bodies instead of trash. The robots bludgeoned those who struggled the most, using the walls, floors, and ceilings to subdue them. At the outset, it didn't look like the machines were set on killing. Most of the captives moaned and even moved, if just a little bit.

The human residents of Crescent were doing far worse things to each other. Horrible acts of violence and mutilation.

Gerald could still hear the muffled sounds of killing through the confining maintenance channel's walls. The collector robots might have been too large for the shafts that he and Ina hustled through, but the crazy people were not, so he was careful to lock each hatch behind them as they went. Small maintenance robots darted this way and that, bouncing off of Gerald and Ina's feet as the two made their way toward the Vault—toward wherever those big robots were hauling their catches. Not exactly a wonderful idea.

After a long elevator descent, Ina and Gerald came out onto L Deck. At the outset, the level appeared dark and ghostly quiet, but the very air was unsettled. It felt charged as it had on Anrar III just before the arrival of the storm. Water dripped from black light panels as they moved through the abandoned residential corridors. Gaping apartment doors watched as Gerald and Ina passed.

The Vault entrance was almost peaceful when Gerald and Ina arrived.

Regardless of the false calm, Gerald's skin crawled with fear and anticipation. Cold air poured out of a large opening that led into a part of Crescent that Gerald had never really thought existed. Yet, there he was, about to dive right into whatever unknown horrors waited on the other side. He opened his mouth to speak and his breath came out as a cloud of vapor.

A whir of motors sounded from directly behind them. Gerald turned, his hands outstretched. A metal behemoth towered above them. Eye nodes burned like hot coals. The machine examined them, titling its bulbous head this way and then that. Gerald braced himself for what would undoubtedly be a grievous death. The thing cocked its head and looked at Ina for several agonizing seconds. It didn't move a centimeter. Ina opened her mouth as if to scream but she only produced a gulping sound that was almost comical. The robot turned and strode past them, dragging a catch of bodies in tow. Some of the bodies had crude lacerations across their torsos.

Gerald thought of his spectral roommate. He should have seen this coming. He looked at Ina. She snapped her mouth shut and peered through the open door after the robot.

"Food," Ina said. "It is going to be weak, and so hungry."

"It? What is going to be hungry, Ina? Just where the hell are you taking me?" He'd come too far to turn back now, but he didn't want to go a step further.

"I could never explain it. But the robots—they are part of the station and this life force controls the station now. It is *becoming* the station." She grabbed him by the arm and pulled him into the dark corridor of the Vault. The tunnel was dimly lit—the only appreciable illumination came from the walls themselves, glazed with a strange, black substance. It looked like tar and glittered with tiny flecks of light. Bulkheads stood out in substance like silver islands. Were these offices? Homes? The edges of the bulkheads bulged with chrome caulking.

Ina and Gerald were passed by a procession of collectors, and were again ignored.

"These bulkheads." Ina ran her finger around the circumference of one oval door. "They're completely sealed."

"Either they didn't want to let something in or... let something out. Let's keep moving," Gerald said. Circular windows were set into the face of the doors, but only darkness was visible on the other side.

"They put people in there to die," Ina said, and then didn't say anything else.

Gerald and Ina moved into a sea of blackness. Phantasmal clouds of weak light drifted past as the pair pushed on.

Ina and Gerald waded free of the darkness and came to an intersection in the corridor.

"Which way?" Ina asked. She looked at him and her brow creased with doubt.

"Left," Gerald said. "First direction that came to mind."

The Aphotic pounced on them the instant Gerald and Ina stepped through the infirmary door. Gerald threw blind punches in every possible direction and combination. His knuckles connected several times, rewarding his effort with a crack or a yelp. Regardless, he was soon overwhelmed. *Why didn't you bring a weapon, asshole?* his conscience spat as he was pulled to the ground. Hands closed around his neck in a death grip; Gerald swatted at them ineffectively. Not far from him, Ina screamed and cried. He could hear her feet kicking at something metal and fought to turn his head. Two cultists were laying her out on a table. Donovan Cortez stepped up to her, a red stone knife in his hand. His skin seemed to be hanging loosely on his bones. He pulled up the hem of his daughter's shirt and her screaming jumped in volume and pitch, but Gerald could only just barely hear her. His heart was pounding too loudly in his ears.

"Maerl... " Gerald gasped as he looked up into the face of the man strangling him. "Maerl... Jesus. Please."

Gerald lost consciousness.

[•••]

It was quiet when Gerald came to. Not even the ceiling vents made a noise. His blurred vision cleared to reveal a dust-covered medical suite. Cult members lay dead around him, their throats crudely slit. They each held a razor blade in their dead hands. *They killed themselves,* Gerald thought, and then heard Ina's voice add, *"It's going to be hungry."*

Maerl's body sat close to the frosted glass exit door, propped against a cream-colored wall panel. The club owner's chin rested on his blood-soaked chest. Gerald probed his own throat with hesitant fingers. It was still intact.

He steeled himself to find Ina. The feat wouldn't be easy solo; not with the zealots wandering in the shadows. He thought of calling Marisa in for backup, but she was more than half a station away. It was a one man show now.

Gerald didn't have to go far to find the archaeologist. She lay on a gleaming surgery table. Her abdomen was opened wide, the incised flaps of skin held in place by four shiny clamps. Gerald hurried to her side. He checked for a pulse, but knew the gesture was meaningless.

She was as dead as the cult members.

His eyes stung with tears that wouldn't come. He took several steps back from the table and shook his head.

"Shit. Ina," he whispered.

Suddenly, Gerald felt a sense of disparity, like two worlds were overlaid one on the other—two worlds that had no business coming together. Whatever Ina and Marisa had been so afraid of happening, was happening. His ears felt like they wanted to pop, but wouldn't.

Small clouds of dim blue light grew out of the air before his eyes. The shifting, glowing clouds effloresced into child-sized ethereal flower shapes, filled with watery light. Gerald gazed into the petals—it was like staring through an undulating window into a stormy, endless sky. The ghostly blooms drifted across the room and disappeared through the far wall. Wraith-like figures rose from the floor panels and joined the floating lights in their ethereal procession. Gerald tore his gaze away and ran from the infirmary. More cult members lay dead in his path. He leapt over them as he hustled down the passageway.

He skidded to a halt at the junction. A light twinkled at the far end of the other corridor. It shone through an unexplainable murkiness, as if from behind dark green water. The light source was not on the station. Gerald gazed into a place that human eyes had never glimpsed. It made his head hurt. The surface of the water rippled and a figure stepped through and into the corridor. The being's mass was insubstantial and so black it seemed to absorb light. The force of its presence froze Gerald where he stood—he could feel the thing reaching out for him and his heart began to slow as if life were being sapped from him.

Ina's words came back to him—*it's going to be weak, and so hungry.* It was feeding time.

Collectors emerged from the wall of water, trundling in his general direction. Their forms were black and ominous in the glare. It was enough to break Gerald's trance. He took a step away from the junction and his movement drew their attention. Robotic heads snapped up and tentacles unfurled. It would be the maintenance shaft, or death.

Gerald ran for it.

The clanking of jointed metal feet became louder with each burning breath that Gerald took. A metal tentacle slashed across his back, cutting through his shirt and his skin. He stumbled, but did not fall. The open hatch into the crawlspace was so close he could almost touch it. Again, the tentacle lashed out. It hit his arm this time and almost found purchase.

A few more steps.

Just a few more steps.

(Part XXIII)

The wounds were mortal—that much was apparent. Dark liquid hemorrhaged from the deep gashes with startling persistence. A gurgling whistle accompanied each of Captain Benedict's labored, ragged breaths. Marisa had found him outside of HQ. How he had managed to hold on for so long was a mystery. Half of his leg was missing, and his exposed torso was a cross-hatch of nasty lacerations. She stroked his blood-soaked hair and whispered all the calming sentiments she could think of. Captain Benedict tried to speak. His lips moved soundlessly and Marisa leaned in to listen. Blood frothed from his mouth; he swallowed it back and tried again, but the light went out of his eyes. Marisa fought back her tears and laid his head down on the blood-soaked office carpet.

There'd be plenty of time to grieve later. She did not have that luxury now.

Marisa turned her attention to the security feeds. She hoped to catch a glimpse of Gerald, but had no such luck. A warning flashed across each one of the displays and filled Marisa with dread, cold and pure. Kendall, that crazy son of a bitch, had set Crescent to gas every living thing onboard. Her stomach dropped and the resulting nausea nearly doubled her over. She sat at a control console, took a slow, deep breath, and then began entering commands on the keyboard. Her fingers moved with deliberate care at first, but each time the display screen taunted her with her lack of clearance and refused her entry to the system, her fingers moved faster. When the computer would not relent, she beat at it with open palms, alternating between shouted curses and sobbing pleas. She was in a full sweat when she finally gave up.

To make matters worse, Nigel was nowhere to be found. As far as Marisa was concerned, he was on his own now. She snapped open her PDA and dialed Gerald. The small LCD indicated that he was not on the station. Interference, Marisa thought dismissively. She set her PDA to keep calling the salvage pilot until it could get through.

Marisa limped out of HQ; her ankle caught fire with each step. A procession of collector robots marched past the T intersection at the end of the corridor. Marisa ducked back into the office before the door had a chance to slide shut. She activated the door lock and pressed her ear to the frosted glass. The sounds of the robots faded. They hadn't seen her. She hazarded a look into the hallway and found it empty. This was her chance—maybe her only one. She made a break for it, ignoring the pain.

Marisa didn't feel safe until she was in the maintenance tunnel, the grate firmly locked in place behind her. She had to shuffle along sideways to move forward. Small maintenance drones bounced off her feet, blipping and chirping. She was a trespasser in their cramped domain, and the little machines did not seem pleased about the intrusion. But at least there was no way the collectors could get her in there. The thought brought her comfort, even if her heart did flutter with claustrophobia. After a short distance, the tunnel grew wider and she was able to pick up the pace, despite her injury.

The passage curved. A body flew around that bend from the opposite direction, colliding with her in a tangle of limbs. Their respective cries of surprise were nearly in unison. She shuffled in reverse and got to her feet. Mayor Kendall lay sprawled flat on his back, breathing hard. She couldn't believe her fucking eyes.

"You!" Kendall growled and struggled to get upright. Marisa did not give him the chance. She grabbed him by the collar and planted her fist in his face. The first punch felt so good, she straddled him and went to town.

No. There's no time. You have to get to Bean.

Marisa dismounted and kicked the former mayor hard in the ribs. One. Two. Three. He cried out each time. Her bad ankle threatened to give with the last blow, but she maintained her balance. The pain was distant now. She moved away.

"I should've… blown you… out the airlock… like your friend Swaren, when I had the chance," Kendall said between big, gulping breaths.

She stopped and turned. Her lips peeled back in a snarl.

"What did you say?"

Kendall caught his breath. He wiped his hand across his mouth and looked at the resulting blood with a smirk.

"You should have seen his face, Marisa. He looked quite surprised when we opened that hangar door."

He wants me to stick around out here. He wants me to get distracted…

"You'll get yours, Kendall. But not from me. There's a higher power playing here now. And you've got no control."

Hatred and pain could wait for some other time.

Marisa ran.

She ran until spots floated in front of her eyes and her lungs burned. She slowed to a halt only when she feared she would pass out, bending over with hands on her knees, struggling to control her breathing. She dry-heaved twice before composure finally returned. She straightened, and realized in dawning horror that she was lost. In her blind flight, she must have missed one of the turns. An important turn. How far back had it been? Marisa looked back the way she had come, but couldn't tell.

Her heart began to hammer in her chest again and she doubled over with more dry heaves.

Relax, Marisa, she thought. *Main Street should be just up ahead.*

The hangars could be reached by crossing the wide thoroughfare—if she survived being out in the open.

Main Street was an embodiment of hell itself. The shops in the bazaar burned. Beyond the sprawling market, jagged holes in the station walls were all that remained of former storefronts. The ruined businesses spewed forth blasts of angry flames. Bodies lay everywhere. The sun globes cycled through color and brightness rapidly. Purple, orange, yellow, orange, purple, white. Shadows, shrunk, lengthened, and changed directions at an alarming rate. It made Marisa's stomach twist into a knot. She wished she could close her eyes and leap the final distance to the big exit tunnel.

Marisa took a deep breath and looked for the collectors. None were to be seen, so she went for it.

An ear-piercing clang rang out from behind her before she could get very far. Marisa turned, not ready for death, but willing to accept it so long as it wasn't too painful or prolonged.

Naheela stood outside what had once been a sidewalk cafe. Mutilated corpses sat propped up at the cafe's tables. Big burning umbrellas lit the grim parody of life in mad, orange light. Naheela stood beyond the tables. She held a metal pipe and trash can lid in her hands. She seemed poised to clang them together again, but when Marisa took notice, the crone dropped them. She waved to Marisa, beckoning for her to come. Marisa jogged to her. Naheela met her at the center of the boulevard.

"Most everyone is either dead or on their way to dead by now. I know that Ina has failed us." Naheela shook her head, her deep-creased features looked impossibly sad. "You have to get out of here very soon. What I have to do next is final."

"You need to leave, yourself. Kendall has the station set to gas everything living within the hour," Marisa said. She breathed through her mouth, but was nearly overcome by the scents of burning hair and flesh.

Naheela chuckled and shook her head. "Don't you worry about me, dearest. What I'm going to do will be more permanent than a little bit of poison gas." She put a finger on her chin. "Though, gassing those who have been brought to the Vault and not yet… processed for supper—that could be a blessing for them." She paused and looked up at Marisa. "No time to listen to me babble. The coast is clear; as far as I can tell, the collectors are all trekking back to the hive now with their last batch for the new-born Other." She waved her hand. "Get off the station. Go!"

Marisa did not have to be told twice.

Crescent's main hangar was in chaos. Straggling survivors fought each other to clamber aboard the few lifeboats that remained docked. The biggest mob of them were clustered around the colony ship, climbing frantically one over the other in an attempt to ascend the wide docking ramp. The evacuation was without order. No one took notice of Marisa as she ran to where Bean sat at the far end of the vast chamber. The hauler's running lights flashed. The engine exhaust ports glowed softly. The vessel was ready for take off, but Bean's hatch was sealed tight when she reached it. She called the ship's name, hoping it would recognize her voice and open up, but it did not.

The PDA vibrated in her chest pocket. She retrieved the device. It almost fell free of her sweat-slicked fingers.

"Gerry," she gasped. On the small display screen, he was drenched in sweat and breathing hard. His face was covered in dirt and blood.

"Where are you? Tell me you're close."

"I think I'm close," he gasped. "Where are you?"

"I'm at Bean."

"Good. I'll be there in five minutes—I'm hoping less."

"Hurry," she said.

The sound of rending metal came through the phone's speaker. Gerald cursed.

"Oh, I'm hurrying."

She closed the phone and looked up. A group of collector robots waded into the crowd of panicked station residents. Blood and rust covered the machines' exteriors. Eye nodes flared through a tacky coating of viscera and oxidation. The bots began hauling people away—soon, they had them all. Marisa marveled at their savage efficiency. She knew it was pointless for her to hide. The creatures had spotted her and four of them were closing in. She wouldn't run. Maybe they would take her and leave, allowing Gerald to get on his ship.

"Hey!" Gerald's voice cried, and she whirled. He was several meters behind her. His head poked out of an open hangar grate. "Talk about a hole in ... holy shit!" The robots had already covered half the distance to Bean. She leaned down with an outstretched arm and yanked Gerald out of the pit.

"Bean. Bean, open up, you motherfucker!" Gerald shouted. The hatch opened on Bean's belly and the docking ladder descended. The collectors were too damn close now. Their metal tentacles whipped out in gleaming arcs.

"You first, Gerald. You have to get this bird in the air before I'm even in my seat." He looked at her but didn't argue. The pilot bolted up the ladder. His head reappeared at the top.

"Come on, Marisa. Quit fucking around."

She started up the ladder, but her hands slipped when a rusted tether grabbed her bad ankle and yanked hard. She cried out. Gerald reached for her hand but missed entirely. He wasn't even fucking close. The collectors dragged her across the deck with a back-jarring pull.

"Go!" she screamed at him. "Go!"

The ladder ascended and the bulkhead sealed. She felt a pang of disappointment, but she knew there was no way he could have helped her. He would have been snagged if he tried.

The pointed tip of a tentacle lanced toward her face. The barbed end missed her by a fraction of a centimeter, but came close enough that Marisa felt a breeze. She closed her eyes and tried to remember the shortest prayer she knew.

[•••]

Gerald practically fell into the control couch. It was all wrong. Why should he be the one to get away unscathed? He could see the collectors dragging Marisa away the through front viewport. All fucking wrong. The collector's tether should have been around *his* ankle.

Inspiration struck and he grabbed the manual controls for Bean's hauling lines. Silvery tentacles flashed out from the underside of the ship. The first thick line hit the collector that had Marisa. It clipped the side of the robot's metal head, knocking it free of the rusty shoulders. The collector's long appendages went limp and Marisa fell to the deck. She began crawling toward the ship. Gerald caught her with one of Bean's other tethers and began to pull her back across the floor. The remaining collector robots changed direction and darted after her with alarming speed. Gerald lashed out again, taking out the legs of one of the big machines. The collector sailed through the air and smashed into the hangar wall with a flash of sparks and smoke. A final robot continued in pursuit, but it was too far behind—nearly half a hangar's length away.

"I've got her on board, Captain," Bean said a heartbeat later.

"Then get us the hell out of here."

The collector robot crashed into the front viewport. Gerald jerked back in the control couch with a yell. *How did that fucker move so fast?* But the robot was mangled. It fell from the viewport, crashing to the deck in a rusted heap. With the window clear, Gerald could see how the robot had closed the gap in a matter of seconds.

It had been launched.

A metal spike had erupted from the hangar floor, sending the robot skyward. The growth was like the murdering shafts that Gerald had glimpsed in Heathen's, but those barbs had been the size of a bee's stinger by comparison. This metal protrusion bisected the flight deck and was easily as wide the hauler's bridge. Another spike burst out of the floor.

It was followed by another. The things continued to sprout from the walls, the floor, and the ceiling. Soon, the hangar was raining with brilliant sparks and falling hunks of twisted metal. The floor ripped open and a mass of black, violet, and red erupted like a living torrent of light and dark. It began to take on a shape. *That's it,* Gerald thought, *it's becoming.*

The colony ship lifted off from the flight deck and careened toward Bean. A second later, a massive spike pierced its belly. The explosion that followed was huge and blinding. Flaming debris bounced off Bean's hull with thundering impacts.

"Bean," Gerald commanded, "Go!"

The hauler took off and rocketed out of the firestorm. The small ship roared down the hangar in reverse as more spikes erupted its wake.

And then they were in open space.

The docking hub's massive glowing portal had become a ring of sharp metal teeth, like the hungry maw of some obscene creature. Before Gerald could consider it further, Marisa was on top of him, peppering his face with kisses.

"You magnificent son of a bitch." She kissed him long and hard enough that he had to push her away to catch his breath. "You smart piece of shit. When did you get so smart? You fucking son of a bitch!" She kissed him again and again. Her lips tasted salty with perspiration.

"Captain," Bean said, "I'm detecting major energy fluctuations coming from Crescent."

[•••]

Kendall staggered into his bed chamber and shrieked when he found Angela sitting at the foot of his large bed. Surprise and fear were quickly replaced by hatred and he lurched toward her with extended arms, intent on strangling the bitch. He would have ripped her throat out if an alarm had not started wailing. Instead, he limped past her and to an emergency closet. There he climbed into a neon orange environment suit and only then did he go to her. He kept his hands at his sides, but could still feel the echo of the snarl contorting his features.

"You look crazy in that suit, you motherfucker. You're going to die looking like an idiot. You're going to—" her words were replaced with gurgling, sputtering noises.

Kendall turned then. The room filled with a heavy white fog. He smiled as he watched her claw at her throat, realizing his providence then. Angela was as fine a canary as she was a whore.

Leaving her body, he went to his personal terminal and entered a string of commands into it. The gas vented from his chamber and was replaced with fresh, clean atmosphere. The display screen above the keypad indicated that his air was safe and breathable again. Now all he had to do was wait for Darros to come and rescue him. Kendall's comm chimed with an incoming message. He removed the environment suit's helmet and played the transmission. It was audio only and riddled with static.

"The Habeos gate has been destroyed. We have taken heavy casualties.

You set us up, Kendall. You are on your own. I hope your death is a long and painful one."

Kendall swallowed hard.

"What are you gonna do now, old man?" a mocking voice called. Kendall swiveled in his seat.

Naheela stood at the foot of his bed; she knelt beside the dead hooker, examining her with wonder. She touched the flesh of the dead girl's stained cheeks and brushed away a trickle of blood that had dribbled from one of Angela's nostrils.

"Still warm," Naheela said, absently. "I ain't one for the speeches. Well. That's a lie. But you ain't worth a speech. I'm tired, Ezra. Even the ageless get weary. I'm done with this place. I'll take my chances with my immortality and erase it all. It is time for me to shed the burden of pride. I've failed here. But it ends now."

"What madness are you prattling about now, crone?"

"This is going to hurt, Ezra. Mortal eyes, they cannot handle looking upon the true face of the ageless."

It occurred to him then that Naheela should have been dead. He saw no signs of an environment suit. The gas should have killed her.

Naheela yawned and her skin started to change. Expanding black spots covered her cheeks and arms. The blossoming patches were fringed by the most brilliant light that Kendall had ever seen. So bright, it hurt his eyes. The spots continued to grow—they looked depthless. The patches filled with shimmering points of light. Each pinprick blossomed into brilliant sun.

"We are the glue that binds all universes together." She smiled and opened her mouth wide. More radiance. God, how his eyes pained him, but he couldn't tear them away.

Soon, Naheela was a figure of pure incandescence. A figure of sable grew up out of the wavering floor to fill the space between Kendall and Naheela. He thought the darkness would soothe his burning eyes, but instead when he looked upon the dark figure, it filled him with a cold that burned far worse by comparison. It was then that Kendall understood the true essence of light and dark, of good and evil. He saw that as a man, he was mortal and nothing.

Suddenly, Naheela's shape flared, Kendall screamed, and something else—something inhuman—screamed along with him. Ezra Kendall had never known so much pain in his life. The world winked out around him. He was blind. He fell to his knees amidst so much heat that his mind couldn't comprehend it. He could, however, comprehend the burning smell. His thin, gray hair was on fire. He cried out again, then inhaled sharply. As he drew his last breath, the air itself caught fire. He was fortunate to die then.

[•••]

Gerald and Marisa sat at the edge of the flight couch, gripping each other's hands with white-knuckled intensity. Crescent erupted with swirling arcs of white light. The blinding streamers wrapped around the curve of station like a cocooning tornado. Red, violet, and black ribbons of light spun out in countering circles, but the ribbons were soon overwhelmed by the white hellfire. There wasn't an explosion but a retina-searing flash of light, and then all that remained of Crescent was a floating afterimage.

"Bean... What the hell was that?"

"I don't know, Captain. I do know that the station is no longer registered on our radar. It is gone."

"It's not there anymore, Gerald," Marisa whispered. "It's not... anywhere."

Debris floated where the station had been—refuse and old, discarded cargo containers. Nothing to indicate the station had blown up. The small leavings retained the shape of the station for a few minutes, but then became dissociated. The only evidence that mankind had built a station above Anrar III began a slow descent into the planet's atmosphere, only to face eventual disintegration.

Bean was silent.

Minutes turned into hours, and they still did not move from Anrar III's shadow. Gerald and Marisa held one another, not out of love, or relief, but just to hold onto something living and real. Gerald felt himself falling asleep and didn't fight it. He was exhausted. Marisa was already snoring softly with her head buried in his neck. She would probably start drooling on him soon.

He didn't care.

[•••]

The next several weeks went by in a haze. There were medical exams and endless questions from Core Sec security officials. They always asked the same questions, and each time Marisa and Gerald were only able to provide the most vague of answers. When they had awakened from their catnap on Bean, memory of what happened on Crescent was fragmented, dreamy, and fast to fade. Bean's memory banks from the past month had been wiped clean. Apparently, Gerald had executed the command himself, but he didn't remember doing it. In the end, those events on Crescent that Gerald remembered most clearly were the ones he believed the least.

"Mr. Evans, we're not accusing you of anything. We really don't think that one man, one woman, and a beat up salvage ship could be capable of making an entire station disappear. We just need your help to piece things together. We need to know if this region is unstable. We need to know if Galatea could suffer the same fate as Crescent."

"Look," Gerald said, "I told you. I don't know what happened. I can't remember, and it causes me pain when I try to. I just want to get out of space altogether. I want to feel the soil of a planet beneath my feet. How many more times do we need to go through this?"

"I apologize, Mr. Evans."

The session went on for another hour, apology notwithstanding.

Marisa was waiting for him in the lounge area outside the Core Sec office. Her back was to him. She stood in front of a large viewport and watched the rolling asteroids and glittering stars. He placed his hands on her shoulders and she leaned back into him.

"How did it go?"

He shrugged.

"They're letting us go on the next colony ship out of here," he said.

"On what condition?"

"That they get to keep Bean for an undetermined amount of time."

"And you're fine with that?" She raised an eyebrow.

"I'm not fine with it, but I do know we need to get out of this part of space for good. When they're done with Bean, they can send the hull to me wherever we end up and we'll use him as a big planter. Don't worry, I'll hang onto the parts that count."

Marisa chuckled. "I'm sure he'll love that."

"I don't think he has much of a choice."

Gerald tapped his breast pocket and the data wafers therein. Bean's personality constructs and memories were close to his heart—where they should be. Core Sec could have Bean's hull, his machinery, and his data banks, but Bean would make a fine estate computer for the house that Gerald had just purchased with the mystery funds in his bank account.

The line to the docking tube remained long and slow as passengers filed onto the colony ship. It seemed that the closer Gerald and Marisa got to leaving, the slower things went. Finally, they reached the security check. Gerald removed his shoes and placed them on a narrow conveyor belt. He proceeded through a metal arch and was scanned for contraband. Once cleared, he stepped out of the checkpoint, retrieved his shoes, and slipped them back onto his feet.

Marisa stepped into the docking tube ahead of him.

"I'm off Galatea before you, sucker." She winked. He turned for one last glance at the station. A young woman with a wild mane of dark hair and cappuccino skin stood watching him. She waved. At him?

"Do we know her?" he asked Marisa.

"Nope," she said and tugged his belt loop. "Come on, Gerry."

In an instant, he remembered. He remembered everything. The woman he saw now was ancient, and he saw the whole story in her face. His mouth fell open and he closed his eyes. Marisa tugged on him again. He opened his eyes and the woman was gone.

"You okay?" Marisa asked as he stepped into the tube.

"Yeah." He hesitated for a moment and then answered honestly. "I'm fine."

The pair boarded the colony ship, and left that piece of space behind them forever.

Epilogue

Gerald was cold.

A violent shiver woke him from a heavy sleep. He was intimate with the fact that it got very cold at night in the desert, but that didn't prevent him from falling asleep with the window open time and again. He rolled onto his back and let out an audible groan. His head pounded. He forced his eyes open. Blue light pushed into the bedroom through wind-blown curtains and pooled on the gray carpet. Gerald realized he was lying on the floor instead of face down in a stack of pillows on his big, cozy bed. And he was naked. He lifted himself onto his knees and his hands came away from the floor wet. He probed the spot with his fingers only to discover the carpet was saturated. He became aware of the shower—it was running. He looked in the direction of the bathroom. The door was closed, but no light shined from the crack beneath it. He looked next toward the large bed. There was a lump under the sheets and a wash of dark hair spread out over a scrunched pillow. A pale, bare foot stuck out from beneath the twisted blanket.

Gerald went into the bathroom and he flipped on the light. He turned off the shower and watched the last of the water trail down the drain, carrying a few grains of red sand with it. A towel in the corner of the bathroom was mostly dry and didn't yet smell of mildew. He used it to rid himself of the excess moisture and then wrapped it around his waist.

Back in the bedroom, he sifted through his discarded clothes for a pack of cigarettes. The beat-up box held only a single stick of tobacco. He shook his head and stuck the final smoke between his lips—he didn't remember going through a whole pack earlier that night, but his lungs did feel tight. It might be time to consider giving the damn things up.

He went to the open window and his gaze trailed up along Cutter's Spine. The low mountains scraped at the glittering stars. His eyes moved out to the mesas and rested on the glowing lights that were the fledgling core mine. If Gerald strained and the wind was right, he could just barely hear the electric generators burning their stinky, liquid fuel. The wind changed direction and all he heard was quiet; all he could smell was dirt. He turned his eyes down to his own stretch of land. To his magnificent dirt gardens. He laughed. Bold salvage pilot turned dirt farmer, he mused. Long boxes of dark, fresh, and very fertile earth stretched out along the flat desert plain. The dirt looked black in the moonlight.

Gerald's PDA flashed on and off where it sat on the floor. Leaving the window, he retrieved the device. The small display told him that Marisa had left him a message during the course of the night. He looked to the bed where the lump remained motionless. The sleeping girl was a stranger to him—even after the hours they had spent getting to know each other. A sigh passed over Gerald's lips and he let the towel drop to the floor. Stepping from the mound of cotton dampness, he slipped into his jeans and a tee shirt that reeked of tobacco and alcohol. Gerald took the PDA and went out onto the back porch of his New Memphis home. There, he slumped into a lawn chair and looked the device in his palm. The PDA's LCD read 4:18 a.m. Marisa's call had come in at 3:34. As he pressed play, her face materialized from a wash of pixels and static.

"Gerry," she said and took a breath. "You're busy right now. Alex said she saw you with somebody at the Depot and that you left with them..." She laughed. It was a small, short, and unsteady sound. "I know what you're thinking. So. Yeah. I'm on the pills tonight. That's not what this about. I'm not calling for...that. You have to listen to me, Gerry." She glanced around. It was dark wherever she was. Gerald had trouble discerning her features. "There is something in me...inside my mind. I'm remembering things that never happened. Things I...think never happened. Things that now I'm wondering if they did happen." She looked off camera and then turned back to lean in. The camera lens was unforgiving. Marisa looked like shit. Her hair was a mess; her eyes were sunken and bloodshot. Gerald filled with both anger and sadness. "I'm not crazy. Gerald. Something followed us here. Something from that place...the place I don't remember. It all has to do with Crescent. I don't know what. Jesus." She popped a pill and followed it with a wash of dark liquid. She waggled the pill bottle in front of the camera. "Maybe Kendall's gas blast did scramble my circuits...maybe I'm only remembering hallucinations from the poison...maybe it's the carthine. But I don't think the memory of the gas is real. Kendall never managed to gas the station—he ran out of time." She laughed. "Time," she repeated and popped another pill. "But, Gerry, I hear a name in the static when I listen close." She smiled and looked sad. "No. This isn't a ploy to get us together. Just... I want to know if you're... experiencing anything. I'll even settle for an email. Please, don't ignore me."

Playback ended. Gerald dropped the cigarette to the patio and watched the smoke trail off into the night. The wind gusted and he wrapped his arms around himself.

"I don't need this shit..." he said.

Gerald was not experiencing anything out of the ordinary on New Memphis. There were no voices whispering in the static. Nothing moved in the corner of his vision. Hell, his few occasional blackouts were self-induced. His index finger hovered above the callback icon for several instants. He looked back toward his bedroom. The desire to crawl back into bed with his new friend had waned completely. He retracted his finger and slid the PDA into the front pocket of his jeans. He didn't want to call Marisa back either. He didn't want to have the conversation she was getting at.

Gerald remembered everything that had happened before they came to New Memphis—from his arrival on Crescent to watching the space hulk disappear before his eyes. He scarcely could believe the memories. Probably, Gerald wouldn't have believed them at all if it weren't for the scars and the accompanying nightmares. He didn't want to have that conversation with Marisa. He didn't want to see her. Every time he looked at her, he saw that place.

The place where two worlds that had no business being acquainted had met, and the door to hell had shuddered open.

He didn't want to go back there.

Not for love. Not for hate. Not for anything in the world.